PRAISE FOR MARY BURTON

THE SHARK
"This romantic thriller is tense, sexy, and pleasingly complex."
—*Publishers Weekly*

"Precise storytelling complete with strong conflict and heightened tension are the highlights of Burton's latest. With a tough, vulnerable heroine in Riley at the story's center, Burton's novel is a well-crafted, suspenseful mystery with a ruthless villain who would put any reader on edge. A thrilling read."
—*RT Book Reviews*, four stars

BEFORE SHE DIES
"Will keep readers sleeping with the lights on."
—*Publishers Weekly* (starred review)

MERCILESS
"Burton keeps getting better!"
—*RT Book Reviews*

YOU'RE NOT SAFE
"Burton once again demonstrates her romantic suspense chops with this taut novel. Burton plays cat and mouse with the reader through a tight plot, credible suspects, and romantic spice keeping it real."
—*Publishers Weekly*

BE AFRAID
"Mary Burton [is] the modern-day queen of romantic suspense."
—Bookreporter.com

BURN
YOU
TWICE

ALSO BY MARY BURTON

BURN YOU TWICE

MARY BURTON

 Montlake

Published by Montlake, Seattle

www.apub.com

Amazon, the Amazon logo, and Montlake are trademarks of Amazon.com, Inc., or its affiliates.

ISBN-13: 9781542021289
ISBN-10: 1542021286

Cover design by Caroline Teagle Johnson

Printed in the United States of America

BURN
YOU
TWICE

PROLOGUE

Missoula, Montana
Thursday, May 13, 2010
1:00 a.m.
Ten Years Ago

The college-campus bar was packed with students celebrating the end of another school year. All eyes were on the small stage, now flashing with blue and white spotlights as a singer gripped the mike and hit the high notes on the song's last chorus. Everyone was mesmerized, including Joan and Ann, who were standing near the bar.

He had been watching the two women for weeks. He knew where they lived, where they hid the spare key to their house, their class schedules, and even what they ate for breakfast. He had been in their house several times, lain on their beds, inhaled the scent of their perfume from their clothes, and dreamed about this night. Over the course of the last few weeks, the rhythm of their lives had become second nature to him.

Now, as Joan and Ann moved seductively to the music's beat, he removed a small vial from his jeans pocket and moved closer to the bar. When the bartender turned to fill a drink order, he quickly squeezed several drops of a sedative into each woman's drink. The drugs would not knock either woman out immediately, but the dosage would be enough to coax each back across campus to the safety of their home.

As he melted back into the crowd and the song ended, Joan and Ann turned back to the bar and gulped from their beer mugs. Their bodies glistened with sweat, and they were laughing. They were so confident and sure of their bright futures.

He had only five minutes to wait before Ann set down her drink. She yawned, said something to Joan, who shook her head as if she wanted to stay. He thought for a moment that Ann might leave alone. Having only Ann at the house was not part of the plan. For it all to work, Joan needed to be in the house as well. Tension rippled through him as he thought about all his plans crumbling. Maybe he should have put more drops in their drinks.

And then, minutes later, Ann spoke to Joan again, and the two stepped out into the cool night air. He followed, careful to keep a safe distance.

"I just need a minute," Ann said as she walked toward the middle of the parking lot. "I'm dizzy."

"I'm a little tired myself," Joan said, yawning.

"Would we be wimps if we called it a night?" Ann said.

"No. We'll both head home." Joan's words sounded a little slurred.

Ann blinked and gently patted her own cheeks with her hands. "But you've been looking forward to hearing this band."

"I've heard enough," Joan said. "And you look dead on your feet."

They walked the three blocks to their small one-story house, located at the edge of the campus. He followed, careful to remain in the shadows. Several times, they paused, drew in breaths as if to clear their heads, and then continued walking.

When they arrived home, Joan fished out the key from under the front doorstep mat and pushed it into the lock. "I didn't think I was that drunk. But I feel like I've been kicked by a mule."

Ann leaned against the house. "We're tired is all. We've been burning the candle at both ends for weeks."

Joan opened the door and clicked on the light. Ann said something he could not hear, and they both giggled as they moved into the living room and plopped onto the couch by the bay window.

Anticipation burned in him as he moved toward his truck, parked across the street. He was anxious to get this party started but knew patience and the details mattered. He pushed back a surge of desire.

"Focus," he whispered. "Stick to the plan."

Through the window, he watched Joan rise and move toward the kitchen. She tripped, righted herself, and then opened the refrigerator door. While she stared, her body swayed, as if standing up straight required too much concentration and effort. Finally, empty-handed, she closed the door and moved past Ann, who had passed out on the couch.

She shut off the light in the living room, and, seconds later, a bedside light in her room clicked on. He watched as she all but fell down on the purple bedspread. She tugged off her shoes, tossed them on the floor, and shut off the light.

He waited another ten minutes before reaching under a tarp covering the bed of his truck. He grabbed the handles of two gallon-size plastic jugs stowed side by side. The containers were each filled with gasoline, and the tops were sealed with fragments of a torn sweatshirt.

The night's inky blackness offered him the cover he needed as he moved with practiced efficiency. He had planned this night for weeks and could picture each and every detail, down to the last moment.

After crossing the small front yard, he ducked around the side of the house. He set the first unlit device under Joan's window and then, moving around the house, placed the second jug by the back door. There was a third gasoline-style bomb under the house's crawl space, positioned near Joan's bedroom.

As he reached for his lighter, he noticed that the back door was unlocked. "Sloppy, girls. Sloppy."

The temptation to see Joan and Ann unconscious and helpless was too strong to resist, so he carefully pushed open the back door. The house was silent as he moved into the small living room toward Ann, who lay on her belly, her hand draped over the side of the couch.

A part of him was sorry for her. Ann was sweet by nature and so pretty.

"You should have listened to me."

He moved more confidently across the room and carefully pushed open Joan's bedroom door. She lay on her back, her body relaxed and boneless. Her breathing was deep and steady. He stood by her bed and gently brushed back her dark hair. She had a pretty face. A very nice body. But she was bossy. Loud. Had a real mouth on her.

"This is all your fault. Ann will suffer because of you. You just don't know when to stop pushing."

As if something deep inside her sensed the danger, she drew in a deep breath and rolled on her side toward him. He stood very still, watching and waiting for her eyes to open. Even as he feared discovery, a part of him wanted her to see him standing over her. He imagined her shock and then her fear. God, how he wanted to see her tremble.

"Joan," he whispered. "Guess who?"

Dark urges burned inside him. It would be so easy now to strip her naked, shove inside her, and show her just how badly she had underestimated him. But that was not part of the plan. His fire would dish out the perfect punishment.

He rose, crossed the room, and closed her bedroom door. He exited the house via the kitchen, carefully centered his device by the door, and adjusted the torn sock deeper into the gasoline. He fished a lighter from his pocket and dragged his thumb over the spark wheel. A flame flickered. For just a moment, he stared at the pretty flame that danced and undulated as it whispered promises of destruction.

He lit the gasoline-soaked cotton cloth, and it caught fire immediately. Practice had taught him that this was the critical time. He had only seconds before the flame reached the gasoline reservoir, so he had to move quickly to the second device, light it, and hurry to his truck.

As he slid behind the wheel and started the engine, the first bomb exploded. Though it was tempting to stay and watch his fire roar to life, he gently pressed the accelerator and slowly drove down the street. The second explosion, under Joan's window, pulled his gaze to the rearview mirror, now illuminated with orange and yellow flames licking up the side of the house. The blaze on the back side of the house cast off dark, billowing smoke that threaded up and through the flames.

God, it was beautiful. Pride swelled in him. He grew hard, sorry now he had not taken Joan.

As he turned the corner, the third bomb detonated, and more flames shot up as a fire engine's siren blared in the distance. Help was on the way. Too bad it would not be in time.

CHAPTER ONE

Philadelphia, Pennsylvania
Friday, September 4, 2020
4:55 p.m.
Present Day

If homicide detective Joan Mason had a superpower, it was her ability to erase memories. Born with a supersize "Delete" key in her brain, she was able to forget grisly homicide scenes, a long-lost mother, a whiskey-soaked father, friends, and lovers. Like little ol' Cinderella, she could scrub the past's stains until they were almost imperceptible.

The noises of the bar hummed around Joan as she reread the letter from the Montana Department of Corrections and sipped her whiskey. Elijah Weston, the man who had set fire to the house she had lived in during her senior year of college, was being released from prison today. She was being notified not out of any professional courtesy but because she had been one of Elijah's intended victims.

She raised her glass and peered through the amber liquid, which cast tawny golds on the letter. She might be many things, but she was not a victim.

"What's turned you so sour?" the bartender asked.

The bar's owner, Ray O'Toole, was a mountain of a man, standing over six foot, five inches. He sported a graying beard that would have made him look fierce if not for the doe eyes outing him as a soft touch. When Joan's father was alive, Ray had given him work when rent money was scarce. When she was in middle school and her old man had accidentally set fire to their apartment, Ray had given them the extra two rooms above the bar. And when Joan's father had finally taken off for good when she was fourteen, Ray met with social services and saw to it that Joan stayed with him.

O'Toole's Pub was still a neighborhood favorite, an everyone-knows-your-name place that also had the added bonus of being within walking distance of her current town house. It was the closest place she had to a home base.

Joan downed the last of her whiskey. "You mean more than usual?"

Ray grinned. "Exactly."

"It's an old case I was involved in. The guy has served his time, and now he's getting out." Joan studied her empty glass, knowing the stain of some memories required more elbow grease than others.

Ray set another whiskey neat in front of her and glanced at the letterhead. "Montana? You have not been out there since . . ."

She met Ray's gaze. "The fire."

"That letter is about Elijah Weston. That psycho is out?"

"Yes, he is."

"Shit. You okay?"

"I'm fine." If her old man had taught Joan anything, it was how to bullshit her way through uncertainty.

More patrons walked through the front door, laughing and joking and drawing Ray away as he swiped a couple of menus and followed them to a booth.

Joan folded up the letter and, needing a distraction, shifted her attention to a reasonably good-looking man sitting at the end of the bar. He had a full head of dark hair, a strong jaw, and carried a few extra pounds that tugged slightly at the lines of his expensive gray suit. She had seen him around the courthouse, and they had exchanged glances once or twice as each checked the other out. She rummaged through her brain, searching for his name. It escaped her, but she was fairly certain he was a prosecutor. Most importantly, he might be a nice distraction over this very long Labor Day weekend.

He raised his gaze and, noting her attention, ordered a beer, came down the bar, and slowly took a seat beside her. He regarded her cropped dark hair, tasteful silk blouse, tailored black suit, and heeled boots. "I've seen you at the courthouse. Cop or lawyer? I usually can tell but can't with you."

"I'm a cop, and you're a lawyer," she said without looking up.

"That's right. Steve Vincent."

She knew immediately Steve liked what he saw. She was not stunningly beautiful but had been described as "striking" by a few suitors. Several workouts a week kept her figure toned. "Detective Joan Mason."

"Joan Mason. Where have I heard . . . ? Damn, you were the lead detective on that arson case," Steve said. "Suspect's name escapes me."

"Avery Newport."

"That's right. Her roommate died in the fire."

"You're well informed."

"Word gets around the courthouse. It's like a small town. You landed one hell of an explosive case."

Joan was the homicide detective to call when arson was involved. "Yes, it was."

Steve accepted a beer from Ray with a quick nod. "The defendant's old man hired a real ballbuster of an attorney. Dug up some facts about you. Said you were biased, based on your history."

"Like me, he was doing his job," Joan said.

"Did the department really suspend you?"

She had never played politics well. And when she'd been told to back off the case, she had not. She knew Avery Newport was guilty, and she did not care about her father's political connections. "Yes, they did, Steve."

He glanced toward her hands, most likely searching for the burn scars the defense attorney had mentioned repeatedly to the media. "He said something about you nearly dying in a fire when you were a kid and then another one while you were in college. He said that's why you couldn't drop this case."

"Those fires were a long time ago." Though they both felt painfully close at this moment.

Feeling Steve's continued attention on her hands, she held them out as she said, "They don't hurt." He now had a full view of the white scars crisscrossing her palms. "Still sensitive to heat, and techs can't roll a decent print, but otherwise fine."

To his credit, Steve did not look away. "Which fire was that one from?"

"College."

"How did you get them?"

"Grabbing a red-hot door handle." She regarded him. "You're a lawyer, Steve, so you'd be the person to ask. Do my past experiences cloud my ability to investigate an arsonist?"

"You're asking a lawyer for a yes-or-no answer?" he said, grinning.

A sense of humor was a point in his column. "You're right, Counselor, but just supposing . . ."

"I'd have used it against you," he said. "Impossible to ignore."

"I would have, too." She pushed the glass away, wishing the whiskey's kick would blur the past.

"Is what they said true, Joan?" Steve asked.

"I don't know, Steve; what did they say?"

He had the good taste to look a little sheepish before he asked, "That the guy who torched your house in college is due to be released from prison this year."

That was another tidbit the defense attorney had used to publicly call her judgment into question. Shrugging her shoulders, Joan decided she needed fresh air. She scrounged up a decent-enough smile as she grabbed the letter and her purse. "It's been nice, Steve."

"Hey, I didn't mean to pry."

"Of course you did." She fished a twenty from her pocket, tossed it on the bar.

He rose. "I thought, maybe—"

"So did I, but you just talked yourself out of what could have been a fun evening."

"I make my living talking." He was the type to argue with the weather. "But I also know how to shut up."

"Apparently not today."

Purse on her shoulder and letter clutched in her hand, she walked outside to discover a sky thick with gray clouds. Mother Nature understood exactly how she felt. As far as she was concerned, it could rain buckets on everyone until Tuesday.

Still, there were people heading to the bars. Many were laughing, as if they had already adapted to the rainy forecast and shifted their weekend plans inside. If only change were that easy.

The air was muggy, and she cursed the sweat running down her back as she made the two-block walk to her town house. As she rounded the corner onto her street, her phone rang. She removed it from her back pocket and glanced at the display. It was her partner, Seth.

"I heard about the suspension."

"Good news travels fast."

"I warned you," Seth's gravelly voice barked on the end of the line. "Can't beat people who are connected. In my younger days, I made that same mistake, but I learned. Just like you have."

Joan flexed her fingers, accepting that he was trying to help. "You and I both know she did it. Even if my witnesses recanted their testimony after I arrested her."

"You are preaching to the choir, Joansie."

"She's going to do it again." Just like she sensed in her bones that Elijah would set more fires.

"We don't arrest people for crimes that haven't happened, and unless you have one big smoking gun, you're not going to hold her for more than five minutes."

"Who gets to die the next time?" Joan asked. "The next woman Avery believes is sleeping with her boyfriend?" *The next woman Elijah Weston fixates on?*

"Look, you got two weeks of what amounts to paid vacation. Use the time to relax. You work harder than anyone I know." Seth sounded tired. "Take a break."

"Right."

He must have heard the fatigue in her voice. "You going to be okay?"

"Don't worry about me," she said carefully.

Seth hesitated. "You sure?"

"Yeah. I'm golden, Seth."

"Don't let the suspension get you down. Two weeks will fly."

Two weeks of no distractions and time to think about how she should have built the Newport case differently. "Like a bird."

"Barb and I are grilling tomorrow. Door's always open."

"Thanks. But don't count on me. I'll be foul company."

After a few more reassurances that she was good to go, she hung up. She climbed the stairs to her town house and unlocked the door. Inside, she picked up the letters dropped through the slot by the mail carrier. She clicked on a light, toed off her shoes, and dropped the mail on a small kitchen table. A card fell out of the stack of envelopes. It was from a reporter. *"Would love to interview you."*

She crumpled the card and tossed it in the trash before she walked to her refrigerator and grabbed a beer. She twisted off the top and took a long pull. Sitting at the small round table by the kitchen window, she pressed the cold bottle to her temple and looked toward her refrigerator, where she had taped a picture of Mandy Kelso, Avery Newport's dead roommate. The picture had been taken at an amusement park and featured eighteen-year-old Mandy flashing a thousand-watt smile. "I'm sorry. But I'll make this right."

The tightness in her chest twisted harder, forcing her to look away. She focused on the mail. Most of it was junk, some were bills, but at the bottom of the pile was a handwritten letter with no return address. She stared at her name printed in the familiar bold handwriting. Heart hammering, she carefully set down the beer, opened the envelope, and removed the letter.

> Dear Joan,
> It's been a while since we exchanged letters, but I wanted you to know I have been following the Newport case . . .

She dropped the letter and closed her eyes. How the hell had Elijah Weston gotten her home address? She could think of nothing more inappropriate than today of all days to receive a letter from the guy who had nearly burned her alive. Karma clearly had a grudge against her.

Needing a moment to gather her thoughts, she moved to her den and sat on a blue vintage midcentury sofa angled toward a nonworking fireplace. A metal-framed mirror over the fireplace reflected the opposite wall and the low shelves showcasing biographies and classic novels. There were more antique pieces, including a coffee table and two walnut lounge chairs sporting cushions covered in a navy-blue fabric. Her decorating style was clean, clutter-free, and incorporated older furnishings not as flammable as their modern counterparts.

She regarded the envelope, again noting her home address written in his very precise handwriting. She had first written to Elijah Weston a year after the fire because she had needed to know why he'd set the fire.

She had provided a PO box, never believing he would answer. But he had written back, denying that he had set the fire. She had exchanged more letters with him over the coming years, hoping he would eventually tell her the truth. But he never had told her why he'd set the fire. Five months ago, she'd closed down the PO box and had stopped writing him.

"How the hell did you find my house?" she whispered.

Dear Joan,

It's been a while since we exchanged letters, but I wanted you to know I have been following the Newport case. I still believe that your instincts about Avery Newport are correct. She did set the fire, and she has escaped justice because she has money and privilege. I know if I had half the resources available to Avery, I would never have gone to prison. Stay strong. Avery will strike again because it is hard for someone like her to ignore the lure of fire.

I didn't mean for this letter to be gloomy. In fact, I have very good news. The State of Montana has ruled that I have served my time and paid my debt to society. By Friday, I will again be a free man and living back in Missoula. I don't know how often you get back to Big Sky Country, but I would love to see you again.

Cheers,

Elijah

"It is hard for someone like her to ignore the lure of fire," she whispered.

Was Elijah talking just about Avery or offering a hint about himself? She reread the letter, trying to wrap her brain around the idea that he had found her. She let her head fall back against the couch.

The last time she had seen Elijah had been a week before the fire. The school year had been nearly over, she'd had her sights set on graduate school, and he had been wrapping up a very successful freshman year. *Her roommate, Ann Bailey, stood at the top of the stairs. "Joan! Chop-chop. We have movie tickets."*

Ann's blond hair was swept into an effortless yet attractive ponytail, and, as always, no makeup covered her peaches-and-cream complexion. A bulky cable-knit sweater skimmed above her trim jeans, proving cold weather lingered a long time in Montana. A pair of well-worn UGGs warmed her feet, and a blue-and-white cable-knit scarf wound around her neck in an offhanded yet stylish way.

"Be right there, Ann," she said before she shifted her attention to Elijah, a freshman standing by her teaching assistant's desk. Elijah had proven to have one of the quickest minds in the entire school.

At the sound of Ann's voice, Elijah had immediately lifted his gaze to Ann. It was not like Joan did not work out or take care of herself, because she did. But Ann was in a different league. When Ann entered the room, men forgot about the other women around. What really sucked was that Ann was sincerely nice and smart.

"Mr. Weston, did you have a question?" Joan knew she sounded more annoyed than she had intended.

Elijah shifted his focus back to her. His hair was thick, blond, and swept back over his forehead as if a breeze had just caught it. It begged to be brushed back. "You shouldn't compare yourself to her."

"What?"

"Comparisons are rarely productive. Women do it all the time. Men do, too. Regardless, they're a waste of time unless there's real value."

Joan felt the color rise in her cheeks, but instead of confirming his wise observation, she went on the offensive. "Did you have a question?"

"No question. You did a great job this semester, and I'm just giving credit where it's due."

"Okay. Thanks. See you around."

"Sure."

Joan gripped the strap of her pack and dashed up the stairs. Halfway up, her foot caught on a loose piece of carpeting, and she stumbled. Adrenaline surging, she quickly righted herself. She refused to look back because she sensed that he was watching.

Ann grinned. "You look flustered."

"I just tripped."

Joan watched as Ann looked toward Elijah, met his gaze, and smiled warmly. "What's Elijah like?"

"Smart. Best student ever."

"He and I are going to be volunteer math tutors this weekend at the student center," Ann said.

"He certainly knows his material."

Ann playfully jabbed Joan in the ribs. Then Joan hustled out of the room, glad Ann was right on her heels. Even after Joan's breakup with Gideon, Ann had remained her friend, and for that reason alone, she would have her back forever.

Ann dropped her voice while glancing around. "He's intense. Smart. Different."

Different. Joan could have practiced all day and not crafted a better understatement. All kinds of rumors swirled around Elijah, but whispers often followed people who did not fit a mold.

"He's hot," Ann said, whispering. "But just a little young for me."

Now, as Joan pushed aside the memory and considered another beer, she wondered for the millionth time if she had missed any warning signs with Elijah. However, replays of their brief interactions had never revealed any lingering omens, and his letters never suggested a motive.

She rose and walked to her laptop, centered on a small desk tucked in the corner. She opened it and checked the weather in Missoula. It was thirty degrees colder than in Philadelphia, and snow would be coming soon.

She tapped her fingers on the keys and then searched airline flights to Missoula. The tickets were not cheap and would mean a dip into the savings she'd been setting aside for a new car. But the car could wait a little longer. And if she called Ann, she knew the lodging would be covered.

Joan had not stayed for Elijah's trial, but Ann had told her later that he had repeatedly professed his innocence. But a history of small arson-related events, multiple eyewitnesses who had placed him near their homes hours before the fire, and forensic evidence that linked his DNA to the crime scene had all resulted in a swift guilty verdict. At his sentencing, Ann had said Elijah had spoken calmly about the imbalanced scales of justice. She said it had not been his words that had troubled her but his expression and tone, which both had hinted of retribution.

In Joan's experience, that kind of anger did not just go away. Ten years of incarceration was plenty of time to plan revenge. The letter Elijah had sent to her home was not meant to be friendly. Hidden behind the chatty conversation was a real threat that she intended to neutralize.

Confessions of an Arsonist
My first fire was a tiny brush fire.

It was nothing big, but it crackled as its flames stretched up and toward the brush around it. It was hungry and wanted to devour the dry land. But I panicked, afraid that it would spread and I would be discovered. So I stomped it out until there was nothing but smoldering black ash. Destroying it made me angry. My fire deserved to run wild and consume everything it wanted. Already, I was anxious to set another fire.

CHAPTER TWO

Missoula, Montana
Saturday, September 5, 2020
4:30 p.m.

As the plane touched down at Missoula International Airport, Joan stared out her window toward the mountain range ablaze with vibrant reds and oranges. She was surprised that the glowing Montana hues conjured memories of the College Fire, which always lurked in the shadows.

The night of the fire, Joan and Ann had been out drinking. Each had broken up with their boyfriends and were anxious to move on with their lives. But a couple of beers had quickly sapped their strength, so they had decided to make it an early night. They had staggered home, and both had fallen into a deep sleep. The next thing Joan remembered was the explosion and Ann's panicked shouts. "Joan, get up! Get up! The house is on fire!"

Ann's voice sounded so far off, and even as she prayed for five more minutes of sleep, the scent of smoke slithered up her nose and rubbed against her nasal passages like sandpaper. She sneezed, pulled in more of the smoke that was quickly filling the air. Her lungs burning, she coughed and sat up as the sound of fire engines wailed in the distance.

"Joan!" Ann's voice grew more desperate and distant.

Her head spun as she looked around the small room filled with dark-gray smoke and coiling fumes. Beyond the door, popping sounds mixed with the roar of a spiraling wind.

Involuntarily, she sucked in a second breath, followed quickly by a new coughing fit. She raised her hands to her mouth as she swung her feet over the side of the bed. For an instant, she was back in the apartment with her father, and the fire was consuming the living room around his recliner as he slept.

The inferno's pop and roar hissed louder as the gray smoke grew darker. She dropped to the floor on her hands and knees, taking refuge in a lingering pocket of breathable air. The smoke thickened and forced her to her belly against the blue shag carpet. Her eyes watered, and she sensed she had minutes to escape. She crawled faster.

Her fingers brushed the edge of a door, and she stood and twisted the knob. She expected to see her living room but instead found herself in her closet. Sweat beaded on her brow and between her shoulder blades. Inside the closet, she sucked in the last of the fresh air and then moved to the door to her right.

Rising again, she reached for the door handle and immediately recoiled as the metal, now molten hot, burned her palm. The pain rocketed through her body and sent a surge of adrenaline, clearing all traces of brain fog. She glanced back toward her bed, thinking she could wrap her body and hands in a coverlet, but the smoke now enveloped her and the bed.

Grabbing the edge of her shirt, she twisted the handle with her left hand. The heat immediately burned through the worn cotton fabric, blistering her skin. She accepted the pain and kept turning the knob. It gave way, and the door swung inward.

Joan gasped at the first sign of the inferno eating through the room and their lives. She looked toward the front door and saw Gideon carrying his sister, Ann, outside. She tried to follow, but the heat held her back.

"Don't leave me!" Joan gasped.

Neither looked back as they rushed out the front door. She dropped to her hands and knees, desperately searching for another pocket of air. The *carpet radiated more heat as wallboards crackled and groaned beneath the fire thundering over her head. When she lifted her gaze, the door had vanished in a cloud of black smoke. Desperate, she crawled back to the closet in her room, choking until finally her head spun, and she passed out.*

The plane came to a stop, and the steward announced the local time. Joan waited as the passengers grabbed their bags from the overhead bins, and when it was her turn, she yanked her backpack free.

Checking her watch, Joan knew that if Ann was as punctual as she had been in college, she would be at baggage claim now. As she made her way through the terminal, she wondered what it would be like to see Ann again. It had been more than ten years since the fire, and though she and Ann had exchanged cards each holiday and had spoken on the phone a few times in the early years, they had not had any real contact in some time. They had been the best of friends during college and had survived a devastating fire. They should have shared a lifelong bond of friendship.

So many times, she had nearly called Ann, but each time she found a reason not to. Dismantling the past was much like poking around a burned-out building. Tug on one board or beam and you risked toppling what structure remained. Pushing through the door, she tamped down her apprehension and followed the sounds of a growing cluster of passengers gathered around the luggage carousel.

Joan's gaze was drawn to a tall, lean woman wrestling a large bag, which she yanked free and pushed toward an elderly man.

Joan recognized Ann's blond hair and compact, athletic body. The hair was shorter, but her body was as fit as it had been in college. Joan tugged her sweater down, remembering her broken promise to get to the gym before her flight today. As Ann turned, she spotted Joan. For a moment, they stared at each other, trying to gauge the other's reaction.

Finally, Joan raised her hand, and they closed the gap between them. She hugged Ann's thinner frame and felt the tension rippling through her body like a rubber band ready to snap.

"Long time no see," Joan said.

"We finally got you back to Missoula. I've missed you."

"Same." Smiling, Ann shoved her fingers through her bangs, a habit Joan remembered from college as a sign of nerves.

To break the ice, Joan produced a red Philadelphia Phillies T-shirt and ball cap from the backpack's side pocket. "Where's your boy? I come bearing gifts."

Ann held up the small T-shirt. "Thank you."

Joan instantly realized her mistake. "Okay, how big is the kid? Any son of Clarke Mead's has to be tall."

"The top of his head comes up to my shoulder."

Joan studied the T-shirt. "Tell me his head will still fit in the ball cap."

Ann laughed, and some of the tension between them eased. "It will. Do you have much luggage?"

"Only the backpack. If I need a change of clothes, I have a brand-spanking-new Phillies T-shirt I can wear."

"Is there a coat in that backpack?"

"It was eighty-five degrees in Philadelphia this morning."

"It'll be close to thirty here by tomorrow evening. I have extra jackets."

"The daytime highs were in the sixties, but I forgot about the cold nights. Winter comes fast out here."

"Yes, it does."

They crossed the terminal and stepped outside into the crisp air. Joan drew in a deep breath, her gaze lingering on the puffy white clouds hovering in the blue sky above the mountain chain to the west. "I'd forgotten how good the air smells out here. And the big sky. Philadelphia is currently locked in haze and humidity."

"I've traveled several times to New York and DC, and I've always found the energy of the cities as intoxicating as it is exhausting. I'm always glad to get back home."

"No more dreams of living in a big city?"

"Not anymore. And if that makes me provincial, then so be it."

"I'm slated to attend a conference in Orlando in January." Assuming she did not get canned from her job. "You and Nate should come and do Disney World."

"I might take you up on that." Ann's acceptance sounded as tentative as the offer. She clicked her key fob, and the lights of a mud-splattered white SUV blinked. "When you called last night, I searched you on the internet. I read about the Newport case."

Joan opened the back door and tossed in her bag. They each slid into the front seats, closed the doors, and clicked their seat belts. "Never arrest the daughter of a very powerful judge. And if you do, and you're warned to back off, do it."

"You could always be stubborn."

"Doesn't matter now. I've officially erased it from my memory bank."

Ann smiled. "You used to do that in college."

"What?"

"Press your 'Delete' key. Bad test, date, or movie, you closed your eyes and said, 'Delete.'"

"Only way to move on." The past was far more powerful than a mystical button, but it was easier to pretend otherwise. "Where's Nate?" Joan asked.

"It's Clarke's weekend to have him."

"Clarke's weekend. Sounds like a divorce."

"We separated six months ago."

"Wow. Sorry to hear that."

Ann's smile was reassuring as she drove to the parking attendant's booth, paid him, and headed north, away from town, toward the family ranch. "It's really going well. We both agreed that a little time apart was a good thing. We married so young, Nate came right away, and neither of us had a chance to be ourselves."

22

Joan leaned back in her seat and crossed her hands over her chest. She had never seen a civil divorce, but if anyone could pull it off, it was Ann, who had earned her PhD in forensic psychology, and then lectured at the university, but also consulted with the police. "You sound very logical, Dr. Bailey."

"Clarke and I are okay with it. Nate loves living on my parents' ranch."

She omitted any mention of Gideon, his wife, or son, and Joan did not ask. "Are you seeing anyone?"

"No," Ann said, laughing and cringing at once. "There's not been enough time for that."

"There's no one? As I remember it, every male over the age of twelve had a thing for you."

"My best offer so far is from a police sergeant to speak at the Montana Highway Patrol."

Joan offered an undeniably sly grin. "Is this guy single?"

"Yes."

"He's got more in mind than forensics."

"He really does have a genuine interest in the psychology of repeat offenders. It's strictly professional."

Joan plucked an imaginary hair from her jeans. "Maybe you're right."

"You're laughing at me," Ann said.

"A little. What would it hurt if he did ask you out?"

The stress visibly melted from Ann's shoulders. "If we're talking about love lives, what's the status of yours?"

"Married to the job."

"That can't be much fun."

"It has its perks."

"It's the job that brought you here, then?"

Joan's vibe shifted from easygoing to brittle. "You know me—I was never good at social calls. Is he really officially out?"

She knew Ann did not need a detailed reference to understand she was talking about Elijah Weston. "I haven't seen him since the trial, but my sources in the prison system tell me that the beautiful boy we knew in college has firmed up into an imposing man during the last decade."

"Brilliant and now strong." Elijah Weston could have been the perfect guy. If he did not have a habit of setting fires. "Where is he now?"

"He moved into a boardinghouse near the university yesterday. He and his lawyer have gone out of their way to keep his release quiet, but you know how that goes. Missoula is a small town in many respects, and people will figure out that he's been released. The state notified me, because I was his victim. Did they do the same for you?"

"Yes. My letter arrived yesterday. Nothing like giving me time to prepare."

"Do you really think that he would come after you or me?" Ann asked.

"I'm not going to wait to find out."

"They tell me he still denies he had anything to do with the College Fire," Ann said.

"Elijah sent a letter to me at my home address."

"What? How did he find you?"

"I don't know. Did he write you, too?"

"He sent two letters to my parents' address years ago, but I never responded. After that, Clarke promised to run interference for me."

"I'd think a psychologist would be all over correspondence with a guy like Elijah. How many people get a glimpse into the mind of an arsonist?"

"Elijah's mind is one place I have never dreamed of traveling." Ann drew in a slow, steady breath. "He's playing a game."

"I'm very aware."

"What do you think you can accomplish, coming back here?"

"Other than catching up with my college pal? I don't know." Elijah had left an indelible mark on her life that would never be erased, even by her magic "Delete" key.

Ann regarded Joan. "You're worried about him, aren't you?"

"He's had ten years to plan his next move."

"What makes you think there is a next move?"

"Gut feeling."

Ann slowed at a T intersection and, tapping the brakes, took a left. Shifting gears, she pressed the accelerator. "What makes you think you can stop him, Joan? You can't watch him twenty-four seven."

"Don't underestimate me. I'm a one-woman wrecking ball." Joan scrounged up a grin, but Ann's grim expression echoed her own sense of dread.

***

The arsonist stood in the shadows inside the beauty shop. It had closed three hours ago, and the space was now silent. The cleaning crew had just swept up the stray piles of hair, polished the mirrors and chrome-trimmed chairs, and dumped the trash.

The Beau-T-Shop was doing well by all accounts. It had more customers than the five hairdressers could handle, so the owner should have been making money hand over fist. But success had a way of tricking people into believing the money would always flow.

He reached for the plastic milk jug of gas siphoned from the borrowed truck's gas tank. Though it was easier to fill up his containers at a gas station, that was a quick way to get noticed by the cops. So, he'd tanked up the truck and then driven to the mountains and siphoned most of the gas into jugs. A trip to another gas station and his vehicle was refilled, with no one the wiser.

He poured a trail of gas along the first salon station. He paused to look at the picture of the stylist and her children, a boy and a girl with white gap-toothed grins standing with their mother in Glacier National Park. He did not know the woman and was a little sorry that she would be out of a job, but if she was any good at what she did, she would quickly find work. It might mean moving to Helena or Bozeman, but no one said life was fair.

He continued to dribble gasoline over each station, only pausing when he reached the last. He knew the woman who worked at this station. She had been a sweet, humble little thing the day they'd met, and he'd been drawn to her from the outset. Like most women, however, she'd proven herself to be a liar.

He continued pouring gas, inhaling the fragrant scent. Just as he'd finished off the first jug, a door opened behind him. Carefully, he set his container down and checked his watch. "You're right on time, darlin'."

Keys rattled and heels clicked across the back room as she approached. She had a petite frame, blond hair cut short on top and long on the sides.

"What are you doing? Why did you call me?" the woman asked.

"What does it look like I'm doing?"

Worry knitted her brow. "You said you wanted to talk." She gripped the keys and took a step toward him. "I smell gas. What are you doing?"

"What do you think? You said you hated your job, right? You said you dreamed of burning this place to the ground. I aim to please, baby."

Her grin faded to horror as the weight of his words settled. "I didn't literally mean *burn* it to the ground."

He moved toward her, smiling, his gaze dropping to her breasts. Lana always did have a great rack. He reached for her left hand and kissed the diamond he had slipped on her finger yesterday. "You said you wanted to see it reduced to ashes."

She searched his face, as if waiting for the punch line. "That was *before*."

"Before what?" he prompted as he reached in his pocket for a packet of matches.

Her gaze shifted to his hands, as if remembering stolen times when she had guided his hand to her breast as she whispered *Fuck me* in his ear. "You know."

He did know. And that was precisely why they were here now. He removed a match from the packet and struck it. "Yes, I do."

"You're scaring me." She took a step back.

"I'm trying to fulfill our fantasy, baby. All you talk about is fire. Now you can see it for yourself." He lit the match, and some of the fear softened in her gaze. "You like it, don't you?" The match burned out. He struck another and held it up for her.

She moistened her lips and touched the burned match.

"You always get excited when I talk about flames."

She pouted her lips, but she stepped closer to him.

"Come on, baby. Do this with me," he cajoled.

"We're going to get arrested."

"Not if we're careful. And I know how to do it right, don't I?"

That coaxed a small, nervous smile. "Yeah, you do."

"Then do this with me. I promise it'll make you horny as hell."

She moistened her lips again. "We won't get caught?"

"No, we won't. I promise."

"Can I light the fire?" she asked in her baby-doll voice.

"Sure, darlin'." He held out the packet.

The tension vanished from her body as she reached for the packet. When she was inches from him, he grabbed her by the wrist and wrapped a rope around her neck. Her keys dropped to the ground as her hands went to his. Blue eyes stared up at him. For a second, her gaze was questioning and even a little turned on.

"You like the danger, right?" he asked.

"Yeah, but . . ."

He tightened his grip on the rope. The tendons in her neck stiffened, and her nails bit into his gloved hands as she tried to pry his fingers free. He had imagined himself doing this so many times, but as detailed as his fantasies had been, nothing compared to this. She kicked him hard, her foot connecting with his shin. The pain felt good, and the bruise to come would be a reminder of all this.

He leaned in closer, savoring the quickening beat of her heart as she struggled to draw in a breath and shout. His excitement picked up even as his arm muscles cramped. Strangling was harder, slower than he imagined. Drawing in a breath, he gritted his teeth as he held steady, knowing he would miss those beautiful breasts the most.

Slowly, her eyes rolled back in her head as her eyelids drifted closed and her lips took on a blue tinge.

"You've never looked so good to me, baby."

When her knees buckled, he loosened his grip and slowly lowered her to the puddle of gasoline under them. The pulsing vein in her neck stilled like a snuffed-out candle flame.

He lingered over her motionless body. He angled her face toward his and kissed her gently on the lips. He removed the diamond ring. "Nothing you didn't deserve, you lying bitch."

Finally, he rose and walked to the back storeroom, where he grabbed two more gasoline jugs. He strategically spread the liquid, careful to douse the back room, filled with chemical dyes and solvents delivered that morning.

Satisfied that he had properly soaked the place, he dug the book of matches from his pocket. He opened the door and looked down either side of the alley, searching for anyone who might have been watching. His gaze roamed over the brick walls and the clapboard siding of the building across the alley. That building housed a law firm. Tonight, the two windows facing the alley were dark, and he saw no sign of movement in the building. It was the random passersby who could ruin the best of plans.

Newbies to arson more often screwed up at this point. Many stood too close to the source of ignition, underestimating the swift and devastating power the fire was poised to blow back on them.

He was no novice.

He not only understood fire; he respected it.

Loved it.

He would use his last reserve jug to trail gasoline down the alley. He tossed the jug back into the beauty shop entrance before running to the end of the trail and striking the match. The flame caught immediately and slithered along the path of gasoline like a fiery snake ready to strike. He had only seconds to wait before a big burst of flames echoed from the building. The fire had reached the large puddle and was headed toward the solvents.

He started walking quickly, knowing the boom would come in seconds. He hustled to the street, crossed to another alley, and ran up to his car. Carefully, he removed his boots and dumped them in a waiting garbage bag. He stripped off his gloves, jeans, and shirt, leaving him wearing running shorts and a T-shirt. The rest went into a bag that he tossed in the bed of his truck. He grabbed clean clothes from the front seat, sliding on worn jeans and a fresh sweatshirt. He had already draped a towel on the truck's seat, knowing that the towel, along with the clothes, would be buried later.

He'd had a lot of time to think about this, and he was not going to let trace evidence trip him up any more than a random witness.

As he started the engine, he heard an explosion in the beauty shop filled with chemicals. The flames would soon jump up the walls and arch over the ceiling. He calculated it would take less than a minute before the entire building exploded. He hoped the attorneys across the alley were paid up on their fire insurance, because they were going to see some damage.

He glanced in his rearview mirror and caught the glow of the flames. In the distance, the fire engine sirens were revving up, and he could picture the men at the station jumping up from dinner and running toward their engines. Wheels rolling in less than sixty seconds. Another two minutes to the fire. Hoses out.

His blaze had enough momentum to gut the building and also eat through the woman's flesh. The human body melted at fifteen hundred degrees, and if he had maybe ten minutes of solid burning, there would be nothing left of her.

But five minutes would do enough damage to hide what he had done.

He grinned.

"You always wanted to go out with a bang, baby. Got your wish."

***

The blast in the back room startled Lana back to consciousness. She gulped in air saturated with chemicals and smoke as the fire roared and licked at her feet.

Her throat burned as she screamed and tried to rise up. But her bruised, nearly crushed throat stung as she drew in the acidic air, thickening with chemicals that she used every day.

She rolled onto her belly, wincing as she crawled toward the front window and away from the unleashed fire dragon consuming the storeroom and the salon. Her escape route was vanishing, and in seconds, this entire building would collapse on her.

Panicking, she rose up on her hands and knees, but another lungful of lethal smoke sent her back to her belly.

She had been so damn obsessed with fire. Setting them had been a game.

The fire, as if it had heard her, jumped up the west wall and rolled over and consumed the posters featuring the newest hairstyles. Long amber fingers crept over the ceiling above her, and she wondered if she were already dead and in hell.

A police car's red and blue lights flashed outside less than twenty feet away.

"Save me!" she screamed.

Timber above her head cracked. Several ceiling tiles fell and hit the floor, releasing a swarm of firefly embers that burned her skin. Flames licked over her feet and spread to her jeans. She howled in pain as her flesh melted.

Confessions of an Arsonist
I burned myself today on the arm, and the pain sent a rush of pleasure through me as potent as sex. Both pleasures create an intimate bond that cannot be duplicated.

CHAPTER THREE

Missoula, Montana
Saturday, September 5, 2020
6:55 p.m.

Detective Gideon Bailey had hoped his first day back on the job would be peaceful. He had expected a call or two. With the students back for the fall semester, trouble was inevitable. And so far, so good. Since his shift had started that morning, he had responded to an overdose and an attempted rape. He had stayed with the victim in the emergency room until the sexual-assault nurse had arrived. Now it looked like his plan to reenter the job after three months of leave was coming off without a hitch.

He had taken three months off to spend time with his ten-year-old son, Kyle. The two had spent the time living in his grandfather Mac's cabin, nestled in the Sapphire Mountain Range. Their days had been filled with fishing, hiking, and rebuilding the stone firepit on the property.

Gideon's ex-wife, Helen, had died in the spring from cancer. Helen had reached out in January and told him what was happening. She was not the type to ask for help, even when their son had been hit by a passing car and suffered a broken arm. But she had sense enough to think of Kyle first and had contacted Gideon.

Gideon had immediately driven to Denver to see her and his son, whom he saw one weekend a month and two weeks during the summer.

Whatever animus he harbored toward his ex-wife vanished when he'd seen her. Helen had aged a decade in the last few months. Her once-full figure had been whittled down to a hundred pounds, her blond hair had thinned, and her skin had turned sallow. She could barely stand. Kyle refused to leave his mother, which meant Gideon traveled back and forth for several months, staying for longer and longer stretches until finally Helen had passed on in early May.

Gideon had packed up his grieving, sullen son and driven back to Missoula. After checking in with his chief, he'd taken leave, and he and Kyle had driven north. The lack of Wi-Fi had been a shock to both their systems. The quiet had created too many opportunities to talk. And the cabin's confined space had offered few places to hide.

That left streams to fish, trails to hike, wood to chop, and a lot of anger and emotions to untangle. They had mended some fences and distance created by the divorce, and he was almost sorry they'd had to come back. But he had a job, and Kyle needed to catch up on the spring's lost schooling.

The car's radio squawked. *"All vehicles in the downtown area, we have a structure fire."*

"Damn it," he muttered as he reached for the radio. "This is Detective Gideon Bailey. I'm a mile away. I'll respond."

"Roger that. Fire crews have been dispatched and deputies en route."

"Roger," he said. He flipped on his lights, did a U-turn at the next intersection, and punched the accelerator. The wails of the fire trucks' sirens quickly grew louder as he hurried through each successive intersection. As he rounded the final corner, his welcome came in the form of flames shooting up toward a dimming sky.

He was out of his vehicle as fire trucks parked and the firefighters scrambled to hook up their hoses to the hydrants. He grabbed his flashlight and raced toward the building, praying that if there were any survivors, he could help.

As Gideon stepped onto the sidewalk, the heat from the building forced him to shield his face with his hands. He angled his body, gripped the flashlight tighter, and edged closer to the front window of the beauty shop, once a favorite of Helen's. Through the window, he saw that the blaze was shooting from the back of the store and heading toward a woman who lay on the floor.

The fingers on her left hand twitched. *Shit.* She was alive.

He rammed the butt of the flashlight into the glass display window. Glass shattered and fell into the shop and around his feet. The extra boost of oxygen energized the fire, making it crackle and wail louder as it dipped down from the ceiling. He thought for a split second that he could get into the building and save the woman. But before he could put the thought into action, all hell broke loose. There was an explosion inside the building, the roof bowed, and ceiling tiles dropped. Cinders danced as heat supercharged the air into a bellowing furnace.

Forced to retreat, he backed up to the vehicle, brushing the burning sparks and soot from his jacket. The firefighters raced toward the blaze, their hoses now shooting at full capacity.

Two patrolmen hurried toward him. The first was Stuart Hughes, who was in his midtwenties and the newest to the department. Tall and lanky with red hair, he still ran almost as fast as he had on the college track team.

Steps behind him was Detective Becca Sullivan, also in her twenties. She stood a few inches over five feet and had thick black hair that she secured in a neat bun. She was one of the department's best shots.

The officers gathered beside Gideon, each staring at the raging flames with a mixture of awe and horror.

"What the hell happened?" Stuart asked, breathless.

"I saw a woman alive inside, lying on the floor." Gideon shouted the words as he jogged over to the fire chief on scene, Clarke Mead.

Clarke was married to his sister, Ann, and the two had recently separated. So far, Gideon had managed to stay out of their separation, which appeared friendly enough, if that was possible. His own divorce had been a nasty, tangled affair that he would not have wished on his worst enemy.

"There's someone inside," Gideon said. "I saw a woman on the floor, near the window. Her fingers moved."

"Are you sure?"

"Yeah."

Clarke raised the radio to his lips and spoke to his crew through their headsets as they wrestled the hose. One team shifted toward the window and sprayed cold water onto the inferno. The flames hissed and spit, not wanting to yield any ground.

"The building is fully engulfed," Clarke said. "I can't send anyone in there now. It would be a death sentence."

"Clarke, she was alive."

Clarke rested his hands on Gideon's shoulders. "If she was, she isn't now. No one could have survived the toxic chemicals and heat."

He stepped back, unable to shake the image of the woman lying unconscious on the floor. "It's like the College Fire."

Clarke stood several inches over six feet, with the broad shoulders of a linebacker. He had short, dark hair and an angled face weathered by the sun. "Don't do that."

Haunting memories, never far away, rushed him. His thoughts went first to his son and nephew, who had been spending the afternoon with Clarke. "Where are Kyle and Nate?"

"They're safe. I dropped both boys off at their friend Tim's house."

Gideon said a word of thanks as he stared at the blaze and prayed the woman had died quickly.

***

Joan settled her backpack in the room assigned to her by Ann, accepted a glass of wine, and was sent to wander around the house as Ann finished dinner. Her gaze was drawn to a picture of Ann, Clarke, and Nate resting on a large raw-edge mantel above the fireplace. The picture looked as if it had been taken a year or two ago. Clarke and Ann both looked much the same, and the boy appeared to be a mix of the two.

The Baileys' front door burst open. Joan automatically reached for the sidearm she'd left behind in Philadelphia as her gaze shifted to the door. Two boys, who appeared to be about ten, stood in the entryway.

"Mom! I'm home! And Kyle is here!"

The child's voice echoed up the stone walls toward the vaulted ceiling, framed by rafters and the mounted stuffed heads of deer and antelope. Joan knew the ever-watching trophies had been placed there decades ago by Ann's father, who had built the place in the midseventies.

As she approached the boys, they skidded to a stop and regarded her with suspicion. She recognized the lean boy as Nate, from the family photo. The high cheekbones and blond hair came from his mother. Clarke's contribution was the dark eyes, though they radiated Ann's intelligence.

The other boy had a similar look, but he was taller and his build sturdier. His relaxed body language suggested he had been here many times and was comfortable in the Bailey home. His dark eyes looked almost familiar.

"Who are you?" Nate demanded.

"I'm Joan. You are Nate, right?"

"Yeah, and this is Kyle."

"Nice to meet you both. I'm a friend of Nate's mother."

"Where's Mom?" Nate's voice was breathless, and his thick hair swept haphazardly over his forehead.

"She's in the kitchen. She's cooking dinner."

Nate's eyes narrowed. This one was not a trusting soul. "Mom!"

"In the kitchen, Nate," Ann called. "You and Kyle wash your hands, and we'll have supper."

Both boys studied Joan just as she might a suspect. The look she shot back had made hardened criminals look away, but neither kid budged.

"How can you be a friend of Mom's? I don't remember you."

"I knew your mother in college, before you were born."

Doubt darkened Nate's gaze. "She's never talked about you."

"How do you know?"

"I remember everything."

"He does," Kyle said. "Ask Aunt Ann."

"Aunt Ann? You two are cousins?" Joan asked.

"Yeah."

Ann had only one sibling, Gideon. And Gideon's son had been born almost nine months to the day after Joan had broken up with him. She could not resent this kid. She had ended things with Gideon. He'd had a right to move on to a new woman.

Joan cleared her throat. "I'm here for a few days."

"Why?" Nate asked.

"You're very inquisitive," she said.

"My teacher says the same thing. She said there are never enough answers for me."

"For you and me both, brother."

"You don't have enough answers?" Kyle asked.

"Never."

"What are your questions?" Nate asked.

"The list is far too long, pal."

Both regarded her for another beat and then moved past her toward the kitchen. Joan followed them into the large kitchen, dominated by a rustic center island trimmed with barnwood that, according to Ann's tour, had come from one of the original structures on the property. Ann had said her parents had tackled a major home renovation last year and were currently in Texas on their first vacation in thirty-five years.

The boys ran toward Ann, and she kissed them both. "I made hot and spicy chili, just the way you like," she said.

Ann was wearing a denim apron and had pulled her blond hair into a ponytail. Joan remembered Mrs. Bailey had worn that apron and had always pulled her hair up the same way. If not for the Baileys, Joan seriously doubted that she would have made it through college. Breaking up with Gideon had meant losing not only a boyfriend but also a family.

Nate reached around his mother and grabbed a freshly cooked biscuit.

"It's hot. Be careful," Ann warned.

Nate bounced the biscuit from hand to hand, then tossed it to Kyle before he grabbed another. "It's not too bad."

"Do me a favor and wash up first," she said, plucking Kyle's biscuit out of midair. "Nate, where is your dad? I thought he had you both this evening."

Nate snatched a second biscuit. "He dropped us off at Tim's. Said a call came in."

"What kind of call?" Ann asked.

"I don't know." Nate bit into his biscuit. "Can we build a fire in the firepit tonight? We could make s'mores."

Ann arched a brow. "Sure. But after dinner. Like I said, wash up."

"Okay."

The boys ran off, leaving Joan to wonder about Clarke's call. "Clarke's a . . ."

"Fire chief. And very good at what he does."

"And Kyle is Gideon's boy."

"Yes."

No sense delaying the inevitable. "How's Gideon doing?"

Ann set out four place settings. "It's been a rough year. You know his ex-wife, Helen, died."

"I did not." She had broken up with Gideon, but that very quick marriage still stung more than it should have.

Ann frowned, as if she had realized another something that she should have shared. "I should have called you."

Joan finished off the wine, hoping it would settle her simmering energy. "How did she die?"

"Cancer. Very aggressive. She was gone within five months."

"How's Gideon taking it?"

"There was no love lost between the two of them after the divorce. But Kyle took it hard."

"Sucks to lose your mother. I feel for the kid," Joan said.

"I don't think I've ever heard you talk about your mother."

Joan glanced into her empty wineglass. "Not much to say. She left when I was two."

"Didn't she die when you were in high school?"

"Yes."

"What about your dad?"

She sighed, realizing they had never talked much about her family because it was so damn depressing. "Dad drank a lot, but he did his best. When I was twelve, he fell asleep in his recliner with a lit cigarette in his hand. The place caught fire. We barely got out. He took off for good a couple of years later. I was raised by a friend of his who owns a bar."

Ann studied her with a mixture of shock and pity. "I didn't realize."

"I never talked about my family because it's a bleak story. I like to think the past doesn't have any power over me."

"Do you really believe that?"

"No."

An understanding smile twisted Ann's lips as she set the chili and the remaining biscuits on the table, along with salt and pepper shakers and pepper jack cheese. Nate and Kyle came hurrying into the room and took their seats across from Joan. Ann sat at the head of the table.

Once each had been served a healthy portion, Joan realized how hungry she was.

Joan took her first bite and almost moaned with pleasure. "This is amazing. I can't remember the last time I ate real food."

"They don't have real food where you live?" Nate asked.

"They do. I'm just not good at finding it. I live on Chinese takeout, street pizza, and hot dogs."

"Why?" Kyle asked.

"I'm busy. I don't slow down much."

"What do you do?" he asked.

"I'm a homicide detective." Fingers crossed she would remain one after the suspension.

Kyle's interest was piqued, and she sensed she had gained a few points with him. "My dad's a detective, too," he said.

"Really?" In college, whenever Joan and Gideon had spoken of potential professions, he had always talked about working on his father's ranch. Law enforcement had never crossed either of their minds. It was ironic that both Gideon and she were now cops.

"Yep, he's one of the best in the state," the boy said with pride.

That was not a surprise. Gideon always gave whatever he did 100 percent. "What grade are you two in?"

"Fifth," Kyle said.

"But I'm also going to audit a class at the college," Nate said.

"It's an experiment we're trying," Ann said.

"That's saying something for a ten-year-old," Joan said. At ten, school and reading had been her safe place. Though she'd made A's, she'd never had a desire to hurry through the grade levels.

"I want to skip middle school and high school and go to college full-time next year, but Mom won't let me," Nate said.

Ann sipped her wine. "There's plenty of time for that. But you also need to be a kid."

"I want to be a neurosurgeon," Nate said.

Of course he did. "Was rocket scientist too tame?"

That coaxed a faint smile from the boys. "Humans are more interesting than machines. More complex."

"I've often said the same." Joan was tempted to refill her glass, but if she kept up this pace, tomorrow would be rough. She reached for her water glass instead. "Your mom wanted to be a medical doctor. She was accepted at several places."

His brow furrowing, Nate looked at his mother as he processed what appeared to be a new piece of information. "Why didn't you go?"

"Because I decided to stay here," Ann said. "I like being close to Grandma and Grandpa."

"Is it because you got pregnant with me?" Nate asked.

It did not take a math genius to backdate his conception to his parents' wedding. "That was part of the reason. And for the record, I made the right choice."

Nate's frown deepened as Kyle asked, "May we build the fire now?"

"Finish your chili and then put your plates in the sink," Ann said.

The boys quickly finished their meals and hurried their dishes into the kitchen. Seconds later, the back door opened and then slammed closed.

"You let them build the fire alone?" Joan asked.

"Yes. But I'm there when they light it."

"In my neighborhood, fires are contained to grills," Joan said. "And even then, I keep my distance."

She glanced out the window and watched as the boys rushed toward the stone firepit with armloads of wood. Both worked together to place kindling in the bottom and build a tripod of wood over it.

"My father says any self-respecting cowboy knows how to handle a fire."

Shifting away from the subject, she asked, "Is Nate really ready for high school, let alone college?"

"Intellectually," she said. "He's still a kid, and I'm trying to give him as normal a life as possible. But he needs the academic stimulation, so he's auditing a class this fall to keep him engaged."

"Clarke on board with this?"

"He's for whatever is good for Nate." Ann set her napkin down by her half-empty bowl. "It's nice outside tonight. Let's have another glass outside."

Joan ate the last of her buttered biscuit. "I shouldn't, but I will."

Ten minutes later, they were on the porch, and she was sitting in a wooden rocker. Nate and Kyle's logs would have made any Boy Scout proud. Ann handed a flint lighter to each boy and took a step back, watching closely as they lit the kindling tucked in the center. The blaze caught quickly among the carefully placed logs.

Joan eased back in her chair and firmly planted her feet on the ground. Tension rippled up her body as the heat from the flames warmed her.

Ann took the chair beside her. "You okay?"

"Sure, I'm fine."

"Joan, I'm a psychologist," she said softly so Nate couldn't hear. "You're uncomfortable."

"I'm tired. Been burning the candle at both ends, no pun intended."

"Can I get more wood?" Nate asked.

"Sure," Ann said. "But we won't be out here more than an hour. It's been a long day."

"Understood," he said before the boys set off in search of wood.

Ann watched as Nate and Kyle vanished into the shadows. "We've never talked about the College Fire."

"It was a near miss for us both. We should count our lucky stars." She tucked her feet in, trying to be relaxed and casual as the fire consumed the wood. She was not in the mood for a counseling session about PTSD or phobias.

"Fire makes you nervous," Ann said.

"No wonder, given my history," Joan said.

"I didn't notice it in college, but Clarke did. He said you always kept your distance at the bonfires."

"We all have our quirks." She heard the boys arguing about which types of wood to collect. Kyle's theories about the proper wood-to-burn ratios were as strong as Nate's. "They're having fun."

"Nate hasn't seen Kyle all summer, and he's missed having his cousin around. The other boys at the elementary school tease Nate about leaving them behind this fall. Some are intimidated by his intelligence, but Kyle doesn't seem to care."

"He has the Bailey good heart." Joan drew in a few breaths, feeling her throat tighten and her palms sweat. "I wish them both happiness."

"I doubt Gideon really has been happy since you left."

Joan stared into her wineglass and the play of light from the fire. "I don't believe that."

"He's always felt like he failed you, Joan. Wished he had tried living back east with you."

Joan had realized her mistake two months after the fire. She had called Ann, fear tangling with hope as she'd asked about Gideon.

"He's married, Joan," Ann had said.

Joan had gripped the phone, certain it was a bad connection. *"What?"*

"He married Helen. She's pregnant."

Joan had sat down, her head spinning. *"What?"*

"She's eight weeks along, and before you say anything, Clarke and I are also married. I'm pregnant, too."

Now, in the distance, an owl hooted and brought Joan back to the present. She cleared her throat, hoping she sounded steadier than she felt. "I'm not sure I can make anyone happy. I'm moody and difficult on my best days, and if you hadn't noticed, I'm a workaholic."

"I hadn't noticed," Ann said, smiling.

Joan allowed a small smile of her own. "Yep, it's true."

They sat in silence for a moment before Ann asked, "What do you think you're going to do about Elijah? He's served his time. He's free to do whatever he wishes."

"I thought about that on the plane. There's nothing I can do legally, but I feel in my bones that he has a bigger agenda."

"What kind of agenda?"

"You told me how angry he was after his conviction and how he still insists he's innocent. He's back in Missoula because he wants something. You think it's revenge?"

Ann paled. "I don't know what Elijah wants."

"If he and I can build a rapport, maybe he'll reveal himself to me. Secrets always have a way of coming out. The trick is to be on the lookout for the signs."

The flames in the pit crackled as they ate through the wood. The tripod Nate had built collapsed in a flurry of sparks and fire.

"I hope you know what you are doing," Ann said.

"I don't. But that's never stopped me before."

Confessions of an Arsonist
Burning brush and wood has its own pleasure, but watching the fire eat through property and destroy what others love . . .

It's a rush beyond measure.

CHAPTER FOUR

Missoula, Montana
Saturday, September 5, 2020
7:15 p.m.

The fire sirens wailed in the distance as Elijah Weston sat on the front porch of his new residence, a boardinghouse five blocks from the university. It was a split-level, five-bedroom house and his home until he could get a better place.

But for now, he would share a bathroom with Rodney DuPree, a recovering drug addict. And if he was really hard up for company, he could sit in the den during the evenings and watch television with the other two residents. Their names escaped him, which suited Elijah just fine.

The owner of the house, Ax Pickett, was a former Vietnam vet who had opened the boardinghouse as a tribute to his dead wife, Delilah. In his early seventies, Pickett had a long, lean frame and weathered features that suggested many years in a saddle.

Though Delilah was long gone, her porcelain cups, blousy pink drapes, and overstuffed furniture covered in rose chintz remained. Her recipes were cooked at mealtime, and her rocker remained beside Pickett's on the porch. Delilah's house rules, which had straightened out Pickett, also still applied. There was no cussing. Smoking was limited to the front porch. And according to Rodney, Pickett did not allow drinking except for the first Saturday of the month, when he indulged in his six-pack limit.

Elijah sat forward, listening as another fire truck's siren raced down one of the central streets. His heartbeat kicked, and a familiar pleasant tension pulsed in his veins as he imagined the flashing lights and the truck racing toward the blaze. Those first few seconds at a fire were always exciting. Fires were an enigma, even to those closest to them.

He drew in a breath and forced himself to sit back in the chair as he stared at the remains of the black graffiti, **ARSONST LEAVE!** spray-painted on the sidewalk. The misspelled warning had been waiting for him when he arrived last night, and he had spent a couple of hours today scrubbing the paint with hot soapy water and a wire brush. A faint outline of the words still remained, but he would see to it again tomorrow.

As tempted as he was to go and witness the fire, the words were a reminder that being seen near a blaze would be his one-way ticket back to prison.

Missoula was one of the biggest towns in Montana, but the reality was it was a small town with fewer than seventy thousand people. There were three fire departments in town. The one on Pine Street served the city, whereas the other two were on the outer edges of town. Of course, all three would respond to any fire that needed all hands on deck.

Hearing the multiple sirens confirmed that the blaze was growing larger and fiercer.

The front door squeaked open, and Elijah looked over his shoulder to see Pickett step out onto the porch. Nodding a greeting, the old man walked toward the porch rail and removed a cigarette packet and lighter from his jeans pocket.

Pickett struck the flint of his lighter, holding it up for a moment before he pressed it to the tip of his cigarette. The tip flared with an orange glow magnified by the graying sky. White smoke puffed and swirled around narrowing eyes that looked toward the direction of the sirens.

Elijah understood this was a test. The town arsonist was living in his house, and fire engines were blaring down the center of the city.

Pickett offered him a smoke.

Elijah held up his hand. "I don't smoke."

Pickett shrugged and tucked the packet into the breast pocket of his jean jacket. "I've been smoking since I was twelve. I hear it can kill me, but given the way I've always lived my life, the smokes are the least of my worries."

Elijah decided to stick to compliments, just as he had with prison guards. "That was a fine dinner you served us tonight."

"As long as you don't get tired of old-fashioned cooking or barbecue, you'll always be happy with what I serve."

"I'm happy to eat anything served to me on this side of the prison wall. I'm a fair cook and willing to help." The reminder of the shared meal was calculated. He wanted everyone to remember where he had been when that fire started.

Pickett inhaled, holding the smoke in his lungs before slowly releasing it. He pointed the cigarette toward the sirens. "What do you think is burning?"

"I haven't a clue."

"Sounds serious."

"I suppose you're right."

"I don't want any trouble." Pickett flicked the glowing tip into an ashtray shaped like New York State. "I'm taking a chance on you. There are a lot of folks in town who don't want you around."

"I doubt I'm wanted anywhere." There was no self-pity or bravado behind the statement. Life was easier to navigate if a man simply accepted what was fact instead of dreaming about what could be.

Pickett faced him. "Should I ask if you're behind that fire?"

"I am not responsible for that fire. I was here eating meat loaf with you."

Pickett regarded him as he inhaled and then exhaled what looked like worry. "Whatever is burning ain't that far from here, and you look fit enough."

"Running the yard relieves stress."

"It can also keep you fit enough to cover distance quickly."

"I didn't set the fire."

He pointed the lit cigarette toward the stain on the sidewalk. "I didn't say you did. But there'll be people who will think you did."

"I have always maintained my innocence."

"The guilty usually do."

"If you think I set the College Fire ten years ago, then why take me in?"

He shrugged, stared at the tip of his cigarette. "Because a part of me believes any man can be redeemed. Change the course of his life for the better." He stubbed out his cigarette on the star marking Albany.

Elijah asked, "Why New York for the ashtray?"

Pickett studied the ashtray, which was already half-full. "You ain't the only one who did time. I pulled mine in New York." He let the rest of the story dangle like a baited hook in a fishing stream.

Elijah did not care but heard himself asking, "What did you do?"

"Murder," he said with no hint of apology. "I was drinking in those days. But I was also defending a lady's honor in a bar."

"Delilah's?"

"I wish. But she drove the two thousand miles to see me. Told me that when I was able to come back home, she would be waiting."

"And she was?"

"Yes, sir. She certainly was."

A flicker of envy sparked in Elijah. "I suppose that's why you married her."

"A loyal woman is hard to find."

"You might be right about that."

Pickett reached for the doorknob. "Delilah gave me a second chance, which is why I'm giving you one. But like she told me nearly thirty years ago, 'If you fuck this up, I'll scalp you.'"

Elijah smiled and went inside the house.

***

As Gideon watched Fire Chief Clarke Mead walk toward him, he thought about the woman he had seen before the blaze destroyed the building. The thunderous flames now hissed as the firefighters sprayed water on the ruins.

Clarke removed his helmet and ran his hand over his salt-and-pepper hair, now damp with sweat despite the cooling temperatures. "It's still too hot to walk the wreckage and conduct any kind of investigation. That's likely to be tomorrow."

"Can you tell what caused the fire?" Gideon asked.

"Hard to say. I did issue the building owner a citation a month ago. Several of her beauticians had rigged electrical outlets to carry a higher load beyond code. They were supposed to hire a licensed electrician to fix the problem. I was due back to check next week. They also improperly stored flammable chemicals, which explains the intensity of the blaze."

"Who owns the building?" Gideon asked.

"Jessica and Darren Halpern."

"Names aren't familiar."

"They are new to the area. Came here about a year ago from California. They liked the idea of Big Sky Country."

The building had gone up quickly and burned to cinder. It could have been electrical, but Gideon was not ruling out arson. "How are the Halperns faring so far?"

"They said they're doing well. Mr. Halpern complained about the winter, but then most of the new folks do."

"This past winter was fairly mild."

"That's what I told him." Amusement briefly softened the frown lines around Clarke's mouth before his brow furrowed. "We haven't had a chance to talk about Elijah Weston. He was released yesterday from prison."

Gideon's face hardened. "I am very aware of that."

"Biggest fire this town has seen in a decade, and Elijah is living less than a mile away."

"We're a long way from making that accusation, Clarke."

"You're the cop, so I'll leave it to you. But I would be paying the man a visit."

"I will."

Gideon and Clarke had both attended college in Missoula and had roomed together three doors down from the house Gideon's parents had rented to Joan and Ann.

Weeks before the fire, Joan had begged him to move back east with her, and he had refused. With tears in her eyes, she had broken up with him. But during their days apart, he had gotten drunk and landed in bed with Helen. That fall from grace had proved to him how much he loved Joan. He had been ready to move east, at least for the summer. That would give them time to sort out their lives. But his plans to fix things between Joan and him had been delayed by the College Fire and then destroyed by Helen's pregnancy.

Regret for the lost love rose up in Gideon's chest. He should have long been over Joan, but thoughts of her still hurt.

His phone rang, and, seeing Kyle's name, he drew in and released a breath and expelled the anger before he answered the call. "Hey, pal."

"Dad, I'm at Aunt Ann's with Nate."

"Great." He and Kyle lived in a house about a half mile from Ann's, on Bailey land. Nate and Kyle had been close as younger boys, and now that they were settled, the first cousins were getting reacquainted. "Be sure you listen to Aunt Ann."

"I will, Dad."

He raised his gaze to the charred structure that had been the beauty shop hours ago and knew he would be on scene for several more hours.

He said goodbye, hung up, and then pushed the phone into his back pocket as he moved toward the rubble. The air was thick with the acrid smell of charred wood and chemicals. "Looks like our boys are having a sleepover at Ann's tonight."

Clarke shifted his stance and rolled his shoulders. "It was my night with Nate, but when I heard the sirens, I knew I'd better drop him off at Tim's."

"Ann's going to have her hands full with those two."

"My wife can juggle more than any woman I've ever met."

"She's always been that way."

"I haven't had the chance to say it yet, but it's good to have you back, Gideon. Missed you this summer."

"Kyle and I needed the break. To unplug. By the end, neither one of us missed the cell phone."

Clarke chuckled. "How long did it take Kyle to reattach to his phone?"

Gideon grinned. "Thirty seconds."

Smiling, Clarke shook his head. "Not sure Nate could survive without his. That boy has his mom's brains and is going to be building his own computers one day."

Gideon's boy was rough-and-tumble. He was plenty smart but would rather play soccer or ride horses than crack a book. Kyle was a chip off the old block, and he liked the idea of Kyle hanging out with his more studious cousin. "Nate will be running the state and then the country one day."

Clarke's grin reflected his pride. "Who's to say the two boys don't partner up and run the state?"

Gideon laughed. "Kyle will be running the ranch, but he'll help your boy whenever he needs assistance."

"Chief Mead!" The callout came from one of the firefighters, Samuel Thompson. "Like you to see something."

As Gideon and Clarke walked toward the building, the radiating heat stopped them before they could get within ten feet. "What is it?"

"Around back," the firefighter said. "One of my men found a purse."

They followed Samuel around the building toward the alley that cut between the Beau-T-Shop and the law offices behind it. Gideon knew the attorneys well enough from his divorce and subsequent custody battle. He had spent a good bit of treasure and time on those folks.

Samuel paused at the mouth of the alley and pointed toward a blue purse leaning against the brick wall. "Seems odd that it would be here."

Gideon reached in his coat pocket and removed a pair of protective gloves. Normally, he might not have been so conscious of forensics with a lady's purse, but it was too close to the fire for it to have been a coincidence. He worked his large hands into the gloves and knelt beside it.

The purse, which did not appear expensive, was sitting upright, as if it had been placed carefully. If it had been stolen, the chances were that it would be lying haphazardly on its side. Thieves, in his experience, did not take the time to carefully set down a stolen purse. It was also zipped closed. Again, that did not fit the profile of a stolen item.

He searched around the purse and then grabbed his phone and took several pictures.

"Why the careful handling?" Clarke asked.

"It just doesn't look right to me." He unzipped the top and noted the wallet inside. He removed it, unfastened the clasp, and discovered three credit cards and thirty-six dollars in cash.

He glanced at the driver's license. It had been issued to Lana Long and listed a Denver address.

"You think she might be the woman you saw inside the shop?" Clarke asked.

Gideon rose and looked at the burned-out structure. "If she was, she's dead now."

Confessions of an Arsonist

Each time I stare at one of my fires, I feel in control.

When I hear the flames roar, I feel power. When I see the black smoke rise toward the heavens, I believe I can accomplish anything. However, when the fire finally dies out, as they all do, that control, power, and optimism vanish.

CHAPTER FIVE

Missoula, Montana
Saturday, September 5, 2020
9:55 p.m.

As Gideon parked, his headlights swept the front of the three-hundred-unit apartment complex located on the outskirts of Missoula. Each of the buildings had three floors, with weathered wood siding and a pitched roof that mimicked a ski resort. Age and too many harsh winters had taken a toll on the buildings, which now looked worn and dated. But because housing in Missoula was not easy to come by, he knew the rents here would have been steep.

He had made a few calls and discovered that Lana Long had held a beautician's license in the states of Colorado and Montana. And it was her Montana beautician's license that had given him her current address. He'd placed calls to Jessica and Darren Halpern, hoping to get background information on Lana Long and to discuss the fire, but so far, his calls had landed in voicemail.

Out of his vehicle, he pushed back his jacket to clear his sidearm for easy access as he strode toward the manager's first-floor apartment.

The curtains were drawn in the front display window, but a television's wavy light leaked out around the edges, suggesting the manager was up and ready for him. He'd called ahead but had not shared specifics of his visit. For all he knew, Lana Long's purse had been stolen, and he was not ready to raise questions about the woman until he had all the facts.

He pounded on the door and stood to the side. The call appeared to be straightforward, but too many cops had been shot or attacked on calls just like this.

Heavy footsteps sounded on the other side of the door. A security chain scraped out of its latch, and the dead bolt turned seconds before the door opened. The man standing in the doorway was midsize and stocky, with a full black beard and thinning long hair tied back at the nape of his neck. A plaid shirt skimmed over a full belly and was tucked into worn jeans. In the background, the television light glowed from a back bedroom and softly broadcast what sounded like old western.

"Mr. Victor Oswald?" Gideon asked.

"That's right." His gaze settled on the seven-pointed gold star pinned to his brown overcoat. "Detective Bailey?"

"That's right. Thank you for seeing me, Mr. Oswald."

What should have been the living room of his apartment had been set up as a leasing office. A pizza box, a couple of dirty blue ceramic plates, and a few beer cans lined the breakfast bar attached to the kitchen.

Following Gideon's line of sight, Mr. Oswald cleared his throat as he moved toward the kitchen and gathered the beer cans and dumped them into the trash.

He sniffed as he tucked in his shirt more securely. "You had a question about one of my residents?"

"That's right. Her name is Lana Long?"

"Long." He shook his head. "I know Lana. She moved in about nine months ago. We don't get that many move-ins in the winter, so I remember her. Pretty little thing. She all right?"

"Her purse was found in town. This is more of a wellness visit to make sure she is."

"The ladies do not like being separated from their purses."

"No, sir, they do not. That's why I'm concerned."

"Did you call her?"

"I was hoping you could give me her phone number."

"Sure. Let me check her records."

The manager went to a computer resting on a desk shoved in a corner and typed several keys. "Ready?"

Gideon opened his phone. "Shoot."

The manager rattled off the number, which Gideon typed into his phone. It rang twice and then, *"This is Lana. You know the drill."*

Gideon left Lana a message instructing her to call him. Next step would be to check with the phone carrier to see if they could locate her cell. "She's not answering. When was the last time you saw her?"

"Oh, it's been a couple of weeks. She's a hairdresser and works long hours."

"Has she had any trouble or complaints?"

"No."

"Can you direct me to her apartment?"

Mr. Oswald scratched the back of his head. "You're going to a lot of trouble over a purse."

"I just need to confirm she's all right."

Mr. Oswald grabbed a lightweight jacket, and as Gideon stepped outside, he closed the door behind him. "She's in building two. It's a quick walk."

The few seconds in the manager's warm apartment had sharpened the bite of the evening chill as they crossed the lot, full of potholes. The air was crisp and ripe with the scent of moisture. Snow in September was not uncommon, and he would bet money they were in for an early winter.

Mr. Oswald fished a ring of keys from his pocket and walked up to the first-floor unit. He knocked hard on the door several times. "Management," he said in a clear, practiced voice. "Ms. Long, are you in there?"

They stood in silence, waiting outside the darkened door. If she was inside, she was either a heavy sleeper or passed out.

"Can you open it?" Gideon asked.

"I don't know. Don't you need a search warrant?"

"I'm just looking for the lady so I can give her back her purse."

A fierce independence ran through Montana residents, as Gideon knew well; they were not fond of the law poking around. "You know exactly what you're looking for?"

"One Ms. Long."

"All right." He selected a key from his ring and unlocked the door. He knocked harder, announced it was management again, and then, after no response, opened the door and switched on the light.

The apartment's interior was dark and silent. The living room was similar to Mr. Oswald's layout, though it appeared this unit had only one bedroom. The living room was furnished with a couple of lawn chairs, a folding table, and several boxes of books that lined the wall. A few of the books dealt with arson and the mindset of an arsonist. Could Lana Long have set the fire at the shop? If she had, she would not be the first arsonist to have underestimated the power of a fire and be consumed by their own blaze.

Gideon unholstered his sidearm. "Ms. Long, police!"

No response.

Mr. Oswald turned on the lights in the kitchen and hallway, calling out as he stayed behind Gideon while they walked toward the bedroom.

Another flip of the switch and they were staring at a single mattress on the floor, covered with a rumpled purple comforter twisted around gray sheets. Butted against the wall was an open suitcase neatly packed with clothes. Either Lana lived out of her suitcase or she was ready to leave town.

There were no pictures on the walls, and the bathroom was cleaned out except for a nearly empty bottle of lavender shampoo in the shower stall. The towels lay in a damp pile in the sink.

"Did she mention she would be moving soon?" Gideon asked.

"No. She signed a year's lease. Said she was going to make a home here. A fresh start. But she wouldn't be the first to skip out on rent."

Gideon wondered how many folks planning on a new start in Big Sky Country ended up in his jail. These people figured moving to the edge of nowhere would solve their problems, until they realized their problems knew no zip code. As tempted as he was to search the open suitcase, he would wait. Better to have a search warrant.

"I should have known she was going to skip on the rent. Too positive and too cheery."

"What makes you think she's left town for good?"

"The skippers either avoid me altogether or smile like a fool whenever they see me. They think they're pulling one over on me, but I've seen it all. Lana was always smiling."

"How long have you managed this place?"

"Fifteen years. Like I said, I've seen it all."

"Did Ms. Long pay on time?"

"A few days late a couple of times, but she always paid the late fine. Never gave me any excuses."

"Did she talk about her job?"

"Said she liked it. Never complained to me. But she can talk."

"The women I know speak when they have something important to say."

"Well then, you're lucky. My ex could talk the ears off a brass monkey."

"Do you have the names of any women Lana works with?"

"Nope."

"Does she have a boyfriend?"

"No idea."

Gideon returned to the living room and knelt in front of the books. He noticed most had not been read. Slipping on gloves, he picked up the only one with a cracked spine. It was a treatise on arson investigation.

"Thank you, Mr. Oswald." He pulled a card from his pocket and handed it to him. "Call me if she comes back."

"Yes, sir. Will do."

"I need to seal this apartment," Gideon said. "No one in or out unless they are law enforcement."

"Because of a purse?"

"Can you seal it for me?"

"Yeah, sure."

As they exited the apartment, Gideon knew it would take at least another twelve hours before the crime scene would be cool enough to walk. If the woman he'd seen in the shop was Lana, then he would have to wait to prove it.

With Kyle at Ann's for the night, he'd have time to conduct a preliminary search into Lana Long and determine if she had any police records. Next, he would pay a visit to Elijah Weston's boardinghouse and properly welcome him back.

***

Elijah was not surprised to see the police car parked in front of Pickett's house. He had spent ten years studying cops and their habits, and he would have been sorely disappointed if no one had come by to visit.

A tiny cinder of excitement flickered in his belly. They were going to talk about the fire, and as much as he did not trust cops, he was going to enjoy every bit of the dialogue.

Elijah recognized Gideon Bailey instantly as he settled his black Stetson and strode up the sidewalk, pausing to study the smudged graffiti before climbing the front porch steps.

In college, Elijah had known about Gideon, the local rancher's boy who had tried his hand at cowboying for a couple of years before returning to college. He had been a receiver on the football team and had earned a partial scholarship, though his athletic talent was not enough to go pro. Not that Gideon would have left Montana. This state and the family ranch were in his blood.

Elijah leaned forward in Delilah's rocker, tracing the rose pattern carved in the armrest with his fingertip. Always important to act calm and helpful, regardless. "Good evening, Detective Bailey."

Gideon rested a foot on the bottom step. The brim of his hat shadowed his face a fraction, making it hard to read his expression, which Elijah supposed was the desired effect. Gideon had filled out in the last decade, but instead of growing soft and doughy like many men after college, his body was lean and rugged.

"Evening, Elijah," Gideon said. "It's been a long time."

Elijah rose from his rocker and stepped to the porch railing. Gideon had attended his two-day trial, sitting in the back of the courtroom, seemingly absorbing every detail. The only time he had shown any emotion had been when Ann had testified. Had Gideon or Ann given him a single thought since then? "Ten years, to be exact."

"You look like you're doing well," Gideon said. "I heard you finished your degree."

So he had been paying attention. "I did. And I'm enrolled in my first master's class. I'll start on Wednesday."

"That so? What are you taking?"

"Psychology 501. Dr. Bailey's teaching it."

"My sister's class?" Gideon's head tipped back a fraction so that Elijah had a full view of his frown.

"I've served my time, so there are no conditions to my release. Besides, she's one of the best teachers at the university. Why would I not?" Elijah wanted to ask about Ann. He'd heard she and her husband had split. Was she relieved to be living apart from Clarke Mead? *Smart women, foolish choices* was the catchphrase, right?

"There isn't another class you could take?"

"None that's of interest." He had served his time and was now completely rehabilitated. He planned to become involved with the community and give back exactly what it deserved.

"How are you paying for the schooling?" His tone was conversational, reserved for friends.

Elijah was surprised Gideon's conversation starter did not focus on the fire. Gideon was always a little smarter than he let on. "There are tuition grants for people like me. And I'll be looking for work to cover the rest. By any chance, is the police department hiring, Detective?"

Gideon nodded, not a bit of emotion showing.

"You come all this way to ask me about my schooling and job prospects?" Elijah asked.

"I did not, as a matter of fact."

"The fire, then, I suppose." When Gideon's expression turned curious, he added, "Hard to miss the sirens."

Gideon took another step closer. "I don't suppose you know anything about it?"

"I do not, Detective. But if you need an alibi, please check with Mr. Pickett. He had eyes on me for most of the afternoon and evening. In case you're curious, tonight's dinner was meat loaf. And Mr. Pickett has a very specific way he likes his late wife's recipe made. Extra bread crumbs and ketchup mixed with honey on top."

"Not that I don't take your word for it, but I'll be checking with Mr. Pickett."

The night air was getting cooler, but the underside of his skin burned hot with an old anger that had never been extinguished. "I didn't set this fire, just as I did not set the College Fire ten years ago."

"You've always maintained your innocence. You're persistent. I'll give you that much," Gideon said.

"Because I am innocent."

"Your DNA was attached to a partially recovered incendiary device found at the scene. Eyewitnesses put you in the vicinity. And the jury found you guilty, Elijah."

He had a list of all the jurors' names and would soon have their addresses. "I was framed."

"Framed?"

"That's right. Someone set me up. I reported my backpack had been stolen days before the fire. When I got it back, I discovered my sweatshirt was missing. That garment was used as a wick. And sure, I was in the area. I went to school there."

Gideon frowned. "Where's Mr. Pickett?"

"Gone to bed. According to the others here, he drinks on the first Saturday of the month. I hear he can't hold his liquor as well as he used to and goes to bed about ten."

"All right, then, I'll talk to him in the morning."

"By the way, what burned down?"

Gideon arched a brow. "The beauty salon on Main Street."

"What type of structure was it?"

"Brick mostly, like the others around it."

His heart rate sped up a beat. "Did the fire spread?" He should not be so curious, but he found the details hard to resist.

"No. Fire department stopped it."

"Injuries?"

"Don't know yet. Rubble is too hot."

Elijah shook his head, sensing that the detective was withholding information. But then, Gideon was a smart one. He would not ask questions until he had a good idea of what the answers were. "I sure hope no one was hurt, Detective. Fire is a terrible way to die."

Gideon's expression darkened with suspicion. "Yes, it is." He touched the brim of his hat. "Good evening, Elijah."

"Yes, sir. You come back anytime. I'll be here or at school."

Elijah watched Gideon stride toward his SUV and then pause at the paint stain. "Trouble?"

"Nothing I can't handle."

With a nod, Gideon left, his long legs chewing up the distance to his vehicle in seconds. Yes, sir, he would have to be careful and not underestimate Detective Gideon Bailey.

Confessions of an Arsonist

Simple is best. No need for fancy devices. I can destroy anything with a milk jug, a cotton cloth, and gasoline. The trick is to remember fire is as dangerous as a wild animal. Pretty to look at, but it'll kill you in a heartbeat.

CHAPTER SIX

Missoula, Montana
Sunday, September 6, 2020
7:00 a.m.

By early morning, Gideon had not gotten a wink of sleep. After leaving Elijah, he'd called over to Ann's to check in. She'd had questions for him about the fire, but he had deflected them, promising she would have answers when he did. He had also given her a heads-up that Elijah had registered for her class. The silence stretched between them before she thanked him for the information.

The next couple of hours were spent trying to obtain a restraining order against Elijah. Though he did not want Elijah within five hundred yards of his sister, the magistrate had made it clear that Elijah had paid his debt, and until he proved otherwise, there was no limiting his comings and goings.

Gideon grabbed a large thermos filled with coffee from the station along with several cups, drove to the scene of the fire, and parked across the street. Two of the three fire engines had returned to their stations, but one truck remained.

While two firefighters continued to spray water on hot spots in the smoking rubble, Clarke roped off the area with yellow crime scene tape. It was a holiday weekend, and the tourists would soon be up for breakfast. He wanted to keep this as low-key as possible.

As Gideon got out of his vehicle, the sunrise bathed the east side of the mountains, showing off brilliant reds and oranges. Within weeks, the entire mountain range would be in full fall colors.

Thermos and cups in hand, Gideon crossed the street, reaching Clarke as he tied off the last of the tape. "How's it going?"

"You missed a local reporter. She shot footage of the fire and promised to have it on this morning's news," Clarke said.

"Not sorry I missed her." Gideon handed him an empty cup.

Clarke sighed as he held it out. "No getting around it."

Gideon filled Clarke's cup. "What about the guys on the truck? They need a hit of java?"

"I made a run for them a half hour ago. They had the lion's share of the coffee, so this is much appreciated." He took a long sip. "Did you find the woman who owned the purse?"

"I visited Lana Long's apartment, which was stripped bare except for a bed and packed suitcase."

"She was planning on leaving town?"

"Looks like it. She also had a few books on arson."

Clarke frowned as he regarded the rubble. "You really think she did this?"

"I can't say yet, but it sure looks like it."

"We'll be on the lookout for the body you saw when we walk this place. So far, no one has spotted any remains, but there's a lot of debris to sort through."

Gideon nodded. "I spoke to Elijah yesterday evening."

Clarke frowned as he sipped his coffee. "And he denies anything to do with the fire."

"That's right."

"You believe him?"

"I'll know better once I confirm his alibi, but he was cool as a cucumber."

"He always was. Never could get a read on that guy."

"I didn't know him, really, until the fire. We were seniors and he was a freshman," Gideon said.

"Smart as hell. Remember he was in Joan's class when she was a teaching assistant," Clarke said, studying Gideon's expression.

Joan Mason. He had not heard that name in a while or seen her in ten years. To say he thought about her every day would be a stretch. Sometimes a few months went by without her trespassing on his thoughts, but she was always there in the shadows.

Though they had been ill matched from the beginning, Gideon and Joan had found something in each other that just fit. They dated all their senior year, and as deep as his roots were sunk into Montana, Joan had nearly coaxed both Gideon and his sister out to the East Coast. But when Elijah had set his fire, it had changed everything.

A week later, with her hands still bandaged, Joan had left without a word to him or any of them. Gideon had called her more times than he could count, and only when he threatened to drive to Philadelphia had she finally called him back.

"Why are you calling?" she had said. *"We were over before the fire."*

"I made a mistake." Memories of his night with Helen lingered close. *"I want to come east with you."*

"You belong in Montana," Joan said. *"I see that now."*

Nothing he had said would convince her otherwise, and he'd finally hung up in frustration. A week later, Helen had told him she was pregnant. They were married July 1 in a courthouse wedding. By the time Kyle was born, they were fighting regularly.

Gideon sipped his coffee. "Elijah met Ann through Joan."

It was Clarke's turn to squirm. "I remember."

"I've been through his police file a few times. He's always denied setting the fire. He even petitioned the Innocence Project to have a look at his case five years ago, but they denied him."

"Because they saw him for what he was," Clarke said. "Psychopaths don't confess."

"Detective Jefferson interrogated him for a long stretch." By Gideon's standards, Jefferson had leaned on Elijah too hard. These days, a defense attorney would have a field day with that kind of law enforcement overreach. But Gideon also understood that Detective Jefferson, like many folks in town, was terrified an arsonist who had nearly killed two coeds would go free.

"Don't forget all those brush fires that popped up that last winter before the College Fire. They stopped completely when Elijah was arrested."

"The arsonist profiles for rural fires are very different from those who execute structural fires."

"That's true in some cases, but I would bet you those fires were meant to relieve stress and provide practice for the main event." Clarke stared into the dark depths of his cup and then took a sip. "You know that son of a bitch wrote to Ann from prison?"

"I didn't know that."

"Upset the hell out of her. I visited him in prison and told him to stop. He didn't seem to care what I thought, so I spoke to the prison officials. They couldn't do anything, so I had the post office hold our mail. From that day forward, I've picked it up from the post office."

"Did he write her again?"

"There were two other letters. He insisted he did not set fire to her house."

"Did you keep the letters?"

"Hell no. I tossed them." Clarke sighed. "He's going to do it again."

"Not if I have any say in it."

Clarke swallowed the last of his coffee and motioned for his two men to join Gideon and him. "The rubble should be cool enough now to walk, as long as you have your boots."

"Let me put my thermos back, and I'll be right there."

Gideon joined the firefighters as they began to search the charred rubble. Hot pockets still gave off some steam, but for the most part, the fire crews had saturated the structure all the way down to the brick foundation. He moved toward the spot where he'd seen the woman through the window. The area was covered in thick debris.

"It'll take time to clear the rubble," Clarke said. "Have a look over here."

Gideon stared at the large window and then at the wreckage. He had been so close to her, just as he had been only a dozen feet from Joan all those years ago. If he had been a minute quicker, the woman might be alive.

He turned toward the melted and scorched beautician chairs and their work areas. All the flammable products at the stations had exploded in the intense heat and had shattered the mirrors behind them.

Gideon paused in the center of the room, where the destruction appeared absolute. "Where did the fire start?"

"Near here. It explains why the woman you saw was trapped in the blaze," Clarke said.

Gideon knew the human body literally melted at fifteen hundred degrees, and, judging by the destruction here, this fire had surpassed that mark.

The water from the fire hoses had turned the ash to a black sludge that squished under Gideon's boots as he walked toward what had been the back of the store.

"This is where the shop stored chemicals like acetone and hair dyes," Clarke said. "An experienced arsonist would have dumped accelerant here and then trailed the remainder out the door down the alley."

"Creating a fuse."

"Exactly. Once the fire trail hit this room, it was game over. All those chemicals are flammable as hell."

"Everything in this structure appears designed to burn," Gideon said.

A firefighter covered in soot and grit approached. "Captain Mead, have a look over here."

Gideon and Clarke crossed the room, mindful of where they stepped and preserving any evidence that might have survived the fire. Following the firefighter's outstretched hand, Gideon dropped his gaze to a pile of rubble. What at first looked like a badly charred mannequin hand peeking out from the ceiling debris was, in fact, human. The fingers and most of the hand had been destroyed, leaving only a blackened stump behind.

Gideon peered into the charred beams, now tangled together like pick-up sticks. As he stared into the gaps, he followed the remains of the arm to a charred torso and head.

He tried to reconcile Lana Long's driver's license image with what lay before him. However, nothing was recognizable.

"I'll put a call in to the medical examiner's office," Gideon said. "The sooner I get an autopsy, the sooner I'll have a cause of death and an identity."

"Maybe it was suicide," Clarke said.

"Could be."

Clarke shook his head, his gaze transfixed on the form before him. "Reminds me of the house fire north of town."

"Three years ago," Gideon said.

"Caused by a dried-out Christmas tree the father had promised to take down, but he put it off several weeks because the kids wanted to keep it up."

Gideon knew Clarke had nearly been killed saving the father and his two young children. He had turned around to go back in for the mother, but the structure had been fully engulfed. The mother had died in the blaze. Clarke had later been decorated by the city, but he'd privately admitted he'd been deeply shaken for months.

"When can you tell me definitely that this was arson?" Gideon asked.

"My boys and I need to thoroughly comb this place and search for traces of accelerants and incendiary devices."

"But you have a theory."

Clarke dropped his voice. "I'd bet my last dollar it's arson."

"Keep me posted. I'll send a deputy by to secure the scene until the medical examiner arrives."

Gideon strode across the blackened debris, and when he stepped out onto the curb and ducked under the crime scene tape, his chest was tight. He drew in a deep breath, expanding the compressed muscles banding his rib cage. He reached for his phone and dialed Detective Becca Sullivan's number.

She picked up on the second ring. "I knew three consecutive hours of sleep was too much to hope for."

"I wish I could let you sleep," he said. "I'm going to need you at the fire scene. We just found the body of the woman I spotted during the fire."

In the background, he heard a light click on. "I'll be there as soon as I can."

"I've put out a few queries about Lana Long. Can you also see if there've been any hits?"

"She connected to the fire?"

"Maybe."

"Will do, boss."

"Appreciate it. I'm going home for a few hours to check on Kyle and talk to Ann. She might have a few insights about this fire."

"Solid police work and forensics is going to solve this, not psychology," Becca said.

"I'll take all the help I can get."

They made promises to touch base by noon before he ended the call. As he tucked his phone in his pocket, a blue pickup truck splashed with dried mud parked behind Gideon's car. A tall man with a thick waist and broad shoulders climbed out. He wore jeans, a flannel shirt, and old work boots. Dark hair was brushed off a square face.

Gideon recognized the man instantly. His name was Dan Tucker Jr. Like his father before him, Dan owned Tucker's Diner, a fairly successful eatery that was popular with the college kids. But his real claim to fame was the creation of a local citizens' action committee dedicated to keeping Elijah Weston out of Missoula. Dan and his followers had made it clear during parole hearings that the ex-con was not welcome, and Gideon would bet money they were behind the faint remains of the sidewalk graffiti in front of the boardinghouse.

"Mr. Tucker." Gideon moved to cut Tucker off as he strode toward the gutted structure. "I'm going to have to ask you to stand back. This is an active crime scene."

Tucker stopped, clenched fists at his sides as his gaze remained rooted on the former beauty shop. "I knew this was going to happen. I been telling you since the day his release was approved that it was a matter of time. I'm only surprised he did it so quickly."

"We don't know how this fire was set," Gideon said. "It's going to take days, perhaps weeks, to determine that."

"I can save the taxpayers a lot of money," he said, turning to Gideon. "Elijah Weston set the fire. He can't help himself."

"We don't know that." Gideon took a step closer to Tucker. "And I want you to stay away from him. No vandalizing and no threats, or I will put you in jail."

Tucker's anger turned sullen. "How many buildings and people does this guy torch before something is done?"

Gideon ignored the comment. "If I end up with a case against Elijah, I don't want a defense attorney getting my charges thrown out because some vigilante compromised the investigation."

"I haven't hurt him."

"Keep it that way. Stay away from him. That includes any more spray-painting stunts. Let me do my job."

Tucker glanced toward the sun gaining distance above the mountain range. "I respect you, Gideon. You're good at what you do, but you haven't been around for months."

"Your point, Mr. Tucker?" Gideon's voice was steady enough to pass for calm.

"Must be nice to take the summer off. I just want to make sure you're with us now that we got a madman living among us."

"I'm not going anywhere, Mr. Tucker." He was committed to the community and the ranch's legacy more than ever.

"I'll leave it to you, then," Tucker said. "But I'm going to be watching, and if you or the law can't act, then someone will."

"What does that mean?"

Tucker shrugged. "Take it any way you want. I care about this town and will do what's necessary to protect it."

Gideon stood in the center of the street, his body tense with fatigue and frustration as he watched Tucker storm to his truck and gun the engine.

He reached for his phone and dialed the medical examiner's office. The situation was going to spiral out of control quickly if this was arson.

CHAPTER SEVEN

Missoula, Montana
Sunday, September 6, 2020
9:55 a.m.

Joan did not understand the concept of a sleepover. Nate and Kyle had barely slept last night, and both still possessed boundless energy.

After pouring a fresh, extra-strong cup of coffee, she took a long sip as Nate and Kyle sat at the kitchen table laughing at another stupid joke. Ann was serving them a second batch of pancakes after they had devoured the first.

Joan used to have that kind of energy. She could go and go like the Energizer Bunny. These days, her idea of pure pleasure was rising on a Sunday, having a coffee, getting back into bed, pulling the covers up over her head, and sleeping. If only she had such a luxury today.

"Joan, can you pull my finger?" Kyle asked, giggling.

"No thanks," Joan said.

"Auntie Joan has not had a full cup of coffee," Ann offered. "Let her drink her witch's brew so it can transform her into Glinda the Good Witch."

Joan arched a brow. "That's very optimistic."

Ann shrugged as she set a platter of blueberry pancakes in the center of the table. "I see the sunny side of life."

Joan topped off her coffee cup. "Can I borrow your car today? I'd like to visit an old friend in town."

"Are you sure you want to do that?" Ann asked.

"Very," Joan said.

"Who's the friend?" Nate asked.

"You don't know him," Joan said.

"I might. Who?" he insisted.

"Never mind," Ann said. "And yes, you can take Mom's car. It's in the garage."

"Great."

The front doorbell rang, and Ann sighed as if she was a little relieved to have this boy party end.

"The cavalry," Joan said.

"From your lips to God's ears."

Joan was anxious to get into town. Elijah had been out of prison only forty-eight hours, and he would still be getting his bearings. In her experience, suspects were more likely to make unintentional, telling comments when they were off balance.

The front door opened, and she heard Ann's light tone mingle with the deep timbre of a man's voice. For a split second, she thought it might have been Clarke, but as she listened closer, she heard a very familiar voice. Her nerves tightened like an archer's bow. Gideon. They had not seen each other in more than a decade, and though his voice was deeper, there was no mistaking it.

A tremor radiated from her tightening belly, shimmying up her back and over her scalp. Her fingers grew unsteady, forcing her to set the half-empty mug on the counter. Most days she could convince herself he was part of her past. But right now, with him so close, she wasn't sure how she felt.

Stepping out the back door was an option, but that would make her look weak, and if anything, she was strong. *Fireproof,* as a paramedic had said years ago.

Squaring her shoulders, Joan came around the corner and into the foyer. Gideon held a familiar black Stetson from his cowboying days in his hand and was smiling as he spoke to Ann. Immediately, she was struck by how tired he looked. Fatigue was part of being a cop. She'd surely pulled her share of all-nighters when she was working a case. But seeing him worn down troubled her more than she would have imagined.

She had a scant second to look Gideon over. Even with the bulky police jacket, she could see that his body remained lean. The once ink-black hair had touches of gray at the temples. She'd hoped he might have grown fat or bald, but he still looked great. She felt her face flush.

She'd pretended that her feelings for him had died when she'd left Montana years ago. But those feelings had never died. They had just curled up into a tight ball and waited for a bit of sunshine and water so they could spring back to life like a bitterroot blossom.

"Gideon." Joan had mastered the art of a clear, crisp voice, because no one respected a cop who sounded like Minnie Mouse.

His gaze, still on Ann, froze. She could not blame the guy. If he had stepped into O'Toole's last week, she might have done the same.

"I was about to tell you," Ann said. "Joan flew in last night. Did you know she's a homicide detective in Philadelphia?"

"I did." Gideon shifted his full attention to her. To his credit, he produced a subtle, almost pleasant smile. "Joan."

He had always been careful with public displays of affection. They both had agreed in college that PDAs were beneath them. But given that it was taking every bit of her to keep her body from melting, she hoped her presence had jostled his apple cart a little.

She held out her hand. "Good to see you."

He took her hand, squeezing gently and slightly frowning as her rough scars brushed his skin. His gaze wavered, suggesting he was taken aback. Good. They could all stand on shaky ground together. "Likewise."

Kyle ran up to his father. "You smell like smoke."

"There was a fire in town last night," he said, dropping his gaze to his son.

"What burned down?" Nate asked.

"A beauty shop." Gideon's voice sounded almost conversational, as if he did not want to alarm the boys.

"Can we go see it?" Kyle asked.

"No."

"I want to see it," Nate said.

"Me too," Kyle piped in.

"Maybe in a few days," Gideon said. "Right now, it's still not safe."

Joan shifted to cop mode. "Do you know how it burned down?"

"We do not," he said.

"Nate said Clarke had a call last night," Ann said.

"That was the one. He was there most of the night."

"Boys, finish your breakfast," Ann said. "We'll go out for a ride in the back range once you're finished."

"Can I ride Whiskey?" Kyle asked.

Ann looked to Gideon, who nodded.

"He's a strong rider," Gideon said with pride. "Whiskey will be fine."

As the boys scurried back toward the kitchen, Joan moved closer to Gideon, more drawn by curiosity over the fire in town than she was cautious of old emotions tangled up with guilt. The scent of smoke clinging to him stopped her a couple of feet away. "Have you spoken to Elijah? Where there's smoke, there's often an arsonist."

He rubbed the brim of his hat, already worn in several spots. "We haven't proven arson yet."

"Just so you know, I came to town to see Elijah," Joan said. "I thought he might act again, but never this fast."

"We don't know if it's him yet," Gideon said.

"Are you defending him?" Ann's anger hardened her tone.

"No. I just follow the facts. And right now, I have a fire with undetermined origins."

"Where was Elijah at the time of the fire?" Joan asked.

"He has an alibi," Gideon said.

"I'll bet," Joan said.

The thunder of the boys' footsteps in the kitchen rumbled through the house and made glasses in an antique cabinet rattle.

"I better go check on that," Ann said.

Ann turned and was calling out the boys' names before her foot landed on the first step.

"I'm going to talk to Elijah," Joan said.

"About what?" Gideon asked.

"I'm not sure. But I'll know when I get there."

"A few questions will reveal the truth in his heart?" he asked, baiting her.

"No. Thinking maybe interrogation skills I've picked up along the way might ferret out a few deceptions."

"And then what? He's already been tried, convicted, and served his time for the last fire."

Joan slid her hands into her pockets. Jesus. She'd been fired up and motivated when she'd boarded the plane yesterday. She had not formulated a clear plan beyond seeing Elijah. Now a suspicious fire had destroyed a building, and there was a crime scene to examine. And whether Gideon liked it or not, she would participate in the investigation.

"I'm borrowing your mother's car," she said.

He shook his head. "The clutch is out."

"Then I'll get Ann to drop me at the rental car place."

He regarded her with a guarded steadiness, as he used to when sizing up a wild bronco. "You can ride with me and save her the trip into town. It'll give us a chance to catch up."

A hint of challenge laced Gideon's tone. He was daring her to spend time with him and perhaps, God forbid, converse about the unfinished business between them.

To beg off would scream *coward*. She might regret the decisions she had made a decade ago, but she would not apologize for them. "I need to grab my coat and purse."

"Chop-chop," he said. "Bus is leaving in five minutes."

"Right." As she passed the hallway mirror, she caught a glimpse of her reflection. Her hair stuck up, and yesterday's mascara was smudged under her eyes. She looked like a cross between a rooster and an anime cartoon character.

Minutes later, teeth brushed and hair tamed by a damp comb, she'd changed into jeans, a dark-brown sweater, and black boots. All work-wardrobe staples. She felt underdressed without her sidearm.

The boys were gathered around Gideon. Both had donned coats and looked ready to head to the stables with Ann. Nate had a calculus book tucked under his arm. Algebra had nearly been Joan's Waterloo in high school. "Some light reading, kid?"

"Yeah," Nate said. "Do you like math?"

A quip died on her lips when she realized it might discourage the boy. "Nice. It's good to be smart."

"Ready?" Gideon asked.

"I am."

The four years Joan had spent in Montana had hovered in the shadows of her life for many reasons. Foolish to think all the baggage had centered on Elijah, when the bulk of it belonged to Gideon.

Walking out the front door, as the boys raced toward the barn, Gideon unlocked the doors to the police-issue SUV.

She slid inside the car, glancing in the side mirror and watching as Gideon hugged his son and whispered something to him. A part of her was glad Gideon had a child to love. Even in college, he had said he wanted children. Even though she had refused to discuss the possibilities of motherhood in those days, a part of her now wished they'd had a child together.

She settled in the seat and hooked her belt. The dash was dust-free, as was the side console. There was a computer mounted between the seats as well as a two-way radio, which must have been convenient for when he was out of cell service.

He slid behind the wheel, clicked his seat belt as he looked in the rearview mirror at the boys to make sure they were clear of the car. She found it strange to think how time and life had made this wild and reckless cowboy more cautious and deliberate.

The engine throttled up as he pulled out of Ann's driveway and onto the rural route.

Joan shifted her attention to the stunning mountain peaks that ran along the entire horizon. The landscape was so vast that it left her feeling exposed and unsure of how to proceed. She missed the urban gray granite walls of Philadelphia that flanked her and blocked out old memories that now nudged to the front of her mind. Joan shifted in her seat and ignored the tightening in her chest. She had been so stubborn and hard on him because she had loved him. She thought if she left him, it wouldn't hurt so much. But she had been wrong.

As she narrowed her eyes, the landscape blurred, and she could pretend it was not so intimidating. She needed to find Elijah, figure out what his strategy was, and get the hell back to Philadelphia before she lost her mind.

Confessions of an Arsonist
This fire should have satisfied my cravings, but it has only created a hunger for more heat and more destruction.

CHAPTER EIGHT

Missoula, Montana
Sunday, September 6, 2020
11:00 a.m.

Gideon noticed Joan shivering but was not surprised, given her flimsy coat. She had forgotten about the weather. He turned up the heat. "I'm assuming the regular rental car place?"

"That'll work." She tapped her finger on her worn jeans, as if unsaid thoughts were scratching against her insides.

"It's about twenty minutes from the ranch," he said.

"How far is the rental car place from the arson scene?"

"Ten minutes in the opposite direction."

When Gideon had first seen her at Ann's, he was too taken aback to notice much about her. Now, with Ann and the boys gone, he'd had time to process. Time to remember what he had loved about her.

Joan was as fit and trim as she had been in college. Her hair was shorter, but he liked the way it showed off her angled face and made her green eyes pop. She did not wear much makeup, but she still did not need it. He had always assumed that if he ever saw her again—and he had fantasized about it—he would not feel really strongly one way or the other about her. Just twenty minutes with her had told him that he'd been wrong.

"Can you take me to the arson scene first?" Joan asked. "I want to see it before I talk to Elijah."

"Why? You can't work it in an official capacity."

"Technically, no. But it may help. I've walked my share of arson scenes in the last few years."

He could drop her off at the rental car terminal now and get on with his investigation, but it would be only an hour before she showed up at the crime scene and started poking around. Better to keep her close.

"Wondering if I'll show up at the fire scene by myself?" she asked.

"I am."

"Good guess. I will. I need to see it."

"You think this person left a calling card?"

"Very few arsonists have signatures, but they leave clues about themselves," she said. "It's just a matter of identifying the patterns." When Gideon did not acquiesce to her request, she challenged, "How many fires have you investigated in the last ten years?"

"On this scale? Only one, and that was ruled an accident."

"You've had other fires in town?" she asked.

"A dumpster fire last year and a few brush fires outside of town over the summer. None of them was particularly destructive." He passed the turn to the rental car place and continued on to the arson scene.

"That's a no to a large-scale arson investigation, isn't it?" she said, glancing up from the map on her phone.

It was, but admitting to shortcomings was not always wise. "You're strictly there as an adviser, Joan. I don't care how much experience you have. Don't touch anything."

A slight smile curled the edges of her lips. "I'll be as good as gold."

He shook his head, fearing he was losing control of this case right out of the gate. "I'm holding you to it."

"When did the fire start?" she asked.

"Last night. The first call came to the police station as I was finishing up my shift. I was less than a mile away, so I took the call. I rolled up on the scene at six fifty-five p.m. The building was fully engulfed. Fire crews arrived within a few minutes, but the building was a total loss."

"They shifted to containing the fire."

"Correct."

"Were there any fatalities?"

Count on Joan to get right to the heart of the case. "Yes."

"Do you have an identity yet?" she asked.

"No."

"Does the evidence suggest the victim was the arsonist?"

"Unsure."

When he pulled up behind Becca's vehicle, he noted a television news crew filming the site. A fire this size in a small city was not going to go unnoticed, and he accepted their presence, even though he did not like it.

Joan visibly tensed when she watched a reporter station herself in front of a news camera. "They're everywhere."

"The press follows the news."

"And when there's no news, they dig up unnecessary dirt to muddy the waters."

"Sounds like personal experience talking." He'd followed her career for a couple of years, but when his marriage had really faltered, he'd had to let his preoccupation with Joan go in order to convince his wife and himself that he was working on their marriage.

"It's a long story," she said.

"I bet it's a good one."

"Not for me." She flexed her fingers. "Do you have gloves?"

He fished black protective gloves from his pocket and handed them to her. "Stick close to me. You're here as my guest."

"Sure."

Out of the vehicle, they crossed the street to where Becca stood watching two firefighters walking the rubble.

"Detective Becca Sullivan, I would like you to meet Joan Mason. She's visiting Ann and is also a detective in Philadelphia."

Becca thrust out her hand. "Good to meet you. You both just missed the medical examiner's team. They transported the remains. The medical examiner on call has been contacted."

"Where was the body found?" Joan asked.

Becca pointed to the front of the building near the display window. "Over there. There used to be a window and exterior door there."

Joan drew in a deep breath as her gaze settled on the site.

Becca's eyes narrowed as she studied Joan. "Do I know you?"

"Not sure."

Becca snapped her fingers as if a memory had materialized. She glanced at Gideon, and he knew she had just assembled the puzzle pieces and connected Joan to him. "Glad to have you, Detective Mason."

"Thank you." Joan worked her hands into the gloves. "May I have a look, Detective Bailey?"

"Follow the flags designating the path."

"Understood."

"I should have updates on the victim later this evening," Becca said.

"Good." As he readied to follow Becca and Joan, his phone rang. "Detective Bailey."

"Detective, this is Jessica Halpern. I understand you've been trying to reach me."

"That's right, Mrs. Halpern." He watched as Joan and Becca stepped over black ash and collapsed timbers. "I have some bad news about your beauty salon. It caught fire last night and is a total loss."

Silence crackled over the line before she stammered, "H-how? I don't understand."

"Still trying to determine the cause of the fire, ma'am. Can you come to the scene?"

"Easier said than done. I'm in Chicago with my husband. He's out for a run now, but when he gets back, I'll tell him." Another sigh. "A total loss? Everything?"

"Yes, ma'am."

"Jesus," she whispered. "What the hell happened?"

"We're working on that."

Mrs. Halpern took a ragged breath. "We put all our money into that place."

"I'm sorry. Mrs. Halpern, did you employ a Lana Long?"

"Yes, why?"

"Her purse was found near the scene."

"I don't know why. She was supposed to be back in Denver by now. What does this have to do with Lana?"

"Can't say right now. I also need a list of current employees who worked at the shop."

"Of course. Darren and I will try to get a flight out tonight, but I might not get back until Monday. You know how the flights can be on a holiday."

"I understand."

The call ended, and a second later, he had a lengthy text including a list of the other salon employees. He went down the list of employees and left messages with two of them and spoke to three others. He heard a mixture of shock over the fire, complaints about where some would work next, and pledges to get in touch with Jessica Halpern. All knew of Lana, but none had spent any real time with her.

Joan stepped over the debris and stripped off her gloves as she approached him. "I want to see Elijah."

"What makes you think Elijah will even talk to you?" he asked.

She looked at him. "Nine years ago, I wrote to him. And he responded. We've been corresponding ever since."

"You're shitting me!" he said, louder than he intended. "Why would you reach out to him?"

She shrugged but did not look away. "I wanted to know why he wanted to burn me alive."

"I'm almost afraid to ask. Did he tell you anything that was of value?"

"No."

"What a surprise."

"I thought a look inside the mind of someone like him would be informative. He started following my cases. He also offered a few interesting insights that helped me solve a couple of cases."

It was a kick in the balls to know she had reached out to Elijah and not him. "So you two are best pals?"

"Hardly. When the parole board asked me three years ago if he should be released, I said no in as many ways as I could think of. But he has now served his full term." She ran her hand through her short hair. "You remember the scorpion and the frog fable?"

"Trusting a predator never ends well."

"Exactly."

"Just make sure you don't forget that."

She rubbed her fingertips over the ribbed white scar on her palm. "I never do."

They got into his car and he started the engine. They drove in silence for a half dozen blocks before he pulled up in front of the boardinghouse.

"It is within walking distance to the fire," Joan remarked.

"Yes, it is."

The two got out of the car and walked up the cracked, freshly scrubbed sidewalk to the front porch. All the faded traces of the graffiti were gone. He rang the bell, and Mr. Pickett answered it. His eyes were bloodshot, but he had shaved, and his shirt looked to be clean. The monthly six-pack appeared to have left him a little hungover.

"Mr. Pickett, could I speak with Elijah?" Gideon asked.

"He's in the kitchen. He's offered to cook up lunch. Making a tomato sauce. And for the record, he was here when that fire started."

"Are you sure?" Gideon asked.

"Very," Mr. Pickett said emphatically.

The scents of oregano and garlic reached out to him as he and Joan moved toward the kitchen. The aroma had a warm, comforting effect, and it surprised him that Elijah could cook.

"He's a great cook," Joan said, as if reading his thoughts again. "He worked in the prison kitchen and decided to improve the culinary standard. He even organized the prisoners to grow herbs in a greenhouse."

"Quite the Renaissance man."

"He can't stand boredom in any shape or form."

They found Elijah at the stove, wearing a yellow apron covered in bouquets of pink bitterroot flowers bound together with twine. He was holding a spoon dripping with red sauce up to the mouth of an older, thinner man.

The man opened his mouth to taste, but when he saw Gideon, he closed his mouth and nodded for Elijah to look. Elijah slurped up the sauce on his spoon. "Can I get you to try my sauce, Detective? The recipe came from a dear friend."

"No, thank you."

Joan stepped around him. Elijah's expression turned quizzical, and then his lips split into a wide grin. He set the spoon down and opened his arms wide. "Joan! God, how I have missed seeing you."

Gideon expected her to retreat. She had been too shaken all those years ago to even talk to him about Elijah or the fire. But instead of fear, her expression softened. It was a far cry from the cool, awkward greeting Gideon had shared with her earlier. "Elijah."

Elijah took her hands in his, and his thumbs rubbed against her palms. He turned them up so that he could study them. "What happened to you in that fire was a travesty. Are you going to help me figure out who set your house on fire?"

"That's why I came," she said.

Elijah's eyes brightened. "I have really missed you, Joan."

She stood silent and then slowly smiled.

"Finally, justice will be served for us both," Elijah whispered.

Tamping down his anger was harder than Gideon had imagined. He had been through the police department's files on the College Fire. He knew Elijah had taken Joan's class in college, had pictures of Joan in his room, and was dumb enough to leave his DNA at the scene. Elijah Weston was all smiles now, but he had the look of a man biding his time. Gideon did not know what Elijah's endgame was, but sooner or later, he would strike.

Confessions of an Arsonist
When the stress rises, I set small fires. They relieve the pressure building in my head, like little safety valves. But when it gets too great, only an inferno will do. And that's exactly what I did. It was glorious.

CHAPTER NINE

Joan knew Elijah was as toxic as the deceptively beautiful milkweed's delicate and bright blossoms. She was not fooled, regardless of what Gideon's expression suggested. It was because Elijah would never break her heart. The same could not be said for Gideon, who threatened a far greater wound if she allowed him to get close.

She stood back. "You look good."

"So do you," he said. "I'm glad to see you're doing so well. The press was very unkind to you in Philadelphia."

She felt Gideon's scrutiny sharpen. "I live to fight another day."

"That's all we can ask. Do you want to try my spaghetti sauce?"

"I would."

He generously filled a tasting spoon with sauce and held it up. She wrapped her lips around the edge of the spoon and genuinely savored the sauce. For a moment, the rich flavors of onion, garlic, and tomato transported her back to Ray's pub. "Marvelous. Reminds me of home," she said.

Elijah smiled, clearly pleased with himself. "It should. It's your mother's recipe that you told me about in one of your letters."

The recipe had been Ray's, and he had scribbled it down on a napkin so she could pass it off as her mother's. She doubted her mother had ever cooked much for her, and her dad's idea of pasta was SpaghettiOs. "I never forget that sauce."

"It won me tremendous goodwill in prison. No one is going to beat the hell out of you if they know you can cook a great meal later that week."

"Glad it helped."

He set the spoon down on a paper towel. "But you didn't come here to talk about food."

She was not reluctant to broach the one topic driving this meeting. "You're right. I'm here about the beauty shop fire."

"I have a solid alibi."

"He's right; he does." Pickett's gruff reminder had her turning to face the older man, as lean and grizzled as any cowboy on the range.

"Mr. Pickett, you were with him at the time of the fire?" she asked casually.

Pickett folded his arms over his chest. "I picked him up from the prison on Friday, and he has stayed in my line of sight since. No way he could have snuck out and set any fire."

"The entire time?" Gideon repeated, locking eyes with the old man.

"That's right," Pickett said.

Elijah shrugged, as if to say, *See, I told you.* She calculated the distance between the boardinghouse and the arson scene and guessed even a fit man like Elijah would need at least ten minutes to sprint over there. Setting the fire took time if an arsonist hoped to survive. And then there was the matter of Lana Long. She would likely have slowed him down. And then the return trip. At the very least, the entire adventure would have taken forty-five minutes.

"Are you sure your Saturday libation didn't start a little early?" Gideon asked.

"It never starts before nine p.m.," Mr. Pickett said, his voice firm with pride. "Never."

"Elijah, did other residents see you in the house?" Joan asked.

"Yes," Elijah said as he looked to the thin man with bloodshot eyes. "Rodney here helped me get settled in my room. And then we played cards up until dinner. Mr. Pickett was with me when we heard the fire trucks about seven fifteen p.m."

Rodney slid his long, bone-thin fingers into the front pocket of his jeans. "He's right. He was here."

Elijah was smart enough to know that if he set a fire, he would land at the top of everyone's suspect list. But Mr. Pickett's solid alibi reminded her that she had to keep an open mind. However, she wondered if the fire fatality had a connection to Elijah. As tempted as she was to ask, compromising what Gideon had told her would be a fast ticket out of the investigation. And she needed him to help her get access to the College Fire files.

"Would you like to stay for lunch?" Elijah offered. "I've made enough food for an army. I would love to serve you now, but Mr. Pickett has strict rules about mealtimes. Translation, we eat at noon."

"I wish I could stay," Joan said. "But I've a rental car to pick up."

"I understand," Elijah said. "Have you seen Ann?"

She felt Gideon stiffen. "I have."

"I hope she's doing well. I'm taking her class starting on Wednesday. I missed the first session, but I've read the textbook, so I should be more than caught up."

"I'm sure you're well ahead of the other students. You always were well prepared in college."

He shrugged again. "It's easy when you enjoy learning."

Elijah must have known she would not be able to resist seeing him after his release. And the spaghetti sauce was proof he had been expecting her. "May I come back and visit again?"

"Anytime," he said with a big smile.

"Great." She thanked Mr. Pickett and Rodney as she and Gideon left the house. Neither spoke until they were in his SUV and pulling away from the house.

"Jesus," Gideon growled.

"Do I look that stupid?" she asked.

He didn't respond.

"I told you we've exchanged letters."

He tightened his hands on the wheel. "Recipes?"

"I'd forgotten all about it."

"He sure as hell did not. He made that sauce because he was expecting you."

"Maybe. Or maybe he planned to make it every opportunity he had until I showed."

Gideon slipped into a stony silence. Oddly, Joan enjoyed seeing Gideon get worked up. Nice to know she was not the only one teetering on the edge.

"When is your medical examiner going to perform the autopsy?" she asked.

"Tomorrow morning." A cutting edge sharpened his words and exposed more frustration. A decade later, he was still red-hot pissed at her.

"I want to attend the autopsy."

"You want?" Annoyance tightened his features.

"I'm a resource. It would be reckless to cut me out. And, like you, I want to make sure Ann stays safe."

He rolled his head from side to side as he took a sharp right and then a left onto another side street. "What happened in Philadelphia, Joan?"

"Does it really matter?"

"Your BF seems to think so."

Joan let the wisecrack go.

"He's going to use it against you. Just like the sauce."

"He will try." She considered telling Gideon that the last letter had been mailed to her home address but decided it would be a distraction at this point.

Gideon slowed as he approached the rental car place. "If you want to attend the autopsy, tell me what happened in Philadelphia."

"Really? We're going to do it this way?"

"We sure as hell are."

Confessing her shortcomings was never easy. And with Gideon, it was downright painful. "I was investigating a fire. I won't bore you with the details, but I was so sure of myself that I made an arrest before enough compelling evidence was obtained. I thought I could get a confession. However, my suspect was tougher and cleverer than I imagined. All the charges were dropped."

"Maybe he is innocent."

"*She*. And no, she is not."

"Charges get dropped all the time."

"Her defense attorney coerced a reporter to do a story on police bias and referenced my experience with an apartment fire when I was in middle school and the College Fire. He also discovered I was writing to Elijah. Pressure quickly mounted online, thanks to the attorney, charges were dropped, and I was put on administrative suspension with pay for two weeks."

"What happens after the suspension?"

"I'm going to be riding a desk for a while. The department is hoping that the news cycle will run its course, and I'll be yesterday's news."

Gideon pulled into the rental car place's parking lot. "You did nothing wrong."

"In my rush, I underestimated my suspect."

"And how will chasing Elijah help you?"

"Would you believe a little redemption would do a lot to soothe my ego?"

"No. Your ego is fine."

"It took a beating." She looked up at him. "Dr. Phil, do I get in on the autopsy or not?"

"Do you know where the medical examiner's office is?"

"I'll find it."

"Nine a.m. Sharp."

"Thanks, Gideon."

"Is there anything you're not telling me?"

"I'm officially an open book." Which was basically true.

"If I get a whiff that you're lying, I'll drive you to the airport myself."

She opened the door and paused. "While you're in a giving mood, can I look at your case files on the College Fire? I've never seen them, and now is as good a time as any."

He sighed. "Sure. They're in storage, so it may take a day or so."

"I have nothing but time right now."

***

It took Joan a half hour to get her rental car lined up. The cost of the car made her cringe, but she had enough savings to handle this additional expense over her two-week suspension. Beyond that, it would be tight.

Returning to the arson scene did not make sense. It would be hours, if not days, before the forensic team had processed all their evidence, and she would only be in the way now.

Joan turned the ignition, took a moment to set the radio to her favorite station that she had listened to in college. It no longer played rock but country and western. "Nothing stays the same," she muttered as she pulled out of the lot.

She drove toward the university, curious to see what was different about it. Would it be like the once-huge elementary school swing set that became ridiculously small over time?

As she drove closer, memories of college drifted back. When she had first arrived in Montana, the place had been so different from anything she had ever seen. The mountains and the enormity of everything were breathtaking. By her senior year, she had become jaded by all this, and like many twenty-two-year-olds, she had become restless and yearned to see new places.

She took a left onto a side street, recognized her old neighborhood, and minutes later found her old address. She stared at the two-story house built on the ashes of the old place. It was painted a dark blue with black shutters and a bright-yellow front door. The house had a wide covered porch perfect for kicking snow off boots on a cold winter day.

There was no garden, but the green grass was neatly cut and peppered with pine cones from a middling ponderosa pine. The wide driveway held three cars, including a four-door Ford, a late-model red truck, and a hard-top Jeep. The license plates were from Idaho, California, and Texas, suggesting this was still student housing.

She closed her eyes and recalled the cute yellow house that Ann's parents had secured for them. Excitement had rolled through her as she thought about living in a real house and not an apartment.

Opening her eyes, she shifted her focus to the neighboring houses on the street. Gideon and Clarke had lived at the end of the block in the brick rancher. God, that had been a fun year.

As she stared at the rancher, a memory flashed. It was January of her senior year, snowing and cold as hell.

Joan was walking home from the rancher, where she had been partying with Gideon, Ann, and Clarke. She could have stayed the night, as Ann had, but she was on the schedule for an early shift at the diner the next day and knew she needed to get some sleep.

Still intoxicated, she left a sleeping Gideon to make her way home. Per usual, she was not dressed for the extreme Montana cold or the never-ending wind cutting through her jacket and stripping her of all warmth. She lost her bearings in the near whiteout, tripped over something on the sidewalk, and did a header into a pile of snow.

Disoriented, she pushed to her hands and knees. Her fingers were numb, and her teeth chattered. Where the hell was her house? Ann had warned her about this unforgiving land, but she thought that after three Montana winters, she could handle a short walk.

Snowflakes fell on her head, soaking her thick green yarn hat, dampening her hair, and drenching her jacket in liquid ice. Shit. Where was her house?

She tried to stand, but her feet were so cold they barely worked. Ray was going to be notified that she had died drunk in a snowbank. And he would shake his head and tell everyone he had tried his best.

Strong hands grabbed her by the shoulders and hauled her wet, cold, and weak body to her feet. She stumbled and would have fallen if a strong grip had not steadied her. Normally, she would have yanked free and insisted she was fine. But even drunk and half-frozen, she realized her ship was sinking in a sea of ice and snow, and if she did not get help, she would perish.

Relaxing into the steady hands, she put one snowbound foot in front of the other. Her legs felt like lead, and her fingers—well, she did not feel them anymore. The hands tightened and pulled her close to a body that was dry and teased her with a warmth she desperately craved.

Blinking, and feeling a sense that she might get out of this alive, she refocused. She looked up and saw the front steps of her house. Her gratitude was palpable.

Gingerly, she raised her weighted feet one after the other until she'd summited the four steps.

"Keys."

"What?" she asked.

"Keys to the door."

"Oh, right." She fumbled wet, gloved fingers into her pocket and produced a key ring attached to a worn purple macramé fob that had been her lucky charm since middle school.

The hands took the keys and opened the front door. A rush of heat greeted her, sending a shiver of pleasure through her body. She stumbled inside, vowing not to leave the house until spring.

The hands stripped off her coat and snatched off her hat. The items were hung by the door in a careful row on horseshoe hangers.

"You better get out of those clothes."

She peeled off her gloves and dropped them on the floor as she toed off her shoes. Her fingers were beet red and trembled slightly as she moved toward a radiator and held them close.

"Thanks," she said.

"That was stupid."

"I know." She turned to face her savior and looked up into the familiar gray eyes of Elijah Weston.

His cheeks were rosy from the cold and his overcoat covered in snow. "Where did you come from?"

A brow arched, amused. "Funny, I was thinking the same question."

She shrugged, staggered a step.

He looked around the entryway, seemed to absorb every detail, and then moved toward the door. "See you in class on Monday."

That distant memory had been lost to Joan for years, and it was funny she recalled it now. Elijah had saved her on that night. But where had he come from? He did not live in the neighborhood, and the campus was several blocks away.

Her drunken, addled mind had not had the desire to seek the answer then. But now she realized Elijah must have been watching her.

Human memories were a tricky thing. Trauma, alcohol, and time had a way of altering the story and imposing impressions gathered from other life events that happened days, months, or years later. She had witnessed this on her job and always took eyewitness testimony with a healthy grain of salt. If Joan were to have interviewed herself about this, she might have called bullshit on it all. *You were drunk. It was dark and snowing heavily.*

She started the car's engine, chasing away a chill worming its way into her bones. Given her experience, she knew she should not trust the memory. "It was Elijah. Right?"

***

By eight thirty in the evening, Gideon had learned from Becca that Lana Long had an arrest record in Denver. Most of her offenses were minor, including two drug-possession charges and one arrest for vandalism. She had been charged with setting fire to a trash can, and the fire had done several thousand dollars' worth of damage to the adjoining structure. The property owner had dropped the charges.

As he pulled up to the ranch, he saw the rental car parked in Ann's driveway. He half hoped to see Joan, but there was no sign of her when Ann answered the door and called to Kyle.

"Are you doing all right?" Gideon asked.

"I'm fine."

"What's your take on Joan?" he asked.

"She's the same in many ways, and yet different. She's just as guarded as she used to be. Did she tell you her family home caught fire when she was in middle school?"

"She skimmed over it."

"I'll bet money the College Fire dredged up a lot of old memories. If she were my patient, I'd be treating her for PTSD."

He had been convinced he and Joan could have solved their problems, until the fire. Now he understood that her running away wasn't all because of him. "Where is she now?" Gideon asked gruffly.

"Sleeping. Time change, nerves, the case back east, and travel all caught up."

"Sleep was the one time she ever seemed to be at peace."

"Have you talked to her about the College Fire?"

"No."

Kyle appeared at the top of the stairs. "Dad, can I stay the night?"

"No. We sleep in our own beds tonight." Sleepovers did not happen unless he had a late-night shift. He and his boy had spent too many nights separated, and they sure were not going to spend unnecessary ones apart.

"Dad, you're not being fair," Kyle said as he stomped around the house.

"Life isn't fair, pal."

"You always say that."

"Get your gear."

"Fine." Heavy, dramatic footsteps faded away.

"You owe it to yourself and Joan to talk, Gideon."

"There's been a lot of water under the bridge, Ann."

"Not as much as you think."

Kyle appeared, and the two drove the short distance to their home. As he walked through the front door of the one-story rancher, Gideon shrugged off his coat, grateful to shut out the world for a few hours. He had become accustomed to the quiet in the backcountry, when all he and Kyle had had to worry about was finding a good fishing spot or splitting logs. Now, he was discovering that balancing the job and single parenthood was trickier than he'd ever thought. He had hoped the time spent at the fishing cabin would reset their relationship, but father and son seemed to be falling back into their old patterns. The kid complained, and Gideon grumbled back, sounding more and more like his old man every day.

"Do I have to go to bed?" Kyle kicked off his boots, leaving them discarded on the floor.

Gideon glared at the shoes. "Put 'em back proper."

Kyle stopped short of rolling his eyes, which he knew now earned him a confiscated phone, but he came damn close as he released a pained sigh and straightened his boots.

"And hang the coat up on the peg."

Kyle yanked off his coat as if it had offended him and hung it up.

The attitude needed work, but Gideon was not in a mood for a fight tonight. "How about you pop some popcorn in the microwave, and we'll watch a little preseason football."

"For real?"

"You can get by on one less hour of sleep, right?"

"Yeah."

He took his son's positive tone as a sign of hope. "Good. Get the kind that has the butter and salt on it, not the healthy stuff Ann gave us."

Nodding, Kyle headed off into the kitchen. The tap turned on, followed by the splash of what sounded like washing hands. A miracle. As he tugged off his sidearm and placed it in a lockbox in the entryway table drawer, he heard the microwave door open and then close with a hard bang. The boy was heavy-handed in just about everything, and Gideon knew every appliance in this house would be worn out by the time Kyle left for college.

Gideon removed his boots, placed them beside his son's, and rolled his head from side to side. He came into the living room and switched on the television as Kyle removed a bowl from the cabinet. The replay featured the Washington Redskins versus the Philadelphia Eagles game. A couple of East Coast teams. Too bad the Denver Broncos weren't playing.

The boy settled near him and offered him the bowl. Gideon scooped up a large handful of popcorn and ate it and then another. Hungrier than he imagined, Gideon realized he had been going nonstop for more than twenty-four hours.

As he watched the game, his thoughts drifted away from downs, penalties, and scores to Joan. She had given him a quick synopsis of what had happened in Philadelphia, but he wanted the entire story.

As the boy watched the game with keen interest, he reached for his phone. Over the last ten years, he had been tempted to look her up again, and had done so, but after a while, he'd stopped. There had been plenty of good reasons not to. But she had come back. Not to him, maybe, but to Missoula.

With one eye on the game and the other on the phone, he typed in *Detective Joan Mason, Philadelphia*. The third search result led with the headline COP PUT ON PAID SUSPENSION. The article was dated September 4.

Kyle's eyes were drifting shut. A few more minutes and the kid would be out like a light. He read through the article detailing the case of Avery Newport, who had been charged with burning down her home. Her roommate had died in the fire. Joan's name did appear in an article about police bias, which quoted unnamed sources who detailed the College Fire and the earlier one in her family's apartment. Unnamed sources told the reporter about the letters to Elijah. Who would have known about their connection? Knowing Joan, that left Elijah and someone in the prison system. Newport's attorney must have been worried about Joan's investigation. Otherwise, why bother with the hit job?

Going back further in the articles, he scrolled through the few mentions of her citations and awards. She was a high-profile cop.

And now Joan was in his jurisdiction. Looking for what? The justice unattainable in Philadelphia? Closure? Redemption? It certainly was not for him.

He laid his phone facedown on the couch and glanced toward his son. Kyle had fallen asleep, the remote in his hand. If things had gone differently between Joan and him, there would be no Kyle.

Life had given him two paths, and he was sorry he could not have taken both.

***

The arsonist squatted by the ring of stones glistening in the moonlight. The night sky was crystal clear, and the stars twinkled above. In the center of the stones, a tripod of sticks leaned lazily against each other. Beneath the small spire was a gathering of dry leaves and shaved bark.

He struck the match in his hand, savoring the brief scent of flint, and then watched the fire blaze bright and tall at the end of the match. The flame swayed in a hypnotic dance. The play of colors seductively spoke to him and whispered promises no woman ever had. He grew hard.

The flame burned down, scorching the tips of his fingers. He held tight to the match, absorbing the pain until the flame had died. He dropped it on the makeshift pyramid of wood, struck another match, and then tossed it on the kindling.

A small flame appeared, and the fibrous strands crackled and glowed. He blew on the smoldering tinder, which greedily accepted his nourishing breath. The flames nibbled at the kindling and then gorged on larger pieces of wood.

His creation grew stronger and hotter by the moment. Gently, he laid a larger piece of wood on the fire as he looked toward the brittle brush blanketing the forest bed beyond the circle of rocks. It would not take much to release his creation into the wild. Given the steady wind and the dry undergrowth, it would dance up and down the mountainside, destroying all in its path within hours.

He sat back on a large stump and poked the fire with a stick from his pile. The embers crackled and floated around like fireflies.

As tempting as it was to let his mistress destroy it all, he had to be careful. With Joan Mason back in town, caution was essential. He had important work to do, and he refused to let her stop him.

CHAPTER TEN

Missoula, Montana
Monday, September 7, 2020
8:50 a.m.

Despite the extra sleep, Joan was still exhausted and overcaffeinated when she arrived at the medical examiner's office at the state crime lab on Palmer Street. The air's crispy coolness had her hunkering down deeper into Ann's coat, which smelled faintly of cinnamon and rose perfume. Look up the word *perfect* in the dictionary, and Ann's smiling face was sure to be right by the definition. Ann's flawlessness contrasted with Joan's chaos-strewn life and was plunging her deeper into her dark mood.

She crossed the parking lot to the front double doors. Normally, she would have reached for her Philadelphia detective's shield and hung it from her neck, but she hesitated, knowing now was not the time to draw attention to her outsider status. She opted to wait.

Gideon's car pulled up and parked. He strode toward her with long, fast strides. "Do you have warm gloves?"

She resisted the urge to rub her hands. "It's still summer back east."

"Montana doesn't give a shit about back east. Borrow a pair from Ann." Gideon opened the door and waited for her to pass. He nodded to the short woman with a round face at the reception desk. "Marge, how did you end up pulling duty today?"

"Cursed, I suppose," Marge said, deadpan. "You?"

His grin was easy and quick. "Same. I'd like you to meet Detective Joan Mason. She's consulting with me on this case."

Marge regarded Joan with a mixture of curiosity and suspicion. "Nice to meet you, Detective Mason."

"Please call me Joan."

"Joan, where are you from?"

"Philadelphia."

"That's a long way."

"I'm here on vacation. I'm friends with Ann Bailey."

Marge's expression softened. "Well, you should have said so. How do you know Ann?"

"We went to college together."

Marge's head tilted a fraction. "You were her roommate during the College Fire."

First Becca and now Marge were proof the past was always near. "That's right."

Gideon patted his hand on Marge's desk. "We came to meet the doc."

"Dr. Christopher didn't look thrilled this morning when he came through here. Said something about fishing."

"He'll get over it," Gideon said. "Thanks, Marge."

They strode down a center hallway and through another set of double doors. He pushed them open, and they were greeted by a man in his late thirties. Tall and lean, he had the bearing of a wrangler, especially the thick mustache that looked straight out of central casting. A white lab coat covered a plaid shirt and worn jeans.

Gideon extended his hand, and they shook. "Thanks for coming in today. Dr. Peter Christopher, I'd like you to meet Detective Joan Mason."

"Heard there was another cop on the scene yesterday," Dr. Christopher said.

"Just happened to be in town," Joan said.

"I've not had a body so badly burned in a long while, so whatever expertise you got is welcome, Detective."

"Thank you," Joan said.

"You two slip on gowns," Dr. Christopher said. "I'll meet you in the suite in a few minutes."

"Will do, Doc," Gideon said.

Gideon fished gowns out of a closet and handed a set to Joan, along with gloves and booties for her shoes. She slid on the paper gown, trying not to think about the last time she had dressed in front of him as she secured the ties at her waist and yanked on the gloves and booties.

She followed Gideon into the exam room as she had followed hundreds of other detectives into suites larger and more sophisticated than this one. Regardless of the room's size, however, they all had a way of shrinking down to the one gurney and the one sheet-draped body.

Dr. Christopher reached for the edge of the sheet, and Joan braced as he carefully pulled it back. Laid bare before them were the charred, blackened remains of this unidentified human. Most people who died in fires were killed by smoke inhalation, but what the fumes did not destroy, the fire did.

"Do you know if the victim is male or female?" she asked.

Annoyance seemed to ripple through Gideon. She had promised not to insert herself into the investigation, but if he was that great of a detective, he would have figured out by now that she played it a little loose with the truth.

"Female," Dr. Christopher said as he moved to the head of the table. "I would say midtwenties."

"Cause of death?" Joan asked.

"That's an interesting question," Dr. Christopher said.

"How so?" Gideon asked.

Dr. Christopher pointed a gloved finger to the victim's blackened neck. "If you look very closely, you'll see what appears to be a ligature mark around her neck. The implement cut into her skin, so whoever was trying to strangle her was not playing around."

Joan leaned closer to the remains, reeking of smoke and chemicals. "It takes strength to make that kind of mark." Avery Newport's roommate had been filled with a cold medicine to make her groggy. "Women as a group tend to favor killing methods that do not involve direct contact. Poison. A gun or knife in a moment of passion or fury. Strangulation is personal and sexual in many ways. Generally, it's done by men."

Gideon shifted his stance. "But I saw her move. I'm sure of that."

"There was a significant amount of smoke and heat trauma in her lungs. Both factors led to her death," Dr. Christopher said.

"Clearly, our boy didn't get the job done," she said. "The question is: Was he sloppy, or did he want her alive, knowing the fire would kill her?"

"Do you think she surprised him while he was torching the place?" Gideon asked.

Pleased his curiosity had elbowed past his annoyance, she said, "Depends on the ligature he used. Did he have it in his pocket, or did he grab an electrical cord that was handy?"

"The ligature was thin," Dr. Christopher said.

"Easy to carry in a pocket. Effective. Painful," Joan said. "He disabled her and then set the blaze."

"She was trying to get out," Gideon said.

"She was tough. A fighter," Joan said with respect. "Any ideas who she might have been? Is this Lana Long?"

"I called all the women who worked at the beauty shop, and none has seen or heard from Ms. Long since her last shift at the salon," Gideon said.

"These remains fit the general size and description on Ms. Long's driver's license," Dr. Christopher said. "I've extracted DNA from her teeth and have sent it off to the lab, but I'll still need a sample of her DNA to compare it to."

"She had a packed bag at her apartment. There might be hair or skin samples. Anything else you can tell me about her?" Gideon asked.

"I took X-rays. There's an old break to her left wrist, and though I can't say for certain until I complete the autopsy, she may have been pregnant."

"Pregnant?" Joan pictured the woman clawing her way across the floor toward safety. Normally, it would have been a five-second walk. But to a semiconscious woman choking on smoke and heat, it would have taken much more time.

"I believe I saw the outline of a fetus on the X-ray," Dr. Christopher said.

"An unwanted pregnancy would be a motive for a man to murder a woman," Joan said. "How pregnant was she?"

"Again, a guess," Dr. Christopher said. "Three or four months."

"Elijah would have been incarcerated when this woman became pregnant," Gideon said.

"Did he have conjugal visits?" she challenged.

"I'll speak to the warden," Gideon said. "What about personal items? Did you find anything on her body?"

Nodding, Dr. Christopher moved to a stainless-steel tray holding metal remnants from a pair of jeans and a melted phone. "The jeans are generic. The phone must have been in her back pocket. It's melted."

"Identifying the body might lead to a phone account, and the phone company can give you texts and call numbers," she said.

"If you can confirm the pregnancy and especially the fetus's DNA, call me," Gideon said. "The majority of women who are murdered are killed by someone they know or who professes to love them."

"I'll see if I can fast-track the DNA test," Dr. Christopher said.

As they pushed through the exam-room doors and stripped off their gowns, Joan's mind churned with facts and frustration. Regardless of the choices this woman had made, she did not deserve to die, and neither did her child. "The forensic team is at the fire scene now?"

"Yes." Gideon wadded up his paper gown and tossed it in the bin on top of hers.

"I want to see if they've discovered anything."

"They don't work for you."

"You going to claim jurisdictional protocol?"

"No. I care more about solving this case than soothing my ego. But a detective on paid suspension would give a defense attorney a field day in court."

His calm logic was irritating. But also correct. "I'll fly under the radar."

He reached for his hat and traced the brim with his fingertips. "Same rules apply, not that you've followed them yet."

"You won't know I'm here," she said innocently.

He muttered a curse and headed to his SUV. In her vehicle, she followed him back into the center of town, and each parked across from the beauty salon.

As she stepped out, she spotted a tall man with broad shoulders. His back was to her, but she recognized him easily enough.

Clarke Mead. He was Ann's estranged husband and the fire chief. In his midthirties, he had dark, close-cropped hair with a matching mustache. He had always rocked that *Magnum, P.I.* vibe, and the extra years now only enhanced the look. Gideon and Clarke had been friends since middle school. Both their families owned ranches, but the Meads had sold years ago. Gideon and Clarke had played ball together, drank beer behind the high school bleachers at football games, and gone to UM together. Two peas in a pod. Both had loved the town enough to stay and serve their community. They would protect it no matter the cost.

Hearing Gideon's footsteps behind her, she did not wait for him but strode toward Clarke. When his head turned, dark eyes narrowed as surprise and questions hiked thick eyebrows. "Joan Mason?"

She thrust out her hand, oddly glad to see the big lug. "As you live and breathe."

He wrapped lean fingers around hers, hesitated briefly before he pretended not to notice her scars. "Damn, I thought you were never coming back."

"I didn't, either. I suppose you can figure out why?" she said.

"I got a good idea why," Clarke said as he looked back at the burned pile of debris. "You been by to see Elijah?"

"I have."

"And?" Clarke kept his focus on Joan as Gideon walked up.

"Cool as a cucumber," Gideon interjected. "Couldn't have been more charming."

"He's a slick bastard," Clarke said. "Don't be fooled by it."

"Have you seen him at all since the fire?" Joan asked.

"Sure. I visited him about nine years ago. Curious, I suppose. Maybe hoping that on some level he was suffering. Of course, he wasn't. He seemed perfectly at peace."

Elijah had never mentioned Clarke's visit in any of his letters. It was a subtle reminder that there was a lot Elijah was not telling.

"Did he ever write you?" Joan asked.

"Hell no," Clarke said. "Why would he?"

"He wrote Joan," Gideon said. "And she wrote him back."

Irritation gnawed. She was not ashamed of the correspondence, but that did not mean she wanted it made public knowledge.

"I bet you didn't learn a damn thing," Clarke said.

"Not about the College Fire," she conceded.

"Is Elijah still insisting he's innocent?" Clarke asked.

"Yeah."

Clarke worked his mouth, like he might if he'd taken a bite of a sour apple. "Any word yet on the body we found in the blaze?"

"None yet," Gideon said.

Clarke shook his head. "My money is on Lana Long. Leaving the purse in the alley suggests she planned to burn the place down but didn't realize her fire was like a wild dog ready to maul her."

Gideon did not respond.

Joan understood he wanted the strangulation detail on Lana's neck kept quiet. She had worked enough investigations to know that certain facts were best kept secret, even from the other professionals working the scene. Cops and fire crews talked to each other, and information got leaked.

"Was anything found on Jane Doe's body?" Clarke asked.

"It was all pretty well destroyed," Gideon said.

"When will the docs get the DNA back?" Clarke asked.

"That's hard to say. They fast-tracked it to the lab in Helena."

A dark-green Jeep parked behind her rental. The driver's side door opened to a tall bleached blonde wearing snug jeans and a fitted sweater that set off a silver-and-turquoise necklace dangling over full breasts that Joan would bet were a plastic surgeon's work. The hair was shoulder length and teased and sprayed enough to resist the Missoula wind.

Her gaze settled on what had been the beauty shop. She blinked, cursed, and blinked again. Custom boots clicked against the asphalt as she neglected to look before crossing the street. "Detective Bailey. I'm Jessica Halpern. What the hell happened? Jesus H. Christ." She walked toward the blackened rubble, stopping just short of the yellow tape.

"We're still investigating," Gideon said.

She turned and faced them, blue eyes glistening in a pool of unshed tears. "This was my life. I sunk my entire life into this place."

"We're very sorry," Gideon said. "And we're doing all we can to get to the bottom of this. Have you heard from Lana Long?"

"No, but I've spoken to all the girls except her." Mrs. Halpern then challenged, "Did she do this?"

"Too early to say," Gideon said.

"Where's your husband?" Joan asked.

Jessica leveled her gaze on Joan as she absently rubbed the naked ring finger on her left hand. "Who are you?"

"Detective Joan Mason."

"I make enough donations to the police funds to stay in tune with the hires and fires. I don't remember your name."

"She's from Philadelphia," Gideon said. "Visiting and lending her expertise."

"You need help from a tourist, Detective?" Jessica asked. "That doesn't instill confidence."

Gideon did not rise to the bait.

"Can you tell me the cause of the fire?" Jessica asked. "My insurance company is already asking. I told them it had to be electrical. The building is nearly a century old, and my girls were always overloading the sockets with their curling irons and hair dryers."

"It wasn't an accident," Clarke said.

"So it was negligence," Jessica countered.

"Where is your husband?" Joan asked. "You're not wearing your wedding band."

Jessica turned to Gideon. "Shouldn't you be asking the questions, Detective?"

"Please answer Detective Mason's question," Gideon said. "Where is Darren?"

"My husband is at the doctor's office. All this really freaked him out, and he's having chest pains. And I was so rattled, I left my rings on my dresser this morning."

Gideon's expression did not change, but Joan sensed frustration simmering. "I want to see him as soon as he's cleared by his doctor."

"Why? He was in Chicago with me when all this happened," she said, waving white-tipped french-manicured fingers. "We're the victims here. We did not burn down our business. Why would we?" Her voice rose, high pitched and sharp. "This is our livelihood!"

"Your insurance company would expect it, and I owe it to you to see that the investigation is done right."

That seemed to appease her. "The sooner this can be wrapped up, the better. I want to rebuild. I can't make money until then." Her fingers slid into the tight pocket of her jeans. "All the girls who work for me have said they're going to have to find other jobs. Do you know how hard it is to find stylists?"

"I've spoken to or left messages with everyone who worked here," Gideon said. "But there will be follow-up interviews."

"Of course." Jessica laid a hand on his forearm, a move that was as decidedly feminine as it was controlling.

The trio watched as Jessica Halpern walked away and slid behind the wheel of her car. When she started the engine, her phone was already pressed to her ear.

Clarke stared after Jessica and then shifted back to Gideon. "We just found the delivery device. One of my men unearthed traces of a plastic milk jug melted by the back door. It was buried under rubble," Clarke said.

"Fill a jug with gasoline and stuff a sock in the top, and you've got a wick and a bomb ready to go off," Gideon said. "Evidence gets consumed by the fire. Leaves no traces, if done correctly."

"Money, revenge, and thrills always top the list of motives for arson."

"Tell me more about that plastic jug," Gideon said.

"Follow me." Clarke guided them around the building's footprint to the alley. "It all happened as I said. Gasoline trail down the alley to the milk jug filled with accelerant and then into the shop."

Gideon's phone rang, and one glance at the display sent him walking a few steps away, head ducked as he listened. Finally nodding, he ended the call and returned. "That was Dr. Christopher. He called the forensic lab and asked if Lana Long had any insurance or medical cards in her purse. We got lucky. She had an old appointment card from a dentist here in Missoula. The doc called Dr. Bischoff, explained his situation, and got the dental X-rays."

Joan was impressed. "And?"

"Dr. Bischoff recognized his work. He compared both sets of X-rays and determined they both belonged to Lana Long."

"Why would a gal who worked in a salon want to burn it down?" Clarke asked.

"Who says she did it?" Joan asked. "Maybe she caught the person who did."

CHAPTER ELEVEN

Missoula, Montana
Monday, September 7, 2020
11:00 a.m.

Joan knew the trail to this arsonist might very well be through Lana Long, but for now, she was leaving that to Gideon, who had been on the phone requesting a search warrant for Lana Long's apartment when she left the arson scene.

Joan decided to take a different angle. She drove toward the edge of Missoula down Bitterroot Road until she reached a blue-and-white sign for the mobile home park. She turned onto the dirt road and drove down the narrow lane past the collection of twenty or so battered homes arranged along a cul-de-sac. The development backed up to the railroad tracks and Hayes Creek. Most of the trailers had fences posted with No Trespassing or No Parking signs and were surrounded by corralled spare car parts, grills, unused propane tanks, and patches of scrub grass.

She checked the address on her phone and followed the occasional posted address numbers until she located the trailer she was looking for in the back. There were three cars parked out front, but the Chevrolet was on blocks, and the muddied white Wrangler beside it had flat tires. The black Ford truck appeared to be the only operational vehicle.

Parking, she realized how vulnerable she was without her sidearm. Domestic calls always made the hair on the back of her neck rise because emotions were high. Serving a warrant, conducting a wellness check, or asking basic questions could turn deadly in a heartbeat. Many cops had been killed by simply knocking on a door.

A dog barked behind the fence as she climbed the three wooden steps to the small porch by the front door. Before she knocked, she took a moment to look around. In the trailer next door, yellow-and-white curtains flickered.

She knocked on the door. Inside she heard canned laughter from a television but saw no signs of movement. She knocked harder and stepped to the side, one foot on the lower step.

Finally, the television silenced, and footsteps vibrated in the trailer, moving with what sounded like annoyed, clipped foot strikes. The door opened to a slim woman in her midfifties. She had long gray hair that draped over narrow shoulders. Wiry hair coupled with sharp brown eyes conjured images of witches and spirits. A black cat strolled near the woman's feet, weaving its scrawny body around worn jeans.

Joan wondered how many trick-or-treaters dared visit this place on Halloween. "Mrs. Weston?"

"Who wants to know?"

She avoided giving her name, fearing the woman would recognize it. "I came to talk to you about your son, Elijah."

"You must be one of those reporters looking for a story about him."

"I'm not a reporter, Mrs. Weston. Do you get a lot of reporters out here?"

"Sure, from time to time. A few last month. And it ain't Mrs. It's Miss. I'll tell you what I told the last folks asking: my boy didn't have nothing to do with the College Fire. He's innocent."

"You've spoken to Elijah recently?"

"No, but I know he's never set any fires. Who did you say you were? I didn't catch it."

She hesitated and then said, "Joan Mason."

Her eyes narrowed as the woman slowly nodded. "From the trial."

"That's right."

"What do you do these days, Joan Mason? You look like a cop."

"I get that a lot. I'm here today to talk about Elijah." A sidestepped question was not exactly a lie.

"I haven't seen my boy since he went to prison. I sent him money when I could, but we don't communicate."

"Did you stay in contact at all?"

"I wrote once or twice."

"In ten years?" Joan said, tamping down her surprise.

"I meant to do better, but time always got away from me."

Joan looked to her left toward a pile of rubbish billowing out of a trash can. A rat circled the can and then quickly vanished into the torn aluminum skirt around the trailer. According to Elijah's juvenile records, he'd had a disdain for trash and clutter. The few fires he had set as a teen had not been motivated by a desire to destroy anything. He'd simply been cleaning up around his home.

"He didn't set the fire in town," she repeated. "I would have sensed it if he had."

"Sense it?"

"That's right. I can sense evil. His daddy had the spirit in him."

"Did you sense anything about Elijah when he was younger?"

The older woman's brow knotted with regret. "I beat the badness out of him. It ain't there no more. The police railroaded him ten years ago. They're going to try it again. Mark my words."

"I can appreciate a mother looking out for her son," Joan said. "I would look after mine."

"You got kids?"

"No. But I watched how my mother worked to take care of me when I was a kid." No rule against a cop lying during questioning. How many times had she made up a story about a hardworking mother or a dead father to win over a witness? She had lost count. "Sometimes she worked three jobs to keep a roof over our heads."

"I did the best I could for Elijah. But he was a challenge from the beginning."

"He's pretty smart."

"Too smart. Got big ideas and went to college. I knew he was reaching too far. That's what happens when you stretch beyond where you belong. The world knocks you back further than you started."

"I don't remember him having a girlfriend in college."

"Why does that matter?"

"Just trying to figure out what happened."

"You sure you're not a cop? Or maybe a reporter?"

"I think I dislike reporters more than you do."

"Why don't you like reporters?"

"They need to mind their own business."

"Exactly what I say," Miss Weston said. "They wrote some bad things about my boy after the College Fire."

"So did he have a girlfriend?" She was pressing the point because arsonists often acted out as a way to relieve stress. Elijah's grades had been the best in his class, so school had not been a problem. A romantic breakup was often a trigger for all kinds of violent behavior.

"He had a girl he liked," Miss Weston said with a slight smile.

"Did you ever meet her?"

"No, but once he was pulling cash out of his wallet, and a picture of a young girl fluttered out. I asked if she was his girlfriend, and he said yes. I tried to get a good look at the picture, but he was guarded. Maybe I shouldn't have, but I teased him about her. He got real pissed."

"What did she look like?"

"Blond hair and real pretty. So pretty I started to wonder if what I'd seen was the picture that comes with a new wallet."

"Was it?"

"No. It wasn't magazine paper but real photo paper."

"Did Elijah mention her name?"

Miss Weston pulled out a packet of rumpled cigarettes and a lighter from her pocket. She lit a cigarette and inhaled deeply. "She looked like she came from money."

"What does money look like?" Joan asked.

"Not like me. Not like you."

Joan grinned. "You're right about that."

"Pretty skin, white teeth, little pearl earrings."

"What happened to her?"

"I don't know. That college house burned, and all hell broke loose."

"The fire and the trial must have been really hard."

Miss Weston glanced back at the television. "I got to go. I taped *The Wendy Williams Show*, and I want to watch it."

"I don't watch television. Who is she?"

"A talk show host." And before she could ask another question, Miss Weston had vanished inside her house.

***

Joan was mulling over what Miss Weston had said as she was driving back toward town when she spotted a small roadside diner. Miss Weston had insisted that Elijah had been framed. But it made sense that a mother would want to believe her son hadn't committed such a heinous crime.

She parked at the café and walked up to a take-out window, ordered a burger, fries, and a chocolate milkshake. She took her food to a small battered picnic table and sat, angling her body toward the mountain range. It would have been warmer if she'd sat in her car, but for some reason, she craved the open air, even if it had a bite. She nibbled a hot fry, greasy and salty in just the right way. She unwrapped the paper to find a fat burger doused in ketchup, mustard, and extra relish, as requested.

She and Gideon used to stop here after their weekend hikes. They would sit at this very table, more worn and weather beaten now but pretty much the same. She had often protested, wondering why anyone would give up a perfectly warm fast-food restaurant to sit in the open and eat food off a paper plate. Memories pressed forward.

Gideon unwrapped his burger and grinned at the sight of the double patties. "Stop being a baby."

"But I like real restaurants."

"This is real." He took a huge bite, chewed for several moments. "This is Montana."

"I know." She glanced around the open sky. "It's everywhere."

"You always complain about long hikes, the snow, and the cold. Why did you come to Montana?"

"The scholarship money," she said. "I didn't think I would actually have to experience the great outdoors to get an education."

Gideon chuckled and scooted closer to her until his shoulder brushed hers. He smelled of fresh air, pine, and a scent that was all his own. Joan almost never felt safe, but in his arms, she did. He was a big guy, strong, and he had a kind of code. He stuck by his responsibilities. Took care of his own. And he was not the type to leave a girl.

And all that had not stopped her from leaving him.

Now, as a cold wind blew up the mountainside and slid under the loose folds of her large cable-knit sweater, she placed her untouched burger down and pushed her fries away. She realized she had not felt safe in a very long time.

She took a pull on the milkshake, tasting the real chocolate syrup they used here. Nothing powdered, nothing canned. Real ice cream and chocolate, with a splash of whole milk.

Joan's phone rang. She rubbed her cold, damp fingers over her jeans. She did not recognize the number, but it had a Montana area code. "Joan Mason."

"It's Gideon. Those files you requested about the College Fire have come back from storage."

"That was fast."

"We're not quite as big an operation as you have back east. Fewer layers to cut through."

"Can I come now?"

"I'll be waiting."

"See you in twenty."

Joan hung up, gathered her uneaten food, and tossed it all in the trash can. A part of her did not want to relive the College Fire. But she had the growing sense that if she did not, there would be more fires and more deaths.

CHAPTER TWELVE

Gideon set the three worn and dusty file boxes on the small round conference table in the police station. The boxes were packed with forensic data, witness statements, crime scene photos, and police reports. As he stared at the collection of boxes, he thought how paltry it was, considering the level of destruction the College Fire had created. In his mind, the files should have filled this room.

His phone rang, and he gratefully turned from the boxes and answered it. "Detective Bailey."

"There's a Joan Mason here to see you," the deputy said.

"I'll be right out."

He strode down the long, tiled hallway, hoping that Joan would find something in these files that would give her peace. Maybe she could leave Missoula and return to her life in Philadelphia, so he could get back to mending the life he was rebuilding for Kyle and himself.

She stood by the front entrance with her arms crossed as she stared at a wanted poster. Energy still snapped from every sinew in her body, as if she were a rocket ready to blast off.

"Joan," he said.

She turned, and her green eyes reflected a tangle of anger, trepidation, and regret. "Hey."

In college, whenever she'd looked at him like that, he had hugged her and reminded her she was not alone. But a hug now would not be appropriate, nor would it repair anything. "I've got the evidence bins in the conference room."

"Terrific. Thank you."

She followed him down the hallway to the small windowless room. Gideon flipped on the light. There was a large table, a half dozen chairs, and a coffeepot emanating a slightly burned scent. In the center of the table were the three dusty brown boxes.

"Not much to go through," he said.

"I've seen homicide files that were thinner." She set her purse down.

He noticed her fingers were red from the cold. When was she going to get gloves?

"It might take me a few hours," she said.

"The room is yours for the rest of the day. But you can't take anything out of here," he gently warned her.

She shrugged off her jacket and draped it over a chair. "Feel free to frisk me when I leave."

His brain immediately flashed to his hands on her body. His groin tightened, and the annoyance tracking him since yesterday amplified.

She rubbed her hands together, either to warm them or maybe express anticipation of the task.

He was tempted to caution her that this material might be tough to see. She was a cop, but that did not make her immune to evidence that had directly affected her life. She always put up a good front, but he knew the person behind the facade was not so tough.

"Don't get all stressed out, Gideon," she said as she removed the top of the first box. "I can handle this."

Christ, could she still read him with just a glance? "I know that."

Mary Burton

"When you're worried, you still purse your lips," she said.

He opened his mouth to relax his lips and voice a denial. "You think you know me?"

Her gaze snared him. "I know you, and you know me more than either of us would like to admit."

"A lot has changed, Joan. We aren't kids anymore."

"I suppose you're right." Now, as before, she hid behind boldness and sarcasm. The fear lurking in the shadows did not surprise him, but it was troubling.

"Remember, you can't take the files."

She shifted her attention to the first box, her fingers skimming over the tabs of the folders. "I get it. Look. Don't take."

He walked to the door and then paused. "Joan, what do you hope to find?"

"I'm not really sure, Gideon." She removed a dusty yellow-white file.

He could not save her now, any more than he could have ten years ago. "Call out if you need me."

"Thanks."

Sighing, he left, hearing the other file box tops hit the conference room table. When he returned to his office, his phone was ringing. He snapped it up, both annoyed and grateful to have his thoughts diverted. "Detective Bailey."

"Becca here. I'm at the jail. Received a drunk-in-public complaint call from the manager at the Double R Bar. A fellow by the name of Ryan Davis, who is now in the drunk tank."

"Why are you telling me this?" He sat in his chair, leaned forward, and began to doodle the letter *J* on his blotter.

"He got drunk because his girlfriend would not answer her cell or her apartment door."

Becca had a punch line, or she would not have bothered with the call. She paused, as if savoring her coup. "The girlfriend's name is Lana Long. Mr. Davis's driver's license gives his last known address in Denver."

He dropped his pen. "I'll be right there."

"He's still pretty drunk."

"I still want to see him."

He grabbed his coat and Stetson and, on the way out, stopped at the front desk. "My sister is dropping off Kyle in two hours. I should be back in plenty of time to take him to his doctor's appointment."

A phone rang, and as the deputy reached for it, he said, "If you're late, we'll look after him."

"He can wait in my office."

The deputy gave him a thumbs-up as his attention shifted to the call.

Fifteen minutes later, Gideon was headed into the jail, removing his hat as he greeted the officer on duty. After checking his weapon in a locker, he hustled to the cell where Davis was being held.

Becca sat across from the cell, her head tilted down toward her phone. As if she'd heard his approach, she closed a few apps and tucked the phone in her back pocket as she rose.

"Have you spoken to Ryan Davis?" Gideon asked.

"Right now, he's sleeping it off, which is an improvement. At least he's calmed down. The sobbing was pitiful. Worse than the vomiting."

Gideon looked through the cell door window. Ryan's long, thin body was curled into the fetal position. His shirt and jeans were stained, his face was as pale as snow, and his mouth hung open. There was a bucket by the cot.

"Like I said, really drunk. He's not going to have much to say for a few hours," Becca said.

"What did he say in the bar?" Gideon asked.

"He was shouting at the bartender. He seemed to know that Lana was a frequent patron through his Find My Friends app. Lana must have forgotten to disable it, or maybe she liked the idea of him tracking her. Either way, Ryan knew Lana had been at the Double R Bar."

The Double R was located a few blocks from the beauty shop. "You said he was crying?"

"Like a baby."

Some of the guilty did cry once the heat of murder had cooled and they realized their loved one was dead or injured. He had arrested a few drunken cowboys who'd mourned the girlfriend or drinking buddy they had assaulted. "Stay here and make sure he doesn't get sprung. Call me when he wakes up. I'm headed to the Double R."

Gideon crossed town in less than fifteen minutes and parked in front of what looked like a nineteenth-century saloon. Painted letters resembling twisted ropes spelled out DOUBLE R BAR across a plate-glass window. A red neon sign flashed OPEN. This time of day, the parking was easy, and the bar would be quiet. Nothing worse than shouting over music or fending off drunks during an interview.

Hat in hand, he pushed through the front door, pausing as his eyes adjusted to the dim light. Behind the bar was a young woman with red hair gathered up in a ponytail. A blue T-shirt, sporting the bar's logo, stretched over large breasts, then whittled down over a narrow waist and into faded jeans.

Drying a glass tumbler, she eyed him suspiciously. "Officer, what can I do for you?"

He reached for his badge and showed it to her. "I'm Detective Gideon Bailey."

"Marcie Cash."

"You called in a disturbance this morning."

"You'll have to do better than that." She placed the glass on the shelf and reached for another damp one in the sanitizer. "I had a couple last night."

"Ryan Davis. He said he was Lana Long's boyfriend."

"Right. The sensitive one. Don't get many of those. Yeah, what can I tell you?"

"He said Lana is a regular here?"

"She was. Liked to sit on the right side of the bar," she said, nodding toward a trio of empty barstools.

"What can you tell me about her?"

"From Denver. Looking to find a little adventure. Had a boyfriend, and I don't mean Ryan. She told me her new guy was local."

"Did he ever come in here?"

"No. She always came in alone all dolled up, flirted a little, had her three Moscow mules, and then left by ten."

"Did she ever mention the boyfriend's name?"

"No, but she hinted once that she might be getting married. I wanted to call bullshit on that, but I keep my mouth shut. Insulting the customers hurts tips," she said.

"Why didn't you believe her?"

"The single boyfriends generally join their ladies. The married ones do not. Why all the questions about Lana? She okay?"

He sidestepped her questions. "You think Lana's boyfriend was married?"

"Either married or in prison," she said carefully, as if she saw the meaning behind his diversion. "And for the record, I'm rarely wrong."

***

Joan thumbed through the files, her fingertips skimming the manila folder tabs identified with typewritten labels trimmed in red. She removed her phone from her bag. She would not remove any physical files from the room, just as she'd promised. But Gideon had said nothing about her taking photos.

The first file contained the crime scene images of her former house, blackened and gutted by fire. The walls remained standing, but the roof had collapsed into the interior. Her room had been on the east side, which coincidentally had sustained the most damage. Puddles from the firefighters' water hoses dotted the scorched front lawn, the gold juniper plants along the foundation had been trampled, and the ten-foot-wide ponderosa pine by the driveway was singed beyond saving.

The photographic evidence moved into what had been her bedroom, and her throat tightened when she saw the outline of her metal-frame bed blackened and crushed by falling beams. A red-and-white MADE IN PHILADELPHIA poster was still thumbtacked to the wall but had been burned up to the cracked Liberty Bell illustration. That poster had been a gift from Ray and one of the few mementos she had brought with her from Philadelphia.

Beside the poster stood her secondhand dresser. The cluster of brushes, hair ties, and makeup had been swept to the floor by the spray of water, and the lone item remaining was a square Chanel No. 5 bottle, which she had purchased at a yard sale for five dollars. Though the scent had never suited her, she liked the idea of having something so fancy. All that destruction, and the perfume bottle still stood where she had placed it.

The ceiling had caved in on her desk, burying her computer, textbooks, papers, and the blue mug she had filled with fresh coffee every morning. Ironically, she remembered feeling grateful, as she had lain on the ambulance gurney hooked up to oxygen and an IV, that she had emailed herself her exam notes. At least she could still pull up her notes on another computer and study.

Joan shifted her attention to the door and the red-hot handle that had scorched her palms as she had desperately tried to get out. Memories crept out of the shadows, bringing with them the heat from the College Fire. For a moment it was hard for her to breathe.

She pressed trembling fingertips to her forehead as she pushed back the rise of panic and concentrated her focus on the image. The fact that the fire crews had reached her in that holy inferno rose to the level of a miracle.

She turned to the next image. The charred and water-soaked living room couch was now cast in sunlight from the collapsed roof. How many nights had she sat on that couch, a large bowl of popcorn cradled in her crossed legs, reading a book or watching *Survivor*?

Ann's room had been damaged, but not to the extent that Joan's had been. The kitchen had also sustained terrible damage. The cabinets, counter, and even its wooden floor had all collapsed into a pile upon the earth foundation.

Joan reached for a file marked *Arson Report* and skimmed a half dozen pages before she found the investigator's official findings.

Three incendiary devices were used. One by the back door leading from the kitchen, the second under the window of the back bedroom, and the third positioned in the crawl space under the same back bedroom occupied by Joan Mason. The combustible devices appeared to have been plastic bottles filled with diesel fuel. The device placed by the back door was not completely incinerated, and forensics identified pieces of a thick cotton sweatshirt that had been wadded into the vessel. The wick was likely ignited by a lighter or match, and because the cotton material was so long, the arsonist had time to clear the property before the explosions. The positions of the vessels appeared to be placed strategically to create maximum damage.

The arson report went on to detail evidence that appeared irrefutable. That recovered strip of a sweatshirt had been tested at the lab, which identified Elijah's DNA on the fabric. Eyewitnesses had spotted Elijah a few nights before the fire leaving their backyard, and he had also been seen walking down their street in the hours preceding the blaze.

"Your DNA was found at the scene," she whispered to herself. Many of the guilty professed their innocence even when faced with overwhelming evidence. But there was something in Elijah's confident tone that rang true.

Footsteps in the hallway had her lifting her gaze to Kyle Bailey. "Kyle?"

"What are you doing here?" he asked.

"Working. What's your excuse?" She welcomed the distraction from the files and pictures chasing too many demons out of the shadows. "Don't tell me—you've been arrested for telling too many bathroom jokes?"

He tipped his lips into a slight grin while still trying to act cool. "No, I'm not in trouble."

"You're not wearing handcuffs, so I guess the other officers agree."

"Cops don't arrest ten-year-old kids." He dropped his backpack in a chair and sat in the one next to it. He dug out a soda and fished a packet of Nabs from his backpack. When he opened the crackers, he offered her one. He may have looked like his mother, but he was quick to share like Gideon.

She took an orange cracker filled with peanut butter. "Thank you."

Freckles were sprinkled across his nose. "You're welcome."

"Seriously, what are you doing here, Kyle? Shouldn't you be out playing soccer or football?"

"It's a holiday, remember? And I'm waiting on Dad. He went to the jail, and I have an appointment at the clinic."

The kid's schedule was none of her business. She bit into the cracker, found she liked the Day-Glo orange and artificial peanut butter. And before she could stop herself, she asked, "Nothing serious at the doctor, I hope."

"I broke my arm last winter." He said it with such authority, as if he was proud of it. "They want to x-ray it and make sure it's growing right." He held up his right arm and bent it in multiple directions. "It's fine. Doctors are a waste of time."

She liked the kid. "I broke my arm when I was twelve. My best friend, Vincent, dared me to ride my bike down ten concrete stairs at the library. Made it almost to the bottom, but the front wheel twisted, and I went flying. Broke my arm at the elbow." Damn thing still hurt when it rained.

"You rode a bike down the library stairs?"

"I wouldn't recommend it, but yeah, I did. I'm not a person to dare. How did you break your arm?"

"I was living with my mom in Denver. I was walking to the corner store to get her some ginger ale and was hit by a car."

"Damn. That had to hurt." Joan intentionally kept her tone calm, just like she did when she rolled up on a crime scene with a hysterical witness or traumatized victim.

"It didn't hurt too bad at first. But it did later in the ambulance." He again rotated his arm in a full circle. "But it's fine now."

"Impressive." She thought about Gideon getting that kind of phone call. It was at least a thirteen-hour drive between Missoula and Denver. "I bet your dad drove all night after he heard."

Kyle's gaze widened with hints of surprise. "Yeah, how did you know?"

"I know your dad. He's like that." She was curious about Helen, the woman who had toyed with Gideon's heart after Joan had split town ten years ago. But grilling the kid about his mother was a pettiness she would not indulge.

"You don't sound like you're from here," Kyle said.

"You know I'm from Philadelphia."

"Why are you looking at case files in this office?"

She closed the folder filled with graphic color images. "I went to college here. Before you were born."

The boy, now looking curious about the file, tried to read the tab. "What was the case?" he asked.

The kid did not appear to be a fan of sugarcoating the truth, but he was still a kid. "There was a fire."

"Did anyone die?"

"No."

"So why do you care about it?"

"Because people shouldn't go around burning down houses."

"There was no arrest?" Kyle challenged.

It was her turn to smile. "You must know a lot about police procedures."

"Some. Dad's told me stories."

"There was an arrest and conviction."

129

"Then why do you care?"

"Good question."

He nodded to her scarring. "What's wrong with your hand?"

"Burn scar." She tucked her hand under the table.

"From that fire?"

The boy was quick. "Yes."

"There was a fire in town on Saturday," he said.

"I know."

"Are you working that case with Dad?"

"Yes. Kind of. Not exactly."

"What's that mean?" He offered her another cracker, but she declined.

"Your dad is letting me nose around."

"He doesn't need your help," Kyle said.

"He doesn't really need me at all." The truth surprised her with a sting.

Quick, determined footsteps sounded in the hallway, and Gideon appeared in the doorway. "Kyle. Why didn't you come by my office?"

"I didn't want to sit there alone. I got a snack and came in here when I saw Joan. We had breakfast together yesterday at Aunt Ann's house."

Gideon lifted his gaze quickly to Joan, as if searching for a sign that she might harbor any resentment toward the boy in any way. Whatever he saw must have calmed him, because he shifted back to Kyle. "Ready to go to the doctor?"

"Yeah. But for the record, I don't need a doctor," Kyle said.

"Once you get your medical degree, I'll stop bugging you about it," Gideon said.

Kyle gathered up his backpack. "Good to see you, Joan. You going to be at Ann's tonight?"

"I'll be there." She pointed her index finger at him. "Show your dad how flexible your arm is."

Kyle rolled his shoulder and then his arm as if he were a major league ballplayer warming up.

"Looks good," Gideon said. "Should be a quick visit, which will give you time to do your math homework."

"I hate math," Kyle said.

"Fractions are his nemesis," Gideon said as he laid his hand on the boy's shoulder. "He's not a fan."

Kyle shrugged. "What's the point? Isn't that what a phone calculator is for?"

"Just between you and me, Kyle," Joan said, "I'm a calculator kind of girl."

"Don't be fooled, Kyle. Joan had a straight-A average in college."

"Is she like Nate?" he asked.

"No. Not quite like Nate, but she's got game."

The offhanded compliment felt surprisingly nice. "Don't make me blush."

Kyle laughed. "See you around, Joan."

"You too, Kyle."

Gideon's expression teetered somewhere between confusion and relief when he and his son left. The room grew heavy with a silence broken only by the gurgle of the coffee maker. She looked at the closed file, her interest in the past waning. Still, she opened the next folder. She found the images that the investigating officer had discovered in Elijah's dorm room. Judging by the location and her outfit, they'd been taken in the late fall of her senior year. She had been at a local bar watching the rodeo on television. She remembered the night and knew Gideon and Ann had been present. Funny, she had no memory of Elijah at the bar. She snapped photos of each with her phone.

She continued to sift through the pictures. Her interest was piqued when the shots shifted from the house to the crowds.

She knew arsonists liked to see their work. It was common to find them lurking among the crowds, watching the flames devour their target. She studied the faces, recognizing a couple of old neighbors and former classmates. Then she spotted Elijah standing behind Clarke and Gideon. Gideon's expression was pained, and his clothes and hands, like Clarke's, were covered in dark soot. She had no memory from the moment she passed out to the instant she woke up coughing in the ambulance. Her memories rested on vague impressions and some sounds.

Joan sank deep into herself and floated in a pool of cool water. She was at peace. Not afraid. Not worried. This sense of well-being suited her, and she wanted to remain exactly wherever this was.

Hot, grimy hands cupped her face and forced her head and neck back. Lips touched hers, and hot air blew into her lungs several times. The air, like a lifeline, dipped below the water's edge and snared her. Before she could resist, the rope was yanking her toward the surface. Her head popped up above the water. She sucked in a deep breath. Her chest hurt, and her throat felt raw.

"Joan!"

Hearing her name shouted out from the past prompted her to open her eyes. She blinked, clearing her vision.

In her mind's eye, a familiar face came into view, but it was not the one she had expected. "It was Clarke," she said to herself. "Why wasn't it you, Gideon?"

***

Ann did not have classes today, but after she'd dropped Kyle off at the police station, she took the opportunity to take Nate by the university campus. The college-level coursework would likely not be a problem for her son, but finding his way to his classes might be. They had made it a habit since kindergarten to visit the school the day before it opened and walk the hallways, and now, in this case, the campus.

Nate stared out the window, his lips pursed.

"You've been here a hundred times before. There's nothing to be worried about."

"I've never been in the math building," he said anxiously.

Last week, Nate was supposed to have visited the building with Clarke, but the boy's father had texted at the last minute and canceled. Sorry, babe, work. "You were there last year for the science fair."

"That was different," Nate said. "I was with a group. Now I'll be alone."

His expression resembled that of a much older man, a far cry from the laughing boy at breakfast yesterday. "Let's have a look at the classroom. By the time we leave, you'll have it committed to memory."

"That's a solid plan."

She smiled, resisting the urge to push the hair from his eyes as she had when he was a toddler. "Let's do this."

Out of the car, the two crossed the nearly empty lot to the four-story brick building. Automatically, she looked to the metal fire escape on the north side. Unbeknownst to Nate, she had walked the building's escape routes last week, double-checking that the exit doors were functioning.

At the front door, she swiped her faculty identification card, and the lock opened. They crossed the tiled hallway to the door marked STAIRS and climbed to the second floor.

"You know the room number. You find it," she said.

Nate's brow furrowed as he nodded and began checking each number over the doors until they reached room 208. "This is it."

She tried the room's closed door and, to her relief, found it open. They stepped inside, and she flipped on the lights, which flickered on over rows of long tables and chairs. There was a lectern at the front of the room, a blackboard, and a screen that could be lowered if the professor needed it.

Nate folded his arms over his chest, walking up and down the aisles. "Where should I sit?"

"Where would you like to sit?"

He drew in a breath and then nodded as he moved to the front. "Here. I don't want to be distracted."

She could count on one hand the number of students she'd had last year who'd willingly chosen the front row. Everyone wanted the back so they could respond to the random text message or avoid her gaze when she was seeking an answer.

"I am satisfied," he said.

"Good. What do you say we get an ice cream?"

Nate regarded her with such soulful eyes that it nearly took her breath away. God, she loved her kid. "Can I get two scoops?"

She grinned. "Yes, you may."

As they walked out of the building and passed a display cabinet filled with school memorabilia, the boy said, "Joan should have a Griz hat so when she goes home, she won't forget us."

"That's a great idea."

They closed the building's front door behind them and returned to her car. Nate settled into the back seat. She slid behind the wheel, turned the ignition, and looked in her rearview mirror. As she pushed in the clutch and shifted into reverse, she spotted a man strolling past the math building. She almost dismissed him, but something about his erect posture made her look twice.

Tall and lean, he had a muscled frame. His jeans, jacket, and dark-blue sweater all appeared new, as did his shoes. He was walking with purpose, as if he had been here before.

She stopped as a nervous chill burned down her spine. Her heart beat faster in her chest. She waited for him to turn so she could see his face.

As if he sensed her gaze, he turned toward her direction, searching. When he spotted her car, she recognized him. It was Elijah Weston.

Heat rose in her cheeks, and her breathing shallowed. She gripped the wheel tighter as she moved quickly into first gear and then pressed the accelerator too hard. The car lurched forward and stalled.

"Shit. Sorry, kiddo. I wasn't thinking."

"Language, Mom."

"You're right." She swiped a strand of hair from her eyes and swallowed another curse.

"Can we see where that building burned?"

"Why?" Ann challenged quickly.

"I don't know. Might be cool."

"We'll see."

Elijah walked toward them, his gait unhurried but steady. The side mirror caught Elijah's stoic expression. He moved closer, as if he had all the time in the world. Her heart continued to beat faster as she tightened her hands on the steering wheel, doing her best to look calm for Nate's sake.

She was not anything close to calm. She was scared and angry. Not only was Elijah out of prison now, but he had registered for her class. When Gideon had called her and told her about Elijah enrolling in her class, she had called her department chair, reminding him of her history with Elijah. The department chair had informed her that Elijah had already threatened a lawsuit if he was denied entry. Faced with Elijah having served his time and receiving a glowing recommendation from the prison warden, the university would have to accept him. If and when he became a threat, they would act.

The financial needs of her separation had made it so she'd had no choice but to accept. Like it or not, she would be facing him in two more days and then every week for the rest of the semester.

But that was another day. And she had learned a long time ago not to steal problems from another day, because today had plenty to go around. Gathering her composure, she pressed the accelerator, leaving him watching her as she drove off.

Confessions of an Arsonist

I am going to plan the mother of all fires. I'm not wasting my time with the small stuff anymore. This one will free me of all my troubles and set me on the righteous course I deserve.

CHAPTER THIRTEEN

Missoula, Montana
Monday, September 7, 2020
3:30 p.m.

Gideon was relieved when the doctor pronounced Kyle fit for duty. His X-ray looked great, the bones in his right arm completely healed and growing as they should. He was a lucky kid, as far as hit-and-run accidents went.

"Ann said you're welcome to have dinner at her place," Gideon said. "Does that work for you?"

"Yeah, sure. Can I spend the night?"

"The plan is for me to pick you up, but this case might keep me late."

Kyle shrugged, already adapting to his dad's busy schedule. "I'm hungry now."

"What do you want?"

"Take-out pizza."

"Done."

"And can we eat it at the station with Joan?"

"What makes you ask that?" Gideon asked.

Kyle shrugged. "Just did."

"I don't know, pal." Gideon did not want his kid falling for Joan Mason. Once her demons were exorcised, she would be on her way.

"Why not? She seems lonely."

Sharing a pizza with Joan would not kill him. Besides, Kyle was asking, and he rarely asked for much. "Sure, why not."

When they pulled up to the Pizza Shack, he ordered two large pizzas. One cheese and pepperoni for Kyle and the other with mushrooms and onions for Joan. Jesus, ten years and he still remembered how she liked her pizza.

When they pushed through the back door of the police station, he was not surprised to find her still hunched over an open file with a picture of her freshly burned hands. He remembered the cop at the hospital taking the picture as she'd sat on the gurney in the emergency room.

When she looked up, her hair looked as if she had been running her fingers through it. She quickly closed the file and carefully tucked it back in the box. "Do I need to clear out? Do you guys need the room?"

"We brought you pizza," Kyle said.

"Pizza?"

"Mine is cheese and yours has mushrooms and onions." Kyle made a face. "I hate onions."

Joan's gaze shifted to Gideon. "You remembered. Thank you."

Gideon set the pizzas on the conference table while Joan removed the file boxes to a corner on the floor. She grabbed a handful of napkins from the credenza. He and Kyle took their seats while Joan passed out napkins. He flipped open both boxes, and the aroma of pizza filled the room.

Joan reached for a large slice, folded the piece in on itself, and took a big bite. "Delicious, guys. Thanks."

"You can thank Kyle," Gideon said. "It was his idea."

"Well, thank you, sir."

Kyle shrugged but pursed his lips, as he did when he was trying not to smile. "Sure."

The three ate in silence for several minutes, until Gideon headed off the coming lull. "Find anything in the files?" he asked.

She finished chewing and swallowed. She looked at Kyle before she nodded. "A very similar device was used to set both the College and salon incidents."

"You can say fire," Kyle said.

Joan raised a brow. "I'm going to have to work harder to talk over your head."

Gideon grinned. "A PG-13 explanation is okay."

"Somewhere between X-Men and Harry Potter?" Joan asked.

"Or *Last Jedi* and *Black Panther*," Gideon said.

"Haven't seen either of those," she said with mock exasperation.

"But you know Harry Potter?" Gideon asked.

"Stupid movie," Kyle grumbled as he shook his head. "Magic is not real."

"My partner has an eight-year-old granddaughter," Joan said. "She just had a birthday, and Hermione appears to be her idol."

"Silly," Kyle said.

Gideon could not picture Joan being attached to anything as fanciful as a fantasy character. But he also had never guessed she would return to Montana. "Tell me what you've learned, and I'll let you know if it's too much."

"Understood. The investigating officer at the time, Henry Jefferson, initially theorized that the fire was random. He found no connection between Ann or me to Elijah Weston, other than I had been a teaching assistant for one of his professors. Elijah never made any threats either in person or in writing to Ann, me, or anyone else. And then the DNA test came back linking Elijah to the device."

"Jefferson later hypothesized that Elijah was targeting the trash can near your window," Gideon said. "We had Elijah's DNA on file as a result of earlier arson episodes targeting rubbish piles."

"He was fixated on overflowing, rat-infested trash cans. Ours was neat and had been dumped the day before."

"One of those early trash fires nearly burned down a trailer."

"The photos of me they found in his house were taken the night we were watching the rodeo finals at the campus bar."

"I remember the night." He and Joan had made love twice that night.

"Do you remember seeing Elijah at the bar?" she asked.

He cleared his throat. "No."

Her lips flattened as she shook her head. If they had been alone, she would have fired back a salty rebuttal. "The College Fire devices were placed in the crawl space, an odd place if trash was the target."

"You said the College and beauty shop devices were similar."

"Very similar," she said. "The 2010 versions were a bit cruder, a first generation. Only one of the three survived for testing, which was where Elijah's DNA was found."

"We've had no other fires with similar delivery mechanisms. And Elijah has been in prison."

She wiped the pizza crumbs from her hands and leaned forward. Kyle paid close attention as he chewed his pizza. "Assume, for a moment, Elijah did not set the College Fire."

"What?" Gideon froze, the next bite inches from his mouth.

"I know it sounds crazy, but hear me out."

"Okay."

"He filed a police report the week prior and claimed his backpack had been stolen. His sweatshirt could have been taken from that pack."

"Or he was building an alibi." He set his pizza down and carefully wiped off his fingers as he struggled to check a surge of jealousy.

"Say the arsonist used Elijah's sweatshirt to throw off the police. Say he has been practicing for the last decade. And has improved. There have been a half dozen brush fires near town in the last few months while Elijah was incarcerated."

Gideon quickly rebutted. "What if Elijah recruited an accomplice to set the brush fires and to help him gather supplies for the salon fire? You weren't his only pen pal while he was in prison. He had a group of women called the Fireflies who followed his case closely." He leaned toward her. "What if he grooms people to help him set fires?"

"What if we're dealing with someone we've never considered? Someone who's been lurking around on the periphery and setting fires in other jurisdictions for years."

Marcie Cash had theorized that Lana was seeing either a married or incarcerated man. If Lana had been seeing Elijah, then that would fit Marcie's theory. He knew that prisons kept records of correspondence and visits. But if Lana had been seeing Joan's mystery arsonist, then that would explain why he did not want to be seen with her publicly. Tracking him would be more difficult.

An unsettled feeling burrowed into the pit of his belly. He sat back, regarding her and then Kyle, who was still riveted.

"We're batting around a lot of what-ifs, Joan."

"Make some calls, Dad," Kyle said. "That's what you do when you're on a case."

"I could reach out to Clarke," Gideon said. "He's tapped into the firefighting community."

"I would keep the circle small, Gideon," she suggested. "No one should get wind that you're looking into the College Fire case."

"I'll make a few calls. And I'll keep everyone out of the loop for now. Kyle, can you keep a secret?"

The boy grinned, clearly pleased to be included in his dad's new circle. "I sure can! I won't even tell Nate!"

***

Joan left the police station feeling as if the answer were only inches out of reach. She parked in front of Elijah's home. She had been speaking off the top of her head to Gideon, but maybe, and that was a big maybe, he really had not set the College Fire.

Out of her car, she crossed the sidewalk and climbed the front porch steps. She rang the bell and out of habit stood to the side of the door. The door opened to Elijah.

He was holding a psychology textbook and a highlighter. He wore thick black-framed glasses that magnified gray eyes that softened when he saw her. "Joan. What a pleasant surprise. What brings you by?"

"Questions about the College Fire," she said.

He opened the door. "I love your honesty. Another cop might have devised some thin pretense to attempt to worm information out of me, but not you. Cut to the chase. Love it. Come in. You know I'm an open book for you."

She stepped inside the house and noted that two of the residents were sitting on the threadbare rose chintz sofa watching a movie. Both sported a few days' growth of beard, and their shirts and pants were worn and stained. They glanced in her direction, and their gazes lingered while they checked her out.

"Back to the movie, boys," Elijah said, closing his book with a hard snap. "Let's go in the kitchen, Joan. I can make you coffee. I remember how much you love my coffee."

"You know the way to a girl's heart."

He chuckled as he pulled off his glasses and set them and the book on the table. "Still take your coffee black?"

"I do." She opened the psychology book and noted that almost every page had a comment or mark on it. "You're thorough."

He opened a wooden coffee tin painted with faded roosters. "Like I said before, I love learning."

"You certainly do."

He poured the coffee in the metal cone and then filled the machine's water well. "I would like to be a professor one day."

"You kept your professors on their toes your freshman year."

"I wasn't totally impressed by most of them. They started to resent my questions." He flipped the coffee maker on.

"Maybe they were embarrassed because you knew more than they did."

He leaned against the counter, folding his muscled arms over his chest. "I did."

She closed the book. "Do you really think it's wise to take Ann's class?"

"She's the only one teaching the subject that I wanted." He regarded her. "You didn't come here to scold me about taking Ann's class, remember?"

The machine hissed and gurgled as she sat. She wished she had a cup in her hands to give her something to do. "You've always maintained that you didn't set the College Fire."

"That's correct."

"Assuming you didn't . . ."

He arched a brow. "What's caused the turnabout?"

"Maybe nothing. Just exploring theories."

"Okay."

"Who do you think could have set it?"

He studied her a long moment and then said, "I don't know. And believe me, I have put a great deal of thought into it."

"You must have some ideas."

"None."

"Why did you really set the fires near your mother's trailer?"

"I was working out rage. My mother was not a very pleasant woman."

"I went by her trailer and met her."

His expression was unreadable. "How is Mom?"

"She's still your number one defender."

"Is she?"

"You don't sound impressed."

He turned to the cabinet and removed two ivory earthenware mugs. He carefully filled each with coffee. "She had her good moments, but unfortunately, when I was a child, they were few and far between." He set a cup in front of her and then sat at the table across from her. His head tilted slightly. "Are you entertaining the theory that I didn't set the College Fire?"

"DNA at the scene is hard to argue with."

"No one believed my backpack was stolen, not even my public defender." His gray eyes focused squarely on hers as he turned his mug until the handle was angled at ninety degrees. "The key to your case is the victim." When her surprise must have shown, he shrugged. "I watch the news. I know there was a fatality."

"What would you say the motivation was?"

The silence that followed was as intentional as a seasoned cop's. He wanted her to put more of her cards on the table.

"We're just spitballing here, you understand," she said.

He regarded her over the rim of his cup. "Anger."

"Anger?"

"This arsonist is angry."

"Angry at what?"

"Not what but whom." He dropped his voice a note. "It might be a long shot, but I'm betting she has something in common with either Ann or you. Maybe both of you."

She absorbed his theory. Lana looked a little like Ann. "What about the owner of the beauty salon? She could have been the target."

"The fire consumed her business, not her body. Big difference. He has also set other fires."

"He? A woman could have set them all."

"Avery Newport is an anomaly. Female arsonists set only ten percent of the fires, and as you know, their fires are generally near their homes."

"Go on."

"The Beau-T-Shop and College Fire were bold statements. Nothing tentative about either one of them. How did your victim die?"

"She's not my victim."

"Did the fire kill her?"

"I can't answer that."

"Oh, but you just did." He shook his head, his eyes glittering with an excitement she had not seen before. "Too bad you don't fully trust me yet. We would be a great crime-fighting team."

Joan pushed her coffee a few inches from her. She had grown far too chummy with Elijah. She needed to remember that they were not on any kind of a team. "This conversation is over. I better go."

"I understand, but I hope you come back soon."

She rose, knowing she would return. Like it or not, for now, their goals could be aligned. "I will."

CHAPTER FOURTEEN

Missoula, Montana
Monday, September 7, 2020
5:00 p.m.

Gideon had been pressing for the search warrant for Lana Long's apartment, but finding a judge today was proving difficult. In the meantime, he had a cold can of soda, aspirin, and crackers when he and Becca opened the cell of Lana Long's ex-boyfriend, Ryan Davis. Enough time had passed for the guy to sleep off most of his inebriation. And Gideon, after hearing Joan's theories on the arsonist, wanted answers.

Ryan Davis sat on his bunk, his head resting in his hands. He wore faded jeans, a sweatshirt dirty and frayed at the cuffs. His lace-up shoes as well as his belt had been taken from him at the time of his arrest. As he lifted his gaze to Gideon, the smell of sweat and vomit stirred around him.

"Have any stomach for a soda?" Gideon asked.

"That would be awesome, man."

Gideon popped the top and filled a paper cup, waiting for the soda fizz to settle before topping it off and handing it to him. He offered the crackers and two aspirin. Ryan took the aspirin and washed them down with soda.

"Do you know why you're here, Ryan?" Gideon asked.

He sipped the soda and then, seemingly deciding he liked it, finished off the cup. He held it out to Gideon, who refilled it with what remained in the can.

"I got drunk," Ryan finally said. "I must have done some damage."

"You've done this before, according to your arrest record in Denver."

"Yeah."

"Why are you in my town, Ryan?"

"I came to see my girlfriend."

"Who's that?" Gideon asked.

"Lana." He took a sip. "Lana Long. I went by her place, but she wouldn't answer her door."

"When is the last time you saw Lana?"

"It was right after Christmas."

If that was true, then Ryan was not the father of her baby. "You didn't visit her here even once over the last nine months?"

"No. She told me to stay away."

"Why did you finally come after her?"

"Out of the blue, she called me last week. She said she wanted to start over. She said she was tired of living out here alone. She said she was in over her head."

"What about the arrest for vandalism in Denver?"

"Lana could get emotional. She saw me talking to another woman and freaked out. She set fire to the garbage cans by the woman's house. She didn't mean for it to get so big."

"And charges were dropped."

"Her mother paid for damages."

"She set any other fires?"

"No."

Gideon shifted his stance. "So she calls and you came running?"

"Yeah. I love her. Do you know where Lana is?" Ryan asked.

Gideon studied the man's bloodshot eyes and hands that trembled slightly but deflected the question. "Why did Lana move to Missoula?"

"I don't know." He ran long fingers through his hair. "She broke up with me, packed up her car, and drove here."

"So she just randomly picked this place on a map?" Gideon asked.

"No. She's had a thing about Montana for a couple of years."

"What kind of thing?"

"She thought it was pretty. That she could be something here."

More than a few people moved to Big Sky Country thinking their troubles would not cross the state line and they could reinvent themselves. But long winters had a way of fanning, not extinguishing, old problems.

On a hunch, Gideon asked, "Was there anyone else in Lana's life? Another man? Another woman?"

Ryan's watery eyes narrowed. "Look, I'm not saying another word until you tell me what happened to Lana."

Gideon never relished moments like this. "I'm sorry to inform you, Ryan, but Lana is dead."

Ryan's head snapped up; then he winced as if the movement had irritated his aching head. "Dead? Not Lana. I just spoke with her on the phone last week."

"What did you two talk about?"

"Like I said, she wanted to see me again. I thought we were going to get back together. That whatever was here had worked its way out of her system."

"Maybe it had," Gideon said. "Maybe she was ready to go back to Denver and be with you."

"Are you sure it's Lana?" Ryan asked in a choked-up voice.

"Yes."

Tears welled in his bloodshot eyes. "How did she die?"

"There was a fire."

"A fire?" Ryan shook his head. "I told her she was playing a danger-ous game."

"What kind of game?"

He sipped his soda, staring at the fizzing bubbles. "She started writ-ing a man in prison about two years ago."

"How did she meet him?"

"She saw him on the news. She became kind of obsessed with him."

Gideon's body stilled. "Does the man have a name?"

"She never told me. She was afraid I would call the prison and get him in trouble."

"Trouble for what?"

"Leading a woman on, I guess. Filling her head with lies."

"A man manipulating a woman's feelings is not against the law. Did he try to solicit money from her, or did he ask her to do anything illegal?"

"I don't think so. He just kept telling her that he was in love with her." Ryan dug a fingernail into the side of the cup. "Do you think he killed her?"

"I don't know."

***

Ann heard the car pull up in front of the ranch and knew by the slight rattle in the engine that it was Clarke's vehicle. He'd had the SUV since his senior year of college and had refused to get rid of it for sentimental reasons. Clarke was loyal by nature and always had trouble cutting ties with the past.

She dried off her hands and carefully laid the dish towel over the edge of the sink before walking toward the front door. Joan had encour-aged Ann to apply to East Coast graduate schools and to take more time before committing to Clarke's marriage proposal. Clarke had been so anxious to marry and had encouraged Ann to study locally. But she had wanted to study at Harvard and to see more of the world before she committed. And then she had found out she was pregnant.

"Nate!" she shouted up the stairs. "Dad is here."

Nate appeared at the top of the stairs. "Why? It's not his day."

No, it was not. She summoned a smile. "I guess he just wants to see you."

Nate shrugged and came down the steps, joining her as the front doorbell rang. When her father had gotten sick over the winter, it had made sense for her and Nate to move back to the ranch. Days spread into a week and then two. And she found she liked being out here and away from Clarke. Finally, after a month, he had confronted her, and she asked him for a trial separation. She just needed a little space. Maybe one day she would clinically analyze her choices, but for now she was simply trying to get by.

Ann opened the door. Clarke stood on the front porch. His soot-covered feet were slightly braced, and he smelled faintly of smoke. "Clarke, is everything all right?"

"Yeah."

"It's not your day."

"I know." A boyish grin tipped the edges of Clarke's lips, reminding her that he was a very attractive man. "I did ring the bell. Respecting your space."

As he leaned in to kiss her on the cheek, she braced but did not pull back. "You smell like fire."

"I'm a firefighter," he said easily. "And the department did a controlled burn today."

"Oh."

"I just came out to check on you two." He winked at Nate. "Hey, pal."

"Hey, Dad."

"As you can see, we're fine," Ann said.

"I figured you were, but I needed to be sure." He dropped his gaze to the calluses on his palms, darkened by more ash.

"What's prompting all this?"

"The fire in town. It reminded me of the other one. And what we could have lost."

The words strengthened the chain forged between them that night. If Gideon had not rushed into the house, there would be no her, no Nate, and if Clarke had not risked his life, Joan would be dead.

"We drove by it today," Nate said. "It was a bad one."

"Yes, it was, pal," Clarke said.

Since Nate was little, he had enjoyed going to work with Clarke. He'd told her that he loved riding the truck and hanging out at the station with the other firefighters. Moving her son out to the ranch had cut down on some of Nate's time with his father, and she felt guilty about that.

"Hey, Mom, does Dad know about Kyle and my half-birthday party?"

The boys had been born in the dead of the Montana winter, and as the boys got into school, they had voted to celebrate their birthdays in September. The kids were back from summer holidays, school was only just starting, and the chance of a snowstorm was greatly reduced.

"No, I haven't told him yet." Every time she'd picked up the phone to call or text Clarke about the party, something else had popped up. Ann smiled. "It's Thursday. Nothing fancy. We'll be out here at the ranch. Four of his other friends are coming. And you are welcome. I should have told you, but I've just been rattled."

"It's okay, Ann. And yes, I would love to attend the party. Why a Thursday?"

"Only day we could get all the boys together."

When he grinned, desire simmered, and she remembered they had always been good together in bed. He knew her body better than any man did, and even if she was not in the mood for sex, he found a way to make her want him.

The term *uncoupling* sounded modern and almost innocent. But whatever ties that bound them were a tangled mess, much like a delicate gold chain left in a pocket too long. As tempted as she was to cut the chain and yank it apart, she could never do that, for Nate's sake.

"It's at four o'clock, right after school," Ann said.

"I'll be here."

"Great."

"What can I bring?" he asked.

"Nothing. Just bring yourself." She knew her tone sounded bright enough to border on overcompensating.

A car pulled up the driveway and parked behind Clarke's. Joan rose out of the car and, her purse strap firmly on her shoulder, strode toward them.

Clarke rustled Nate's hair and smiled at Ann. "Good to see you again, Joan."

"You as well."

"I better get going," he said. "I'll see you on Thursday, and good luck in school, pal."

"Clarke," Joan said, clearing her throat. "I owe you a big thank-you."

"For what?" Clarke asked.

"I was reviewing the College Fire files. As I was looking at the pictures, I realized you pulled me out of the fire."

Clarke shrugged. "Yeah, I did. I thought you knew."

"I had passed out. And I guess I didn't try too hard to remember any of it. I always assumed it was a firefighter who saved me. Anyway, thank you."

"You're welcome, Joan." He tossed one last wave to Nate and then headed to his car. Joan watched him back around her car and drive off.

"Nate, can you set the table for dinner?" Ann asked.

"Sure."

As he ran back into the house, Ann asked, "You okay?"

"How did Clarke know where to find me in the fire?" she asked.

"Gideon told him he had last seen you by the back bedroom."

"That house was about to come down around me in those last seconds."

"Clarke has never lacked for courage," Ann said. "And for the record, Gideon handed me off to the first firefighter he saw and ran back to the house. Clarke was coming out with you over his shoulder just as Gideon reached the door."

"No one ever told me."

"We all thought you knew. And then you were gone. That moment has haunted both of us for a long time."

Joan drew in a deep breath. "I don't seem to be getting anything right. I've been suspended from my job, and my new pal is a convicted arsonist, so it would be nice if I could let that day go forever."

Ann shook her head. "Let me know if you figure out how to do it."

***

Dan Tucker parked his car across the street from what remained of the Beau-T-Shop. Tightening his hands on the steering wheel, he could barely contain his simmering rage. This meaningless destruction was Elijah Weston's doing. He had seen this trouble coming and had been warning the cops for months. But they had not been listening and were now scrambling to do a full homicide and arson investigation to cover their asses. Anyone with half a brain could have solved this crime.

Cursing, he drove the few blocks to the boardinghouse. It was going to take more than a few spray-painted words to chase away Elijah. But he could arrange whatever trouble it would take to deal with that bastard.

He picked up his phone and dialed a familiar number.

"Yeah," the gruff voice on the other end said.

"It's Tucker. I'm outside his house."

"Why?"

"I can't stop thinking about the fire and him. He set it. He killed whoever it is the cops aren't talking about. I fucking know it."

"What do you have in mind, Dan?"

As tempting as it was to shoot Elijah between the eyes and dump his body in the wilderness, he wasn't ready to cross that line yet. A good beating was more fitting, and though he could do it alone, there was safety in numbers. "I want to give him a message that will make him rethink living here."

"More paint?" In the background, the television blared.

"Not this time. Thinking maybe he should get a dose of his own medicine." He reached in his pocket and pulled out the lighter. He struck the flint and lit the flame until it got too hot to hold.

"What do you want from me?"

"It might take two of us. He's bigger and stronger than I remember from high school." Elijah had been quiet, in a know-it-all kind of way. It had been easy to push him around then.

"You almost sound afraid of him."

The challenge stoked Dan's frustration and anger. "I'm not."

"You're still pissed about what he did to you in high school."

Dan remembered walking outside his home to discover fire licking up all four wheels of his new truck. The flames had scorched the white paint, popped his tires, and melted his side-view mirror. As he'd tried to beat the flames out with his shirt, the smoke had scorched his mouth, nose, and lungs. Coughing, he had run to the side of his parents' house and grabbed the hose. His hands trembling, he'd squeezed the nozzle. To this day, he could remember the sound of the flames hissing like a viper as he shot them with cold water. Later, the truck was towed to a body shop that had soon slapped him with a $4,000 repair bill, half of which he'd had to eat because insurance did not cover it.

The cops later decided it was arson. No shit. And said the fire had started in a plastic milk jug filled with gas. A rag had been used as a wick. At the time, they'd had no idea who'd set the fire.

After the College Fire, the cops had come to talk to him, but there was no proof linking Elijah to his truck fire. Dan knew it was that weirdo Elijah. Who the fuck else would have been crazy enough to mess with him?

"I just want to make a smart play," Dan said. "In this PC world, too many people don't fully grasp the old brand of justice."

A heavy silence lingered on the line, and then he heard the swig of beer. "I'm in."

Confessions of an Arsonist
I miss the days I saw fire burn in my lover's eyes.

CHAPTER FIFTEEN

Missoula, Montana
Monday, September 7, 2020
8:00 p.m.

Enough evidence was pulled from the Beau-T-Shop fire to suggest that Gideon was dealing with an experienced arsonist. Whether it was Lana Long working with Elijah or someone else, this perpetrator had been skilled enough to fashion low-tech incendiary devices and then place them for maximum effect.

However, before he talked to Elijah or the warden at Montana State Prison, he wanted a complete record of recent arson reports across the state. He glanced up the darkened stairwell of his home, listening for signs of Kyle. The quiet suggested he was asleep, but Gideon still closed the door to his home office before placing a call to Bryce McCabe, an agent with the Montana Highway Patrol. He had known Bryce for years, and if his theory was full of holes, Bryce would say so immediately. As the phone rang, he reached for a yellow legal pad and pen.

Bryce picked up on the third ring. "Gideon."

"Bryce, how are you?" Gideon asked as he leaned forward at his desk.

"Can't complain. What's up? Not like you to call on a holiday weekend without a good reason."

Gideon uncapped his pen and drew a *#1* at the top of the yellow pad. He circled it once. "Did you hear about the fire we had on Saturday?"

"I did," he said. "I also understand your newest resident is a convicted arsonist."

"That's correct." He circled the number a couple more times. "I have a few questions that may seem off base, but bear with me."

"Have at it."

"Have you had any significant fires in your area in the last few years?" Gideon asked.

"You mean while Elijah Weston was incarcerated?"

Gideon sat back and wondered what the hell path he had set out on. "That's correct."

Bryce was silent a moment. "You don't think Elijah Weston is responsible for your fire?"

"He's on my radar, that's for damn sure."

"Fair enough. Let me get to my computer. Hang on."

"Got all the time."

In the background, a door opened and closed, and a light switch clicked. "Here we go," Bryce said. "We had a warehouse fire eighteen months ago in Helena. The structure burned to the ground."

"Cause of the fire?" He jotted down the incident by the number one.

"Electrical. No fatalities, but the damage and losses totaled more than a million dollars. That's all the structural fires we've had recently. In 2018, there were four dumpster fires in Bozeman. No real property damage sustained in those events, beyond the dumpsters."

Gideon made a notation. "Any rural fires?"

"Funny you should mention that. Statistics show a thirty percent increase in brush fires. The causes range from unmonitored campfires to electrical line failure."

"How many were undetermined?"

"Of the seventy-four fires reported, sixty-two weren't resolved."

"Where were they?"

"I would have to get back to you on that one. I just have overall statistical data."

"I'd appreciate the locations."

"Sure. What are you going after, Gideon?"

He ran his hand over the top of his head. "Just a hunch."

More computer keys clicked at a slow, steady pace. "Okay, I missed two Butte house fires in 2018. One was caused by a Christmas tree, and the other one was ruled arson."

"Do you know how the arson fire started?"

"Plastic jug filled with gasoline and a rag. No arrests."

In 2018, Gideon had just signed divorce papers, and Helen and Kyle had moved out of their home. If there was a year that he would have happily erased, it was 2018.

"What was the cause of your beauty shop fire?" Bryce asked.

"Plastic jug filled with gasoline."

The silence grew heavy. "All the materials are easy to get, and it's impossible to trace the source."

"Very true," Gideon said.

"Want me to poke around?" Bryce offered.

"I've taken up enough of your time on a holiday weekend."

"It's a holiday, and if I knew how to have fun, I would not be sitting around," Bryce joked.

"I appreciate this."

"No worries. I'll call if I find something."

Gideon kept digging in the surrounding states of Wyoming and Idaho. He located several fires on the Wyoming and Montana border, and within a half hour, Bryce had texted him the locations of all the urban and rural fires.

Most of these incidents had been small and involved dumpsters, trash cans, and rubbish piles. In the rural areas, the brush fires had each destroyed less than an acre of woodland. Several had mysteriously extinguished themselves, which many had reported as minor miracles.

As he thumbed through the yellow notepad, he realized he needed to map out the fires. The only large map he had was the one Kyle had used for a Montana history project two years ago. He found it rolled up in a closet, and he flattened it out and pinned it to his wall.

He did not have pushpins to indicate locations, so he cut Post-it notes into small strips and began to mark each fire's location. Green indicated rural fires, and purple denoted urban fires. It took more than an hour to geo mark all the events, but by the time he was finished, he could see distinct patterns.

Near Helena in 2018–19 was the large warehouse fire, and also dozens of rural fires in the surrounding counties in the months leading up to the fire. In 2016–17, several rural fires near Bozeman had ended up burning a few residences. And in 2019–20, a similar cluster had appeared in the Missoula area.

As Gideon stood back, staring at his makeshift geo-profiling system, he reached for his coffee, discovered it was cold, and went into his kitchen to make a fresh pot.

"He's practicing. Building up his nerve in the country before coming into town," he said to himself.

And if these fires had been started by the same man, then that definitely ruled out Elijah. No way he could have done any of them.

He took a picture of the map and prepared to text it to Joan. He paused. He knew his desire to share his findings with Joan was due to fatigue. Normally, he would not have considered it. If he could get a couple of hours of sleep, he would think more clearly. He deleted the text.

He sat on the couch, and the softness immediately coaxed him back. As he put his feet up, he glanced at his watch, noted the time. He just wanted to close his eyes and steal a few minutes of rest. The instant he did, his mind tripped back in time to a moment he had shared with Joan.

She was pulling the Christmas Day shift at Tucker's Diner, and Gideon had skipped the family festivities so he could spend time with her. She always took the Christmas and New Year's shifts because airfare home was expensive, and the double-time holiday pay was too rich to resist.

He sat at the breakfast bar decorated with silver garland. He made no secret that he liked watching Joan move about the diner in her pink uniform. The red Santa hat and earrings were a cute touch.

A dozen folks dotted the seats at the breakfast bar, and she moved down the row of customers with practiced efficiency. She chatted with everyone while staying on the go, setting down platters of food and refilling coffee cups.

When she came to fill his coffee, he grinned at her, liking the way the pink skirt hugged her hips and the apron nipped at her narrow waist. "Like the earrings."

"They're Ann's." She filled the cup. "Said they would help with the tips."

The beaded earrings dangled and brushed the side of her jaw. "Have they?"

"Can't complain. What are you doing here? Doesn't your mother have a big dinner planned?"

"I wanted to see you."

A ghost of a smile tipped the edges of her lips. "Your mom can't be happy about that. She had a feast planned."

His mother had started decorating for Christmas the day after Thanksgiving, transforming the house into a holiday extravaganza. "Do you get any time off? Mom invited you to dinner."

"That's nice. Tell her thank you. But I promised Mr. Tucker I would close up at ten p.m."

"Where are Tucker and his dad?"

"Hunting. It's their Christmas tradition."

He kept his hands on his lap so he would not be tempted to touch her. He loved the feel of her skin. A bell behind her dinged, and she turned toward the cook as he put out two hot plates of pancakes. She gathered both and set them in front of two cowboys sitting at the end of the bar.

Joan made the rounds, dispensing butter packets, extra napkins, and coffee before she returned to him. "I'll be back at the house by eleven."

"Why don't you come out to the ranch? Ann's there this week."

"Thanks, but I'm also scheduled to open the diner early. But you can swing by my house after my shift," she offered with a sly grin.

"I'd like that."

Just watching her in her pink uniform with the tiny white apron made him so hard that he was pretty sure there was no blood left in his brain.

The cook's bell rang again, and Joan was off for more platters of food. Another lost soul with no place to be on Christmas arrived and took a seat at the end of the bar. Joan chatted easily with him, lingering an extra moment to make his holiday a little better. Gideon recognized Elijah Weston.

Later, while he was alone with Joan in her house, he asked, "What's the deal with Weston?"

"I know him from school." As she released her dark hair from its ponytail, the slight scent of pancakes and maple syrup made him even more attracted to her.

"You're comfortable with him."

She unbuttoned the uniform's pearl buttons that trailed down between her breasts, and then she shrugged off her dress. When she stepped out of it, her smooth skin glistened in the soft light. He caressed her shoulder, hooking his thumb in her bra strap. "You like him?"

"I want you." The clasp between her breasts unhooked, and just like that, coherent thought abandoned him completely.

Weston had been woven tighter into Gideon's past than he had ever realized. Like a spider, he was always there, lurking.

Ten years of perspective now exposed Joan and Elijah's strong connection in college. They were two lost souls with no real family. Loneliness was a potent connection that could bind tighter than the best sex. Gideon sat up and walked over to his map. He was not sure if

Joan was under Elijah's spell or if she simply saw something others did not. Either way, he wanted to keep her close until he could untangle this case.

He texted Joan the image of his map. I'm headed to Helena to investigate a fire tomorrow. You in?

Bubbles appeared immediately. Yes.

CHAPTER SIXTEEN

Missoula, Montana
Tuesday, September 8, 2020
8:00 a.m.

Joan parked in front of the police station and glanced at the fire map Gideon had texted her. His makeshift collection of Post-it notes on a child's map was a very powerful graphic detailing the regional fires over the last ten-plus years. The clusters were unmistakable, though whether the fires were the work of one or multiple arsonists was impossible to tell. But it was a pattern that could not be ignored.

Out of the car, she hoisted her purse on her shoulder and pushed through the front door. At the front window, she introduced herself to a deputy she had not met before. "I'm here for Detective Bailey."

The deputy picked up the phone and announced her arrival. "He'll be right out."

"Thanks." She turned toward a bulletin board filled with wanted posters, resisting the urge to pace.

The door opened to Gideon, who regarded her with a mixture of distrust and keen awareness. Cowboy lean, he wore jeans, a light-blue dress shirt with no tie, a black leather jacket, and scuffed boots. His weapon and cuffs were attached to a handmade belt buckled with a silver medallion sporting the BB brand of the family ranch. Shit, why did he have to look so good?

"We have a stop to make before we go."

"Where?"

"The search warrant for Lana Long's apartment just came through."

"I can come, too?"

"Try to hang back."

She grinned. "Always."

They drove across town and pulled up in front of the older apartment complex. She followed Gideon up to the second floor, and when they rounded the corner, they spotted the yellow crime scene tape and the two techs. The first tech, Hank, was in his late fifties, with thinning red hair. The other tech, Doug, looked to be in his thirties, and he wore his thick, dark hair slicked back off his face.

Gideon shook hands with both. "Did the manager give you any trouble?"

"Not after we showed him the warrant," Hank said.

Doug doled out gloves and booties, and when they were all geared up, he let them into the apartment.

Joan worked her fingers into her gloves as she stepped inside. She stood for a moment, allowing her gaze to survey the small space. She moved toward the bookshelf and pointed to the book on arson. "I've actually read this one," she said as she bent down and snapped a picture with her phone. "Covers the motivations and case studies."

"Don't think she was studying to be an arson investigator one day," Gideon said.

Joan rose and moved past the sparse kitchen toward the bedroom. An air mattress worked well on a tight budget. She had slept on her share.

They watched as Doug lifted a pair of neatly folded jeans from the suitcase. They smelled of laundry soap, as if they had just been washed. Lana did not appear to have owned many clothes, but what she had was well cared for. Doug checked the suitcase's inside pocket. "It's an itinerary for a flight dated for today. It was bound for Denver."

"Why call her boyfriend if she was planning to fly out?" Gideon asked.

"Maybe she got spooked," Joan said.

Doug carefully documented and photographed as he went through the contents. Once the suitcase was empty, Doug reached in a side pocket and removed a picture. It was of Joan and Ann, taken in front of their college house.

"Wow," Joan said, too stunned to add much more.

Gideon muttered under his breath, "What the hell?"

"The picture was taken at the beginning of our senior year."

"I should know," Gideon said. "I took it."

"Where did she get it?" Joan asked. "The last time I saw that photo was on the refrigerator of our house. Did you have copies?"

"No," Gideon said. "But I had other versions of the same photo at my house. I haven't seen it for years."

Doug dropped the photo into a clear plastic bag. "We'll dust it for prints back at the lab."

She smoothed her hands down her thighs. "If that doesn't tie the two fires together, I don't know what does. Seems very convenient."

A woman appeared as they were leaving Lana's apartment. In her midthirties, she wore faded jeans and a leather jacket, and her dark hair was swept into a ponytail. "Why are the cops in Lana's apartment?"

Gideon introduced himself, then asked, "And who are you?"

"I'm Penny Rae," she said. "I live a couple doors down. Lana and I are friends."

"How long have you known Lana?" Gideon asked.

"About a year. We met at a concert in Helena last year. She said she wanted to move to Montana, so I told her to try Missoula. She took me up on my offer to see the city and decided she liked it."

"When exactly did you see her in Helena?" Joan asked.

"Early last summer. Why does that matter?" Penny asked.

"Was she with anyone at the time?" Gideon asked.

"No, she was all alone. Said she had just visited her boyfriend." Penny tried to look around Gideon into the apartment. "What's going on?"

"There was a fire at the salon where she worked," Gideon said. "You think Lana had something to do with it?"

"Why would you say that?" Penny asked.

"Just asking," Gideon said.

Penny pursed her lips. "Is Lana okay? I don't want to get her in trouble."

"Tell me what you know about Lana," Gideon said.

Penny slid her hand into her pocket. "There was a guy. She didn't see him much, but he wrote her letters, which I thought was a little old-fashioned."

"Did you get a look at any of the letters?" Gideon asked.

"She read a few to me. He was pretty sexy."

"Sexy how?" Joan asked.

"Not in an obvious kind of way. He just seemed totally focused on her." She shrugged. "I started to pretend he was writing me."

"It's something to have someone feel that strongly about you," Joan said.

"Yeah."

"So Lana was hooked?" Joan asked.

"She would have done anything for him. And some of his requests were kind of weird."

"Weird how?"

"He asked her to light a candle for him each night. Said the fire would remind her of him."

"What else?"

"She burned her arm on the stove. She said it was an accident."

"And you don't think it was?" Joan asked.

"The first few times, but by the fifth time, I knew it was more than that."

"Her boyfriend was asking her to burn herself?" Gideon asked.

"*I hope you burn for me like I burn for you.* She told me he said that in a letter," Penny said.

"What was his name?" Gideon said.

"He only signed all his letters E."

"E. Are you sure?"

"Yeah. You never said if Lana was okay?"

"When I can say, I'll let you know." Gideon thanked Penny. "Doug, we're going to get out of your way. Call me with any updates." He took Joan by the arm. "We need to get going."

"I want to stay," she said.

"No," Gideon said. "We'll get a recap later."

Outside, Gideon settled his black Stetson on his head as he reached for his phone and searched his contacts for Warden Martin's number. The number rang three times and went to voicemail.

"Warden, this is Detective Gideon Bailey in Missoula. I have a few questions for you about a former inmate, Elijah Weston. Can you call me back?" He hung up the phone.

"None of this makes sense, Gideon," Joan said.

"No, but it will. Eventually."

"We need to tell Ann. She needs to know about that picture."

"Agreed."

"What's the next move? Helena?" she asked. "It's less than two hours away."

If he was annoyed that she had jumped into his investigation with both feet, he did not seem to mind. "Okay. Let's go."

In his car, he tossed his Stetson into the back seat and sat behind the wheel as she climbed into the passenger seat. As he slid on dark glasses, she unzipped her jacket and clicked her seat belt.

He easily maneuvered through town to I-90 North with the practiced ease of a man who had spent his entire life here. She missed that kind of familiarity. In Philadelphia, she knew almost every side street, shortcut, and back alley. Here it had all changed enough that she was constantly rechecking her bearings.

"A warehouse caught on fire in Helena?" she prompted.

"Leading with arson first. No small talk?"

"What?"

"Small talk would involve asking me about Kyle. What I had for breakfast. The status of the ranch."

She considered her options. "Kyle is fine, or you would not be here. Unless you've changed, you still don't eat breakfast, and I hear you have a very competent ranch manager."

"Still not good with the small talk?"

"Worse, if you can believe it. Let's stick to the fire in Helena."

He wove around a slower family van and zoomed ahead in the left lane. "Owned by John Pollock," he said. "Pollock was in Texas when his warehouse burned early in 2019."

"Out of town like the Halperns," she mused. "I bet he had a solid alibi."

"He did."

"What was the cause of the fire?"

"It was undetermined. The local fire chief finally ruled it an electrical fire despite the fact that there were two ignition points."

"That alone should have raised a red flag."

"It did. But in the end, the investigator was pressured to make a call. The destruction was quite extensive."

"How certain are they that it was an accident?"

"Enough to authorize the insurance payout."

"Does Pollock know we're coming?"

"No. I've spoken to my buddy with highway patrol, Sergeant Bryce McCabe. He's fully apprised of what I'm looking for."

"What's his judgment on the Helena warehouse fire?"

"He's given me free rein to ask as many questions as I want."

"Which means he has suspicions."

"Maybe."

"Speaking of the Halperns, do you have their financials yet?"

"They've been slow to respond. I should have my court order later today so Detective Sullivan can start pulling them."

She looked out the window at the rolling landscape, watching the distant mountains trail past. The air was thick with the promise of snow.

"Speaking of Kyle . . . ," she said.

"Yes?"

"He's a good kid."

His expression softened. "I know. Thanks."

"Sorry to hear about his mother. I knew Helen in school."

Gideon remained silent. "You two didn't get along."

"I didn't get along with a lot of people. Doesn't mean I wished her harm. It's not like she stole my man." Though it had sure felt like it when Ann had told Joan they'd married.

He shot a glance her way, and, though dark glasses concealed his eyes, his deepening frown suggested her comment had hit its mark.

"Sorry," she said. "That was petty."

"I begged you not to leave, Joan. I called you a dozen times. You shut me out completely."

"I was running scared," she said.

"I wanted to help you."

"I know. But I didn't have a solid foundation like you and Ann. You two could weather storms. I couldn't. Maybe still can't."

"We all wanted to be there for you."

"Believe it or not, I came to my senses within two months of leaving. I called Ann, and she told me you had gotten married."

"She never told me."

"Because I asked her not to. I couldn't face knowing I'd screwed up the best thing in my life."

A muscle pulsed in his jaw. "We always had shitty timing."

"Tell me about it."

She switched on the radio and found a station with clear-enough reception so that the silence would not be so awkward.

When they arrived in Helena half an hour later, she was anxious to be out of the SUV and back in her own head.

Gideon parked in front of the highway patrol headquarters, and the two made their way inside. They were met by Sergeant Bryce McCabe, a tall, lean man with a thick shock of black hair. In his late thirties, he wore the dark suit, white shirt, and blue tie that seemed to come with all state and federal jobs. Gideon made the introductions, and they all shook hands.

McCabe led them to a conference room and closed the door. Once they were all sitting at the round table, he threaded his fingers together. "I couldn't sleep after we talked last night. I've been thinking about the fires. We never connected the urban and rural events."

"I'm not sure I would have, either," Gideon said. "But we had a similar cluster of fires in the spring near Missoula. The patterns tell me there's nothing random about the buildup to the fires. But I can't speak to the motive yet. That will likely take financial records."

"I'll warn you now," McCabe said. "Pollock is connected in the area. He's donated heavily to the local fire department's fund and is a real personable guy, with a solid alibi."

"You have described the couple in Missoula who just lost their business to arson," Gideon said.

Joan's temper rose. Whether it was Philadelphia or the Wild West, connections always mattered. "Did you ever get a look at Pollock's finances?"

"According to his insurance filing, he's heavily invested in all types of properties around the state. Land rich, cash poor."

"There's no law against that," Gideon said.

"Half the state would be in jail if it were," McCabe replied.

"Did Pollock have any kind of an arrest record?" Gideon asked.

"No. Neither did his wife or his oldest son," McCabe said.

"What would be the motive for the arson?" Joan asked.

"Other than the million-dollar payout?" McCabe asked. "I can't think of one."

"Land rich and cash poor," Joan said. "Now he's flush."

"Detective Mason and I are headed out to talk to Pollock," Gideon said.

"Keep me posted."

After the trio shook hands, Joan and Gideon exited the building to his car. They drove to the site that had been Pollock's former warehouse. It had been cleared, construction crews were on-site, and a new foundation had been laid. There was a large flatbed carrying steel structural beams.

"Mr. Pollock is wasting no time rebuilding."

"There's money to be made."

Joan and Gideon crossed the street to one of the crewmen. He asked about Pollock and was instructed to visit the construction trailer.

Gideon banged his fist on the trailer door, and a man shouted for him to come inside. Joan went first and found herself facing down a trio of men gathered around blueprints spread out on a long, wide table.

"I'm looking for Mr. Pollock," she said.

The men looked at each other and then back at her, grinning.

"Who wants to know, doll?" the oldest of the three asked.

"Detective Joan Mason."

"And Detective Bailey." Gideon's voice reverberated directly behind her.

She had seen Pollock's kind before on the streets of Philadelphia. They were quick to underestimate a female, especially one with a small frame. Almost all had shit-eating grins on their faces right up until the moment she clicked handcuffs on their wrists.

"We're here to talk to you about the fire," Gideon said.

The older of the men stepped away from the trio and came around the table. He moved past Joan toward Gideon. "The fire was more than a year and a half ago."

"We understand. But walk me through what happened again."

"What's bringing all this up now?" Pollock challenged.

"I have a similar case in Missoula. Perhaps there's a common thread," Gideon said.

"I don't see how one has to do with the other. Besides, my fire was ruled an accident."

"Then you won't mind answering a few questions. Otherwise I can take it up with your insurance carrier, if you're too busy for me," Gideon said.

Pollock motioned the other two men to leave the trailer, and once they'd closed the door behind them, Pollock said, "There's not much more I can tell you. I was out of town. San Francisco. On business."

Joan could picture him standing in front of a mirror saying the words. *I am innocent. I was out of town.*

"Sergeant McCabe told me exactly that," Gideon said. "Did you receive any threats or have any trouble before the fire?"

"No," Pollock said. "One minute I'm staring at the Golden Gate Bridge and the next I'm getting a call from the police."

Joan shifted her stance, already knowing this guy was going to feed them a story vetted by his attorney. "What would have happened if the insurance company didn't pay out?"

Pollock's eyes narrowed. "What's that mean?"

"How much of a financial hit would it have been if they clawed back the payout?" Joan pressed.

"Something tells me you know the answer," Pollock said.

"A million dollars is a fortune for some and pocket change for others. Which one are you?" she said, studying the blueprints.

Pollock's grin looked feral. "I don't like your tone. And unless you have proof to back up whatever it is that you're suggesting, then I suggest you back off. In fact, who do you work for? I want to file a complaint."

That prompted a smirk from Joan. She was already in hot water, likely would not get her job back, and knew her boss would welcome a complaint out of another jurisdiction that would be the final nail in her coffin. He had her name, and he could dig for the captain's name if he wanted it.

"What was the cause of the fire?" Gideon asked, redirecting him.

"Electrical," Pollock said, his gaze still on Joan.

Gideon looked out the window toward the fresh slab of concrete. "There were two ignition sites."

"It was a surge in power that overloaded the old wiring," Pollock said. "Read the fire report."

"Was it as large as this new project?"

"No. The new building is twice the size. The area is booming, and I have the land to expand. Now's as good a time as any to go bigger."

"The old warehouse would have cost a fortune to renovate or tear down," Joan said. "The fire was a stroke of luck."

"Time for you both to leave," Pollock said. "If you have any more questions, you can talk to my attorney."

"You think you need an attorney?" Joan asked.

"I don't cross the street without one," Pollock replied. "Now leave."

Both stood their ground, ignoring the bluff.

Gideon searched his phone and then held up a picture of Lana Long. "Do you know her?"

"No."

"Take a long look," Gideon said.

"I don't know her."

"If we need to come back, we will," Gideon said as he handed his card to Pollock. "Might want to give your attorney a heads-up."

Outside, neither spoke until they'd crossed to his SUV. "Not sure if it's my winning personality, but I torqued him up," Joan said.

"You always had a knack for irritating people. Direct as an ax," he said.

"Pissed-off people usually open their mouths and incriminate themselves."

Gideon drove them back to Missoula, and both sat in silence, each lost in their thoughts. When he pulled into town, he asked, "Are you hungry?"

"Starving."

"I know a place." He pulled up in front of Tucker's Diner.

"Ah Jesus, Gideon. Is there no other place to eat?"

"Old times' sake," he said with a grin.

"The good old days weren't that great. I worked my ass off here."

"My treat. Indulge me."

Joan stared at the door she had pushed through so many times. "I'm afraid I'll end up in that pink uniform again and behind the counter."

Gideon opened it for her. "You won't."

The diner was quiet, but she knew it was the lull before the usual lunch crowd. They each grabbed menus from a star-shaped holder and gave their order to a waitress dressed in the restaurant's traditional pink uniform. The pretty young woman returned quickly with their drinks and a smile.

"This your first time back here?" Gideon asked.

She sipped her soda. "Yes. I've avoided it since my return."

He shook his head as he stirred the ice in his soda with the straw. "You put in some long hours. Holidays, too."

"I had no choice."

He looked toward the counter. "Did Elijah eat here often?"

"At least four or five times a week. He always ordered the same thing. Pancakes, bacon, and eggs. Never varied once."

He studied her over his cup. "I'm surprised you would remember that."

"I liked him. He was a nice guy. I know he didn't fit in well with most, but that's probably why I liked him."

"What did you talk about?"

"Everyday stuff. Classes and books mostly. We never talked about life beyond graduation. I just assumed we would find a way and it would work out."

"It did. In its own way."

His silence felt troubled until finally he shifted back to the case. "What do you think of Pollock?"

"Giving him the benefit of the doubt, he's been through the wringer the last year. Fire generates a lot of paperwork and is a pain in the ass. He could just be tired of the questions."

"Now tell me what you really think."

She grinned. "Arson is an accepted business practice in some communities. It can be the most cost-effective strategy in the long run, assuming you don't get caught."

"Maybe we'll get lucky and see similarities between the Halpern and Pollock books."

Ignoring the *we*, Joan sipped her soda. "He sincerely seemed to not recognize Lana Long's face."

"She was in Denver when his place burned. But I thought it was worth a try."

"Assuming the Beau-T-Shop and warehouse fires are connected. Are you saying we're dealing with an arsonist for hire? Someone has a problem with a building and hires our boy?"

Their burgers arrived, and each said little as they ate. Finally, Joan said, "Elijah could not have set the Pollock fire."

"Agreed." He shoved out a breath and sat back.

"And it would have been a hell of a stretch for him to set the Beau-T-Shop fire."

"Maybe he had a proxy," Gideon said.

"Lana Long."

"This guy turned on his charm, and according to her former boyfriend, Ryan, Lana fell for it hook, line, and sinker."

"Sounds like Elijah."

"You need to watch yourself around him."

She arched a brow. "Do you think I've fallen for Elijah's charm as well?"

"You did come halfway across the country twenty-four hours after his release." He sat back, balling his paper napkin and then setting it on the plate.

She leaned forward, not knowing whether to slap him or laugh. Finally, she said, "You really think I'm that gullible?"

"When you spent time with Elijah at the diner, what did you talk about?"

"School. I was the teaching assistant in his class. Books. Gossip."

"You didn't date?"

"You mean, did I cheat on you? No. I did not. And since we're being very honest, when did you start to date Helen? Was it really after I left, or had you two taken up before?"

His face hardened into a stiff mask. Her comment had hit its mark, and she was glad. Hit her and she hit back.

"I didn't go out with her until after you broke up with me," he said.

"You didn't wait more than a day or two."

"How long was I supposed to wait, Joan?"

What he had done after she left was his business, not hers. But it still stung that he had moved on from her so quickly. She could feel her own damn emotions welling up, and she feared if she stayed in this diner much longer, she would say something stupid that would make her look weak.

She fished a twenty-dollar bill out of her purse and tossed it on the table. "You're right. None of my business. I'll find my way back."

As she rose, his hand came out, and he captured her wrist. "It's been ten years. Why are you so upset?"

"I'm not upset."

"You are."

Her pulse beat fast and hard against his calloused fingertips. She had always made it a policy not to stir up the ghosts and demons from the shadows. But here they were, examining past mistakes and injuries. Maybe one day, she would discover this had been cathartic. But that day was not today. "I'm not Lana."

"I didn't say you were."

"You implied I've fallen for Elijah like Lana did."

"Have you?" He studied her closely.

She snatched her hand away and left the diner.

Confessions of an Arsonist
A cleansing fire hides so many sins.

CHAPTER SEVENTEEN

Joan grabbed an Uber back to her car at the police station and then drove to the ranch. Her head was pounding by the time she pulled into Ann's driveway. The sun still burned hot, but the light was softening. She was bone-tired, but not so much from the day itself.

What had drained her was the time with Gideon. The old wounds had been ripped wide open today. And for him to suggest she was like Lana pissed her off. If her partner or a stranger had lobbed such an accusation, she would have been pissed but not hurt. But Gideon striking such a low blow had all but drained her of her resolve.

She got out of her car, and gravel crunched under her feet as she crossed the circular drive and tried the front door. It was locked.

Joan rang the bell and waited as Ann's patient, steady steps clicked through the house.

When the door opened, Ann was smiling. "Sorry about that."

"No, it's fine. It's smart to lock your doors. I wouldn't work so many cases if more people did."

Ann stepped to the side, studying Joan. "Is everything all right?"

"I feel a little ragged." She placed her purse by the door where Ann's and Nate's shoes were neatly lined up and then toed off her own.

"I just opened a bottle of wine."

"I'll take a large glass, please."

"Coming up."

Joan followed Ann toward the kitchen. "How did school go today?"

"Nate had a great day. After school, I picked him up and brought him to the university. He audited a class."

"Did he like it?"

Ann reached for the open bottle of red on the counter, poured a glass, and handed it to Joan. "He couldn't stop talking about it."

"What was the class?"

"Advanced math. I'll spare you the details."

"Wow. Good for him." She sipped. "And Elijah?"

"I see him Wednesday."

"And how are you doing with that?"

"Not great. I'm not looking forward to it."

"He is. He's read the textbook at least twice."

"Really?"

"When I was his TA, he always gave me a run for my money." Ann sipped. "Terrific. How did it go with Gideon today?"

"Interesting."

A timer on the stove dinged, and Ann reached for oven mitts and removed a roasted chicken from the stove. "In a good or bad way?"

"Both." Joan fished her phone from her back pocket and handed it to Ann. "He compiled a list of fires in the state during the last decade and marked them on a map."

Ann studied the map, enlarging the image with a swipe of her fingers. "Does he really think they're all related?"

"I doubt they all are, but there're enough clusters to suggest a pattern. Check out the Helena area. It's had quite the collection in the rural areas as well as a significant fire last year in town."

She frowned. "We had a few small fires in the hills this summer."

Joan glanced in her glass, swirling the wine gently. "Nobody has a better alibi than Elijah."

"For only those fires," Ann said.

"Gideon thinks Elijah might be working with an apprentice. Lana Long may have been one of them."

Ann handed Joan back the phone. "That would make sense."

"How well did you know Elijah?" Joan asked.

"I knew of him," she said carefully. "Just like everyone else."

"Do you remember him hanging out with any girls?"

"No."

"Anyone who might have been a little too devoted to him?" Miss Weston had said he'd carried a picture of a pretty girl from money.

"I don't understand where this is going," Ann said.

"Maybe Elijah really wasn't near our house the night of the College Fire. Maybe he sent someone to do his bidding."

"I'm sure the cops would have asked around about Elijah's associates."

"I would assume so, too. But there's always someone who slips between the cracks. We all think we know people, and in the end, we really don't."

"You sound like a psychologist." Ann smiled, but it had a nervous edge to it.

Joan had been a cop too long not to notice. "That makes you nervous."

"No."

Joan shook her head. "It does. Why?"

"Maybe I don't like the idea that someone else was working with Elijah. Bad enough there's one crazy running around. Now we might have two? And this person, if he or she exists, didn't get arrested."

"No, they did not. But that doesn't mean they still can't be." Joan met Ann's gaze. "A picture was found in Lana Long's apartment. It was of you and me."

"What?"

"It was taken our senior year."

Ann's face paled as she seemed to absorb the information. "How could she get ahold of that?"

"I have no idea. But you need to be careful."

"We both do."

***

Gideon sat in his study, listening as Kyle finished washing his hands and brushing his teeth. He sipped his beer, wishing it had enough punch to blot out his last conversation with Joan. Now that he'd had a couple of hours to cool off and replay the shocked look on her face, he knew he had overstepped in a major way.

"Dad?" Kyle asked.

He looked toward the doorway. Kyle was dressed in pajama pants and the T-shirt he had worn to school that day. His hair was wet and stood straight up on end. "Did you take a bath?"

"Yes. See, my hair is wet."

He considered pointing out the day-old shirt but let it go. "Good job, pal. And homework is finished?"

"Yep."

"Do I need to sign anything for school tomorrow?"

"Teacher said a bunch are coming this week."

He had learned the hard way to have specific questions for the kid; otherwise his yes-no answers did not always tell the full story. "Great."

Kyle crossed the room and hugged Gideon. He set down his beer and hugged the boy back. As much as he wanted to take back sleeping with Helen right after Joan had left, he would never do that because then Kyle would not have been in his life. "Love you, kid."

"You too, Dad." Kyle scratched his head.

When Kyle turned the light off in his room, Gideon glanced at his phone and noticed the missed call from the prison warden. He took another swig of beer and hit "Redial." On the third ring, he heard a brusque "Detective Bailey."

"Warden Martin," he said. "Thanks for the return call. I know it's getting late."

"I'm still at the office. Got your voicemail and was intrigued. I pulled Elijah Weston's file to refresh my memory."

Gideon's chair squeaked as he leaned back. "I'm guessing he was a model prisoner."

"That he was. In fact, he's one of the inmates we like to brag about. He started working in the kitchens, moved to the library, and finally was an assistant in my office. He's already promised to come back and speak to the inmates about making life on the outside work. Please tell me he's not already in trouble."

Gideon rubbed his finger over his eyebrow. "No. From what I can see, he has been a model citizen."

"Then why are you calling?"

"We had a fire in town over the weekend. It was the day he was released from prison. But Elijah does have a solid alibi."

"I understand, given his history, why you have to look at him, but make sure you don't get tunnel vision."

"I understand."

"So how can I be of assistance?"

"I had a woman die in the fire. Her name was Lana Long. Her boyfriend said she carried on a correspondence with one of your prisoners."

Gideon could hear papers flipping in the background. "Yes, Lana Long did write to him. But he had several women who wrote to him."

"Can you name them for me?"

"For starters, Scottie Winter, Sarah Rogers, and Jennifer Caldwell. There're about a half dozen more. I can email you the full list."

Joan Mason was also on that list. "Can you send me copies of the letters?" He knew the prison opened and searched inmate mail and, in some cases, kept copies on file.

"I'll send you what I have first thing in the morning."

"That would be great."

"May I ask why the interest?"

"We're fairly sure he did not set this recent fire, and we know he didn't set a series of smaller fires across the state in the last decade. But that doesn't mean he wasn't working with someone."

"He wouldn't be the first to get a woman on the outside to do his bidding. He's charismatic as hell."

"What else can you tell me about him?"

"Always insisted he was innocent, but that's standard with a lot of these guys. Has one hell of a memory. The last couple of years, he worked in the main office and was always professional."

"Did he have visitors?"

More papers rustled. "Lana Long saw him six times this year. Approved visitors are allowed once a month."

"Was Elijah allowed conjugal visits?"

"He was not."

"He was never alone with Lana Long? Perhaps a blind spot on the cameras?"

"We're very careful."

"Did he get any work release jobs because of his good behavior?" Gideon asked.

"No, all his jobs were on the prison property."

"You said he worked for you in your office."

"He did. He was a great help." Warden Martin cleared his throat and lowered his tone. "Why are you pressing this?"

"I'd rather not say now. But as soon as I know more on this end, I'll give you a full brief."

"I'm going to hold you to that."

***

He stood in the darkness, staring at the Bailey ranch house, waiting for all the lights to go out. The boy's room had been the first to go dark, at about 9:00, and after that, the mother's room at 10:15. But the guest, she was a stubborn one. Her light stayed on till almost 11:00.

Picking up the plastic milk jug full of gasoline, he crossed the large lawn toward the house. Out here, there were no neighbors to see him, and under a moonless sky, he was nearly invisible to the naked eye. Thankfully, there was no dog to contend with, although he had managed quite easily with them in the past.

In a low crawl, he moved toward a shed located near the woods. He was tempted to set fire to the house, but this was meant as a warning, and he always stuck to the plan.

As he approached the shed, he realized the door was ajar. Not smart to leave a shed unlocked. Even this far out, thieves turned up. He reached inside the door, set the lock, and then gently closed the door. He tested the handle and made sure it was locked.

He removed a sock from his pocket and twisted it into a spiral before shoving it in the gallon-size plastic milk jug filled with gas. He then fished out a lighter from his pocket.

He flicked the lighter, and when the flame caught, he paused for a moment and admired the dancing flame. "So pure," he whispered.

He held the flame to the cloth, which had already wicked up the gasoline. It immediately embraced the cloth and enveloped it in a blue-and-orange flame. Its heat warmed his face and chased away the evening chill. In these few seconds, he understood completely the danger. It was the one last intimate moment he shared with his creation before releasing it.

After setting the jug down in the mulch, he quickly backed away as the flame snaked down the sock. He held his breath.

He counted. One. Two . . .

The flame ignited the gasoline, and the plastic jug exploded in a fireball that was nothing short of perfection. How could he not love something like this?

CHAPTER EIGHTEEN

Missoula, Montana
Tuesday, September 8, 2020
11:50 p.m.

The explosion jerked Joan out of a restless sleep. She sat up in her bed, her heart pounding and the glow of flames dancing on the walls of her room. She thought for a moment that she was dreaming. Despite the decade that had passed, the College Fire had never been far away. It lurked in her subconscious and sometimes invaded her dreams. She blinked, but even as her head cleared, the flames did not die down. She realized this was no dream.

She quickly reached for her phone and swung her legs over the side of the bed, grabbing her jeans, boots, and shirt. Her clothes were always within reach since the College Fire, and then later, when she became a detective, she was always ready to respond to a call and primed and ready to run for her life.

She bolted into the living room and shouted to Ann as she pulled her shirt over her head and shrugged on her pants. "Fire! Ann, wake up. Fire!"

The lights upstairs flicked on as Joan shoved her feet into her boots.

"Joan!" Ann appeared at her bedroom door, still wearing her pajamas. "What's going on?"

"There's a fire outside my window. I think it's the shed. Is there a hose outside?"

"Yes." Her voice sounded heavy with sleep. "I'm getting Nate."

Joan ran out the front door, bracing as the cold wind slapped her face. Adrenaline pumping through her body, she ran along the side of the house until she saw the hose and the spigot. Another couple of weeks and the hose would have been winterized and the exterior faucet turned off.

She wrapped her fingers around the cold metal and turned. The knob was stuck, forcing her to tug her sleeve down over her palm for traction. Gritting her teeth, she put her weight and energy into the handle. The heat of the flames warmed her back, and when she looked over her shoulder, it was licking up the side of the shed. "Turn on, you son of a bitch."

The handle budged slightly, and she renewed her efforts. She twisted again, and this time it gave way. Water spurted out, and she dragged the stubborn coil of hose with her. She opened the nozzle and hit the fire with water. The fire hissed and spit but resisted any attempts to quell its fury.

Joan's heart hammered in her chest as she took a step closer, the heat so hot now that her cheeks felt blistered.

"I can't find Nate!" Ann shouted behind her. "He's not in his room."

Joan stretched the hose as far as it would reach and then squeezed the nozzle harder. "Have you checked the entire house?"

"Yes!"

She peered into the blaze, praying the boy had not slipped outside to build one of his bonfires and ended up trapped in the burning shed. "Would he have come outside?"

"No! Why would he do that?"

"I don't know! What about the closets and under the beds?"

When a fire broke out, children, in an effort to save themselves, often hid from the flames, not realizing that the insidious smoke would coil around them and take their lives long before the fire did.

"I didn't search them all. I'll go back inside."

Joan realized the flames were now succumbing to the water.

As Ann turned, Joan caught a flutter of movement to her right. She looked out toward the expansive yard and saw a figure of a child standing and staring at the shed.

"Ann. Look over there! Is that Nate?" Joan asked.

Ann shouted her son's name as she ran barefoot across the lawn. The boy did not respond to his mother but stared at the fire with an intensity she had never seen before.

The cold water from the nozzle dripped over her fingers and onto her clothes. The growing cold was sapping her strength, but she kept shooting the water at the fire. The fire howled as if it sensed it was losing this battle.

She glanced back to see Ann rush up to her son. He was dressed in light-blue pajamas that made him appear much younger than ten. Ann wrapped her arms around the boy, hugging him close to her body and then hurriedly drawing him back as she ran her hands over his arms, torso, and legs. The trance was broken, and he shifted his attention back to his mother.

When Ann hugged her son to her again, Joan decided the boy was physically fine. She looked back to the fire, which had curled in on itself and retreated. She remained vigilant, however, determined to eradicate every trace of the devil's breath.

She lost track of time until a strong hand gripped her shoulder. Startled, she turned to see Gideon standing there. The fire was all but gone, taking with it its heat and allowing a chill to burrow into her bones. Her teeth chattered when she asked, "Where's Ann?"

"She's in my car getting warm with Nate." He took the nozzle from her and stopped the stream of water. "The fire is gone, Joan. It's okay."

Her fingers were red from the cold as she shivered. He shrugged off his jacket and wrapped it around her. A rush of warmth vibrated through her body. "How did you know?"

"Ann called me."

She tensed and dug her heel into the muddy mulch. "We need to take pictures. Preserve evidence."

"The fire department is on the way. So is Clarke. There will be plenty of people to figure out what happened here."

Her fingers had taken on a gray cast, but they still trembled, not with cold but with a surging adrenaline that she knew would keep her wired for hours, if not days. She looked back at the shed's exterior, still smoldering and streaked in soot. The siding had melted and curled.

"I woke when I heard an explosion," she said.

Gideon coaxed her forward. "Thank God you did. If that had spread to the woods, we'd have had a much bigger problem on our hands."

She expelled the stale air in her lungs and pulled in her first deep breath since she had awoken. "How did it happen?"

"I don't know."

"Nate was out here just watching the fire. He wasn't screaming or running for help or trying to approach the flames. He was simply standing there and staring."

"I haven't talked to Nate yet. But I will."

"He could have seen who did this."

Moonlight glittered over the brim of his hat, shadowing his face. "Joan, you have to get in the car and get warm. You're going to go into shock."

"I'm fine."

He grabbed her by the arm. "You're *not* fine. Accept the goddamn help, Joan."

The temptation to surrender was palpable. But lowering her guard would accomplish nothing. "I know what I need." She gritted her teeth so they would not chatter.

"Sometimes. But not now. Now you need to get warm and out of wet clothes. Once you're stable, then you can micromanage this entire investigation."

"I'm detail oriented. I don't micromanage." But she started walking toward him, and when she closed the gap, he fell in step beside her. When they reached his car, a fire engine siren wailed in the distance. Ann got out of the car and immediately wrapped a blanket around Joan.

"Joan, you feel like ice," Ann said.

"The irony," Joan said, attempting a smile. "Is Nate okay?"

"He's fine. He's in the back seat with Kyle."

"Did Nate explain why he was outside?" Joan asked.

"He said he saw the flames."

"From where?" Joan demanded.

"He won't say."

"Let me talk to him," Joan said.

"He's fallen asleep." Ann sounded defensive and on guard.

"I won't upset him," Joan said. "I just want to know if he saw anyone."

"It's too much for him," Ann said. "We'll talk to him in the morning."

"By morning, whoever did this could be long gone."

"I know."

"She needs to get in the car," Gideon said.

The fire engine lights appeared in the distance, flinging yellows and reds on the trees. The sirens grew louder.

Gideon reached for the door handle on the front passenger seat and opened the door. A rush of warm air beckoned her inside.

"You need to get out of your wet clothes," Ann said. "I'll hold up a blanket so you can strip."

Whatever modesty she felt was outweighed by the practical matter of getting warm. She reached for the hem of her shirt and, as she pulled it up, noted that Gideon's gaze lingered only a moment before he turned away. She peeled off her boots and jeans and left both in a wet, cold pile by the car.

Ann wrapped the blanket around her, and again her body shuddered, expelling the chill inside her. She slipped into the passenger seat, and Ann closed the door.

She watched as Ann and Gideon spoke to each other. Their voices were low, but she could see by the agitated looks on their faces that both were shaken.

Joan tipped her head back against the seat and closed her eyes. Who the hell would set that fire? It was not lost on her that the fire had started in a shed that was easily visible from her window.

"I didn't set the fire." Nate's quiet voice came from the back seat.

She looked in the rearview mirror and caught his wise gaze staring at her.

Kyle was beside him, nodding his agreement. "He didn't set the fire."

"I believe you." Keeping her voice low and calm, she asked, "Do you know who set it?"

"No," Nate said.

"What woke you?"

"I was hungry," Nate said.

"He's always hungry," Kyle offered.

Joan could not tell if Kyle was giving him an excuse or really explaining. "What did you eat?"

"I saw the fire before I got to the kitchen." Nate burrowed deeper into his blanket, making it impossible to really see him well.

"Why didn't you tell your mom? It could have caught the woods on fire."

"I didn't think about that; I just ran outside. Then you came out."

She stared into his gaze, trying to decipher what was going on in that head of his. "Did you see who set the fire, Nate?" she asked again.

Instead of answering, Nate closed his eyes and tugged the blanket up close to his chin. "I'm tired."

Most children were not good at masking their thoughts and feelings, but she suspected Nate was far more mature and capable than she had realized.

***

The fire crews arrived minutes later, and the single-engine crew quickly unloaded their hoses and went around the side of the house. With more power than her garden hose, they quickly doused whatever embers remained. Clarke pulled up behind the truck and got out of the car.

Joan tightened her blanket around her. She was warm, and the comfort of the wool now scratched her skin. She was anxious to get clothes back on so that she would be more comfortable and freer to move.

She opened the door, glancing back to see that Nate and Kyle were sleeping. Gingerly, she stepped out of the car, the graveled driveway digging into her bare feet. The night's chill had more bite now that her blood had warmed.

She closed the car door gently, watching as Gideon, Clarke, and Ann all spoke to each other. She crossed the driveway and hurried up the front path, past two firefighters.

"Sorry, fellas," she said as she kept moving. "I'm buck naked and need my pants."

Their gazes shifted to her hand gripping the wool blanket, and no doubt they were wondering what was underneath it. Let them wonder. As long as she got her clothes.

The heavy scent of smoke had infiltrated the house. She hurried down the hallway toward her bedroom and ducked inside.

She snapped up the bag and slid into a clean pair of jeans and a black V-neck sweater. She quickly ran her fingers through her damp hair, which stuck up and refused to be tamed. There was nothing to be done about it, so she slipped on her other pair of shoes and headed toward the front door. She grabbed one of Ann's jackets and headed outside. Gideon was waiting for her on the front porch.

"What are you doing?" he asked.

"Getting clothes. Hard to investigate when you don't have pants on."

The sound of a man's voice rose before he could respond, and they looked to see Clarke and Ann arguing. She was keeping her voice low but was standing toe to toe with him.

Joan moved past Gideon and crossed to the couple. "What's going on?"

"It's none of your business," Clarke said.

"I just spent a half hour putting out a fire, so I would say all of this is my business," Joan replied.

Ann looked pale and tired. "I don't want you two getting into it. I want to go back inside my house with my son and maybe get a shower and an hour or two of sleep."

"You're not going into that house," Clarke said. "You and Nate need to move back to town into our house. At least in town, you'll have better access to fire and rescue if this nut strikes again."

"I'm not moving back into our house," Ann said.

"I will move out," Clarke said quickly. "I'll stay at the fire station. I just want you and my son safe."

"We're fine," Ann said.

"The shed was torched!" Clarke shouted. "Next time it might be the house."

"Dad? Why are you fighting with Mom?" Nate asked.

They all turned to see Nate and Kyle standing in the driveway, wool blankets wrapped around their pajamas.

Clarke moved to Nate and knelt in front of him, hands resting on his shoulders. "Mom and I aren't fighting, buddy. We're worried."

Nate looked toward the smoking remains of the shed. "Why? The fire wasn't that bad."

"It could have been much worse," Clarke said calmly. "That's what worries me."

Nate yawned. "I want to go to bed."

"I can put you in your old room," Clarke said.

"I don't want that room. I like the one here better."

Ann stood beside Nate. "Gideon is on the property. Joan is here. We aren't alone."

"That's not the point." Frustration simmered under Clarke's words. "You're my family. My responsibility. This break you put us on needs to end."

"The house is untouched," Gideon said. "And I'm just down the road."

"See? We'll be fine," Ann said. "But I agree—we'll have to talk soon."

Clarke kept his hand on Nate's shoulder. "Ann, it's safer for you both in town, and you know it."

"We're staying here," she insisted. "I won't be run out of my home by some coward who thinks he can scare me."

"I'll be here as well," Joan said.

"But you might be the reason that my family is in danger," Clarke said, his gaze cutting to her. "What the hell is it with you and fire, Joan?"

"What do you mean?" Gideon asked.

"Wherever she goes, disaster strikes. This is the second time she's been near Ann when a major arson event happened. Three if you count the Beau-T-Shop fire, which happened within hours of her arrival."

Tamping down her anger, Joan refused to let Clarke see he had gotten to her. The Beau-T-Shop fire might have just coincided with her arrival, but this fire was a direct message.

She was not comfortable with the thought, but better her than Ann and Nate. "I'll get my gear and find a room in town first thing in the morning. That way the threat will be removed."

"I appreciate that, but what if you're wrong?" Clarke asked.

Gideon looked at her, his expression a mixture of annoyance and frustration. "I have a spare room at my house," he said. "It's over the garage."

"It's nice," Kyle offered. "Dad and I used to live there."

"Thanks, Kyle. But I'll get a hotel room," Joan said.

"It will cost you a fortune," Gideon said. "Besides, you're only staying a few more days, correct?"

Her return ticket was booked for Sunday, which gave her less than a week to clean up whatever mess was here before she returned home to the other mess she had left behind. "I'm here until early next week. But it's better I stay in town."

"I'm sorry, but the sooner you leave, the better," Clarke said.

Ann wrapped her arms around Nate's shoulders. "I want to get to bed. We'll sort it out later."

"I'll stand watch tonight and leave first thing in the morning," Joan said.

Neither Gideon nor Clarke appeared happy with the solution, but when the fire crews announced the shed extinguished, neither could argue.

"My house is a half mile down the driveway, Clarke," Gideon said. "I can be here in five minutes if Ann or Nate needs me."

That seemed to soften Clarke's hardened features. "I want you to call me if anything happens," he said. "I can also be here in less than twenty minutes."

Ann moved toward Clarke and kissed him on the cheek. "We'll get through this."

Clarke's hands came up to her arms, and he gently hugged her. "I'll do anything to protect you two."

"I know. We'll be fine."

Clarke was calm enough to leave, and when his car vanished around the corner, Gideon approached Ann. "Ann, I haven't told you everything."

"If you're going to tell me about the picture found with Lana, Joan already told me."

Gideon glanced toward Joan, his gaze a mixture of frustration, anger, and worry. "How well did you know Lana?" he asked.

Ann drew in a breath, as she did when she was stressed. "She did my hair once in the spring. Cut it too short. I wasn't happy. I haven't been back to the salon since."

"Did she say anything to you?" Gideon asked.

"She chatted about how much she liked Montana. Hinted that she had a boyfriend. I didn't press her for details. Why would she have a picture of Joan and me?"

"We don't know," Gideon said.

Ann flexed her fingers. "I have no idea who would give her a picture like that."

"Is there anything else she might have mentioned about her boy-friend?" he asked.

"I wasn't paying attention to her. Clarke and I had recently sepa-rated, and I was very distracted."

"If you think of anything about Lana, let me know."

"Of course. And if you find anything else that connects my son or me to any of this, keep me informed."

"I will." Gideon turned and left with Kyle.

Joan followed Ann inside and went into the kitchen. Ann took Nate upstairs. Needing something to do, she made a pot of coffee. As the machine gurgled, she stared out the window at the smoking remains of the shed.

She poured herself a cup and set out another mug for Ann, guess-ing she would come downstairs instead of sleep. Ten minutes later, Ann appeared in the kitchen and poured herself a cup.

Joan sat on the barstool, cradling her cup. "That was quite the evening."

"I still can't believe it," Ann said. "Makes me think about the College Fire."

Joan looked at her fingernails, still darkened with soot. "The flames brought it all back."

"Who could have set the fire?" Ann asked.

Joan carefully set her cup down. "Nate and I spoke while we were sitting in the car. He said he saw me come out, which means he was outside before I was."

"That doesn't make sense."

"He wasn't in the house, and we were both in a panic until I saw him watching the fire."

"He would have no reason to be outside."

"He told me he wakes up a lot at night from hunger. Kyle confirmed it."

Shaking her head, Ann dropped her gaze to her cup. "He's just a kid."

"He's a really smart kid with a very active mind."

Ann drew in a breath, rising and moving almost robotically to the refrigerator. She paused to stare at a picture of Nate held in place by a Montana state flag magnet. Finally, she opened the door, removed a carton of half-and-half, and took her seat back at the island. She did not bother to pour the cream in her coffee.

"Ann, what aren't you telling me?" Joan asked softly. "Why would he be outside?"

"I don't know." Her foot pulsed nervously against the rung of her stool.

Joan had interviewed enough suspects to recognize deceptive behavior, and Ann was showing signs of it. Retrieving the cream was a delay tactic, and though Ann could almost hide her unease behind a stoic expression, she could not control the nervous leg movements.

"Did Nate set the fire?" Joan asked.

Ann's green gaze turned watery, as if a dark secret had been spoken. "Why would you ask that?"

"Why aren't you denying it?"

"He's just a kid," Ann said. "And he has never had any history of setting fires or troubling behavior. He's smart and a little geeky, which sometimes gives kids and teachers a reason to single him out."

This burst of righteous outrage was a deflection, another sign of deception. Ann had also yet to deny Joan's assertion that the boy might have played a role in the fire.

"What aren't you telling me?" Joan asked.

"I don't know what you're talking about."

"I haven't pressed about your separation from Clarke, but what I saw out there tells me he doesn't want it. He really wants you back."

"No separation is easy."

"Is that what it is? This isn't about your dad's health anymore?"

"I've been avoiding talking about our marriage," she said.

"Whatever you're calling this living arrangement, it's a huge stressor, not only for you and Clarke but also for Nate. No one would be shocked that a boy missing his firefighter father would set a fire. Nate, of all people, would know that a few flames would bring Dad running. Maybe he didn't intend for the fire to get so big."

"That's ridiculous," Ann said. And then, as if noticing her cream, she poured a splash in her cup and took extra time to stir it with a spoon. The metal clanked against the earthenware mug, but Ann said nothing.

"I'm your friend," Joan said.

"You're also a cop."

"Who's on leave," she joked. "That makes me more friend than cop."

Ann shook her head. "You won't be here for long."

This latest deflection deepened Joan's suspicion that there was something bigger at play. "Ann, Nate likes setting fires."

"He's a boy. His father is a firefighter."

"When I showed up here and saw Nate, my first impression was that he did not look much like Clarke."

"He takes after my family."

"Not really," Joan said.

Ann folded her arms. "This is ridiculous."

The tension tightening Ann's features reminded Joan of someone with a secret. "Nate is smart. Very smart."

She dropped her gaze and shook her head. "So?"

Joan had never been afraid of making outlandish statements to provoke a reaction. "He loves Clarke, but he isn't anything like his father."

Ann's body went rigid. "I don't like whatever it is you are getting at."

And in that moment, Joan realized she had struck a nerve. It was a good thing she was leaving Ann's house, because if her suspicion was right, her next question was likely to get her kicked out. "Is Nate Clarke's son?"

Ann's eyes widened with a mixture of fear and dread. "Of course he's Clarke's son. That boy adores his father."

"I'm talking about biology now, Ann. Biologically, Nate is nothing like Clarke." She thought back to the moment in college when appreciation had shone in Ann's eyes as she'd looked past her toward Elijah. She softened her tone, as she did when she sensed she might be close to a confession. "At first, I thought Nate just favored you. But when I saw him outside staring at the fire, he reminded me of someone else."

Ann held up her hand, silent and staring as she shook her head. "Stop right there."

And this was the moment, suspended or not, Joan knew she had to be a cop first. "Is Elijah Nate's biological father?"

Confessions of an Arsonist
Fire has no bias. It has no worries. It simply consumes
all that it can. The great equalizer.

CHAPTER NINETEEN

Missoula, Montana
Wednesday, September 9, 2020
12:50 a.m.

Joan waited for Ann's wrath. But Ann remained silent, her face growing more ashen by the moment as she stared into her pale, creamy coffee. When she finally looked up, the reflected pain was reminiscent of a cornered animal.

Ann cleared her throat and lifted her chin. "I love my son. I would do anything to protect him."

"I know that. He's a great kid." It was not hard to sound genuine. She really did like the boy. "You got pregnant in the spring of 2010. Tell me what happened."

Ann glanced up the stairs and then beckoned Joan out onto the front porch. The cold night air bit and snapped, but Ann clearly did not want to take a chance Nate would hear them.

"I was tutoring at the student center with Elijah. We were working with other freshmen studying for the math finals," she said in a voice that sounded as if it were already traveling to the past.

"Nate was born in January," Joan said.

Ann shook her head. "We were in almost whiteout blizzard conditions when I went into labor. And Clarke was great. He was cool and calm as he put the chains on his tires. And he couldn't have done more for me."

Because he was getting exactly what he thought he wanted: Ann and a son.

Joan backed up the calendar nine months. "You and Clarke were on a break from each other in April," Joan said.

"Clarke was pressing me to get engaged, but I just wasn't ready for that."

"Did you tell any of this to Elijah?" Joan asked.

"No." She glanced at her palm, tracing a callus likely earned keeping the ranch going. "Elijah mentioned several times that I looked upset."

"He noticed a lot of things about you."

When Ann looked up, her surprise was genuine.

"I saw the way Elijah stared at you. He started tutoring when he realized you did."

"He was patient with the students," she said. "And we got along really well."

"And then . . ."

Ann's brow arched. "I was feeling alone after Clarke and I broke up. I felt like I had blown up my life. The students had left the center for the day, and Elijah was waiting around while I locked up. I was laughing about a joke he had recently told, and when I turned, he was right there. We stared at each other for I don't know how long. And then he kissed me very gently on the lips. And then I wrapped my arms around his neck and kissed him back harder."

"And one thing led to another."

"Yes." Ann pressed her fingertips to her forehead. "He walked me home and asked if he could see me again, but I told him I couldn't. I tried to soften the blow, but I could see that he was hurt. He asked me to reconsider, and I said I would, only because I felt so bad for him.

But the instant I woke up the next morning, I knew I had made a terrible mistake."

"Did you tell him that?"

"I called him and told him I had thought about it, but I really couldn't see him. I needed time to myself after the breakup with Clarke."

"How did Elijah take it?" Joan asked.

"He was calm about it. Said he would be there for me, whenever I was ready."

"That all sounds rational and mature." And if Joan distrusted anything, it was how accepting Elijah had been.

"I was so relieved. I thought I could just put what happened in the past, and we could all move on."

"And Elijah stuck to his promise to respect your decision?"

"Elijah was truly kind to me, and I respected him for it."

"Kindness can be more potent than roses or chocolates."

Ann gripped the handle of her mug and raised her coffee slowly to her lips.

"So at the time of the fire, Clarke and you were not reunited?" Joan asked.

"We slept together once after I was with Elijah."

"Did Elijah know that?"

"I don't know."

"Maybe Elijah decided if he couldn't have you, then no one could. If you had died in the fire, Elijah would have been assured you and Clarke would never be reunited."

"I didn't see Elijah once in the days leading up to the fire. I received no threatening notes, calls, or anything from anyone."

"Did you tell the police or anyone else about Elijah?"

"Not a soul. Until now."

"And Clarke was there for you after the fire." She was surprised to hear the bitterness in her tone.

Ann seemed to pick up on it as well. "The fire brought us together."

And it had driven Gideon and her apart. Was that not irony? She rolled her head from side to side. "When did you find out you were pregnant?"

Ann sat straighter. "The ambulance took me to the hospital, and the emergency room doctor ran a pregnancy test as a matter of protocol. When it came back positive, I nearly fainted."

"Did you know Elijah was Nate's father?"

"I knew it was a possibility." Ann shook her head. "It sounds terrible."

"It sounds human."

"Clarke appeared seconds after I found out about the baby. I tried to hide the news from him, but he realized something was wrong and pressed me to tell. I told him, and he was thrilled. We were married two weeks later by the justice of the peace in town."

By then, Joan had flown back to Philadelphia. She had been sleeping on Ray's sofa, and Gideon had been blowing up her phone with calls. "Clarke does love that kid."

"He adores Nate."

"Nate looks like you."

"Clarke says the same. And he has always attributed Nate's intelligence to me."

"Did you always wonder if he wasn't Clarke's?"

"I pushed the idea out of my mind until a couple of years ago. Nate was talking about math and how fun equations are for him. It was something about the way he lifted his chin that reminded me of Elijah. I just knew."

"Did you run a DNA test?"

"I took a cheek swab while Nate was sleeping. I sent it off to an out-of-state lab. The results were definitive. There's no way Clarke could be Nate's father."

Joan rose and walked to the porch railing overlooking the moonlit mountains and woods. "You're worried Nate set the fire because he's Elijah's, aren't you?"

Ann did not speak, folding her arms over her chest as she came to stand beside Joan. "I smelled his pajamas when he was showering. There was no hint of gasoline."

She faced Ann. "If he's as smart as you say, he could have set the jug out earlier. Easy to come back and light it."

Ann's face tightened with pain and worry. "Do you think he set it?"

"I don't know," Joan said. "He was so mesmerized by the flames."

"You cannot tell Clarke or Gideon." Ann's eyes were pleading. "No one can know this."

"I won't say a word, but I want to talk to Nate."

"Oh God, no. I don't want you asking him any questions."

"I can be subtle, Ann." Joan now shifted to a professional tone she used with her bosses and the press.

"He'll see you coming a mile away."

"He's smart, Ann. But he's also ten. I might not be as bright as you two, but I have a few tricks up my sleeve. Either way, you and I have to figure out if he set it. If he did, that means he's going to need some help."

Tears welled in Ann's eyes and rolled down her cheeks. "I thought the past was all behind us."

"Believe me, it's always been there."

***

Joan spent most of the night on Ann's couch, tugging at a short wool blanket, convincing herself the throw pillow was really comfortable, and staring at the vaulted ceiling braced by hand-hewn logs as she thought about Nate. Whether the boy set the fire, or Elijah, or God knows who else, they had started back up when she'd arrived in town.

She reached for her phone and checked the time. It was 5:50 a.m. Accepting that sleep was never going to happen, she capitulated and decided to take a shower.

She yanked out her one last clean shirt, the red Phillies shirt she had bought for Nate, and turned on the shower. Steam rose up in the room as she stared into the mirror at a soot stain slashing across her cheek and her eyes, red with fatigue. How had she gotten to this point in her life? Slowly, the mirror fogged up, and her image vanished. She stepped into the shower.

Joan ducked her head under the hot spray and let the heat work through her hair and wash away the ash and smoke. She planted both her hands on the shower wall, leaning in as the water beat against her tight shoulder blades.

She finally stepped out of the shower, dried off, and shrugged on her shirt and jeans. She combed out her short hair until it was reasonably presentable again.

Feeling a little more human, she went into the kitchen and made a pot of coffee. As the machine gurgled, the sound of footsteps had her turning to see Nate walk in. Without a word, he went to the cabinet and retrieved a box of Cheerios and then grabbed a half carton of milk from the refrigerator. He set both on the kitchen island before getting two bowls and two spoons. He filled one bowl with cereal, milk, and a couple of teaspoons of sugar.

"That second bowl for me?" Joan asked.

Scrambling on the barstool, he reached for his spoon. "Yes, but I don't know how you like your cereal."

She could not remember the last time she had eaten breakfast, but the boy was offering, and she could not afford to refuse. Mirroring his choice, she put sugar on her cereal and then a splash of milk.

"That's not enough milk to cover all the cereal," he said. "Your ratios are wrong."

"Depends on your goal. I don't like chasing my cereal in a sea of milk. I want it damp but immobile."

He grinned as he lifted another milk-soaked spoon to his mouth and took a bite. "Logical."

"Your mom still asleep?" Joan asked.

"Yeah. She's sleeping in the other twin bed in my room. She looked tired, so I let her sleep."

"Good plan. Your mom used to eat this exact brand of cereal in college every day without fail."

"I do, too."

"They say breakfast is the most important meal of the day."

"Who is *they*?"

"No idea."

"You still have a price tag on your shirt."

She glanced down and spotted the green sticker. At the airport, she had assumed Clarke's DNA had produced a tall ten-year-old, and Ann had allowed her to believe it. "I got this for you, but your mom said it was too small."

"Maybe."

"I can still give it to you?"

"Naw, I don't need any more shirts."

They both continued to eat in silence. Joan had forgotten how much she liked the cereal's malty taste, which now reminded her of school and a young life filled with possibilities.

She set down her spoon and shifted to the stark task of questioning the boy about the fire. With his mother still asleep, now was the best time. Once Ann was around, her mama-bear claws were going to come out and censor everything the boy said.

She chased around a few dried Cheerios, realizing her milk-to-cereal ratio might have indeed been too low. "What did you think about the fire?"

He finished chewing. "Bright."

For all his brains, he had come up with a fairly weak descriptor.

"It was more than that. It was pretty destructive and dangerous."

"I know."

"I asked you this last night, but Kyle was there. Now it's just the two of us. Why were you outside?"

"I told you, I couldn't sleep."

"Do you set fires in the firepit when you can't sleep?"

His eyes widened in surprise, as if he had been caught stealing cookies from a jar. "No."

"But you think about it, don't you?"

"Yeah. But Mom would freak out if I did, and I don't want to upset her. *Ever*."

"Okay, okay." Joan shifted her line of questioning. "What kind of noise did you hear outside last night?"

"Crunching leaves." He refilled his bowl with more cereal, milk, and sugar. "I thought it was a bear. I was going to investigate. We have horses in the barn that are easily spooked by them."

"The barn is down the road, along with the foreman, who takes care of the horses."

"He drinks and also sleeps hard. If I had told Mom about the sound, she wouldn't have let me go. She doesn't want to admit it, but I'm grown up."

She resisted a smile. "Okay, you hear a sound and go out to investigate. Did you see a bear?"

"I saw something big and dark running toward the woods. And then I heard the big whoosh and then saw the flames."

She had heard the same sound. By her calculation, it had taken her at least a minute to put on her clothes and shoes and get out the door. "Why didn't you call for help?"

His brow furrowed. "I don't know. The fire was so interesting. I couldn't stop staring at it."

"The figure who was running away, was it a man?"

"I think so."

"Was he carrying something?"

"I didn't see anything."

"Did you smell anything?"

"Like an accelerant?" the boy asked wisely. "No, I don't think so."

"You know about accelerants?"

"Gasoline, diesel, and thermite. Sure. Who doesn't?"

She could name a hundred. She set down her spoon and picked up her coffee, sipping as she tried to keep this entire conversation light and easy, as if that were possible with arson. "Are you sure you didn't set the fire by accident?"

He looked at her, his gaze widening a fraction. "Yes, I'm sure."

"Because if you did, I wouldn't be mad."

"My mom would be mad. She's not crazy about fire because her house burned down when she was in college."

"I wouldn't tell her." Which was not true. In fact, Ann would be the first she would tell. Like it or not, lying was a trick cops used to get a suspect to tell them what they needed.

"I didn't set it!" His voice rose, and he dropped the spoon into the bowl, creating a loud clank.

"Set what?" The question came from Ann, who was standing in the doorway. She looked both bleary eyed and suspicious.

"I asked Nate if he set the fire," Joan said.

"Why would you do that?" Ann asked as she came up behind her son.

"He was on the scene when I arrived."

"He's a child, and you were not a cop rolling up on a crime scene last night. You're my guest."

"It was a crime scene. Still is. And I am a cop." Maybe not in Philadelphia much longer, but somehow, somewhere else, she would be.

"Nate, finish your breakfast. Then get dressed. I've laid out fresh clothes for you."

"I didn't set the fire," he repeated.

"I know, baby."

Ann touched him gently on top of his head, but he angled slightly out of her reach. "I'm not a baby."

"I'm well aware," Ann said.

Nate took several more bites and then picked up his bowl and set it in the sink. "We're still going to school today, right?"

"Yes," Ann said, smiling.

He ran off, his feet thudding against the wood floors as he made his way upstairs.

"That's the second time you have spoken to him without me," Ann said. "Don't do it again."

"Your presence would have prejudiced his comments. He knows you dislike fire."

Color rose in Ann's face. "And you don't? You could barely stand by the firepit the other night. The College Fire sent you running back east!"

Joan set her cup down. "For what it's worth, I don't think he set the fire. He said he saw someone or something running away from the house."

Frustration turned to relief and then curiosity. "Did he say anything else?"

"No."

"So why don't you think he did it?"

"He doesn't want to disappoint you." She thought about the crime scene pictures taken at the College Fire and Elijah staring at the flames from the crowd. Nate was still a young boy, despite all his intelligence, but one day he would grow up and, as all boys do, grow independent of his mother.

"Whereas Elijah never had such limitations," she said.

"You've met Miss Weston?"

"A couple of times in town. I'm not fond of her, and a part of me always felt sorry for Elijah, knowing he grew up with her as a mother. He didn't have a chance."

"Do you believe you're all that stands between Nate becoming . . ." Joan hesitated and dropped her voice. "Elijah?"

Her shoulders stooped, as if for the first time she had released a heavy weight. "Yes."

"You don't have to do this alone, Ann."

"I can't tell Clarke. Jesus, he would be devastated."

"Clarke is returning today to work the fire scene, correct?"

"Yes."

"He's good at his job. He'll figure out how the fire started. And he'll look out for Nate, if he should find anything that contradicts the boy's story."

"You don't have to go into town," Ann said. "Whatever happened here was not your fault."

"The College Fire began outside my bedroom window, and the third incendiary device was under my room. Elijah had pictures of me in his dorm room. And this fire could only be viewed from my window. Like it or not, I am a possible target."

"I was on both properties with you each time. And Lana had a picture of both of us. Besides, Elijah never disliked you," Ann said. "He might have had a twisted idea of him and me, but you were his friend. He wouldn't hurt you."

"Regardless of who's unhappy with me, it's best I still leave. I would never forgive myself if something happened to you or Nate."

"Do you really think someone wants to kill you?"

"I didn't used to think so. But now, hell yes."

Confessions of an Arsonist
I've seen how the boy looks at fire.
    And I see in him the blaze that burns in me. Pride.

CHAPTER TWENTY

Missoula, Montana
Wednesday, September 9, 2020
9:15 a.m.

Tension rippled up Ann's back as she stood behind the lectern at the head of the class. She glanced up toward the clock; her nine-thirty class would not arrive for another fifteen minutes, but she was already wishing away the next hour. Normally, she did not arrive to her classroom so early, like she had when she was a new teacher. But today, sitting in her office was nearly unbearable.

The secrets of the past were clawing their way to the surface, and she was terrified what it would mean for Nate.

She glanced at her notes, tried to focus on the day's lecture. She had given this class and its lectures twice during the last academic year and was so well versed in the subject that she did not really need notes. But as she stared at the neatly typed words, her thoughts jumped back in time to the night she had been alone with Elijah at the student center.

He had been a gentle lover, handling her as if she were made of a fine china. That had bothered her, because she had craved something rougher, more primal, the kind of joining an anonymous couple might share.

When it was over, she had not found the release she had been seeking. And Elijah had stared at her with eyes that reflected a kind of puppy love that only made her feel worse. She had been his first, he whispered, and he wanted to see her again.

Ann had dressed quickly, gathered her books, and told him it would not be possible. She was already practicing her denials, but he insisted on walking her home, which she allowed in order to avoid a scene.

Ann had not been totally honest with Joan. She had seen Elijah again a few days later . . .

"I did it wrong the last time," he said, closing the door behind him.

All traces of the sensitive young man were gone, and in his place was a darker, edgier persona. "What?"

Nerves in her belly tightened, even as a thrill of excitement shot through her. Last night, Clarke had come by. They had had sex, but she had gone through the motions.

"You want it different." There was emotion. "I saw."

"What?" She moistened her lips.

"Take your shirt off."

"What?"

"Do it."

Intrigued, she reached for the hem of her blouse and pulled it over her head. Her nipples hardened under the thin fabric of her bra.

"Take all of it off," he said.

"What about you?"

"This is what you want, isn't it?"

She hesitated before whispering, "Yes."

"Then get naked."

She slid off her bra and then her jeans and panties. When she stood bare before him, he smoothed his hands over her shoulders and then turned her toward the wall. He did not hurt her but held her firmly in place as he leaned down and kissed the nape of her neck. His pants zipper opened, and then he pushed into her hard. She gasped, curling her fingers into fists, and arched toward him.

When she came, she went limp against the wall, her heart pounding fast.

"You won't forget this fuck. Ever," he said.

And then her house had burned to the ground. And then the doctor told her she was pregnant. And then Clarke and she were married. And then . . .

Steady footsteps sounded in the hallway outside her room, and she knew it was Clarke. His heels always struck the ground as if he were rushing to the next fire.

Color rose in Ann's cheeks, as if she had been caught recalling the forbidden. She closed her notebook and braced for another sales pitch involving her moving back into town. His wide shoulders filled the doorway, and he was dressed in his uniform.

He strode down the aisle between the long tables set up classroom-style. His aftershave curled around a lingering scent of smoke and reached out for her. Ann had always loved his scent. For a second, he was the old Clarke, and she was the old Ann. Surprised and troubled, she cleared her throat.

"Your office said you came to the classroom early," he said. "You didn't answer your cell."

"It's on silent."

"What if Nate needs you?"

"I can see his texts."

"Is he all right?" Clarke asked.

"He's fine." Nate had been curious about the damage and insisted on inspecting it before school. Boys his age were naturally inquisitive, so she'd chalked up his curiosity to his gender. "I dropped him off at school and will pick him up by one thirty so he can audit his university math class."

"He wasn't traumatized?"

"Not at all."

That seemed to please him. "A chip off the old block."

"Yes," she said carefully. "He's not afraid."

Dark eyes glistened with pride. "You're sure he's fine?"

"Positive."

"He's spending next Wednesday night with me, right?"

"He's looking forward to it." Which was true. Nate and Clarke were very different in so many ways, but that did not undercut the love.

"Have you thought any more about returning to town permanently? If you come back to town, we'd have a better chance of figuring this all out, whatever it is. I can find an apartment for a few months."

"We're staying put, Clarke."

"We have to talk about all this soon."

"I know. And we will. I promise."

He looked as if he wanted to pull her into an embrace but instead cleared his throat. "What about the damage at the ranch?"

She was relieved to be off the topic of them. "I've already called the ranch manager, and he's coming out midday with his crew to see what he can do about the cleanup. Have you inspected the damage?"

"I'm headed out there now."

She did not like the idea of him on her property without her there. It was not that she expected him to do anything nefarious, but the ranch was her space, not theirs, and he did not belong there.

"Okay."

"I'll warn you now, Ann, that last night's fire had all the hallmarks of the College Fire." As he stepped toward her, she sensed the restrained energy. He was trying to maintain a calm front, like a cowboy wooing a wild mare, but it was a struggle. "Elijah set that fire."

"You don't know that."

"I can't prove it yet. But I will."

"Joan believes he might not have set the College Fire."

His gaze darkened. "Then she's a damn fool. What the hell is it with her?"

"She's trying to make sure no one else gets hurt."

He rubbed his hand over the back of his neck. "You know why she's out here, right?"

"Because Elijah was released from prison."

"That's a convenient excuse. She's been put on leave by the Philadelphia police. She'll likely lose her job soon."

"How do you know that?"

"I made some calls. She screwed up an investigation. Miscalculated her interviewing prowess, which led to the release of a crazy woman who'd burned her roommate alive. Joan is fast and loose with the facts now, just as she was in college."

"That's not true."

"I know she painted me as some kind of albatross around your neck in college."

"Joan had nothing to do with our breakup. You wanted to get married, and I wanted to wait. You pushed, and I felt backed into a corner." Footsteps sounded outside the classroom. "I don't want to get into this with you now."

"We need to talk about this."

"There's nothing to talk about."

"*My* son was in *your* home when the shed caught fire."

A muscle pulsed in his jaw, as it did when he regrouped. "Come to dinner with Nate and me next Wednesday. It would be nice for the three of us to share a meal as a family."

"We'll have family time at his birthday party. It'll be fun." She added the last bit just as much to convince herself as him.

"That's not the same. I want the three of us to share at least one meal."

She drew in a slow breath. "All right. Next Wednesday. Got it."

His frown softened into a grin. "Thank you."

"Sure. Of course."

The classroom door opened, and two young women walked in. Clarke stepped back. "I'll pick Nate up after his class and see you later tonight when I drop him off," he said quietly.

"Nate finishes with class at three."

"Good." He glanced over his shoulder at another set of students. "See you then."

"Terrific."

Clarke strode down the center, pausing for several girls to pass, and then went out the door. Ann carefully opened her lecture material and tried to refocus.

A few whispers rose up among the women and men, and she raised her gaze to see Elijah walking in, his textbook tucked under his arm. If he was aware of the comments, he did not show it. His pace was unhurried and his posture relaxed as he took a seat in the front row. He carefully opened his notebook and clicked the end of his pen before he looked up and smiled at her. "Good morning, Professor Bailey."

***

Gideon returned to the jail as Ryan was being processed out. It had taken the young man a day to recover from his binge and another to find a bondsman before he could post bail with the magistrate.

Ryan looked up, his still-bloodshot eyes reflecting grief and anger. "Thanks for coming."

"You had something important to tell me?" Gideon asked.

"Yeah." Ryan threaded his belt into the loops on his pants and fastened the buckle. "I've been thinking about Lana."

Gideon escorted Ryan out of the holding area and through the security doors to the lobby. "Are you hungry?"

"Starving."

"I know a diner."

Ryan nodded, sliding into the front seat of Gideon's SUV without a word. Gideon drove across town and parked in front of the Buffalo Café. Inside, the sweet scents of cinnamon and maple syrup blended with the crispy tang of bacon. A tall waitress with red hair poured coffee for both and took their orders.

After she left, Gideon asked, "What did you want to tell me, Ryan?"

Ryan set his cup down. "Lana always had a thing about texting through encoded apps. She didn't want her mother snooping, which she did a lot when we were dating. When Lana told me that she wanted to see me again, she sounded off, so I logged into her account." Ryan fished his cell from his pocket. "I figured she'd changed her password and username and stuff, but she hadn't. She could be lazy about that kind of thing."

The boy had a nervous edge that came with a juicy discovery.

Ryan turned the phone around, his face hardening as the meaning of his find settled. "It looks like she was pregnant, and her boyfriend didn't want it. That explains now why she called me. She always came back to me when she was having a hard time."

"Did she name the boyfriend?"

"The name he used was Roger."

Gideon took the phone and dropped his gaze to Lana's exchange.

Lana: Don't pull that shit with me. The baby is yours.

And DNA will prove it. Step up or I'm going public.

Roger: Don't do that.

Lana: Why shouldn't I? You made it clear you don't care about me or the baby.

Roger: I care. I do. Let's meet. We can talk. I have a ring for you.

Lana: What?

Roger: That's right. I love you.

Lana must have accepted the ring, because in subsequent texts she said how much she loved it.

Roger: I have a surprise for you.

Lana: Really?

Roger: Meet me at the Beau-T-Shop?

Lana: Time?

Roger: Now. I need to see you.

Lana: Okay.

The last text was sent at 6:15 p.m. on Saturday. The fire crews estimated that the blaze had started about 6:45 p.m.

"Do you have any idea who Roger is?" Gideon asked.

"No. I never heard the name until I read the texts."

A DNA test would create a profile for the father of Lana's unborn child, but whether that individual was in any DNA database was impossible to tell. Still, it was a solid lead in the process of solving who had strangled Lana and then left her to burn alive in the fire.

"Can you give me Lana's password and username? I want to read all her messages to Roger." He removed a pen and pad from his coat pocket and pushed them toward Ryan, who wrote down both. "Thanks, Ryan. This could be a big help."

Their food arrived, and they both ate in silence. Ryan all but cleaned his plate in less than five minutes, and Gideon gave him his extra bacon and toast.

When Ryan seemed to have had his fill, he sat back and said, "Lana and I were once really good together. I would have taken her back even with the baby." He stared down at the empty plate, trying to hide his tears.

Gideon wanted to promise that he would solve this case, but he had learned a long time ago that sweeping promises were a recipe for disappointment. "Are you staying in town?"

"There's a bus to Denver in two hours. I'm going to be on it."

"I can drive you to the station."

"Thanks, man. I appreciate that."

"Sure."

"You'll call me when this is solved, Detective?"

"As soon as I have an update I can share, you'll be getting a call from me personally."

Confessions of an Arsonist
Out of all the destruction caused by fire, there is always new growth eventually. New bonds.
Death before life.

CHAPTER
TWENTY-ONE

Missoula, Montana
Wednesday, September 9, 2020
10:30 a.m.

When Ann and Nate left for school, Joan had every intention of following them into town. But the fire last night and the lack of sleep had left her exhausted.

She swallowed a couple of aspirin and sat on the couch for a quick break until the throbbing in her head eased. But her eyes quickly drifted closed, and this time she fell into a deep sleep, only to be awakened by pounding on the front door.

She jumped to her feet, fingers fisted, ready to fight as she quickly oriented herself. She glanced at her phone, groaned at the lost couple of hours, and then hustled toward the door. She opened it to find Gideon and Clarke standing on the front porch steps. "Hey, fellas."

Gideon's gaze pried into her, as if he was searching for a nugget of information that would answer questions that went back more than a decade. "Did we wake you?"

Joan moistened her lips and drew in a breath. "No. Just about to make a second pot of coffee. You guys want any?"

"No," Gideon said.

"Can we come in?" Clarke asked.

Joan stepped aside. "Sure. I figured you'd be back this morning. You boys know where the fire started, so I'll leave you to it while I make coffee."

"Did you sleep at all last night?" Gideon asked.

"I don't need much."

"What about Ann and Nate?" Clarke asked.

"Both got to bed. Nate went right off to sleep, and Ann finally gave up and grabbed a few hours."

"Did you have any other problems last night?" Gideon asked.

"No," she said. "Very quiet."

"Any calls afterward?" Gideon asked.

"No contact of any kind."

"Did Nate or Ann see anyone before the fire?" Clarke asked.

She had not really thought how she was going to juggle Ann's paternity reveal and also the boy's presence at the fire. But for now, she would not tell. "No."

Clarke accepted her comment with a nod and headed toward the bedroom. Gideon lingered a beat. Those dark eyes searched her face for any hint of deception. Finally, both men walked out the back door and crossed the yard toward the crime scene tape.

She moved to the kitchen and made a single cup of coffee, figuring if the dynamic duo wanted coffee now, they could make it themselves. Cup in hand, she trailed them outside. The air was still cool, but the sun was bright and warmed her skin. She burrowed deeper into another one of Ann's jackets.

"What woke you up last night?" Gideon asked.

"An explosion." Last night's memory had mirrored the long-ago past far too well. But to her credit, her voice did not break. "Then I put on my boots, ran outside, and grabbed the hose."

"And you saw no one?" Clarke asked.

"Wish I had. It would have made last night a lot calmer." She sipped her coffee. "It's always the unknown that eats at you."

"I'm going to walk the woods and see if there's anything," Clarke said.

Joan shoved her hands in her pockets, promising herself to buy gloves before the day was out. "Have at it."

When Clarke vanished into the woods and they were alone, Gideon said, "You're very calm."

"Why wouldn't I be?" she challenged.

"Last night had to be traumatic. A reminder."

She crossed her fingers. "Haunting memories and I are well acquainted. I don't run from them anymore."

His brows knotted together. "Are you still troubled by the College Fire?"

"*Troubled* is a strong word."

"You said *haunting memories*."

"A figure of speech." The emotional scars, unlike the physical ones on her hands, were very much alive and painful.

"What aren't you telling me?" he asked.

Again, Gideon lingered, his head cocked, as if searching for any small clue lurking behind her expression and tone. Her skin tingled, and a restless energy surged inside her. Finally, he shook his head as if whatever he had been stalking had eluded him.

Clarke returned from the woods and strode toward the burn site. Gideon joined him, and the two poked through the ashes. Clarke stopped in what had been the center of the shed and knelt down.

"See anything?" she asked.

Clarke held up a blackened, twisted blob covered in charred mulch and dirt. "It's plastic. Likely the delivery device for the accelerant." He held it up to his nose. "Gasoline. And there's a burn track in the grass. The arsonist trailed the gasoline from the shed to the woods."

She imagined someone placing the jug in the shed and setting it on fire knowing she had a front-row seat. She tried to imagine Nate at the center of this storm, but the more she thought about him as an arsonist, the less it made sense. Christ, if genetics were a precursor to trouble, she and a lot of other folks were screwed.

"If there's any chance of pulling prints or DNA, our best bet is the state lab or the FBI lab at Quantico," Gideon said.

Clarke carefully bagged the remnants of the homemade device and handed them to Gideon. "It's got to be similar to the other one. Joan, you might want to find out where your pen pal Elijah was last night."

***

There were several cars parked in front of Elijah's boardinghouse when Joan arrived. She had decided to make this visit without Gideon because she sensed that Elijah would be more forthcoming if it was just her asking the questions.

Striding across the front and up the steps, she rang the bell and was shown to the den by Mr. Pickett. She found Elijah on his laptop studying video clips of arson events.

"You do this for fun?" she asked.

His gaze did not waver from the screen, but a smile curled the edges of his lips. "Back so soon? People might start to talk, Joan."

She moved into the room and took a seat next to him. "Don't you have class today?"

"I did. Class was an hour ago. When did you start sleeping in late? And why do you smell like smoke?"

223

Despite a shower and a clean shirt, her jeans still reeked and would until she could wash them a few times. "Someone torched Ann's shed last night. I had the pleasure of putting it out."

He paused the video and faced her. All traces of humor had vanished. "What happened?"

"Fire set outside my window."

"How?"

"I'm not supposed to say. It's an active investigation."

"I didn't set it."

She held up her hands. "I suppose you have an alibi."

"For last night? Yes, I do. Was anyone hurt?"

"No." She searched for traces of Nate in Elijah's features and found several. "How old were you when you set those dumpsters on fire?"

"Are we relitigating old news?"

"Humor me."

"Twelve and thirteen."

"Why did you do it?"

"My mother had kicked my stepfather out and begun to invite the first of many boyfriends into our home."

"What did you hope to accomplish by the fires?"

"The prison psychologist asked me that very same question, and I've had ten years to think about it." He shifted, crossing his legs. "I was angry. I didn't know how to articulate it."

If she were back in Philadelphia, she would not have hesitated to use the information Ann had given her. But this was not back east, and Ann was her friend, maybe the only one she had in Montana. "What are you watching now?"

"This is research."

"On?"

"You." He hit "Play," and the fire began rolling again. As she looked closer, she saw this fire was eating through Avery Newport's house. The footage had been recorded by a neighbor's cell phone. "Amazing what you can find on YouTube."

"Why would you care about the Newport fire in Philadelphia?"

"This fire reminded you of the College Fire, didn't it? Two young women home alone. Fire breaks out, and one dies."

"Newport is a cold-blooded killer. End of story." Joan watched as the flames ate into the house, consuming it like a roaring dragon would. Her attention shifted to the left side of the screen, where she knew the roommate had slept.

His brow knitted with curiosity. "This really bothers you, doesn't it?"

"A young woman died in that fire." She reached over and closed the laptop.

"You'll get another chance to catch her."

"Really? How can you be so sure?"

"I know Ms. Newport better than she knows herself," he said.

"How?"

"The footage captured Newport at the scene, but her expression was all wrong for an innocent victim. All they saw was her crying, but the tears weren't for her roommate. They were for her child, the fire."

A sense of vindication rose up in Joan. "Unfortunately, that's not enough for the prosecutor to file charges. And the evidence I collected was all circumstantial."

The smile returned, warming his eyes. "I do have some theories, if you wish to hear them?"

"Yes, I would."

"Well then, once we figure out who was behind the College Fire and the two most recent ones, I'll share all I have on Avery Newport with you."

"And if the evidence still points to you, then I don't get the evidence on Avery Newport?"

"I'm not that petty, Joan. You know me much better than that."

She drew in a breath, punching down her frustration. Like it or not, he had a talent for identifying patterns. Showing him the map Gideon had made of the recent fires was a risk, but if anyone understood the mind of an arsonist, it would be Elijah. "Gideon mapped the fires. I'd like to show it to you."

"I would like to see it."

She handed him her phone, and he studied the image for a good minute. He rose up from the couch and moved to a desk, where he'd stacked his textbooks. He opened the top one and pulled out notes. "I could get used to this detective work. I can already tell it's going to be rewarding."

"You're not an official detective until we've done an all-night stakeout with only stale doughnuts and cold coffee."

A smile tugged his lips. "Not all glamorous like the movies."

"I wish." She nodded to the paper. "See anything on the map that tells you something about our arsonist, *Detective*?"

He enlarged the photo on her phone. "These areas around Missoula and Helena are the same guy. The others have no statistical significance, meaning they're random."

"Why these?"

"It's just a gut feeling at this point. Can you get me the official reports?"

"I can't." She leaned closer and looked again at the map. "Were the rural fires practice? Was the guy building up his courage?"

"I would say he has plenty of both. He's letting off steam until game day."

"How do you know?"

"Again, a feeling," he said.

"I trust my gut, but I find DAs like evidence."

"You have two distinct patterns. Now it's a matter of figuring out who was in both these areas at this time."

"You weren't."

"No, I was not."

"Do arsonists recognize others? Maybe some kind of tell?"

The easy smile faded. "I am not one of them."

She was surprised by the edge sharpening his words. "So what's this guy's deal?"

"He's not a crazy kid working out anger. He likes the fires, and he's turned it into a money-making operation."

"How do you know about the money?"

"I didn't until you just confirmed it for me."

Joan could have tried to backpedal and deny she had given him anything, but she had. "The Helena fire did involve a payout."

"I'm assuming the Halperns also took out a hefty plan. Were the Halperns and the Helena business owner out of town when their businesses burned?"

"Yes."

He nodded thoughtfully. "The owners travel to a distant city, their places get torched, and both parties come home looking innocent."

"You're saying that the fires are financially motivated?"

"For the business owners, yes."

"And for the arsonist?"

"The thrill. The control. The power. The danger."

"You can slip into this guy's mind pretty easily. Maybe you're behind the fires," she challenged.

"We established I was in prison."

"That didn't stop you from finding my home address."

He nodded slowly. "I admit to taking liberties when I worked in the prison warden's office."

"What other liberties did you take?"

"None."

That she did not believe but for now let it lie. "Maybe you used one of your little Fireflies."

"Interesting theory."

"A local woman, Lana Long, came to see you in prison several times. You also wrote to her multiple times."

"Yes, she did. She was an entertaining diversion."

"How did you two connect?"

"I didn't reach out to her; she found me. There are women who are fascinated by men behind bars. Several women came to see me while I was incarcerated."

"You're a good-looking guy."

"I am." No bravado, simply a statement of fact. "These women can build elaborate fantasy worlds because they know I'm locked away. They always know where to find me, and I can't get involved in their worlds unless they want me to."

"That's what Lana wanted? To talk to a handsome man behind bars."

"Yes."

"It appears you two were never alone. Is that true? Prison wardens don't always know what's going on in their facilities."

"We always had three inches of glass between us."

"A trustee in the warden's office must have extra freedoms."

"Not that kind."

"Did she ever mention a boyfriend?"

"Other than Ryan, no."

She studied him closely, searching for signs of deception. "No one here in Missoula?"

"None."

"Did you get her to set the Beau-T-Shop fire? Maybe she was the one up in the hills practicing techniques you'd taught her."

"Why don't you ask her?"

She ignored the question. "Did she lose her nerve in the beauty shop? Is that why you had to kill her?"

His frown deepened as if he had been presented with a new math problem. "Lana's dead?"

"Burned to a crisp." She was intentionally blunt to shock him and perhaps provoke a reaction.

He closed his eyes for a moment and seemed genuinely shaken. "I didn't know she was the fatality."

"Really?"

"I liked Lana. I would never wish her harm. Check the prison records. You'll see that Lana and I first made contact back in January. They have samples of my correspondence."

"How many girls like Lana did you know?"

"You're suggesting I have this stable of women who set fires for me."

"You wouldn't be the first Svengali to get women to do your bidding."

His quick laugh was tainted with a bitter tone. "You should write for television."

Confessions of an Arsonist
I need more fire to burn the ice she has wrapped herself in. Soon. Soon. Soon.

CHAPTER
TWENTY-TWO

Missoula, Montana
Wednesday, September 9, 2020
2:00 p.m.

Joan pushed through the doors of Tucker's Diner, hearing the bell above her head as she entered. If only she had a nickel for every time she'd heard that damn bell or stood behind the counter and served coffee until 2:00 a.m. At least the late-night hours were quiet and allowed her to do the bulk of her studying. In fact, the regulars back then had toned down their chatter while she did her homework.

Dan Tucker stood behind the counter just as his father had ten years ago. The younger Tucker was fatter, his skin blotchier. She guessed the heavy drinking he did back in the day had finally caught up to him.

She took a seat at the end of the bar, waiting as he served up a platter of pancakes to a customer. On autopilot, he reached for a coffeepot and an ivory stoneware mug. But when his gaze crossed her face, he froze. "Well, look what the cat dragged in."

"Dragged me all the way from the East Coast."

He set the mug in front of her and smiled as he filled it. "It's good to see you, Joan."

She sipped. "Still the best coffee I've ever had."

"Damn right." He set the pot down. "I don't need any guesses to figure out why you're back in town, Detective. Mr. Weston should be worried."

"He doesn't seem too rattled."

"No, he never did. Always had a smirk on his face." He regarded her. "You didn't come here just for my coffee."

"I have questions, if you don't mind answering them."

"I'm an open book."

That she doubted. "I understand someone painted a few unkind words on the sidewalk outside his residence."

"I heard something about that," he said easily. "Are you here because of the graffiti?"

"I have bigger fish to fry."

"You going to prove Elijah set the Beau-T-Shop fire?"

"I have no jurisdiction here."

He laughed. "When did not having the authority ever stop you?"

"Never." She reached for a sugar packet, shook it, but did not bother to tear it open. "Why are you so against him, Dan? One thing to not like a guy but another to set up a citizens' action committee against him."

"You of all people should understand. He nearly burned you alive. He is a danger, and he will end up killing someone. It's a matter of time."

"I know why I should have a beef, but why you?"

"Maybe I don't like the idea of his kind of trouble. He doesn't belong here. The Halperns have lost their business, and if I lost the diner, I would be screwed."

"Why would he come after you?"

"Because my stuff burns as good as the next guy's."

"You set up your citizens' group long before the Halpern fire. There has to be more to what's motivating you."

"Do I need a personal reason?"

"No, but I'd bet you have one. Tell me why."

Dan sighed. "We went to high school together."

"Spit it out."

"Someone set my truck on fire in high school."

"Are you saying it was Elijah?"

"Yes!"

"But Elijah was never arrested or charged with that crime."

"But he did it. I know he did."

"How can you be so sure?"

"Because I was a little rough on Elijah in high school. I gave him a hard time. It was all fun and games, but he must have taken it personally."

Joan remembered that Tucker used to tease her when she worked at the diner. If it wasn't her Philly accent, it was the way she dressed or her plans to go to graduate school. He went out of his way to point out that she was an outsider. His teasing had quickly stopped being funny, and though she was good at ignoring him, someone less stable might have reacted differently.

"Your teasing is the reason Elijah set fire to your truck?"

"Yeah."

"Maybe you made someone else angry? You do have a gift for finding someone's weakness and pressing."

"You never seemed to mind."

"We're not talking about me."

"I knew from the beginning that Elijah was off. He was never like regular kids in high school. It was a matter of time before Elijah caused trouble then, and it's the same now," Tucker said. "The cops don't seem to be willing to do anything."

"The police don't have any evidence that he set the fire. Our judicial system is a little fussy about that."

"I don't need proof to make my case."

The underlying threat was clear, but she did not challenge it. "Did you know Lana Long?"

"Sure. Nice gal. Came in here from time to time."

She tore open the sugar packet and slowly poured it into her cup. "Did she date anyone that you know of?"

"I don't track the love lives of my customers."

Joan cocked her head. "Dan, you pay attention to everything."

He shrugged and pulled the dish towel tossed over his shoulder to wipe his hands. "Lana came in last week. It was a slow time of day."

"And?"

"She was dressed in tight jeans and had her hair done up. She was a handsome woman and didn't mind showing off her goods."

"And?"

"Ordered pancakes. Said she was celebrating, according to Nora."

"Nora?"

"Nora O'Neil. The waitress serving Lana's table."

"What did Lana tell Nora?"

"She said she was getting married."

"I don't suppose there was a name attached to that statement?"

"Nora asked, but Lana didn't say. Nora said she was sporting a big engagement ring on her ring finger."

"When was this?"

"Last week. Friday, maybe."

There had been no mention of a ring on Lana's body. "But she didn't say who gave it to her?"

"Whoever it was had money." He sniffed. "You should ask Darren."

"Darren Halpern. He owns the beauty shop with his wife."

"That's right."

"Why Darren?"

"He joined Lana at her booth table just as she was finishing up. They chatted. Looked like a boss talking to an employee. Aboveboard."

"Was it?"

He shrugged. "You'll have to ask him."

Joan leaned forward, catching a lingering scent of bacon on his white T-shirt. "Between us girls, Dan, how's the Halperns' marriage?"

"It's seen better times. They've shared a few silent and stony breakfasts."

"Lana's name ever come up in conjunction with either of them?"

"Not in front of me." His eyes narrowed. "Do you think she had something to do with the fire?"

"I have no idea." Lana died in the fire and had been connected to the Halpern couple. Had she been having an affair with Darren? A fire would be the perfect way to take care of financial issues and a mistress making trouble. "Can I get the Mountain High Pancakes?"

His grin did not reach his eyes. "You think you can handle them?"

"I know I can."

His easy expression hardened. "You're smart, and Gideon does a fine job of keeping the peace, but if you two don't get to the bottom of that fire *tout suite*, someone just might go after Elijah."

"Tell *someone* to hold off for a few days."

He studied her a beat and then tapped the counter with his fingers. "I'll get those pancakes."

Hardly a ringing acceptance, but it was the best she could hope for. She knew her brokered truce with him would not last long.

She ate the pancakes once they came, proud to leave Dan a clean plate. But when she reached for her wallet, he insisted her money was no good in his establishment. She thanked him and headed directly to the Halperns' office on State Street.

The brick building was a plain one-story structure with no distinguishable features. It looked as if it had been built fifty years ago and was in need of a major renovation. In Montana, real estate was at a premium, and she bet it was still expensive to rent.

She pushed through the front door and walked up to an empty receptionist station and waited a few seconds before knocking on the desk. "Anyone here?"

In the back, she heard papers shuffle, so she followed the sound to a small room in the back where a man knelt by a copier. He had opened the machine's front access door and was yanking on sheets of crumpled paper jammed inside.

Joan knocked on the doorjamb. "I'm looking for Darren Halpern."

The man glanced over his shoulder. He had salt-and-pepper hair, a face weathered by the sun, and bright-green eyes that peered over a pair of reading glasses. "I'm Darren."

She reached for her police ID out of habit but caught herself. "My name is Joan Mason."

He rubbed the back of his hand against his damp forehead. "What can I do for you?"

"I'm a cop and in town for a few days. I know a few things about arson, and I'm assisting Detective Bailey."

He placed a hand on his knee and, as he rose, stifled a groan. "I've driven by the shop. It's awful."

"What's with the knee? Looks like it hurts."

"Twisted it while I was hiking a few weeks ago. I always underestimate the terrain out here."

"It's beautiful country, but it does take its toll."

Darren was not swayed by her less-than-stellar attempt at small talk. "What do you want from me?"

"What can you tell me about Lana Long?"

"I didn't usually see much of her when I came by the shop."

"How many businesses do you and your wife own?"

"The beauty shop and a dozen houses in town that we're renovating."

"Are they doing well?"

"Yeah, sure. The beauty shop had great cash flow and was supposed to keep us afloat until the rental properties came online. Ask Becca Sullivan. She should have our bank statements now."

"When were these properties going to be available for rent?"

"Three months, four at the latest."

"Were you highly leveraged?"

Halpern shook his head. "Sounds like I should have a lawyer with me."

Instead of pressing, Joan shifted her line of questioning. "I'm trying to track down Lana Long," she lied. "Someone said she might be holed up with her boyfriend."

"I didn't realize she had a boyfriend, but I didn't know her that well."

"Apparently, she was sporting an engagement ring at the diner late last week. Dan Tucker said you two shared a booth."

"She texted Jessica and wanted to meet."

"But you met her?"

"My wife was packing for our trip to Chicago."

"What did Lana want to talk about?"

"She was quitting her job and heading back to Denver."

"Did you notice her ring?"

"I did not. She kept her hands in her lap, I think."

Darren's face projected a mixture of boredom and annoyance, but she could not tell if the reaction was genuine. "How much do you and your wife stand to make from the insurance company when the claim is settled?"

"You'll have to ask my wife. She handles all the finances. I handle the renovations."

"Would she tell you if there was a financial problem with the company?"

"There wasn't a problem." He tapped his index finger on the copier as his expression tightened. "I'm not answering any more questions without a lawyer."

As she turned to leave, she paused at the door and looked back at him. "You know what strikes me about Lana?"

"No, what?"

"She looks like a younger version of your wife."

"Get out," Darren said through clenched teeth. "Or I'm calling the cops."

She had hit a nerve. Good.

***

An express package was waiting for Gideon when he returned to his desk. It was from the warden of Montana State Prison. He shrugged off his jacket, hung it over the back of his chair, and sat. He ripped open the tab and removed the thin bundle of copied letters that had been written to Elijah James Weston, prisoner #2317104. There were letters from five women.

The warden indicated that Elijah had received many more letters in the last decade, but these were the only ones in Elijah's file. His staff was searching for the remaining letters.

Gideon knew the letters would never be found. The warden had said Elijah had worked in his office during his last year in prison. He likely had removed the letters.

The warden also indicated that because of Elijah's excellent record within the prison, he had been allowed six contact visits a year. These visits allowed the prisoner to hug or shake hands with the visitor and to sit across from each other at a table, not separated by glass. The women who visited Elijah Weston were Scottie Winter in 2014, Sarah Rogers in 2019, and Lana Long, who had visited him six times in 2020.

According to the warden, all the women were required to submit a questionnaire detailing not only basic facts about their lives but also if they had prison records. All Weston's visitors had been incarcerated at one point in their lives. Infractions included prostitution, identity theft, and narcotics possession.

There was nothing of real note in any of the letters. Given the strict guidelines of the prison, the letters simply detailed their day-to-day lives. On several occasions, the women would send books to Elijah via a mail-order book service. All the women except Joan were on Elijah's preapproved visitor list and were able to send him money via the prison systems.

Gideon set Joan's letters on top of the pile and studied her bold cursive handwriting. She had asked him several times in different ways why he had set the College Fire, but each time he had vehemently denied it. Finally, she had stopped asking, as if she hoped he would reveal his motivations. Elijah had never revealed anything significant about himself, and yet she had continued to write him right up to this year. Her last letter read:

> Elijah,
> It's been a few months. What can I say? Work's been crazy. I have a tough case on my docket. I am digging into case facts and motivations, but it seems the deeper I go, the more I come up empty. I want to solve this case badly, but as a friend of mine once said, "There are no guarantees in life," and that includes finding the answers that explain painful events.
>
> Excuse this grim, short letter. Perhaps my next one will be more upbeat when I am less reflective.
> Sincerely,
> Joan Mason

He glanced at the date. The letter had been written on February 7, 2020. He shifted to his computer and searched Avery Newport's name. Newport's house had burned down February 1, and Joan would have been in the early and, most would argue, ugliest stage of the investigation.

He pictured her sitting alone writing this letter. Was she pouring out her frustration to a man thousands of miles away and locked in prison? It didn't sound like she was working him as an asset at this point.

A knock on his door had him looking up to find Detective Sullivan. "Got a second? I have some of the Halperns' financials."

Gideon rose, and when she took the seat by his desk, he sat again. "Are they in debt?"

"Technically no. But they own several properties around the city that they're renovating. Right now, they're seeing negative cash flow, but by the first of the year, that should turn around."

"But . . ."

"They have a balloon payment due on the Beau-T-Shop building in December. That's going to be a tough payment for them to make unless they have a secret stash of cash that the IRS doesn't know about."

"If the insurance policy Jessica took out in February of 2020 pays out, they would be flush with legitimate cash."

"To the tune of two million dollars."

***

When Gideon saw Joan pull up in his driveway, he was somewhat surprised. She had said she wanted a hotel, but after a day of checking around, she'd likely realized it would cost a fortune. With the leaves turning and the air now crisp and clean, Missoula was inundated with tourists willing to pay high hotel rates.

"Is that Joan?" Kyle asked.

Gideon pushed away from the laptop he had placed on the dining room table next to Kyle and his homework. "It is."

"She's come to stay in the apartment?"

"I think so." If she was a target, Gideon liked the idea of having her near. He already knew he would be sleeping with one eye open until she left town.

"Is she going to eat with us?" Kyle asked. "It seems like the polite thing to do."

"Yes, it does." He watched Joan hoist her backpack on her shoulder and run her fingers through her short hair. It had been longer in college, soft as silk, and as thick as a horse's mane. He had liked the way it skimmed the top of her breasts when she was on top of him.

He shoved the memory aside, recalling that her hair had been scorched in the College Fire and that she had cropped it short. Why she had kept it that way over the years, he did not know, but it seemed to suit the person she was now.

Her head bowed, she glanced at her phone and then walked up to the front door. Kyle moved past him, opening it just as she'd rung the bell.

When she looked at Kyle, Gideon sensed she was again searching for signs of Helen. He was not sure how he would have reacted if he were staring at a child Joan had given birth to just nine months after they had broken up.

"Hey, kid," she said with a smile. "Have you gotten taller since I saw you last?"

Kyle rose up a fraction. "People don't grow that fast."

"Grown people don't, but ten-year-olds do." She scrutinized him. "Yep, definitely taller."

Kyle wrinkled his nose. "You smell like smoke."

"I can't seem to shake the smell."

"Come on inside," Gideon said. "I can give you something to wear while we run your clothes through the washer."

She tightened her hand on the strap of her backpack, and he wondered if she was remembering the times when she'd worn his shirt as they'd sat together on a rare Sunday morning drinking coffee and doing homework.

"Sounds like a plan." Joan stepped inside and looked around at the vaulted ceiling. "Nice place. Wasn't this your grandfather's house?"

"Good memory. It was the original house on the property. My dad and mom built their own place after they married. That's where Ann lives now."

"Ah. You were right about hotel prices. Ouch."

"We're known for our sticker shock," he said.

"Offer still open to crash?" she asked.

"It is," he said.

Joan gripped her backpack's worn strap. "Can you show me where you want me? And I'll get out of your hair. I don't want to intrude more than I have."

"I can take her to the garage apartment," Kyle offered.

"We'll both go," Gideon said.

"A formal escort," she said. "I like it."

The trio moved through the house and out the back door. Across a large graveled area, he led her to the three-car garage and the side door that led to the apartment.

They climbed the stairs to the second floor, and he switched on the light. The apartment, which extended across the top of the garage, had been his home for several years after his divorce. He had been strapped financially, and his grandfather needed an extra set of eyes on him, so it had worked out for everyone. When he subsequently inherited the property, it had been good for Kyle to have a firm home base.

The apartment was almost twelve hundred square feet. There were two bedrooms, with a bathroom, a small kitchen, and a living area with a wide-screen television and overstuffed sofas. It was decorated solely to a man's taste.

"Wow, some garage," Joan said. "I was thinking tiny."

"It's Montana," Gideon said.

She smiled. "Right."

"Dad said when I'm a teenager, I can live here," Kyle said.

"Dad said he would think about it," Gideon said easily.

"That's only three years away," Kyle pointed out.

"I'm very aware," Gideon said, feeling his age. "Joan, there are extra clothes in the front bedroom, in the dresser. Plenty of soap and shampoo, towels, the whole deal in the bathroom."

She walked to the back door and stared out its window. "Don't suppose you have a fire escape?"

Gideon moved to the closet and pointed to a boxed fire ladder that could be hung off the windowsill in seconds. "I always do."

"Thanks," she said.

"Are you having dinner with us?" Kyle asked.

Joan looked to Gideon. "You don't have to feed me."

"It's hamburgers on the grill and salad. Nothing fancy."

"Sounds good to me. Give me fifteen minutes."

"Take your time." Gideon laid his hand on Kyle's shoulder and guided the boy toward the door. A part of him wished he could have Joan all to himself for a few hours. He wanted to talk to her about the investigation, find out more about what she had done the last ten years, why she had pressed so hard on the Newport investigation, and a million other things.

But he was not alone. Kyle was there, and the three of them would have to make the best of it.

Confessions of an Arsonist

The time has come. My patience is extinguished. She will die.

CHAPTER
TWENTY-THREE

Missoula, Montana
Wednesday, September 9, 2020
6:00 p.m.

Joan's washed hair was damp and brushed flat, and her smoky clothes were in the washer, now agitating on the heavy-duty cycle. Gideon's oversize flannel shirt, drawstring sweats, and wool socks swallowed Joan's frame as she stood in front of the dresser mirror.

She raised the shirtsleeve to her nose and inhaled a scent she remembered clearly as Gideon's. She closed her eyes and wished she could turn back the clock and make different choices. Most days, she never allowed those kinds of thoughts, because wallowing in the past accomplished nothing. But to have his scent literally touching every square inch of her body made it impossible to ignore what they used to have.

"Shit," she muttered. "Keep moving forward and don't look back."

She quickly headed down the stairs and across the driveway to the main house. She considered knocking but then opted to just push right into the house. Warmth and the scent of burgers grilling coaxed her toward the kitchen, where Gideon was serving them up on huge buns. There was a large kitchen island with three place settings.

"Smells good," she said.

"I cooked yours medium rare. You still eat it that way?"

"I do."

"And no cheese, right?" he asked as he reached for a stack of individually wrapped slices of orange cheese.

She shrugged as she stood next to a chair at the island. "As I've grown older, I've become more open to cheese."

"It happens to the best of us."

"Can I help you with anything?" Joan asked.

"Get whatever you want to drink out of the refrigerator and then pick a seat."

"Will do." She opened the refrigerator. "What can I get for you and Kyle?"

"Beer for me and milk for Kyle. He'll be down in a minute."

She snagged two cold bottles of beer and the carton of milk. She grabbed a glass from the cabinet and filled it with milk. After she'd set the milk glass on the table, she twisted off the beer tops. She handed a beer to Gideon. "Where is he?"

"Finishing up homework."

"How's it going with the investigation? Any updates on the Halperns' financials?"

Gideon carefully peeled off the first cheese's plastic wrapper. "A couple of financial reports came in today. The Halperns have countless credit cards and have been moving balances from one to the other. They are up to date on the minimum payments."

"What about insurance?"

"The salon is insured for up to two million dollars."

Joan sipped her beer. "Dan saw Darren with Lana at the diner late last week. When I went to see Darren, he said Lana wanted to give her notice."

Gideon paused, the fingers of his right hand curling and flexing. "You talked to Darren?"

She took a pull on her beer, ignoring the tension humming under his words. "In for a penny, in for a pound." She grinned.

"Joan, this is my investigation. You are a guest."

"You can be mad, or you can listen. I don't have a lot of time in Missoula and can't waste an opportunity."

He drew in a slow, steady breath. She knew he was still pissed, but he was also too practical to ignore good evidence. "Did Dan give you any idea why he despises Elijah?"

"Seems there was an arson incident back in high school. Someone torched Dan's new truck. He reported it, but the police never linked it to Elijah. You must have known Dan in high school."

"Yeah, sure. He played ball along with Clarke and me."

"What was he like?"

"Dan was a hotshot in those days. That truck was a gift from his dad because Dan caught a winning touchdown. Turned him into a town hero for a couple of months. He had big dreams, but after high school, he ended up working at the diner."

"He used to talk about his glory days when I worked with him."

"Dan understands that he needs to stay clear of Elijah, correct?"

"I strongly encouraged him to give us time."

"And will he?"

"For now." Joan's gaze was drawn to Gideon's wrist and his black watch face. The sweep-second hand ticked past the date, reminding her that her time here was fading. "Don't suppose the medical examiner received any preliminary DNA results on the fetus?"

"Not yet. He's fighting the backlog at the state laboratory." He sipped his beer. "I was able to pull up a text message chain between Lana and an unknown boyfriend."

"Really? Is he here in town?"

"Seems that way. She was threatening to expose their affair. This was early last week."

"For what it's worth, my theory is fairly simple. Darren starts an affair with Lana, she threatens to tell the missus, and he decides to kill two birds with one stone."

"Great theory, but he was in Chicago at the time of the fire," Gideon said.

"According to whom? His wife? Maybe she liked the idea of taking care of two problems at once." She rubbed her thumb against her index and middle fingers. "Money, money, money."

"She's provided me with a list of places where they were in Chicago, as well as credit card receipts."

"Do you have security footage at these establishments corroborating the purchases? Otherwise, anyone could have swiped their credit cards for them."

"I'm working on that. I've been on the phone most of the day requesting security footage."

"The DNA of Lana's baby will be the ace in the hole."

"I hope you're right."

The boy's heavy footfalls reminded Joan of how her dad's liquor bottles would rattle when she raced in after school.

Kyle hurried into the room as Gideon was pulling a sheet pan of french fries from the oven. The boy washed his hands and, drying them quickly, tossed the towel in a ball on the counter. He plopped in his chair with a big grin.

She was tempted to assign him the nickname Bamm-Bamm but decided to keep her distance, knowing she was leaving on Sunday. They each grabbed burgers, fries, and whatever condiment seemed to suit. Ketchup was the winner, hands down.

As they ate, she listened to Kyle chatter about his day as Gideon asked pointed questions that displayed real interest in his son's life. She remembered now why she had been so drawn to the Bailey family, and most especially Gideon. What would it have been like if Gideon had gotten her pregnant and Kyle was their child? She quickly chased away the answer.

"Nate just texted me a picture of the burned shed," Kyle said.

Joan had been careful not to question Kyle about Nate, knowing Gideon would be as touchy as Ann had been when she'd interviewed Nate. But she was paying close attention.

Gideon cleared his throat as he grabbed a french fry. "What did he say?"

"Not much. He said it's still warm in spots."

"Yeah," she said easily. "It was tough to put out."

"That's what Nate said." His tone was a mixture of wonder and skepticism. "He said the hose almost didn't reach all the way."

She let the boy's comment dangle like bait for Gideon. She had promised not to tell, but if Nate had told Kyle and Kyle told his father . . .

"How much of the fire did Nate see?" Gideon asked.

"He didn't start it," Kyle said.

"Okay." Gideon's gaze immediately shifted to Joan. "Did Nate see how it started?"

"Nope, he was just outside and saw it go up."

"What was he doing outside, pal?" Gideon asked.

Kyle shrugged as if he realized he might have said something wrong. "I don't know."

"Yeah, you do," Gideon said.

Kyle dropped the last half of his burger to the plate. He looked as if he might argue but then sighed. "When he can't sleep, he goes to the firepit and hangs out."

"Does he set fires?" Gideon asked.

"No," Kyle rushed to say. "Aunt Ann would kill him."

"Yes, she would," Gideon said.

"Why does he like the idea of setting fires?"

"I don't know. He didn't say. Is he in trouble?" Kyle asked.

"No, he's not in trouble." Gideon shifted the conversation toward sports, and soon the three were arguing the merits of the Denver Broncos versus the Philadelphia Eagles.

When Kyle asked to be excused and cleared his plate, Joan sat, feeling all Gideon's unasked questions bubbling below the surface.

"You didn't tell me Nate was outside before the fire," he said.

"Ann asked me to keep it between us."

He was quiet for a moment, staring at her with an expression reserved for suspects. "I understand the need to protect your own child. Ann loves Nate. And we all know he's bright as hell, a little quirky, and we all love him. He and Kyle are best friends."

"I'm waiting for the *but*." She sipped the last of her beer, knowing she would soon need another one.

"I know Nate loves the bonfires at the games. I admit, there've been times I thought that was the only reason he came."

"His dad's a firefighter. Makes sense, I suppose."

"Joan, did Nate set that fire?"

Joan had asked herself that question a dozen times since last night. "I don't believe so. He thought he saw someone run off into the woods."

"He saw someone?"

"That's what he said. He didn't see the person's face and can't identify him."

"It was a man."

"He thinks so."

"And Nate was outside because he has trouble sleeping?"

She thought about Elijah in college and all the reading he did at the diner when he could not sleep.

"What aren't you telling me?" he asked.

She met his gaze head-on. "You know everything I know."

"Bull."

She shrugged. "I can't help it if you don't believe me."

He sat back, still regarding her. "Elijah's warden sent me the letters he had on file from the women who wrote him."

She folded her arms. "And?"

"You wrote to him a few days after the Newport fire."

"I've written to him plenty of times. Feel free to read all of them."

"I've read a few."

She arched a brow. "And what was your impression?"

He dodged the question. "Why did you write him?"

A half smile tugged at the edge of her lips. "Like I've said. Insight."

"His letters offered insight into your case?"

She rubbed her temple with her fingertips. "And that's when I cut off contact."

"Do you want to talk about the Newport case?"

"Why? The charges against Avery Newport have been dropped. I gambled that an arrest and an interrogation would get me a confession. Instead, they got me a suspension."

"We've all miscalculated. It makes us human."

Her gaze softened, and for a second, he saw the woman who had trusted him and loved him until he had left her behind in a fire. "That still doesn't make it acceptable."

***

Jessica Halpern had been ignoring the cops and her husband all day. And now, as she drove up to the mountain cabin, far out of cell service, she could finally get a status report. She was anxious to see him and ask what the hell she was supposed to do about Gideon. The detective was digging deeper into the fire than she had ever expected. The cops had not announced the identity of the fire fatality, but she knew it had to have been Lana.

Too bad for Lana, if she was the one who had gotten cooked in the fire. The girl reminded her a little of herself at that age. She knew how to cut hair, she had a knack for hair color, and she was ambitious. But when she was not working, she was stirring shit up and creating problems among the other girls.

She parked, leaving the car engine on and the headlights shining on the rustic cabin that had been built as overnight lodging for hunters. Heat came from a wood-burning stove, and the water source was the stream that she had passed a few hundred feet below the cabin.

When she and Darren had married, they had shared a weekend here. To say it had been fun would be a lie. Both were in serious creature-comfort detox within the hour, and even though Darren kept the fire banked high, it had been one of the coldest nights of her life. They had packed up first thing the next morning and returned to town. Still, she had not gotten around to selling the place, because there was no better place to meet in secret.

She honked the horn three times, their signal that it was her.

A figure passed in front of the window, and the front door opened. He stayed back in the shadows just out of reach of her headlights. All this cloak-and-dagger shit annoyed her. They both had a reason to keep their mouths shut, so hiding in the shadows seemed unnecessary. She shut off the engine.

"Come inside," he said.

She grabbed the paper bag on the front seat and walked to the open front door. "Do you have my ring?"

"I do."

"The last thing I need is for the cops to figure out that Lana was wearing my ring."

"She promised she would keep our engagement a secret."

She chuckled. "Really? You give a rock to a girl like that, and you think she's not going to tell anyone?" For the first time, he looked slightly dumbfounded. Men. "We need to wrap up our business. It's cold, and I want to get back to town."

"I have something for you."

She held up the paper bag. "This is for you, as we agreed upon. Now, give me back my ring."

He fished the ring out of his pocket and held it out. When she stepped toward him, she had to look up to meet his gaze. She was tall for a woman and liked a good-size man.

He took her hand and carefully threaded the ring on her finger. His calloused touch sent a ripple through her, and she remembered how good those hands had felt on her body. If only she had time for a session between the sheets.

He grabbed her by the wrist, tightened his hold. He was not hurting her, but he was showing her who was boss. She had always liked it when he manned up.

"Let go of me," she said.

He yanked her toward him until her breasts were pressed against his chest. His hot breath brushed her neck, and she knew his gaze had dropped to her full cleavage.

"Step inside," he ordered.

His voice had a smoky quality that made her tingle a little. Every time they fucked, it was always so good.

Thrusting her lip out into a small pout, she flicked her head back as she traced her finger down the center of his chest. "What are we going to do inside?"

"Find out."

He turned and went into the cabin, confident that she would follow. And she did. She liked what the wild woods did to him and what he then did to her.

The interior was dark except for several flickering candles on the hearth of the large woodstove that dominated the cabin's single room. He closed the door behind her and took her hand in his. He pulled her toward the small bed in the corner of the room, and she willingly lay down and angled her body up on pillows. The moonlight caught the contoured edges of his face as he straddled her. She ran her hands up and down his hard thighs.

"I don't have long," she said.

"This won't take any time at all."

Before she could question him, he'd wrapped his hands around her neck and had begun to squeeze. They had played games like this before, but this time was different. He was rougher, and there was a darkness in his gaze she had never seen before. "What are you doing?"

He smiled and squeezed tighter. "Killing you."

She waited a beat to see if this was just another twist to one of their past fantasies. But as the pressure grew tighter and her air supply stopped, survival instincts took over. She arched back, connecting her knee with his groin.

He grunted while his grip slackened enough for her to roll toward the edge of the bed. "This is not funny," she gasped.

"It's not meant to be." Pain strained his voice, even as he recovered quickly.

As her feet hit the floor, he grabbed a handful of her hair and yanked her back. "Stop it! You're hurting me."

"You never complained before," he said. He was enjoying this.

"You were never like this before." Panic echoed from every syllable. She struck out, connecting the flat of her hand with his jaw.

He grinned and pinned her arms down with his legs. She tried to sit up, determined to bite and scratch to stop him. She just needed to get out of there and to her car.

"What the hell?" she shouted. "Why are you doing this? We are on the same side."

"I can't have you telling." He punched her hard in the mouth, snapping her head back. The pain was blinding, and she could feel her grip on consciousness slipping along with the pain.

The blow stunned her. Her anger vanished as fear took hold. She tried to free her hands to claw his eyes, but he drove his knees deeper into the flesh of her arms.

His hands came around her neck again, and this time she felt him grow hard. Was this a game for him? He'd had trouble getting it up the last time. God, she prayed it was a game.

But his grip banded her neck like a vise, and again her airflow stopped. She stared into his eyes, seeing a grim determination. As the seconds passed and the pressure intensified, she realized she had gambled with the devil and lost.

***

He stepped outside the cabin, his heart striking his chest like a boxer's fist. Adrenaline coursed through his body as he thought about Jessica and his hands around her throat. "Damn, it was better than sex."

He hurried to the trunk of his car and grabbed three gallon-size plastic jugs of gasoline and then started in the bedroom, carefully dousing her face and body with the gasoline before he trailed a stream of it through the living room and out onto the porch. He opened all the cabin windows, knowing his fires fed best on a large supply of fresh air.

"You pushed too hard, Jessica," he said. "You made too many demands and forgot who was really in charge."

He stood over her lifeless body, perhaps a little sorry he did not get some before offing her. Gently, he lifted her hand and stared at the ring that he had used to convince Lana they were on the same side, so she'd stay quiet.

Once outside, he backed up a good dozen feet and lit the gasoline trail. The blue-and-white flame sprinted along the accelerant up the porch stairs and into the open front door. He fished a camera from his car and trained it on the fire, documenting the way the flames grew taller and angrier.

CHAPTER
TWENTY-FOUR

"A call came in from Darren Halpern," Becca said over the phone.

Gideon shifted the phone to his left hand as he rose up out of his bed and glanced at the clock on his bedside table. On a typical day, he should have gotten another half hour of sleep, but typical was rare in his line of work.

He sat up and swung his legs over the side of the bed. "What did he say?"

"His wife is missing, so he said he drove up to the family cabin in the hills. Instead of finding her, he discovered the cabin had burned to the ground."

"What?" he asked, rubbing sleep from his eyes. "When was he there?" The cold from the floor crept into his bones.

"About two a.m. He had to drive to the nearest gas station to get cell service. An officer is bringing him into town."

"Good. Keep him at the station. I'll be out as quickly as I can."

He dressed in minutes and, when he emerged from his room, walked down to Kyle's room. He crossed the boy's bedroom floor, littered with yesterday's discarded clothes, socks, and shoes, and sat on the edge of his bed. The boy lay on his belly, his arm flung over the side with his mouth open. His face was relaxed, as if he had not a care in the world.

Gideon rubbed him on the back. "Kyle, you're going to have to get up. Got to take you to Aunt Ann's."

"I'm sleeping."

"I know, buddy. I got a call."

He yanked the pillow over his head.

Gideon tugged back his covers. "Rise and shine."

"Can I stay with Joan?"

"No. Aunt Ann."

The boy's groans of complaint followed him as he strode out of the room and flipped on the light.

As Gideon hurried down the stairs, he was hit by the scent of coffee. Joan, never a good sleeper, was addicted to the brew.

Leaning on the kitchen counter, she stared at the pot, probably willing it to work faster. His attention shifted to her bottom, still as round and firm as he remembered.

Gideon cleared his throat.

She straightened, turning as if he was interrupting a private moment. "Your little apartment has a good bed but no coffee."

"How did you get in the house?"

"You have a set of keys in the apartment. I had to try three before the back door opened. You really should consider color coding them. They all look alike in the dark." She had drawn back behind her trademark humor and sarcasm.

Maybe she was right. Distance was better for everyone. He reached for his phone and texted Ann. Her reply was quick. She would be glad to drive Kyle to school. "I'll keep that in mind."

"The house rises early."

"I got a call." He did not hesitate to fill her in. "Jessica Halpern is missing. Darren drove to his cabin last night and discovered it burned to the ground."

She folded her arms and blinked. "Really? And where is Mr. Halpern now?"

"An officer is bringing him into town. I'm headed to the cabin to survey the damage."

"I want to come."

No *may I* or *please*. "I leave in fifteen minutes. First stop is Ann's so I can drop Kyle off."

"I'll be ready."

"You ride with me. Hate to lose you in the dark up in the mountains."

He reached around her for his travel mug. She smelled like the lilac shampoo left behind by Christie, a gal he had dated when he lived in the apartment. The scent had always suited Christie but smelled too fussy on Joan. Something spicy would have befitted her.

Gideon grabbed the travel mug, and as he reached for the pot, she did not shift out of his way, and his arm brushed against hers. Under the soft knit sleeve was sculpted muscle. He was not sure if she was just lost in thought or wanted him to touch her. That was the way it was with Joan. She always had him in a pretzel of emotion.

As if she had made her point, she pushed away from the counter and crossed to the refrigerator. She hefted the gallon-size jug and jostled the remaining contents around. "Does Kyle take milk with his cereal?"

"Yes."

She replaced the milk without taking any.

"Go ahead and drink it. I can make him toast."

"No, I'll save what remains for him. It doesn't feel right disrupting his routine. It's his world. Not mine."

No truer words. She was a visitor in his world, and he would be smart to remember it.

***

As Gideon drove, Joan watched as the sun rose above the eastern horizon and remembered her first winter in Missoula. It had been miserable. She had always thought Philly winters were brutal, but out here, the weatherman measured snow in feet rather than inches, and extreme wind drove temps well below zero. She had never really gotten warm that first winter, and by late January, she had been compiling transfer applications to colleges in Florida, Texas, and Arizona.

But a lack of funds to pay for her transfer applications had led to the diner job. The work was hard, but she liked Old Man Tucker. By spring break, she had her application money and had sent off her forms. In late May, she was accepted to both the University of Arizona and the University of Central Florida, but by then, the weather had warmed, bringing with it blooming flowers. Montana had seduced her into staying for another year. The cycle replayed during her sophomore year and her junior year. And then she had met Gideon, and the winters no longer felt the least bit cold.

Gideon downshifted and slowed to make the turn on a dirt road she would have missed if she were driving. "How did you find this place?"

"This county is my beat. You know all the back alleys and side streets in your jurisdiction."

"Point taken."

He wound up the washed-out road, and when he rounded the final corner, she saw the log structure. The walls were intact, but a portion of the roof had collapsed, allowing tendrils of smoke to hiss out. There was a fire truck on scene, with two firefighters pumping water into what had been the front door of the cabin.

"The old logs are harder to burn than most realize," he said. "The inside can be devastated with an exterior still standing."

Out of the car, Joan accepted a pair of protective gloves from Gideon. She worked her fingers inside and slipped on the mask.

"Rick," Gideon said. "This is Joan Mason. Joan, this is Sheriff Rick Sexton."

"Pleasure," she said.

Rick was in his early thirties, tall, lean, and sporting thick blond hair. His gaze was wary, as if he was wondering what the hell she was doing there.

"What can you tell me?" Gideon asked.

"Fire was set in the living room. Appears to have been a small plastic tub of gasoline that was ignited. The flames caught the curtains and rug on fire. However, the furniture is ancient and stuffed with horsehair. It's not as flammable as the modern stuff we buy."

Joan looked toward the blue tarp that covered the shape of a human form. "Who's that?"

Rick looked at Joan. "Who are you, Joan Mason?"

"She's a homicide detective from Philadelphia," Gideon said. "She's worked several arson cases back east and is assisting."

Rick did not look like the answer satisfied him. "The purse and ID we found in the vehicle matches Jessica Halpern; however, the body was badly burned. Whoever torched the place doused her body with gasoline first. She's not recognizable, so the medical examiner will have to confirm the identification with dental records."

"Any idea of the cause of death?" Gideon asked.

"Impossible for me to tell," Rick said.

"By now, Darren should be at my office waiting to be questioned," Gideon said. "I sent my officer to go get him."

"He called in the fire," Rick said.

"Many arsonists do," Joan offered.

"You're getting ahead of yourself," Gideon said.

"Perhaps," she conceded.

"Can we walk inside?" Gideon asked.

"The fire is out, but it'll be hot. I can't speak to the integrity of the building."

"I'll take my chances," Gideon said.

"Fine. But she stays out."

"Why?" Joan demanded.

"Because this isn't Missoula but Granite County, and they have vastly different rules," Gideon explained.

"Out here, you're a civilian," Rick said.

"How about some professional curiosity?" Sure, she was on leave, but they had not taken her badge yet.

"Nope," Rick said. "Too much liability."

"Do I look like someone who would sue?" she asked.

"Doesn't matter," Rick said.

"Stay," Gideon said. "I'll be right back."

As Gideon stepped inside the water-soaked living room, Rick received a call that took him back to his vehicle. Joan immediately moved closer to the house, stopping short of stepping inside. She watched as Gideon approached the blue tarp. He squatted and carefully lifted the edge, his face drawing into a frown as he studied the body.

When he glanced her way, she shouted, "What does her neck look like?"

He dropped his gaze and then reached for his phone and took several pictures. Finally, he covered the body and rose. When he joined her out on the porch, his face was grim and a shade paler. One more image to carry.

"Do you think it's Jessica Halpern?" she asked as they stepped away from the cabin. "How did her neck look?"

"Her head was twisted at an odd angle, but the skin was too blackened to make any visual determination. The damage to the body was extensive."

Joan nodded as she followed Gideon's train of thought. "This time, the killer wanted to make damn sure she was dead."

"Her face was all but gone," he said.

"Jessica took out the insurance policy, knowing she needed money. Darren could have snuck out of Chicago, killed Lana, burned the beauty shop down, and then returned. We have credit card receipts but no footage yet of him swiping any of his cards."

"Jessica could have also hired someone to do the dirty work," he said. "Burn down her business while she's out of town, and then they return as the victims."

"If we go that route, Jessica hadn't counted on Lana's death, and maybe she panicked. Maybe she got cold feet and said she was going to the cops."

"You saw Darren when?" Gideon asked.

"Yesterday afternoon at about three. I brought up Lana but didn't mention she was dead. My questions could have spooked him. Maybe he calls Jessica and they plan to meet up here. She's no shrinking violet and calls him out for Lana. She suspects the affair with Lana, and their fight gets ugly. He strangles her and burns the place down."

"Easy for him to get up here, kill Jessica, change, and return to the store to call for help."

"Though why would Darren set the fire at the Bailey ranch?" she asked.

"Maybe he wants to shift the blame to Elijah, who is a very convenient scapegoat. Not a coincidence that the beauty shop burned after Elijah's prison release. A fire at the ranch near you and Ann would circle back to the College Fire."

"It's plausible, but crime is rarely that complicated or that well planned," Joan said. "Motivations, like most people, are generally simple."

"That's basically true," Gideon said. "Wonder if John Pollock knew the Halperns?"

Joan shrugged. "Each agrees to torch the other's property and provide an alibi."

Gideon rubbed the back of his neck. "Now you're straying back into complicated."

***

When Gideon and Joan arrived in town, Becca greeted them in the hallway by the stairs. "Darren Halpern is waiting in the conference room. He keeps asking about his wife."

"There was a body in the cabin," Gideon said to Becca.

"Is it Mrs. Halpern?" Becca asked.

"We've not made an ID yet."

Becca's expression turned grim. "When a wife goes missing, my money is always on the husband," Becca said.

"We'll follow the facts, Becca," Gideon said.

"You're the boss," Becca said.

"I'd like to be present when you talk to Darren," Joan said.

"It's one thing to walk a scene but another to participate in an official interview," Gideon said.

"Darren has not been charged." She hung up her jacket on a peg and rubbed her hands together. "We're just having an informal chat, right?"

Gideon realized he liked working with Joan. She had a sharp mind, and it turned in directions his did not. He could follow A to B to C and could dig deep into the details. She saw the same facts but through a different prism. "Right."

"Then why not have me along? He might be the type who underestimates a woman. Most men do."

Becca's eyes widened with amusement, but she did not comment.

Gideon shook his head. "Anyone who underestimates you does so at their own risk."

Her grin contained a rare glimpse of humor. "I tend to agree."

"I'll let you in, but don't talk."

She held up her first two fingers. "I swear I will be quiet."

"You're not a Scout," Becca said.

"The oath thing applies to everyone, right?" Joan asked.

"Don't say a word, Joan," Gideon warned.

"I promise." She followed him down the hallway and paused while he made two cups of coffee.

"I don't need coffee," she said.

"It's not for you. It's for him."

"And here I was assuming." She shook her head.

"Can't do that."

"Won't again."

Inside the room, they found Darren sitting at the end of the table reading his phone as he tapped his foot. Gideon closed the door, and Darren rose immediately. "Did you find my wife?"

Gideon set the coffee cup in front of Darren and waited as Joan took a seat in the far corner. He sat and asked the man to do the same. "When was the last time you saw your wife?"

"Yesterday," he said. "We were staying in town. She was very upset about the fire. She'd been on the phone most of the morning with the insurance company. I told her to be calm, but she lost it. She took off and said she needed time alone."

"And you thought she went to the cabin?"

"It's where she goes from time to time when she needs quiet."

"Does she need quiet a lot?" Gideon asked.

"More lately."

"No cell service ensures quiet," Gideon said.

"The cabin is off the grid completely."

"When did you decide to drive up to see if your wife was there?"

"After she visited me," he said, nodding to Joan. "I knew it was a matter of time before the cops blamed us for the fire."

"And now your cabin has burned," Joan said quietly.

Gideon tamped down a rush of frustration as he shifted his chair, deliberately dragging the metal feet against the floor. "Go on, Mr. Halpern?"

"I saw the smoke above the trees as I was driving to the cabin," Darren said quickly. "I floored it and raced toward it. I could see the fire had destroyed the building."

"Did you go inside?" Gideon asked.

"It was still too hot. I drove back to the nearest landline and called the cops. Look, I've been calling my wife for hours, and no answer. I need to find her."

Gideon sipped his coffee, taking an extra beat to gather his thoughts. "We're looking for her. But if you don't mind, I want to circle back to the Beau-T-Shop fire and Lana," he said.

Darren's brow furrowed. "What does Lana have to do with this?"

Gideon dropped his voice a fraction, as if he and Darren were allies and confidants. "Turns out she was pregnant."

"Pregnant. Okay. A couple of the girls in the store have gotten pregnant."

Darren was tense, but his lower limbs remained still and his hands relaxed. When folks lied, they might be able to control their face and hands, but the lower body had a tendency to shift and move, as if the truth needed to get released somehow.

"She was about eight to ten weeks pregnant," Gideon said.

"What does that have to do with Jessica or the fires? Is there something you aren't telling me?"

Gideon ignored the question. "Would Jessica have known about the pregnancy?"

"Sure. It's possible. The ladies in the shop told her things, and they came to her when they were in trouble. Look, if you want to know more about Lana's life, talk to Nora O'Neil. I think they were friends."

"Where can I find Nora O'Neil?"

"She lives on the west side of town." He reached for his phone and pulled up her contact information and then texted it to Gideon. "Call her. She works at Tucker's Diner."

His phone dinged with the text. "I'll talk to her today." He turned his phone facedown on the table. "Tell me about John Pollock."

"Who?"

"Pollock. He said he knew you." Lying was a tool in his arsenal he used whenever necessary.

Darren shrugged. "I have no idea who he is."

"He lives up in Helena. He told me to tell you to say hi when I saw you."

"Okay. But I still don't know the name. Should I?" Darren asked.

"His business burned to the ground last year," Gideon said.

"What are you saying?"

"Both of you had similar fires and significant insurance coverage."

"Are you saying I had something to do with any of the fires?"

"Now that you brought it up, did you?"

Darren sat back and held up his hands. "I don't like the turn of this conversation. You still have not told me about Jessica. Have you found her?"

"We found a body in the cabin," Gideon said. "We cannot make a visual identification. The medical examiner will have to ID the body."

Darren raised his fingers to his lips as his eyes widened. "It can't be Jessica. I just spoke to her yesterday."

"We have transported the body to the medical examiner and are waiting on Jessica's dental records."

"Dental records?" He closed his eyes. "Jesus."

"You'll need to stay in town and keep your phone with you," Gideon said.

He fingered his phone as if it were a lifeline. "Do I need an attorney?"

"That's your call," Gideon said, matter of fact.

"You've accused me of arson."

"I have not," Gideon said. "I'm just gathering facts now."

"You both think I had something to do with all this."

"Two women you know are dead," Gideon said.

"I didn't kill them!" Darren shouted.

Gideon stood. "I hope not."

Darren's gaze shot to Joan, and he pointed at her. "She grilled me yesterday at my office. Is she a cop?"

Gideon tossed a half glance toward Joan. "She's a detective, and a very good one."

"Mr. Tucker said you and Lana met at the diner last week," Joan said.

"I told you she was giving me her notice!" Darren said.

"Did Lana say why she was quitting?" Gideon asked.

Darren stabbed his fingers through his hair. "I have no idea. Girls come and go in this business."

"Tucker said he saw you and your wife fighting at the diner," Joan said calmly.

Gideon realized Joan was baiting Halpern. Sometimes it was a smart play to go easy on a witness and other times better to stoke their temper. He decided to let the next few seconds play out before he shut it down.

Darren rose. "Unless I'm under arrest, I'm leaving."

"You're not under arrest," Gideon said.

"Then I'm leaving." Darren marched out of the conference room, and when he reached the main door, he opened it and then slammed it shut.

"We touched a few nerves," Joan said with a grin. "The question is, which one lit his fuse?"

***

Elijah was filled with a restless energy that made it impossible for him to read another word. So he closed his book and started walking. Paying no attention to the time or direction he was headed, he looked up, spotted Joan and Ann's old street, and made his way to their former address.

Of course, the house had been rebuilt. And by the looks of it, it was an improvement over the last. No doubt it still housed college students, just as it had before.

He closed his eyes, imagining what the old place looked like, but he found the memory shrouded in haze. What was not lost in time was the night he had spent with Ann. He had replayed their lovemaking so many times over the last ten years. He remembered every touch, kiss, taste, and sound.

He had served his sentence and was technically free, but he still remained locked out of Ann's life. Elijah was no longer a kid who was unsure of himself. He was now a man who knew exactly what he wanted and how to get it. It would not be long before he'd find a way to shatter that glass wall keeping Ann and him apart.

"I'm coming, Ann," he whispered.

As he rounded the corner and walked back to the boardinghouse, footsteps raced up behind him. The hurried, almost frantic sounds had his body tensing as his hands curled into fists. The good thing about prison: you learned to fight, or you got the shit beat out of you.

As he turned, ready to fight, a baseball bat connected with his shoulder. The pain rocketed through his body, but as he struggled to right himself, he was violently shoved off balance and fell to the ground. Experience kicked into high gear, and he reached for the knife in his pocket.

A booted foot connected with his ribs, giving him an opportunity to flick open the switchblade. He wasted no time plunging it into the attacker's inner thigh. Warm blood on his hand told him he had sliced flesh.

The footsteps immediately retreated, and he looked up to see the man's hooded face, covered with a black ski mask. The eyes glistened, but he could not identify the man.

Elijah's ribs jabbed with pain, but he forced himself to stand so he could face his enemy. "Don't leave. We are just getting started."

The man took a step back. "Get the fuck out of town."

"I'm not going anywhere." This was his home, and he was prepared to kill anyone to prove it.

Confessions of an Arsonist
Burning her pictures gives me some satisfaction.
Too bad it's not her flesh.

CHAPTER
TWENTY-FIVE

Joan knew Gideon was annoyed with her as they left the interview room. But considering she'd sensed downright hostility from him just a few days ago, she saw this as progress. Love was not in the cards for them again, but a friendship would definitely be welcome.

"What happened to 'I'm not going to talk'?" he said.

"I didn't talk that much. In fact, I was damn near silent."

Before he could unload his thoughts, his phone rang.

"Detective Bailey."

His annoyed expression darkened. "We'll be right there."

He hung up. "You're coming with me."

"Where?"

"Missoula Montana Hospital. Elijah was admitted a half hour ago. He was assaulted." She knew Gideon did not trust or like Elijah, but he sure as hell would not sit by and have a vigilante assault him.

Joan's expression tightened with worry. "Is he going to be okay?"

"He'll survive. He has two broken ribs and a few contusions."

"Does he know his attacker?" Joan asked.

"Apparently not."

"I want to talk to him," she said.

"You're in luck. He's asking for you. Guy's got a thing for you."

"It's not romantic. He sees us as kindred spirits."

"I disagree. He's using you."

Unwilling to argue now, she followed him toward the station's exit and was already zipping up her jacket as she stepped outside. She and Montana were getting used to each other.

He drove them across town and parked in the spot reserved for law enforcement. Inside, he presented his ID and was sent to a room on the second floor.

"Let me do the talking," she said as she hurried to keep up with his long strides. "I'm the one he trusts."

Gideon paused and looked at her. "Does he?"

She shoved out a breath. "Maybe not, but I might be the one person he tolerates."

"I'll let you kick it off. Then we'll see."

"No. Let me go in alone."

"Why?"

"Stand outside the door if you're so worried. And if you discover a burning question—"

"Pun intended?"

"Text me." Joan continued down the hallway to Elijah's room. She knocked on the door and slowly opened it.

The room's lights had been dimmed and the shades closed. Elijah lay in his bed, hands at his sides with eyes closed. She moved toward the bed, noting there were no bruises on his face.

"Elijah?" she whispered.

"Joan," he said without opening his eyes. "I heard you coming down the hallway. You have a very distinctive gait, and you still smell faintly like smoke."

She pulled up a chair and sat. "I've been told it sounds like a stampede when I walk. Rushed and angry."

"That about sums it up." He opened his eyes and turned toward her. "You don't look too bad."

"My ribs would say otherwise. It hurts to breathe."

"Do you know who attacked you?" she asked.

"No. He wore a ski mask."

"You're certain it was a man?"

"Very. He spoke to me. Something about me getting out of town. The kind of bad dialogue you find in an old western."

"Was high noon referenced?" she quipped.

A slight smile tweaked his lips. "Almost."

"You aren't leaving, are you?"

"You know me too well."

"Why stay?" She thought of Ann's confession about Nate and wondered for the first time if Elijah had pieced together the truth.

"It's home."

"You're smart. You can go anywhere."

"My alleged past always follows. At least if I'm here, there's no time wasted with awkward explanations. We all know where we stand."

She reached to straighten his pillow. "Can I help? Is there anything else I can do? Get a nurse maybe."

"No. But thank you."

"Well, now that I'm here, I do want to talk to you about the fire out at Ann's place."

He turned his head toward her. All traces of humor had vanished. "I assume still no suspects."

"None."

"Ann and the boy?"

"She's still shaken."

"And the boy? How is he doing?"

"He's fine."

"He's not upset by it?"

"No."

That triggered interest. "How did he react to the fire?"

"What do you mean?"

"Was he fascinated by it?"

"Yes. That would be a way of describing his reaction."

"Was it speaking to him?" Elijah asked.

Instead of answering, she asked, "If the fire were speaking to him, what would it say?"

Elijah rolled his head and gazed back toward the ceiling. "Fires are like people. They show different motivations. Some are set as a demonstration of power, while others are an expression of passion, and many are simply designed for destruction."

"Did your fires speak to you?"

"You mean the dumpster fires when I was twelve?"

"Of course."

"They reminded me that I was still in control. That I could do anything I wanted."

"Those are things a twelve-year-old in a challenging home would need to hear."

"Yes."

"Do you have to be the fire's creator for it to talk to you?"

"No." He tried to sit forward and reach for the cup and straw, but he winced and lay down. She took the cup and held the straw to his mouth. He raised his gaze to her, wrapped his lips around the straw, and sucked. Once he'd drained the cup, he released the straw and leaned back.

"How is Detective Bailey doing?" he asked. "He's out there somewhere skulking and worrying, but I like him."

She smiled. "Do you?"

"Want to hear a secret?" he asked.

"Sure."

"Gideon's still in love with you."

She stilled, calculating where this was coming from. "What?"

His eyes lightened with humor. "Don't look so surprised, Detective."

She glanced toward the door, wondering if Gideon had heard. Heat rose in her cheeks as she thought about him overhearing this conversation. Would he be angry or embarrassed or accepting? The thought concerned her more than she had expected. "That's bull."

The door opened, and Gideon strode in, his hat in hand.

"And now it's a party," Elijah said with a grin.

Gideon stood beside Joan. "One of my deputies is going door to door to see if there are any witnesses to your attack."

"Then they'll tell you what I told the deputy. Masked man. Worn jeans. Scuffed boots. It could describe many of the males in the area."

"The officer tells me there was blood at the scene," Gideon said.

"I have no doubt. We had quite the tussle."

"You have no idea who did this?" Gideon said.

"No."

Elijah's quick answer rang like an alarm bell in Joan's head. If he knew more than he was saying, then why not tell Gideon who had attacked him? She knew the answer. Elijah was guarding the attacker's identity for his own reasons.

***

Gideon left Elijah's hospital room and waited in the hallway for Joan. She was refilling Elijah's water cup and making sure the phone and channel selector were close at hand, given his limited mobility.

When she came out, they exchanged glances, and together left the hospital. In the front seat of his car, they sat in silence for a moment.

"What did Elijah say to you?" Gideon asked.

"What do you mean?"

"He said something to you right before I came in. You were pale."

"I don't like hospitals."

Gideon was willing to sit here for as long as it took. "Again, what did he say?"

Joan stared out her window at the clouds hovering over the ring of distant mountains. She turned toward him. "He said you're still in love with me."

There were few times in his life when he wanted nothing more than to turn and run. But each and every time, he'd stood his ground, more out of stubbornness than bravery. "He's trying to get in your head."

Her expression struggled to remain stoic, but a mixture of relief and disappointment tugged at her features. "You might be right. I get that we're water under the bridge," she said carefully.

If he had learned anything about Elijah, it was that he was good at exploiting targets. What had he seen in Joan that prompted him to take aim? "Did he get under your skin?"

"I'm not sure what you're looking for, Gideon."

Her lack of an answer suggested an option Gideon had long given up on. Could she still be in love with him? And why did the idea frighten the hell out of him?

Gideon started the engine, turning up the heater to chase away the chill. Cracking the door to their past was a dangerous move he could not afford to make. Joan would find whatever answers she wanted and then leave. He would then get on with his life. And this time their break would be for good.

So why did his gaze drop to her fingers as they moved back and forth on her thigh? Why did he want to take her hand in his and trace the scars she tried to hide? He understood the fire had changed her. It had changed him. Different was not necessarily bad. Good came from change. Maybe they could . . .

"If you can drop me at the station, I'll grab an Uber and get out of your hair," she said. "I know you have work to do."

He shifted into drive. "Where are you going?"

"Thought I might pay a visit to Dan. I have a craving for one of his burgers."

"Stay out of Elijah's assault investigation."

"I'm just getting a burger. Maybe a milkshake."

His phone dinged with a text. It was from the medical examiner. The body from the cabin was ready for autopsy. "Or you can come with me to the medical examiner's office."

"For the autopsy?"

"Yes. Jessica Halpern was identified by her dental records an hour ago."

She seemed to relax, as if forensics were a welcome respite from feelings. "You're talking my language."

"Good." If Gideon kept to himself, he might come out of this intact. The last few years had had productive, satisfying moments. But he had not tasted the excitement he'd enjoyed while being with Joan these last few days.

But if he was really honest with himself, he would admit that his life was lackluster because he still missed Joan.

***

Joan and Gideon stood in front of the medical examiner's computer screen and watched as Dr. Christopher opened a file. The digital image of the body appeared on screen, and a familiar sense of discomfort washed over her. When would she ever shake that damn College Fire?

The heat and fire had damaged the body, melting muscle and eating into bone. The carnage was more complete than it had been with Lana. Either the killer was wrapping up loose ends, or his destructive behavior was escalating. Either way, his quickened pace was putting him at risk of exposure. Good for the cops, if they could catch him before the next homicide and arson.

"As you can see, these are dental X-rays I took of the victim's mouth," Dr. Christopher said. "And on the left are Jessica Halpern's records, which I obtained from her dentist. Both sets of teeth have the same patterns of fillings on the back molars, as well as both sets have caps on the front-right incisor. This is definitely Jessica Halpern."

"Do you have a cause of death?" Gideon asked.

"Strangulation," the doctor said. "Her killer all but crushed the hyoid bone in her neck."

"No smoke in the lungs?"

"None. She was not alive when the fire was set."

"Who knows that Lana died of smoke inhalation?" Joan asked.

"I told rescue and police crews that I saw Lana move before the fire reached her," Gideon said.

"Overkill, with some pent-up rage, or fear of another mistake?" Joan asked.

"Fear of a mistake suggests a leak," Gideon said.

"Cops gossip," she said. "Good luck with that."

Gideon frowned, as if wondering how many layers removed the killer was from the first responders. "Can you estimate the time of death?"

"Within the last couple of days, but the fire damage makes it nearly impossible to be more accurate," Dr. Christopher cautioned.

"Her husband said he spoke to her yesterday," Joan said. "Of course, that's assuming he didn't kill her earlier and is lying. Gideon, did she return any of your calls?"

"No. Detective Sullivan checked her phone records, and her last text was thirty-six hours ago," Gideon said. "Assuming she sent the text."

"Who did she text?" Joan asked.

"A travel agent. She was planning a trip to Mexico."

"When?" Joan asked.

"Tomorrow."

"Not sticking around for the investigation," she said. "Was it a trip for one or two?"

"One."

"She was worried. You should have your friend Bryce McCabe keep an eye on Mr. Pollock in Helena. He might also be spooked now."

"Already took care of that," Gideon said.

"What about Lana Long's fetus?" Joan asked. "Do you have DNA results back?"

"I do, as a matter of fact," Dr. Christopher said. "Just came in today." The doctor adjusted his glasses and shifted his attention to a different set of files on the screen. He pressed several keys, and a series of DNA markers appeared. "These belong to the biological father. The other set belongs to Darren Halpern."

Joan leaned in. She was no expert on DNA but knew enough to recognize a match. "Darren is not the daddy."

"Correct," the doctor said.

"If Lana was seeing Darren, she was also busy with someone else," Gideon said.

"She would not have been the first woman to pass another man's baby off as his own," Joan said.

"Whatever game Lana was playing, she pissed off the wrong guy," Gideon said. "Doc, could you compare these results to Elijah Weston's DNA?"

"But you said yourself the two would not have been in physical contact," Dr. Christopher said, looking puzzled.

"She was obsessed with him." Gideon shifted his gaze from the body to the doctor. "And if I've learned anything about prisoners, they are incredibly resourceful. Elijah did work in the warden's office, so he might have had more access than most prisoners. Also check the DNA against Ryan Davis's. He's playing the part of the wronged boyfriend, but I've been surprised before."

"Was a diamond engagement ring ever found with Lana's body?" Joan asked.

"No. But one was found with Jessica Halpern's remains," Dr. Christopher said. He moved to a bin filled with the few personal belongings that had not been destroyed by the fire. He held up three baggies, each containing rings. Two were melted beyond recognition, and though the third was also misshapen, the trio of diamonds was clearly visible. She snapped several pictures.

They each thanked Dr. Christopher and, in the adjoining room, stripped off their gowns and gloves. Outside, they stepped into the sunshine and drank in fresh mountain air.

"Tucker said Lana was showing off her big engagement ring to a waitress named Nora last week. A ring like that, if it was real, required deep pockets."

"That suggests that Lana's boyfriend had money."

"Let's talk with Nora," Joan said. "It's critical we find this mystery boyfriend."

***

Gideon called the diner and discovered that Nora's shift would not begin for another hour, so he and Joan headed to the woman's apartment, hoping to head her off.

They pulled up in front of the apartment building a few minutes before four. As they were getting out of the car, a woman was exiting the building. She was wearing a pink Tucker's uniform, a heavy black sweater, and sensible white shoes.

"That must be Nora O'Neil," he said.

"You think, Detective? If I had a nickel for all the times I put on that pink dress," Joan said, shaking her head. "I guess if one good thing came out of the College Fire, it was that it destroyed those uniforms."

"Too bad," he said, almost in a whisper. "I always thought they looked good on you."

"You're kidding."

He shrugged. "Nope."

They started moving toward Nora, a tall, shapely woman with thick, dark hair tied back in a ponytail. "Ms. O'Neil," Gideon said as he held up his badge.

Nora came to a stop, her fingers tightening around her keys, but said nothing.

"I'm Detective Gideon Bailey, and this is Joan Mason."

"Detective," Joan corrected. "We came to ask you a few questions about Lana Long."

Nora's expression did not relax. "She ate at the diner sometimes."

"Tucker said she showed you an engagement ring at the diner last week."

"Yeah, it was something to see. Three big diamonds. She was proud of it." Jessica Halpern's ring had sported three large diamonds, but when Jessica had visited the incinerated salon, she had not been wearing the diamonds.

"Do you know who gave it to her?" Joan asked.

"No clue. She hardly talked about her guy, like it was a big mystery. But she sure was thrilled to say she was getting married."

Joan opened the photo featuring the Halpern ring. "Did it look like this?"

Nora studied the picture. "Yeah. That's the ring."

"How can you be sure?" Gideon asked.

"Because of the three diamonds, and the setting was high like that one."

That ring was not cheap, and the chances of two similar ones floating around town were slim to none. "You and Lana must have talked about something," Joan said. "Tucker said she ate at the diner a lot."

"I asked her once why she came there, and she said her boyfriend lived nearby, in Deer Lodge."

"That's over an hour away," Gideon said. "Why would she not live there or in Helena?"

"Because her beau was planning on moving back to Missoula."

"Was he a prisoner?" Gideon asked.

"That wouldn't surprise me. Highest concentration of men in Deer Lodge are locked up."

"Did he give her the ring, or did she pick it out?" Joan asked.

"I don't know. I had orders to fill, and Dan hates it when I talk to the customers too long." She glanced at her watch. "Speaking of which, I got to go. Dan's not at the diner right now."

"Where is he?" Gideon asked.

"He took the afternoon off to help my mom, if you can believe it."

"What's he doing?" Gideon asked.

"Mom's been after him to help set up her iPad."

"That's some boss," Joan said.

"Little secret," Nora said. "We're dating."

"Where was he last night?" Gideon asked.

"Don't know. You'll have to ask him. He'll be back at the diner tomorrow."

Gideon handed her his card. "Call me if you think of anything."

She shoved the card in her apron pocket, already sporting her order pad. "Sure thing."

***

Dan Tucker winced as he slowly slid off his blood-soaked pants and eased into the recliner in his living room. The knife wound in his thigh still oozed blood and showed no signs of letting up. Reaching for a handful of paper towels sitting on the side table along with gauze and a six-pack, he pressed the wad to the injury. As pain shot up his leg, he hissed in a breath. "Motherfucker."

Absorbing the burn, he grabbed a beer, popped the top, and gulped the full can. He glanced at the paper towels, now soaked in blood, and tossed them in the trash. He grabbed another wad and a fresh beer. He repeated this process for nearly a half hour before the blood had slowed enough for him to be able to wind the gauze around the wound. He damn near could have bled out.

He fished his cell from his pants and hit "Redial." Seconds later, he heard a slurred "Yeah."

"Where were you?" Dan asked.

"What do you mean?"

"What the hell do you think I mean? We were going after him. You were supposed to have my back."

"Yeah, I got hung up at work."

Dan tipped his head back, pissed at the lame excuse.

"Did you go after him without me?"

"Yeah," Dan said.

"How did it go? Did you teach him a lesson?"

Dan glanced down at the white gauze wrapped around his thigh. "It went great."

"Seriously?"

"No."

"So what's next?"

Dan popped his last beer. "Next time, I'm going to kill that motherfucker."

Confessions of an Arsonist
All the blazes that I have set have been rehearsal for my final act.

CHAPTER
TWENTY-SIX

Missoula, Montana
Thursday, September 10, 2020
4:15 p.m.

Joan pulled up to the Baileys' to a large inflatable bouncy house, a cotton-candy machine, and blaring music. There was no sign of the birthday boys or the party guys, but she suspected kickoff time had to be any minute.

She pushed through the front door to find Ann standing in the center of dozens of red, white, and blue balloons dangling from the ceiling.

"Isn't he a little old for this?" Joan asked.

"He might be, but I have one last year before he won't want anything like this."

"Even if he thinks he's too big, he'll still secretly appreciate the gesture." Joan plucked a potato chip from a bowl. "Where are the half-birthday boys?"

"Upstairs. The other kids should be here in about a half hour."

A car pulled up outside, and both turned to see Clarke's SUV parking in the circular driveway. Out of the car, he glanced at the house, frowned, and then reached inside for two neatly wrapped packages. He strode toward the house and rang the bell.

Ann glanced at Joan and then forced a smile. "Here we go."

"It'll be fine."

"Nate!" Ann shouted from the bottom of the stairs. "Your dad is here."

"Coming."

Joan strode to the door and opened it. "Clarke."

The smile on his face stiffened. "Joan. You're becoming a real fixture here."

"I'm like a bad penny," she joked.

He didn't look amused. "Is Ann here?"

"Right here," Ann said from behind Joan.

"Is the shed still fully extinguished?" Clarke asked.

"I spoke to the ranch manager, and he's having it cleared away this weekend. Thankfully, we didn't have much equipment stored there, so the loss was minimal."

"The damage might have been minimal this time, but the threat is still here," he said.

Joan grimaced. "By separating myself from Ann, we'll at least know who the real target is."

"That's little comfort. Ann is still in danger," Clarke said.

"Clarke, I am being careful," Ann said.

"Have you two heard about the cabin fire?" Clarke challenged.

"I haven't," Ann said as her expression became more serious.

"My buddy in Granite County said that the Halpern cabin burned, with Jessica Halpern in it."

"That's awful," Ann said. "Joan, you knew about this?"

"I was with Gideon when the call came in. He allowed me to tag along. Professional curiosity."

"But that's not your jurisdiction," Clarke said.

Joan ignored the comment. "By the way, Clarke, did you hear Elijah was assaulted? He's in the hospital."

Ann's wide-eyed expression gave away her surprise, but Clarke's perpetually annoyed scowl was harder to read.

"Elijah shouldn't be in town," Clarke said. "He's asking for trouble. I'm not the only one who thinks he's the arsonist."

"Have you found evidence that proves it?" Joan asked.

"Not yet. But it's a matter of time, and then everyone will see that he has not reformed one bit."

Hurried footsteps hustled down the stairs. "Hey, Dad!"

"Hey, Uncle Clarke," Kyle said.

Clarke's expression softened as the boys approached the stairs. "Hey, guys. Happy half birthday."

"Thanks!" Nate, the serious and thoughtful boy, actually looked excited. "Is that for me?"

Clarke held up a wrapped box. "Sure is. Want to open it before everyone arrives?"

"Can I, Mom?" Nate asked.

"You sure can."

Clarke handed the other box to Kyle. "And this one is for you, pal. I know you'll like it."

Clarke followed the boys toward the large dining table, set with paper plates, napkins, and spoons. In the center was a birthday cake covered with mathematical symbols and horses. Clarke looked pleased as the boys ripped the wrapping paper away. It quickly became clear that Nate's gift was an expensive computer that must have cost at least a grand. A chunk of change for a municipal employee.

"Is this for me?" Nate asked.

"All yours, pal. I thought about getting you a desktop, but with you ready to skip high school and go to college, it seems a laptop would suit better."

"I'm not in college," Nate said. "I'm auditing a class."

"Which is as good as it gets for a ten-year-old," Clarke said.

"That's very generous." Ann's emphasis on the last word spoke to her disapproval.

"He deserves the best," Clarke said. "He's smart, and I want him to go as far as he can."

"What did you get, Kyle?" Joan asked. Kyle held up an electric car. "Sweet!"

"I know how you like to race them," Clarke said.

"Thanks, Uncle Clarke."

Nate looked up at his mother, his eyes glowing with excitement. "This is awesome! Can I set it up now?"

"Your dad is here, and your guests are arriving soon."

"I can't stay," Clarke said. "I have to take a shift tonight. But we're still on for dinner next Wednesday, right?"

Ann nodded. "That's right."

"Thanks again, Dad!"

"Anything for you, pal."

"Why don't you two boys set up the car outside? I'll hold on to the computer," Clarke offered.

Nate and Kyle seemed pleased with the compromise and ran outside, slamming the front door behind them.

"That computer and the car were very, very generous gifts," Ann said. "I thought finances were a little tight."

"They were, but not now." He leaned toward her a fraction, as if hoping she would meet him halfway for a kiss, but when she did not, he made up the distance and kissed her gently on the lips. "I want you to really consider moving back into town. It's not safe here."

"We've been through this."

Joan ducked her head and reached to pick up the discarded wrapping paper. She should have given them privacy but was curious about Clarke's recent change in finances.

"We'll talk next week," he offered.

She hesitated and then nodded. "Sure."

"Great." He strode toward the door and yanked it open. "Stay out of trouble, Joan."

She crumpled the wrapping paper into a tight wad. "I'll do my best."

"You do that."

Joan tossed the paper in the trash. "Where do you think he got the money? That computer is at least a grand. And that car was close to five hundred."

"Noncustodial parents like Clarke are known to compensate with expensive gifts, as if that will make up for their lost time."

She shook her head. Clarke did not appear to have any suspicions about the boy's paternity. But that did not mean that, on some level, he didn't sense he could be in a competition with the very intelligent Elijah Weston. Could he suspect that Ann had slept with Elijah? "I suppose that's it."

Just then, several cars pulled into the driveway. "Let the fun begin."

***

If volume of noise was a measure of success, then Joan decided that Nate and Kyle's half-birthday party was a hit. The six boys ran around the house, and when Nate nearly crashed into a coffee table, Ann ordered them all outside.

For the first time since Gideon had arrived two hours ago, they looked at each other and laughed.

"I need a drink," Joan said.

"What? The noise getting to you?" Gideon asked.

"Yes." She held a cold beer bottle to the side of her head. "How does so much sound come out of such young humans?"

Gideon sipped his soda. "It's a mystery."

"Did you hear about the gifts Clarke gave Nate and Kyle?" Joan asked.

"Something about a computer and a car."

"A really expensive computer and remote-control car."

Gideon was silent for a moment. "He's always wanted to provide the best."

"A sentiment I can appreciate. But where does a firefighter get that kind of dough?"

"Credit cards. Sold one of his hunting rifles. I don't know. Why does that bother you?" he asked.

"I don't know."

"Clarke is rough around the edges. But he has always been a straight shooter, and he's always treated Kyle like a son."

"Why hasn't Ann moved back home?" Joan asked.

"I don't delve into the love lives of other couples. I've got enough on my own plate."

"You've known Clarke since middle school, right?" Joan asked.

"That's right. Why the sudden interest in Clarke?"

"I don't know. I question everything and everyone. It's just habit. Never mind. I was just thinking out loud."

"Are you staying at the guesthouse tonight?"

"If you'll still have me." She had packed her things this morning, just in case.

"You're welcome as long as you want to stay."

"I'll be out of your hair by Sunday."

"There's absolutely no rush."

***

Joan stayed behind to help Ann clean up after the boys while Gideon drove the overly sugared, rowdy kids back to town. Kyle and Nate were upstairs, excited about their sleepover. The house breathed a sigh of relief.

She pulled the overstuffed trash bag from the can in the kitchen and carried it outside to the garage, where there was a locked box for the garbage. Philadelphia had rats. Montana had bears.

Back inside, she washed her hands and wiped down the counter for the evening.

Ann filled the empty trash can with a new bag. "You don't have to go back to Gideon's," Ann said.

"I want to. It's easier."

"Did you and Gideon start something again?" Ann asked.

"No. We're older and wiser and both know that I won't stick around."

"You could stay out here. Big Sky Country had its moments for you."

"Live here again?" Joan had not even toyed with the idea. She was here to figure out Elijah, and now the other fires. Once that was solved, it would be time to go home and face the music of her off-key life.

"Consider it," Ann said.

"And how would I support myself?" Joan asked. "I doubt anyone in the Philadelphia Police Department will give me a recommendation."

"Enough people know you. I would vouch for you." Ann added, "The police department's always hiring. I also hear the medical examiner needs an investigator."

"I doubt I could work for Gideon."

Ann closed the door to the utility room. "Then call Dr. Christopher."

"Before we get carried away with ourselves, I need to get going. I want to see Elijah again before visiting hours are over and figure out how he's doing."

Ann's good humor faded. "I'm sorry he was assaulted."

"He's taking it in stride. Though he doesn't strike me as the type who lets something like this pass."

"Have you ever sensed that he, well, knows?" Ann asked.

"About?" Joan did not mention Nate's name, but they both understood his paternity was the topic. When Ann nodded slowly, Joan said carefully, "He's not stupid, and little gets past him."

Ann's face tightened with worry. "Nate and I were at the university on Monday checking out his classroom. We saw Elijah."

"Did you speak?"

"No. But I know he saw us. When we pulled away, he spotted my car."

"What was he doing there?" Joan asked.

"I don't know."

"Maybe he was scoping out the school layout so he would be ready for his class."

"I suppose," Ann said.

"Don't worry about him. Let me do that, okay?"

"Okay."

Joan opened her phone and scrolled to the picture they'd found of Ann and her in Lana's suitcase. "Gideon took the picture using Clarke's camera, right?"

"Yeah, and he also took one of Clarke and me. Clarke keeps it in our bedroom. That's the picture Lana had, right?"

"Yes."

"What are you saying?"

"Clarke had the pictures and the negatives. And then Lana ends up with a copy."

"Maybe someone else had a copy," Ann said.

Before Joan could answer, the boys called out to Ann. "Mom, you said we could build a fire!" Nate shouted.

Ann's brow furrowed. "Be right there."

"I'll give you the rundown in the morning. Go keep an eye on the boys."

"Right."

Joan got into her car, and in the quiet, she was able to think. Who had given Lana the picture of Joan and Ann? And how had Lana ended up with an engagement ring that looked like Jessica's? Clarke had taken the original picture, and he had also done a fire inspection on the salon recently. Several had suggested that Lana had a boyfriend who made a point not to be seen in public with her. Clarke was separated from Ann, and if he had been seeing Lana, it would likely have ended whatever chances he'd had with Ann. Clarke was also an expert on fires.

None of these suppositions proved anything, but they also all pointed to Clarke. But something about Clarke troubled her. Sure, the two had never gotten along great, but the guy had pulled her from the College Fire and saved her life. He could have sold a rifle for the birthday-present cash. And if that were a crime, most of the country would be in jail.

Until she had solid proof, she could not make a move against Clarke. If Philadelphia and the Newport case had taught Joan anything, it was to have an ironclad case before making any kind of arrest. Maybe it was time to quietly poke around in Clarke's history.

She kept driving, and by the time she approached the intersection that cut one way to the hospital and the other to Clarke's house, she paused for just a moment before taking the road toward the small residential neighborhood where Ann and Clarke had lived.

She slowed as she pulled into the subdivision. Though the homes were much smaller than the ranch, they were close to the schools, grocery stores, and all the other civilized things not found farther out of town.

Joan located the one-level rancher that Clarke, Ann, and Nate had recently shared. The house was dark and silent. She parked across the street and studied its features. Fall leaves coated the yard, and the flowerpots that surely had been filled with vibrant blossoms while Ann was here now sat empty.

Clarke's car was not in the driveway. He had said to Ann he was working tonight. He was not home. And she would need more evidence before she could even utter any suspicions about him.

Breaking into Clarke's house would be crossing a line. If she was caught, she could not only kiss her job goodbye, but she could also end up in serious legal trouble. Not to mention losing Gideon and Ann.

She drove around the block and parked at a convenience store a half mile away.

Whoever had set the fires knew what they were doing. The same low-tech milk jug filled with gasoline was simple, hard to trace, and brutally effective. The buildings that had burned in Missoula and Helena had been heavily insured. Both owners had been out of town, with solid alibis.

Joan went inside the store and bought a few items she did not really want in order to provide a good reason why she was in the area.

Out of the convenience store's door, Joan went around to her car and tossed her groceries in the back. Instead of getting behind the wheel, she ducked into the woods, got her bearings, and set off for Clarke's house.

In the darkness, she weaved in and out of heavy thickets and fallen trees. When she emerged, she was staring into a lit-up house. She stopped, her heart pounding as she backed into the woods. At the kitchen table was a couple and a few kids. She had overshot her approach. "Terrific. Wrong house. Smooth, Joan. Really smooth."

She moved to her right and made her way along the edge of the yard until she emerged from the woods to face the back of Clarke's still house.

Her gaze was drawn to dark shadows for a long moment, hoping a solid reason would present itself and she could stand down from this crazy idea that she was about to undertake.

Finally, when reason stood her up, she glanced from left to right, hurried toward the back door, and peered through one of its glass panes that gave her a view of the kitchen. The sink was filled with unwashed dishes. Par for the course for a separated man. Hell, her own sink looked like this.

She tried the doorknob but found it locked. As she looked along the back of the house, she spotted what appeared to be a slightly open window. She slinked down to the window and peered inside. With no search warrant, anything in this house would be inadmissible in court. She could get herself arrested, and whatever chance she had of catching Avery Newport would go up in smoke.

Reason screamed for her not to go inside.

"Jesus, Joan, you've lost your mind," she whispered.

She pushed open the window and listened for the beep of an alarm system. The house remained silent as she glanced left and right and then hoisted herself through the window and onto the floor.

She had landed in Clarke and Ann's bedroom. The large king-size mattress was directly on the floor and covered in a tangle of blankets and sheets. Clothes were scattered about, and a couple of pairs of boots lay in the corner.

Joan picked up one of the shirts and raised it to her nose. The scent of smoke clung to the rough cotton, but she could already hear the defense attorney arguing it was common for firefighters to have clothes that smelled of smoke.

She walked over to a bureau and saw the collection of framed pictures. There were several of Ann and Nate. And there was also the picture taken of Ann and Clarke in college all those years ago.

She moved through the darkened house, listening for any signs that she was not alone. A clock ticked in the house, and a refrigerator hummed.

In the living room was a wide-screen television, recliner, and TV tray. She could tell the furnishings had been selected by Ann, but Clarke had made no effort to keep it clean.

In the kitchen, she opened the refrigerator and noted there were two large milk jugs. Clarke did not strike her as the type to gulp down milk, but it was plausible, given he had a son. She could also argue that the jugs could be easily drained and filled with gasoline. Nice theory that was not even remotely strong enough to support a search warrant.

She opened the kitchen pantry and found a box of heavy-duty rags, five empty gallon-size milk jugs, and a ten-day supply of boxed macaroni and cheese. She snapped pictures of the rags and then the milk jugs.

Why had he stockpiled the jugs? Was he really into recycling, or was he saving the jugs for another fire?

Outside, a flash of headlights swiped across the front of the house. Closing the pantry, she dashed to the bedroom window, exited, and lowered it to where she had found it. Behind her, she could hear the front door open.

She raced across the yard and into the woods, crouching as she watched the house. The kitchen light clicked on, and she saw Clarke standing at the sink. He stared into the woods, almost as if he knew someone had been in his house. She ducked down, lowering her gaze, fearing he would somehow sense her presence.

He opened the back door and stepped out onto the patio, peering into the darkness. He was holding a paper bag.

Finally, he turned and opened a side shed. Stacked inside were three gas cans. He chose one, opened the grill, and dumped the paper contents of the bag onto it. He poured a liberal portion of gasoline on the debris and then pulled a packet of matches from his pocket. He struck one, stared at it a beat, and then tossed it onto the grill.

The flames shot up in an angry, explosive whoosh. Any sane person would have stepped back, but Clarke held his position. She could not tell if he was daring the flames or if he was simply drawn to the heat.

The night chill seeped into her bones, and as tempted as she was to leave, she did not dare make a sound.

As she watched, the flames slowly died down. Clarke stoked the flames with a stick several times.

He had all the elements of the incendiary devices that had set fire to the beauty shop, Ann's shed, and the Halpern cabin. Lots of pieces that any good defense attorney would argue were strictly benign, just as Avery Newport's lawyer had done. Who did not have milk, rags, and gasoline? It was not a crime to burn papers on a grill. Or to have a picture of your wife from college.

Clarke remained by the fire, the glow of the embers shadowing his firm jaw and hooded brows. After about fifteen minutes, he closed the lid and glanced back at the woods one last time before entering the house. The lights shut off in the kitchen, and soon his car drove away.

She waited until the headlights had completely vanished before she ran back to the patio to inspect the grill. She lifted the lid and stared at the hot, smoldering embers. Whatever he had burned had been reduced to blackened ashes. What was so important to bring him home just to burn one stack of papers? She grabbed a stick from the yard and burrowed through the ashes. She found a fragment of a picture featuring what looked like a blue blouse very similar to the one she had been wearing in the pictures found all those years ago in Elijah's dorm room after the College Fire. She knew those pictures had been taken in the bar, but even now, she did not remember seeing Elijah there. But Clarke had been present that night with Ann, Gideon, and her.

She replaced the lid and tucked the picture fragment in her pocket. If Clarke had set the recent fires, then it was plausible that he had also set the College Fire. Framing Elijah would have been the perfect way to eliminate a rival.

The same gut feeling that had convinced her that Avery had set her fire was even stronger now. But in a court of law, feelings meant nothing.

***

Dan was not sure what had woken him up from his drunken stupor. He reached for a beer but found only empty cans on the side table. He glanced at the sweatpants covering the thick bandage and was pleased to see that the bleeding had finally stopped. He had been lucky. Elijah had been so quick with the blade that he never saw it.

That would be the last time he brought a baseball bat to an ambush. The next time it would be a gun and a lot more caution.

The back of his neck tingled, and he had the faintest sensation that something was off. But before he could process the feeling, a plastic bag was slipped over his head and quickly tightened around his neck.

He sucked in air, using up what little remained inside the bag. He reached up for the hands holding the bag, but the booze combined with a lack of oxygen made his movements sloppy and ineffective.

The air gone, his senses screamed as panic cut through him, his head dropped back, and his world went black.

***

Joan called the hospital and discovered that Elijah had been released, so she drove to the boardinghouse, where she found him sitting on the front porch.

When she walked up, he moved to rise and winced, so she beckoned him to sit. "I thought they were going to keep you another day."

"As you already know, I'm not fond of confinement." He shifted in his rocker and leaned back until he seemed to settle on a comfortable spot.

"Do your doctors know you left?" she asked.

"I'm sure they do by now." He sniffed. "How was the half-birthday party?" he asked.

"You know about that?"

He shrugged. "I keep up."

She sat in the rocker beside him and steered the conversation away from the boys. "I would like to run a hypothetical scenario past you."

His eyes brightened with interest. "All ears."

"If someone had several empty milk jugs, rags, and gasoline in their house, what conclusion would you draw about them?"

"You have not given me enough variables," he said. "What else can you tell me about the individual?"

"All those elements could be put together to make an incendiary device."

"Sure. But it's certainly not a given."

"This person burned papers on a backyard grill."

"Nothing out of the ordinary there, either, Joan."

"Could a small, controlled fire on a grill be a way of a guy letting off steam?"

"Maybe. It's also an efficient way to dispose of important papers. Identity theft is a real problem these days. My cellmate was doing time for that very crime."

She should have been having this conversation with Gideon, but he would never have approved of her methods. And he had been Clarke's friend since childhood. Their boys were best friends. As much as she wanted to do it all by the book, she wanted—no, needed—to catch the arsonist more.

"We can keep playing this game of guess who," Elijah said. "Or you can tell me what you've really been up to."

It was so tempting to trust him and tell him about her suspicions of Clarke. He had a calm voice that lulled her into believing that they had somehow become friends. But they were not friends. She sensed in her gut that though he might not have set the fires, he had an agenda that might one day put them at odds. She recalled the scorpion and the frog fable and was damn sure she was not going to end up the poor, trusting frog.

"Maybe later. I need more before I name names."

"Be very careful, Joan. If you know about this individual, chances are you're on his radar."

***

"Where have you been?"

Gideon's rough voice reached out from the darkness, halting Joan midstep as she approached the side entrance to the garage apartment. She paused and turned slowly, doing her best to look casual.

"You startled me."

He stepped out of the shadows. "Where have you been? Ann said you left a couple of hours ago."

"Checking up on me?"

"I thought you might have gotten lost on the road."

"You could have called me."

"I did. Twice."

She reached for her phone and glanced at the *Two missed calls*. She turned her ringer back on. "Sorry about that. I must have turned it off during the party."

"Were you with Elijah?"

"I did go visit him. I wanted to see how he was doing."

Moonlight slashed across his face, sharpening the hard angles. He had always been attractive, but the last decade had brought a few gray hairs and deepened the lines around his eyes. All looked good on him.

"If I told you the truth, you would not be happy," she said.

"That's almost a given," he said. "I still want to hear it."

A cold wind blew across the open land and coiled around her. "How about we talk in hypotheticals for a bit."

"I'd rather you just spill it."

"It would be better if we spoke about potential situations. Otherwise, we don't talk at all, Gideon."

His feet braced, as if he were ready for a hard tackle. "Okay. Let me have it."

She considered her words, knowing honesty was likely going to get her booted out of town. "What if a town had an arsonist?"

"Okay."

"And this arsonist was good at what he did. He didn't leave traces of himself behind. In fact, he was so careful about what he did, he killed two women who could have told the world the truth about him."

Gideon stared at her, silent, his gaze unwavering.

"What if this arsonist not only burned structures for money but also because he loved to see things consumed by fire. Fire energizes him. Fire makes him feel in control when his life is out of control."

"You're describing Elijah."

And here was where the rubber met the road. "I'm also talking about Clarke."

That provoked a mirthless smile and a shake of the head. "You're joking. Clarke is a firefighter."

"Some of the most prolific arsonists have been attached to fire prevention. They set the fires and then get the glory when they put them out."

Gideon shook his head. "You're wrong, Joan. Clarke is a straight shooter. I've known him for almost twenty years."

"How well do you know him beyond sports, work, and the boys?"

"He's a good father. He loves Ann."

"I have no doubt he loves them very much, and he would do anything for them."

"That's not a bad thing. I'm the same with Kyle."

She was sorry that she was about to torch the fragile bridges they had cobbled together these last few days. "Consider the College Fire. Ann had just broken up with Clarke. She was on the verge of moving east to study."

Gideon's frown deepened, as if his mind had tripped back to that time. Joan wondered if Clarke had said or done something that now struck Gideon as odd.

"And then her house burns down. Clarke rescues me from the flames, and then he rides in the ambulance with Ann to the hospital, where she soon learns she is pregnant. Mr. Superhero."

"Elijah's DNA was found at the scene."

"He also reported to campus police a week earlier that his backpack had been stolen."

"We've been through this. The backpack was found twenty-four hours later, which was nearly a week before the College Fire."

"Elijah insists a sweatshirt was missing from the backpack after it was recovered. A portion of it was used as the wick for one of the incendiary devices."

"What are you saying? Clarke framed Elijah? Why would he do that?"

She fished the fragment of the photo from her pocket and then scrolled on her phone to the picture she had found on Clarke's grill. "Look at this remnant of a photo. It looks like one of the pictures found of me in Elijah's dorm room."

He studied the image on the phone. "I told you no evidence was to leave that conference room."

"It didn't. Technically. And yes, I bent the rules, but for now, can you put that aside and just compare the two?"

He glared at her and then dropped his gaze to the phone image and the fragment. "Where did you get this?"

"Perhaps I found it on the barbecue on Clarke's back porch."

"Damn it, Joan!"

"I know. I know. But before we get into a fight about that, I have something else."

He kicked the dirt with his boot as he shook his head. "Okay."

And here was the trickiest part. Should Joan break Ann's confidence and tell Gideon what she knew? She trusted that Gideon would never tell Clarke if it were Kyle. "What if Ann had been going out with Elijah?"

"Ann and Elijah?" Disbelief mingled with humor. "I don't see it."

"What if she didn't want you to see it? What if she wanted it to stay a secret forever?"

Gideon's head cocked slightly, as if an idea he had never considered had blindsided him. "Nate?"

Joan drew in a breath. "She loves her boy more than anything."

Gideon stared at her with a mixture of horror and disbelief. "And Clarke figured this out?"

"Not yet would be my assessment. But I think Clarke must have sensed that Elijah was a rival."

"How could he? Ann and Elijah never openly dated."

"But he seemed to be around us a lot. And if I noticed how Elijah looked at Ann, Clarke must have as well."

"Okay, assuming he noticed."

"Then he decided to drive a stake in the heart of his competition. He steals the backpack, plants the pictures, sets the fire, and then is on the scene to play hero. You got to Ann first, and I was saved only in the nick of time."

"I begged him to save you as I was coming out with Ann." A muscle pulsed in Gideon's jaw. "They got married six weeks after the fire."

"Exactly. The fire drove Ann right into her hero's arms. Your sister got played by your best friend, Gideon."

He dropped his gaze and pushed the gravel around with the tip of his boot. "And the recent fires?"

"The beauty shop was a job for hire and I think purposefully timed for just after Elijah's release. He becomes a suspect all over again. Ann's shed fire was a warning to me, and I think the cabin fire was a way of cleaning up a loose end."

"You're saying Jessica hired Clarke to burn down her salon?"

"She had a cash-flow problem and a big insurance policy."

"If Jessica hired Clarke, why would she turn on him?"

"She wasn't banking on someone dying in the fire."

"And Lana?" Gideon challenged.

"We know she was in contact with Elijah, and she was sporting a ring similar to the one we found on Jessica's body."

Gideon ran his hand over his head. "That's not anywhere near solid evidence."

"You're right. Which is why I think you need to test the DNA of Lana's baby against Clarke's."

"Clarke and Lana were having an affair," he said, looking like he was trying to wrap his brain around the idea.

"It would explain why Lana had the picture of Ann and me."

"All Clarke has talked about is fixing his marriage."

"I suggest you check Clarke's phone records to see if he was in Helena at the time of the warehouse fire."

"Joan, this is out of left field."

"You need to consider it, Gideon."

Gideon's phone rang, and he looked almost relieved for the interruption. "Becca." He listened for several seconds and then said, "Leaving now."

"What?" Joan asked.

"Dan Tucker is dead."

Minutes later, they were in his car and headed to town. Neither spoke as Gideon drove the back roads into town. He did not mention Clarke, and Joan did not press the point. He was still keeping her in the loop, and she took that as a sign he was considering what she had told him.

Gideon pulled up in front of the one-story rancher with the sloped roof. There were two other police cars parked out front, their flashing lights drawing the attention of curious neighbors who must have decided the blue lights trumped the week's entertainment options.

They each donned rubber gloves. Someone commented about Joan entering the secured space, but Gideon vouched for her with a few terse words. They then stepped under the yellow crime scene tape that separated the insiders from the rest of the world.

She tugged at the edges of her gloves, working her fingers in deeper as she entered. The air temperature in the house was cold, which she knew would retard decomposition and the scent of death. She gave props to the killer for having the sense to turn off the furnace.

She followed Gideon down a narrow hallway that opened into a living room with closed curtains and a thick shag carpet. The main furniture piece was a worn brown recliner and a large television set playing a documentary on gold miners.

Beside the chair was a coffee table sporting six empty beer cans, gauze, and bloodied paper towels.

"You said his girlfriend found him?" Gideon asked.

"Yes. She's in the back of my car," Becca said. "Figured you'd want to talk to her there rather than in here."

"I do," he said.

Joan walked around the chair and studied Dan's body. His face was covered in a clear plastic bag. His jaw was slack, his lips blue with eyes half-closed over glazed irises.

"Windows or doors open?" Gideon asked.

"No. All closed and locked," Becca said.

"Any witnesses?" Gideon asked.

"My partner is knocking on doors as we speak. So far, he's come up empty. Weather was cold and everyone had burrowed in—closed curtains, TVs, and such."

She knelt in front of Dan, seeing hints of the guy who had once been attractive before a decade of long hours, no exercise, and a poor diet. She looked at the side table and noted there was also antibiotic cream and discarded gauze-bandage packages. In the trash were wads of more bloody paper towels.

"He was hurt recently." Joan touched his thigh and felt the raised edge of a bandage under the sweats.

"I know he could be an ass, but why kill him?" Becca asked.

"Gambling, drugs, a pissed-off neighbor," she said.

Gideon kept his comments to himself, but Joan sensed he was still mulling what she had said about Clarke.

Whoever had gotten into Dan's home had killed him without leaving any signs of forced entry or signs of a struggle. This guy was strong and prepared.

Gideon and Joan left the house and paused to speak to Dan's girlfriend, Nora. She had changed out of her uniform into a snug-fitting blue T-shirt, fur-trimmed blue jacket, and jeans.

Gideon tapped on the window and then opened the door. She rose, sniffed, and glanced toward the house as if it were a house of horrors.

"When did you stop by?" he asked.

"About an hour ago. We were supposed to eat pizza and drink beer and stuff."

"I thought he was at your mother's," Gideon said.

"No. He asked me to tell people that. He wasn't feeling well."

"Looks like he was hurt," Gideon said. "Do you know how?"

"He said it was an accident. Said he cut it on a barbed-wire fence he was fixing."

"Did you see anything when you arrived?" Gideon asked.

"I used my key to get in. The TV was on, the room was dark, and I saw him in the chair. When I walked up and saw the plastic bag, I freaked." Nora shook her head. "I called 9-1-1."

"What did Dan think of Elijah?" Gideon asked.

"Hated him. Especially after the beauty shop burned. It dredged up bad memories of his truck. He thought his diner was going to be next."

"Did you hear Elijah was beaten up?" Joan asked.

"Yeah, I heard, but what does that have to do with this?"

"Did Dan decide to give Elijah a reason to leave town?" Joan asked.

"He wouldn't do that," Nora said.

"Why not?" Gideon pressed.

"Dan's all talk. He makes a big fuss but never follows through."

"Maybe he decided this time was going to be different," she said.

"No." She shook her head, causing hoop earrings to tangle in her hair. "That's not Dan."

"Was there anyone who didn't like Dan?" Gideon asked.

"He got along with most folks," she said. "He just didn't like having criminals living in a town full of good folks."

"Did Dan know Lana Long well?"

"Like I told you before, he knew her from the diner. She wasn't here long enough for most people to get a chance to know her." Nora shifted her stance, as if working the warmth back into her limbs. "Is that all you got for me? I'm tired and want to go home. You know how to find me if you need me."

"Sure," Gideon said.

They watched as Nora slid behind the wheel of her red pickup truck and drove off.

"Elijah has broken ribs," Joan said. "Suffocating a guy like Dan would be really painful."

"Elijah could have surprised him. Dan could have been dozing in his chair. And you saw the bandages. Maybe he'd taken a few painkillers with those beers. Bag slips over Dan's head, and before he realizes what's happening, it's lights out."

Joan wanted to believe Elijah had not done this, but wanting and knowing were two different things.

A uniformed police officer approached Becca, the two talked, and then she approached them.

"No one has seen anything so far," she said.

"Whoever did this must have left something behind," Gideon said. "They always do."

***

Gideon and Joan again fell into silence as he drove them back to his ranch. Joan had made a logical argument, but it was so outrageous. Clarke an arsonist. Until a DNA test came back proving Clarke had fathered Lana's fetus, Gideon would reserve judgment.

The more time he spent with Joan, the more aware he became of her. The curve of her neck. The way she tapped her thumb and index finger together when she was thinking.

He slowed as they approached his driveway and passed under the double-B brand. As they grew closer to the house, he was tempted to slow-walk his approach so they could spend a little more time together. She was a puzzle he had not cracked.

"Home sweet home." Bitterness dripped from her words.

"Why do you say it that way?"

She shook her head. "Just being sarcastic."

"Say what you mean, Joan."

The heater blew gently on her face, teasing the edges of her bangs. She moistened her lips, making them glisten. As he looked at her face, he was tempted to kiss her and see if she still tasted the same. Still, he was smart enough to know some territories were better undiscovered.

"I've got to get back to Philadelphia. My union rep and boss want a meeting next week. Rep says I'll be back on the job soon, though it'll be desk duty for a while."

"That's what you want, right?"

"That's where I'm headed."

"Then why the 'Home sweet home' comment?"

"Because there's no such thing. No place feels like home. It's all temporary."

"That's up to you. You can put down roots anywhere you want."

She turned toward him. For once, her frown was gone, as if she had released a secret that had been weighing her down. "I once thought I could live out here. Then I realized it's no different from back east."

Gideon was so rooted in the Montana soil that he doubted he could ever break its tethers. "I'm sorry you feel that way. I can't imagine."

"That's what drew me to you back in college. It was a certainty that you knew where you belonged. You never questioned it."

"Is that the only reason you went out on that first date with me?" he asked, feigning surprise.

A small smile tipped the edges of her lips. "You also had a nice ass."

He laughed. "Hopefully I've not lost my girlish figure."

"No. You still got game." For a moment, they locked gazes, and he was so tempted to brush the strands of hair off her forehead. Her body was rigid, as if she could not decide whether to stay or go. He waited, knowing she wanted to invite him up to that little apartment.

She parked, reached for the door handle, and opened it. Cold air rushed into the cab. "You need to stay on top of Clarke."

"I hear you."

Gideon watched her walk toward the house, hoping she would turn back and beckon him. Foolish to think she would suddenly reconsider. If whatever had joined them in the past was not enough to make her stick around, a short trip would not do it now.

She vanished into the garage, the lights in the stairwell soon turning on. He pictured her lingering by the door, kicking herself for not being with him. That image was enough to give him hope to wait another beat.

But she never came back out the door.

He parked and tried to picture Clarke setting fires for money and killing women, one of whom might be carrying his child. It was an outrageous theory.

Inside the house, he hung up his coat, his attention shifting to a picture taken of Clarke, Nate, Kyle, and himself. They had been fishing back in June. As he stared at father and son side by side, he saw the differences more than the similarities now. "Shit."

He grabbed a beer from the refrigerator and sat at his home office computer. He twisted off the bottle top and took a pull as he thought back to the trips Clarke had taken to various fire-training conferences around the country in recent years. There'd been one in San Diego, California, and another in Washington, DC. Next he searched for fires in those areas matching the time frame. Nothing came up.

He refined the search, digging into news reports in the outlying counties. After an hour of reading local crime reports around San Diego, he found articles detailing several shelter fires at a park thirty miles east of the city. The fires could have been caused by anyone. He read down three paragraphs into one article and noted the fires had been started with a cup full of gasoline. The heavy-duty plastic had melted, and whatever the arsonist had used as a wick had vanished in the flames.

He shifted his attention to the DC metro area. Another forty-five minutes of reading and he discovered a series of dumpster fires in Fredericksburg, Virginia. The site was less than an hour south of Clarke's conference and easily reached off I-95 South.

Gideon sat back, rubbing his eyes. Though two fires had aligned with Clarke's travel schedule, that did not mean there was enough evidence to request a DNA test on Clarke.

He reached into the side drawer and pulled out the old Bible his grandfather had left him. He thumbed through the thin pages until he reached the picture that he'd tucked in there years ago.

The image was of Joan and him, taken in the spring of their senior year. They were dressed for the spring formal. He had rented a tux, and she wore a red halter dress that showed off her figure. It had been cold as hell that night, and this picture had been snapped seconds before she had been forced to swap the heels for boots and slide on a thick overcoat. She looked sexy as hell in that gown and boots. *But even better now,* he thought as he slowly put the picture back in the Bible.

His phone rang, with the medical examiner on the other end. There was no way he could have picked up Tucker's body and had any information yet.

"Doc."

"I got your message about the DNA. Elijah Weston is not the baby's father."

Gideon pulled in a slow breath. "I got one more test for you."

Confessions of an Arsonist
The time has come. She will die tonight.

CHAPTER
TWENTY-SEVEN

Missoula, Montana
Friday, September 11, 2020
1:00 a.m.

Under the moonless sky, he stood outside the garage apartment and stared up at the window near where he knew Joan was sleeping. His last fire for her had been a gentle message. It was his nice way of telling her she needed to leave town and let the folks here live the lives they were meant to live.

But she would not leave. She kept pressing. And she would keep on pushing and turning over every rock until she exposed him. And that was not going to happen. Ever.

Gasoline had sloshed in the milk jugs as he walked up to the main entrance of the property. This fire was not going to be a warning. It was going to be his final message to Joan.

He set two jugs by the side and primary entrance into the apartment upstairs. Once the flames caught, they would travel up the stairs, bringing along a black smoke and flames that would chew up the oxygen. The garage would burn nicely before Gideon would be alerted in the main house. And as long as the wind did not pick up, poor Gideon would not lose his house because of this bitch.

He moved around to the back side of the structure and set the remaining two jugs by the back exit. Whether she ran down the front or the back stairs, his fire would be there to greet her like an old friend.

He struck the first match and tossed it at the jug of gasoline. The vapors caught on fire instantly and flames jumped, whooshing like a dragon taking flight. His creature had taken its first breath.

Confessions of an Arsonist
"And I will be to her a wall of fire all around, declares the Lord, and I will be the glory in her midst." Zechariah 2:5.

CHAPTER TWENTY-EIGHT

Missoula, Montana
Friday, September 11, 2020
1:05 a.m.

The smoke detector woke Joan up out of a deep sleep. She had barely slept in weeks, but tonight when her head hit the pillow, she had felt that all the pieces of the fires were coming together.

The alarm blaring, she jumped out of bed, heart jackhammering into her ribs, and ran to the door. Black smoke was angrily marching up the main staircase. It would be only a matter of seconds before it breached the room. She raised her arm to her nose and stepped back, turning to the back staircase. She opened the exit and was immediately hit by the heat of a second fire.

Coughing, she hurried into the kitchen and turned on the cold tap. Grabbing a dish towel, she soaked it with water and draped it over her head before she dropped to her knees and crawled to the utility cabinet. She grabbed the fire ladder Gideon had showed her in the closet and dragged it back toward the window.

Her lungs and eyes burned with acrid smoke. It was nearly impossible to see as she pried open the side of the box and yanked out the ladder. She forced herself to her feet and flipped the lock on the window. The window sash, however, was stuck in place from a recent paint job.

She grabbed one of the stools at the counter and rammed it into the window. A couple of the panes broke, but the wood frame did not give way. Gritting her teeth, she tightened her grip and hit the window again. More glass shattered, but it was still not a big enough opening for her to fit through.

The cool air rushed in, and even as she greedily breathed in the fresh air, the fire behind her bellowed and pulled as it consumed the oxygen. She struck the window again, and this time the frame gave way and fell to the ground below.

Her head spinning, she reached for the end of the ladder, hooked it onto the ledge, and tossed it over the side. The rungs rolled down and caught halfway as the heat behind her scorched her back.

As she climbed onto the ledge, she saw someone near the corner of the big house.

A sudden explosion sounded behind her, blasting hot embers across the room and against her back. The damp cloth was helping, but she would be lucky to have another few seconds.

As she gripped the sill, shattered glass cut into the palms of her hands. She felt nothing as the blood poured over her fingers and she slung herself over the sill. With her foot, she desperately searched for the first rung of the ladder, which shifted and swayed against the house.

Looking back into the apartment, she glared at the fire, an angry red beast that snarled back, almost grinning as if it knew she'd been seconds away from dying. She froze, unable to shift her attention away from the formidable creature that was almost mesmerizing.

The ladder shifted under her feet as the ceiling beams in the apartment began to collapse. The spell broke, and she skipped the next rung down to get away as fast as she could.

Blood made her palms slick, and gripping the ladder became difficult. Her hands slipped twice as she struggled to keep her feet on the twisting rungs swaying in the wind. Heat from above rained over her as glowing debris tumbled down.

When she was five feet from the ground, the window ledge above gave way, and the right hook disengaged. Her grip tightened, but the chain ladder twisted violently, knocking her against the side of the garage. The siding cut into her ribs, knocking the air from her. Her fingers slipped, and she lost her grip completely and fell to the ground.

She landed on her feet hard. Her ankle rolled, but she did not go down. The fire howled and glowed above her as the structure began to collapse in on itself.

Joan pushed up to her feet, teetering as she struggled to put distance between her and the fire. Her legs wobbled, and pain from her ribs knifed her from within. Still, she stumbled back several steps. She was not going to let this damn fire kill her.

As she took another step and then another, she felt hope that she would survive this. Her gaze on her feet, she never saw the blow that came at her from behind. She took a strike to her lower back that dropped her to her knees.

"Fucking bitch!" a deep voice growled. "What's it going to take to kill you?"

She tried to rise, but a heavy boot kicked her forward. Her face hit the ground, dirt and blood filling her mouth.

"You're going to burn alive if it's the last thing I do."

She looked up into Clarke's lifeless eyes, which mirrored the growing flames behind him. "You gutless shit," she spat out.

"Yeah, aren't you the smart one?" he hissed. "You were in my house."

She winced as she pushed farther back from him and the burning structure.

Clarke stepped toward her. "I have tiny bits of paper stuck in the doors and windows. I always know if anyone has disturbed them."

She pushed back a few more inches, gritting her teeth as her body screamed in pain. "You set the fires, didn't you? All of them."

He grabbed her by the arm and yanked her to her feet. Twisting it behind her back, he shoved her toward the fully engulfed building. "Maybe not all, but nearly all. It was going so well. And then you came back."

Her gaze locked on the raging fire as its heat scorched her skin.

"In case you're wondering, I set the College Fire. It was all me, baby. I showed Ann how much she needed *me*, and I taught you a lesson about meddling. But you forgot that lesson and now are back and hell-bent on taking Ann away again." He dragged her closer to the fire that loomed over them both. "She's beautiful, isn't she? And she's all mine."

He whirled her around and wrapped his fingers around her neck and started to squeeze. She coughed, knowing the building could come down on them at any second. But Clarke was in a blind rage. She knew he would rather die killing her than survive.

Joan kicked her feet hard, her foot connecting with his shin, but he seemed to enjoy the fight she had in her. She could feel herself passing out and her knees buckling. Her vision narrowed as her fingers fell free of his hands.

When she collapsed to the ground, she was dimly aware he grabbed her by the ankle and dragged her faceup toward the flames. She somehow sensed Clarke did not want her to die at his hands, but wanted the smoke and flames to take her.

As her fingers dug into the ground, she clawed at the dirt, grabbing a handful, and threw it in his face. Her wild aim was off, and the dirt only caught the side of his left eye. But the strike forced him to blink and turn his head away. His grip on her ankle slackened, and she tried to kick free.

His fingernails dug into her skin as he swiped the debris from his eyes. "I can't wait to see you burn."

A gunshot rang out from behind her. Through her hazy vision, she saw Clarke stumble. For a moment, he dug his fingers deeper into her flesh, as if killing her was all that mattered now. But in the next second, blood bloomed on his shirt, and he reeled backward. His fingers slackened, and he released her. He looked past her, staring a moment, and then staggered toward the inferno and vanished into the flames.

The fire roared louder as it consumed the building, and flaming pieces fell to the ground around her. She turned onto her belly and started to crawl away from the heat consuming her.

Strong hands banded around her, hauled her up, and tossed her over a wide set of shoulders. She lay limp like a rag doll and struggled to catch her breath.

She watched the ground move under her and felt distance grow between her and the flames. When they were at least a hundred feet from the blaze, her savior laid her gently on the front porch. The building garage cracked and broke, and the structure collapsed.

"Joan." Gideon's sharp tone cut through her mind's haze. "Joan."

She coughed and tried to sit up. Through her blurred vision, she stared into Gideon's intense gaze. Her throat was raw, and the scent of burned hair filled her nostrils. Her voice was barely a whisper. "It was Clarke."

"I know."

"He wanted to burn me alive."

Gideon gathered her up in his arms and held her close. She raised her hand to his arm and gripped his shoulder. He leaned down and kissed her on the forehead. "I thought I was going to lose you."

"Me too." Her voice was rough with smoke inhalation and emotion.

"This time we figure it out together."

"Yes."

CHAPTER
TWENTY-NINE

Missoula, Montana
Friday, September 11, 2020
5:00 a.m.

Gideon had ridden in the ambulance to the hospital with Joan and had been at her side as the doctors examined her and treated her for burns and bruising. When she'd finally fallen into a deep sleep, he had called Ann and told her about the fire and his trip to the emergency room with Joan.

When Ann pushed through the emergency room doors, her face was flushed and her eyes bright with panic. She spotted Gideon and rushed toward him. "Gideon. I dropped the boys off with Tim's mother like you asked."

He crossed to her, searching for the right words. Finding none, he said, "Clarke is dead."

"What?"

He watched the play of shock and disbelief on her face as she searched his gaze. He thought back to the moment when he had told Kyle his mother had died. Delivering the news had gutted him. And now he had to tell his sister that he had shot and killed her husband. He would have done anything to spare his sister this kind of pain. But the truth had to be told, and he wanted her to hear this from him and no one else. "I shot him."

"I don't understand." Her eyes darkened with questions and confusion.

Gideon shifted his stance but kept his focus on Ann. "Clarke was trying to kill Joan. He set fire to the garage apartment."

"Clarke?" She shook her head and hesitated, as if she expected some kind of punch line. When none came, she said, "No, he wouldn't do that."

"I promise you, he did."

She raised a trembling hand to her forehead. "I don't understand why he would do something like that."

"I don't understand it all yet, either. But I'm headed out to get a search warrant so I can go through his house."

"It's my house, too. You don't need a warrant. You have my permission."

"I'm still getting a search warrant. I don't want any confusion later."

A female uniformed officer approached them, and he motioned for her to come closer.

Tears welled in Ann's eyes. He kissed her on the forehead. "This is Officer Wilson. She's going to take care of you."

"I don't need taking care of."

"Yes, you do, and I can't do it right now. When I have more answers, you'll be the first person I call."

Ann looked at him a long moment and then slowly nodded. She fished her keys from her purse. "Take my keys."

"Thanks."

Gideon left Ann with the uniformed officer. It took another hour to get his warrant and arrive at Clarke's residence with Becca and a forensic tech. The keys Ann had given him did not work in the door. It was not a surprise that Clarke had changed the locks. A half hour later, he had a locksmith on scene.

Becca shook her head as she regarded the house. "I was just here last year for a cookout that Ann and Clarke had for the Fourth of July. Clarke seemed so in love with Ann."

"Love or obsession?"

"Clearly the latter," she said.

A car pulled up, and Gideon turned to see Ann get out. He cursed. "I told her to stay at the hospital."

"She has a right to be here," Becca said. "This is her life imploding."

Ann rushed toward him, her face pale and her features tight with anger. "Joan is still unconscious, and I cannot just sit and wait. What is going on?"

"I don't know. I'm hoping the answers are inside."

"Have you gone in yet?" she asked.

"About to. We're working on the lock."

"Why aren't you using my keys to get into the house?"

"The lock's been changed," Gideon said.

"Why would he do that? He kept saying he wanted me to move home. Why would he change the locks?"

The locksmith worked his implements into the lock, and it clicked open. He twisted the knob and pushed the door open. "There you go."

"I want to be there," Ann said.

"No," Gideon said as he blocked her path.

"This house was my home for so many years," she protested.

"Right now, it is a crime scene investigation. So you will stand on the curb and wait. I don't want you anywhere near this investigation."

"He is . . . was my husband."

"I know, Ann. I know he was a good father and he loved you. But I'm not sure if we ever really knew him."

"I knew him," she said, frowning. "Or at least I thought I did."

"We were all fooled." He laid his hand on her shoulder. "Now, I need to ask you to step back. This is a criminal investigation, Ann."

She wrapped her arms around her chest. "It can't be happening. I'm going to wake up and this nightmare will be over."

"Ann, have you spoken to Nate?"

"Not yet. I will soon. I just need to get my head around all this."

"You should be with him. You two need to talk. Let me take care of this."

Tears welled in her eyes and spilled down her cheeks. "Call me when you know something."

"I will. You should go and see Nate."

"This is all too much. I still can't process it," Ann said. "How's Joan ever going to forgive me?"

"You didn't do anything wrong, Ann. Don't take any responsibility for what Clarke did."

She shook her head. "I should have listened to her years ago. I should have left and moved east."

"Don't do that. No good will come of it. Go home to Nate. Let me figure this out."

Ann drew in a breath and squared her shoulders. "Thank you, Gideon."

He watched as she got in her car and drove off.

"I got it," the locksmith said. "Have a look at this."

"Thanks, Bill."

Gideon followed the locksmith's finger to a small piece of tape secured to the door and jamb. It was unbroken. He pulled on protective gloves and summoned the tech over. She collected the piece of tape and bagged it.

"Check it for fingerprints."

"Will do, boss."

Gideon stepped over the threshold. He moved into the kitchen, opening the pantry. There were no empty milk jugs or rags as Joan had said.

He looked around the kitchen, searching the corners and the vents for any sign of a camera. But security could have been as low-tech as a piece of tape on the front door or a back window to have alerted Clarke.

He moved to the bedroom overlooking the patio and tried the window. On the dresser was a framed picture of Clarke, Ann, and Nate. Beside it was a picture of Ann that had been taken the same day the other image of Joan, Ann, and Gideon had. If Clarke had taken these pictures, he was likely the source of the picture Lana had had in her suitcase.

As he searched Clarke's face in the first picture, he wanted to see signs of the evil in the man. But there was nothing that appeared to lurk behind the smiling eyes.

He turned to the window and studied the lock. On the top sash was a clear piece of tape that had been dislodged. If this was how Joan had accessed the house, Clarke would have discovered it. "You were made in seconds, Joan."

He looked around the bedroom, taking in the unmade bed and the scattered clothes. He moved to the closet, where Clarke had lined up a collection of books next to a small cabinet secured with a combination lock.

Given that Clarke had been caught trying to commit murder, Gideon's search warrant allowed him access to every corner and drawer in this house. He spoke to the forensic tech, who retrieved a pair of bolt cutters. Wrapping the sharp ends around the lock, Gideon shoved the handles together. The lock snapped open.

As the tech filmed the process, Gideon opened the cabinet door. Inside was a collection of DVDs, and each was marked in Clarke's neat, bold handwriting. Gideon selected the first recording, identified with the description "Practice fire #1."

***

When Joan woke up in a hospital bed, she was aware of the beep of a monitor, the IV in her arm, and the bright sunshine. When she raised her hand to shield her eyes, she noted that both her palms were bandaged.

As she shoved through the haze in her brain, she struggled to remember the day and then the year. Her throat was raw, and her skin felt tender, as if she had a bad sunburn.

"Welcome back."

She turned to see Elijah sitting in the corner of her room. He carefully closed a large textbook already filled with multicolored tabs.

He set the book aside, rose, and walked gingerly up to her bed. As she had done for him yesterday, he held up a cup of water and a straw so she could drink. The water scraped against her raw throat, but her body was greedy for the hydration. She drank the entire glass.

"Aren't you the good little patient," he said.

"I aim to please." Her voice sounded ragged, as if she were recovering from a cold. "How long have I been sleeping?"

"A few hours," he said. "The good detective was here for a while, but duty called. Ann was also here for a time. When they both left, I decided to visit."

"How long have you been here?"

"Not long." He grinned. "And for the record, you don't drool or snore when you're asleep."

"Good to know," she said.

"I owe you my thanks."

"Why?" she asked.

"Clarke."

"He's dead?"

"Very. From what I'm hearing from the nurses, Detective Bailey shot him, but that was before he burned up."

Memories of last night emerged from the fog. "Yep, I was there, unfortunately. You said Gideon got called away."

"My sources tell me he and his team are searching Clarke's house."

She remembered her own search of the house. Nothing she had found would have been admissible, and Gideon could never have legally acted on her discoveries if Clarke had not attacked her. And even still, Gideon was a stickler for the rules.

"It's been a productive twenty-four hours for you. Dan and now Clarke are dead," Elijah said.

"Pretty busy for a small town."

Joan understood why Clarke had come after her, but why would he go after Dan? If anything, Dan would have been the perfect fall guy for eliminating Elijah. "Where were you when Dan died?"

"Always the cop," he said carefully.

She wanted to sit up and reach for the controls on the side of the bed. Elijah brushed her fingers away and pressed the button until she signaled for him to stop.

"I was taking a walk," Elijah said. "The doctor said I would heal faster if I moved."

"Where did you walk?"

"Around. And I have no witnesses to prove or disprove that statement. Am I still the go-to suspect in this town?"

"No, the cops are totally focused on Clarke now."

Elijah nodded, looking only mildly surprised. "Good. It will be nice to have the fires solved and maybe get my name cleared." He studied her an extra moment. "Why did Clarke come after you?"

"He said I was trying to take Ann away."

"Ann's rooted in this state. She's not going anywhere."

"You might be sure of that, but Clarke wasn't." Mention of Ann shifted her perspective. "Ann and Nate must be devastated. I should call her." She looked around her bed. "Do you know where my cell phone is?"

Elijah pushed her hand away. "I'll find Ann. You stay put."

"I don't know if you should be the one, Elijah."

"Why not?" He watched her closely.

"She's Gideon's sister. He'll take care of it."

"Ah, right. Gideon."

"You don't care for him much, do you?"

"On the contrary: I respect him quite a bit. He's the man of the hour." He stepped back. "He saved your life, Detective."

"I do owe him."

He smiled, turned, and picked up his book. "We all do. Take care, and let me know if I can help," he said as he walked into the hallway.

"You don't appear to be surprised by Clarke. Did you know about him all along?"

He stilled. "I had no proof, and if prison taught me anything, it's to keep my mouth shut."

"Lana loved you, or at least she thought she did. And yet she ended up with Clarke."

"I never had any control over Lana. She made her own choices."

"I don't think so." Joan moistened her cracked, dried lips. "I think she loved you so much that she was willing to sleep with Clarke to get you the proof you wanted about the fire."

"That's an ambitious plan."

"How did you come to suspect Clarke?"

"Joan, you have been severely traumatized. And it's easy to see Clarke as the ultimate bad guy."

"He took ten years of your life."

"I've had ten years of living, just like you and everyone else. I consider my years behind bars to have been very productive. They taught me so much."

She realized now that Elijah was a master chess player. His mind always advanced to at least five moves ahead. "That's not an answer."

He pushed back the curtain. "I think I hear Prince Charming right now."

As he moved to leave, she tried to rise up. This was far from finished. But when Gideon appeared in the door, she was overcome with relief and emotion.

Gideon's frown deepened when he looked at Elijah. "What are you doing here?"

Elijah nodded to him. "I was just visiting with Joan."

"As soon as I get this sorted out, I want to talk to you," Gideon said.

"I'll be here," Elijah said easily as he offered a small salute and left.

Gideon stood in the doorway watching until finally he pulled up a chair beside her. "That guy is everywhere. I still don't trust him."

She didn't, either. In her bones, she sensed that Elijah had a plan that was far from played out. She tried to sit up as Gideon approached, but her broken ribs forced her to remain still. "You might be right."

A ghost of a smile tipped the edges of his lips as he sat beside her bed. He brushed her bangs back, staring at her. "You take too many chances."

She would have leaned over and kissed him if not for the cracked ribs. "I would literally be toast now if not for you."

"I'm sorry I wasn't there faster."

"The fire ladder was a nice touch."

He tipped his head back, his eyes darkening with the fear of what could have happened. "I'm so sorry. I should have seen this coming."

"No one figured it out."

"You did."

"You can pay me back."

His brow arched. "How?"

"Kiss me. I'd do it myself, but the ribs aren't having it." When he hesitated, she added, "Please tell me I haven't misread the sexual tension."

He cleared his throat as he rose and leaned toward her. "You haven't." He gently kissed her on the lips, and she raised her hand to his arm.

"I still love you," she whispered. "I always have."

He drew back, searching her gaze. "I thought I could get over you, but I never did."

Her chest tightened as she thought about all the years she had tried to convince herself they were done. There were times she could almost believe she had moved on, but then something would trigger an old memory, and then she was right back to missing him.

She gripped his arm. "You don't have to try anymore."

He grinned. "Good. I'm tired of running away from the one person I've always wanted the most."

EPILOGUE

Missoula, Montana
Saturday, October 31, 2020
6:15 p.m.

In the end, it had been easy to quit the Philadelphia Police Department. Joan had flown back east and met with her boss and learned she would have desk duty indefinitely. Her boss was not going to fire her but had presented an option he knew she would never accept. She had politely shaken his hand and quit.

It had taken a couple of weeks to pack up, to give away what she did not want, and to find someone to sublet her apartment. Finally, she had hugged Ray, who'd stood on the sidewalk waving as she drove off in a car packed with the few possessions she cared about.

Now, as she pulled into Missoula, she knew by the darkening sky that she had barely beaten the weather. Within hours, snow would be blanketing everything and announcing winter was here to stay. There was no turning back now.

She drove down the familiar road to the Bailey ranch. The sun had all but set, and whatever light remained was blocked by the thick, dark clouds.

She pulled up in front of Ann's house, shut off the engine, and silenced a moment of doubt. She had not given up a life to be here.

Out of the car, the first small flakes began to fall. She hugged her coat around her and dashed to the front door, where Ann was waiting. It was Halloween, and the house was decorated with all the fixings.

"I hope there's a party here," Joan said.

Ann wrapped her arms around Joan. "You made it!"

"The last two days were killer."

"I told you not to rush," Ann said.

"Couldn't help it."

Gideon's deep voice mingled with Kyle's and Nate's. The three were watching a football game.

"He's missed you," Ann whispered, looking over her shoulder with a grin. "We all have missed you."

"How are you doing?"

Ann smiled. "One foot in front of the other. Nate is hurting, but Gideon is helping."

Joan shrugged off her coat and lowered her voice. "What about Elijah?"

Ann's demeanor grew more guarded as she took the coat and hung it up. "He's still my best student."

"That's not what I mean."

"He's been nothing but the perfect student. I have no complaints."

He was patient and good at playing the long game. The problem was, no one knew his real goal. "He hasn't tried to make contact with Nate?"

"No."

"Good." How long would it be before Elijah realized the truth about Nate? And what would he do?

Joan and Gideon had spoken on the phone almost daily over the last seven weeks. He had updated her whenever he could on the investigation into Clarke's fires. Cell phone data had placed Clarke in Helena at the time of the warehouse fire, and when the insurance company had insisted on another investigation, its report had unearthed traces of incendiary devices like the ones Clarke had used. Bryce had arrested Pollock for arson just last week.

The DNA of Lana's baby indeed matched Clarke's. The two had been having an affair, but as much as Gideon pressed, Elijah insisted that she had acted alone. Gideon theorized that Lana had set out to seduce Clarke so that she could get insight into the origin of the College Fire. Somewhere along the way, Clarke must have won her over with an engagement ring he had taken or borrowed from Jessica Halpern.

Jessica's cell phone texts revealed that she had been in direct contact with Clarke for eight months. Motel records suggested the two had been having an affair for at least six months.

The cops had found Clarke's DNA in the form of hair fibers on Dan's body. They had theorized that Clarke had broken into Dan's home and killed him. Cell phone records confirmed that the two had traded several phone calls on the day Elijah had been attacked. Whether Clarke had helped rough up Elijah was not confirmed, but it appeared that Dan could have become another loose end to Clarke.

Beyond the regular updates, Gideon had given Joan some space while she was in Philadelphia. He had not told her he loved her and had not pressed her to return to Montana. But after three days back east in her apartment, she had realized her place was out west with him. When she'd floated the idea, Gideon was thrilled.

"Come on into the den," Ann said. "We knew the snow was coming, so we decided to keep the party here. Gideon will be relieved to see you. He was worried about you in the weather."

They had spoken two hours ago, but excitement rushed through her as she thought about seeing him.

"Look who I found," Ann said.

Gideon was sitting in the center of the couch, a boy on each side, as they watched the college game. All three turned around at the sound of Ann's voice, and the boys hopped up immediately.

Gideon rose quickly, but he smoothed his hands down his thighs, as if he might be nervous. He leaned in and kissed her on the lips. "Right on time."

The boys spoke to Joan almost too fast for her to take it all in, but she loved their enthusiasm.

"All right, you two," Ann said. "Help me get the table set for dinner."

The boys and Ann rushed out of the room, leaving Joan and Gideon to themselves.

She slid her hands in her pockets, then decided that made her look too on edge. "Long time no see. Sorry it took me so long."

Gideon took her hands in his. "Doesn't matter. You finally made it."

She stepped toward him, and when he embraced her, Joan felt a sense of belonging she had not felt in a long time, and, in ways she could not articulate, she knew she was home.

ABOUT THE AUTHOR

Photo © 2015 Studio FBJ

New York Times and *USA Today* bestselling novelist Mary Burton is the popular author of thirty-five romance and suspense novels, as well as short stories and five novellas. She currently lives in Virginia with her husband and three miniature dachshunds. Visit her at www.maryburton.com.